One Heart
to Win

JOHANNA LINDSEY

One Heart to Win

G

Gallery Books

New York   London   Toronto   Sydney   New Delhi

Gallery Books
A Division of Simon & Schuster, Inc.
1230 Avenue of the Americas
New York, NY 10020

First Gallery Books hardcover edition June 2013

GALLERY BOOKS and colophon are registered trademarks of Simon & Schuster, Inc.

For information about special discounts for bulk purchases, please contact Simon & Schuster Special Sales at 1-866-506-1949 or business@simonandschuster.com.

The Simon & Schuster Speakers Bureau can bring authors to your live event. For more information or to book an event contact the Simon & Schuster Speakers Bureau at 1-866-248-3049 or visit our website at www.simonspeakers.com.

Manufactured in the United States of America

10 9 8 7 6 5 4 3 2 1

Library of Congress Cataloging-in-Publication Data

Lindsey, Johanna
   One heart to win / Johanna Lindsey. — First Gallery Books hardcover edition.
       pages   cm
   I. Title.
   PS3562.I5123O53 2013
   813'.54—dc23   2013011681

ISBN 978-1-4767-1426-4
ISBN 978-1-4767-1430-1 (ebook)

One Heart
to Win

Chapter One

Rose Warren stopped crying before her daughter, Tiffany, opened the front door of their brownstone town house, but she couldn't get out of her mind the words that had provoked the tears. *Come with her, Rose. It's been fifteen years, haven't you tortured us long enough?*

She usually let her daughter, who had turned eighteen last month, read the letters from Franklin Warren. Frank usually kept them impersonal so she could share them with their daughter. This time he didn't, and she wadded the letter up in her fist and stuffed it in her pocket as soon as she heard Tiffany's voice in the hall. The girl didn't know the real reason her parents didn't live together. Frank didn't even know the real reason she'd had to leave him. After all these years, it was best it remain that way.

"Tiffany, join me in the parlor, please!" Rose called out before Tiffany could go upstairs to her room.

The afternoon light glinting in her shiny reddish-blond hair, Tiffany removed her bonnet as she entered the parlor, then the short, thin cape from her shoulders. The weather was too warm now for a coat, yet a lady in New York City still had to be respectably dressed when she left the house.

As Rose gazed at Tiffany, she was once again reminded that her little darling was not so little anymore. Ever since Tiffany had turned eighteen, Rose had said more than one prayer that her daughter would stop growing. She was already well above average height at five feet eight inches and often complained about it. Tiffany got that height from her father, Franklin, and got his emerald green eyes, too, she just didn't know it. She got fine bones from Rose and delicate features that made her more than pretty, but she'd only partially gotten Rose's red hair; Tiffany's was more a coppery hue.

"I've had a letter from your father."

No response.

Tiffany used to get so excited over one of Frank's letters, but that had been so long ago—about the time she'd stopped asking when he would visit.

It broke Rose's heart to see the indifferent attitude her daughter had adopted toward her father. She knew Tiffany had no memories of him. She'd been too young when she and Rose had left Nashart, Montana. Rose knew she should have let them meet over the years. Frank had been magnanimous in sending the boys to her, though she was sure he had done it to make her feel guilty for not reciprocating and allowing their daughter to visit him. She'd been too afraid Frank wouldn't let Tiffany return home to her. It wasn't a groundless fear, it was her worst nightmare. In his rage he'd threatened to keep their daughter. He'd threatened so many things to try to make his family whole again. And she couldn't even blame him for that effort! But it wasn't going to happen, it couldn't. And now she was going to face her greatest fear: that once Tiffany got to Montana, Rose would never again see her.

She should have insisted that Tiffany's fiancé come to New York to court her. But that would have been the last straw for Frank. He'd honored Rose's wishes for fifteen years and stayed away, but this was the year she'd promised him Tiffany would live under his roof again. Rose couldn't, in good conscience, keep them apart any longer.

Tiffany stopped in front of her and held out her hand for the letter. Rose directed her to the sofa instead. "Sit down."

Tiffany raised her brow at being denied the letter, but took the seat across from Rose. The room was large. The town house was large. Rose's parents had come from old-world wealth, all of which was hers now. When Rose had returned from Montana Territory with her three-year-old daughter, she'd found her mother recuperating from a series of illnesses that had left her an invalid during the five years Rose had been away. Rose's mother had only lasted four more years, but at least Tiffany had gotten to know her grandmother.

That had been a painful time in Rose's life. She'd had to give up her husband, give up her three sons, then she'd lost her only remaining parent. But at least she'd had Tiffany. She would probably have gone mad with grief if she'd had to give up Tiffany, too. But now the day for that had come as well. . . .

"Is it time for the Talk again?" Tiffany asked in a bored tone.

"You've gotten sassy since you turned eighteen," Rose noted.

"If that's what you want to call this resentment that's been eating away at me, fine. Sassy it is."

"Tiffany—"

"I won't go to Montana, Mama. I don't care if it means bloodshed. I don't care if it means I won't ever see my brothers again. I refuse to marry someone I've never met." Tiffany crossed her arms over her chest and jutted out her chin defiantly. "There, I've finally said it and I'm not changing my mind."

"I quite agree."

Tiffany's eyes widened before she squealed in relief. "Thank you! You can't imagine how miserable I've been over the prospect—"

"You should let me finish. I agree you're not going to marry a man you've never met. You're going to go to Montana to meet him. You will have several months to get to know him. At the end of that time if you have no liking for him, then, yes, you can end this engagement and come back to New York before the weather turns bad. I give you my word on that, Tiffany."

"*Why* did you never tell me I would have a choice about this marriage you and my father arranged for me when I was just a baby?"

"Because I hoped you would honor this commitment I made for you of your own volition. I wanted you to grow accustomed to the idea, hoped you might even be looking forward to it by now."

"But Montana isn't even civilized yet!"

"Can we have this conversation without the shouting, please?" Then Rose added with a slight grin, "The Territory of Montana is not as uncivilized as you think. I thought your brothers convinced you of that. And it's some of the most beautiful country I've ever seen. You might actually like it there."

"I like it here, where I've grown up, where my friends live, where you live," Tiffany mumbled, then said louder, "where

men don't wear guns on their hips because there's always something that needs shooting, including people. How could you
even agree to this arrangement in the first place, Mama?"

"I'm the one who suggested it." She'd never told her daughter that before, and looking at Tiffany's widely rounded emerald eyes now, she wished she'd been able to explain some other
way. But there was no other way.

"So you're the one throwing me to the wolves?"

"Oh, good grief, Tiff, don't be so melodramatic. It was the
only thing I could think of to end the feud between the Callahans and the Warrens. That strip of land with the water on it
between the two properties isn't even what started it, but both
sides are using it to keep the feud alive, both claiming it's theirs.
I've never seen such pigheadedness, on both sides. Anytime
they got near that water at the same time, shots were fired. If
any cows wandered across it, they weren't given back, which
caused more shooting. Giving it to you and Hunter Callahan
as part of your marriage agreement will end the contention
over it."

"So you took it upon yourself to end a feud you didn't start
by sacrificing your only daughter?"

Rose made a sound of exasperation. "For your information,
young lady, Zachary Callahan is one of the most handsome
men I've ever met. I had no doubt that his young sons would
grow up to be just as handsome, considering the pretty wife he
married. I didn't think I was sacrificing you at all, I was quite
sure you'd be thrilled with a Callahan for a husband. But then
as an outsider, I saw things differently. The ranchers were aggressive, even possessive, yes, but I don't think that was unique
to the area. Frank and Zachary were just two strong-willed men
who weren't willing to concede an inch. Bad history started it,

and that water on the border between the two ranches wouldn't let it end. Personally, I don't think the Callahans are bad people. Zachary might be a competitive, ornery cattleman, but he has a reputation of being a devoted husband and a good father, which says a lot for a family."

"It wasn't up to you to end the feud, Mama. Why did you even try?"

She wasn't going to burden Tiffany with the horrors she'd lived through back then. Shots were fired so often she was afraid one of her children was going to catch the next bullet. Then a simple idea had occurred to her: to end that feud through marriage. When she'd first brought up the idea to Frank, she didn't know that she and Tiffany wouldn't remain in Montana. She'd imagined Tiffany and Hunter growing up together, being friends first, then falling in love naturally . . .

She tried to explain in simpler terms. "I hated that feud, but, yes, I tried to ignore it, until the night your father was carried home half-dead. It wasn't a Callahan that shot him, but one of the Callahans' hired hands. A funny thing about the West: employees take sides, too, and some of them don't follow orders too well. But regardless, your father came close to dying, and I was so desperate to put an end to the bloodshed that I'd try anything. And the betrothal did exactly that. There's been a truce ever since. Your brothers got to grow up without having bullets flying at them every time they went out on the range."

Rose waited breathlessly for Tiffany's response. What she'd told her daughter wasn't all a lie, only partial truths. But it was exactly what they'd all thought when Frank had been shot. But the shooter didn't work for the Callahans. He had another employer, one much more ruthless, who was pulling his strings. When she found that out and learned she couldn't put the blame where it belonged, she did the only thing she could think of to stop Frank from retaliating once he recovered: she brought up the idea of a truce through marriage again, a sure means of ending that deplorable feud for good, and insisted on it this time.

She was the only one who knew what really happened that night and why. It had to remain that way. But Tiffany's accepting an arranged marriage could really be the salvation of two neighboring families that were too stubborn to agree to share water rights instead of fighting over them. But Rose wouldn't force her daughter to solve a generations-old problem. She could only ask her daughter to give Montana and Hunter Callahan a chance.

Thankfully, Tiffany's expression turned a little curious. "So what happens if I do call the marriage off? They're back to trying to kill each other?"

Rose cringed. "I don't know. I'm hoping these fifteen years of getting along has made them realize they never should have carried on a fight their grandparents started that has nothing to do with them."

"What did start it?"

"I'm not even sure. Something about a wedding that turned into a shooting instead."

"You mean the two families were supposed to have been joined through marriage two generations ago?"

"Apparently."

"That doesn't portend well for your idea of trying it again," Tiffany pointed out. "In fact, a marriage between the two families is more likely fated to never happen."

Rose gave her daughter a stern look. "It won't happen with that attitude. Will you at least meet this man without prejudice? Give him a chance, Tiffany. He could make you very happy."

Tiffany mulled that over for a few moments before she allowed, "Now that I know I don't have to marry him if I don't want to, I suppose I can try and look at this from a new perspective—as a two-month summer holiday in a different part of the country. When are we leaving?"

"I'm not going—well, not all the way. I'll accompany you as far as Chicago and stay there to await the outcome of your courtship."

Tiffany's shoulders slumped with that news. "Why bother, if you're not going all the way?"

"Because I want to be relatively close by in case you need me, and with the rail lines connecting all the way to Nashart now, Chicago is pretty darn close. Anna will be going with you, of course. And I've arranged for a retired US marshal to meet us in Chicago to escort you on the last leg of the journey, right to your father's door."

Rose was going to start crying in a moment if Tiffany didn't stop looking so sad about this impending separation. "You aren't even a little excited about this trip?" she asked hopefully.

"No," Tiffany replied tonelessly as she stood up to leave the room.

"About seeing your father again?"

"Again?!" Tiffany swung around with a snarl. "I don't remember him, and you and he made sure I'd have no memories of him. So I'll be honest, Mama. If I could get this over with without laying eyes on Franklin Warren, I would."

"Tiffany!"

"I'm not kidding, and don't give me all those excuses about why I've grown up without a father. If he'd really wanted to see me, he would have found a way. But he didn't. And as far as I'm concerned, now it's too late."

Rose saw the angry tears welling in Tiffany's eyes before Tiffany bolted out of the parlor. God, what had she done to the people she loved the most?

Chapter Two

TIFFANY HATED FIGHTING WITH her mother, hated it so much the painful lump of emotion was still in her chest when she went downstairs for dinner that night. But her mother took one look at her and understood, holding out her arms. Tiffany flew into them for a hug. Both of them laughed after a moment because Tiffany, who was above average in height, had to bend over slightly to get her hug.

Rose put her arm around Tiffany's waist and led her into the dining room. Dinners were formal in the Warren household, guests or no, and mother and daughter dressed accordingly. Tiffany's evening gown was coral with ivory sequins outlining the square neckline. Rose's was navy blue with black lace, but her bright red hair countered the rather somber colors. Only one of the four Warren siblings had Rose's dark-red hair, Roy, the third oldest. The other two boys were blond like their father. Only Tiffany with her reddish-gold hair got a blending of both parents' hair colors.

"We won't talk about it anymore until it's time to pack,"

Rose assured Tiffany as they took their seats at one end of the long table.

"It's all right, Mama. I convinced myself I wouldn't be going. Now that I am, I have a few questions that are long overdue."

Tiffany realized she probably shouldn't have added the overdue part. A flash of wariness crossed her mother's face before Rose smiled and said, "Of course."

"I know that the Transcontinental Express can cross the country all the way to California in a record-breaking four days, and Chicago isn't even half that distance. I appreciate that you're going to travel with me that far, but why are you really going to stay in Chicago rather than return home to await the outcome of this courtship?"

"Is that really what's on your mind?"

Tiffany chuckled. "No. I just feel if you're going to go that far, I don't see why you can't go all the way to Nashart. Why spend two months in a hotel when—"

"Chicago is the closest big city that offers the comforts I'm accustomed to."

"Fine, but doesn't Nashart have a hotel?"

"It didn't the last time I was there, just a boardinghouse. It might have one now, but I can't hide in a town that size. Too many people will remember me. Frank would find out and he'd be breaking down doors."

Tiffany looked at her mother incredulously. "Breaking down doors? You're exaggerating, right?"

"No."

"Then why didn't he come here and break our door down?" Tiffany demanded, her tone taking on an angry note that, fortunately, her mother didn't seem to notice.

"Because he knew I'd have him thrown in jail." Then Rose added in disgust, "In Nashart, no one would blink an eye over such rambunctious behavior."

"Why not?"

"Because I'm still his wife and they all know it."

"Why is that, Mama?"

There it was, floating in the air between them, the question that interested Tiffany most and that had never been answered to her satisfaction. Her parents had been separated for fifteen years but they hadn't gotten a divorce so they could remarry. And Rose was still a beautiful woman. She wasn't even forty yet.

Tiffany's parents had met in Chicago when Rose had gone to visit her great-aunt, now deceased. Her last evening in the city, Rose had gone to a dinner party given by a friend of her aunt's, who was the lawyer Franklin Warren had hired to negotiate some cattle contracts he'd come to the city to arrange, so he'd been invited to the dinner, too. After talking with each other that evening—all evening, actually—Frank impulsively got on her train the next day and followed her all the way to New York and began a whirlwind courtship that swept Rose off her feet. They were married a month later. And that's about all Tiffany knew about her parents' marriage.

When Rose didn't answer the question, Tiffany added reproachfully, "I assumed when I turned eighteen, you'd finally tell me why I'm living here with you and my brothers are living in Montana with our father."

"There's nothing to tell," Rose said evasively, and began eating her soup, which had just been served. "Your father and I just weren't suited to each other."

"You were suited long enough to get married and have four children."

"Don't be impertinent."

Tiffany flinched. "I'm sorry. That really was uncalled for. But, Mama, please, I'm old enough to hear the truth, and I'd like to hear it before I actually meet him."

Rose continued eating. It looked as if she was going to pretend they weren't having this conversation. Tiffany hadn't touched her own soup yet.

She was debating whether to turn mulish or give up when Rose finally said, "We married too quickly, Tiffany, before we found out how little we had in common. And he didn't warn me ahead of time about that feud that was going to intrude on our marriage. I still tried to make a go of it. I did love him, you know."

And still did, Tiffany guessed, but she didn't say that. Rose was still evading the question. Telling her that she and Frank had nothing in common was purely an excuse so she wouldn't have to discuss the real reason she'd left her husband.

Rose added, "I would have divorced your father if I'd found a reason to."

"You mean another man?"

"Yes. But that never happened. And actually, I'm not sure I can even get a divorce. Not long after I snuck off, taking you with me, he said he would fight a divorce."

"You *snuck* off?"

"Yes, in the middle of the night, so I could catch the stage first thing in the morning to get a head start on Frank. The rail-road hadn't connected to Montana yet. And my maid delayed him from finding out I'd left by telling him I wasn't feeling well."

Tiffany was fascinated. This was the first she'd heard that her mother had fled Montana stealthily. But if Frank hadn't woken up and found her gone, then . . .

"You weren't—sharing the same room?"

"No, not by that point."

Tiffany wasn't blushing over the subject, but she wondered why her mother suddenly was. Rose hadn't blushed even once a couple of years ago when she'd given Tiffany all the information she would need to know about married life. But if her parents' marriage had deteriorated to the point of their not even sharing the same bed, then Tiffany pretty much had part of the answer. Rose must have stopped wanting her husband—in that way. Either that or Franklin Warren had simply turned into a bad husband, one that Rose couldn't stand living with anymore. And the latter was something Tiffany wanted to know *before* she showed up at his ranch. What if he prevented her from leaving if she decided not to marry Hunter Callahan, the same way he'd tried to prevent Rose from leaving?

But she gave her mother a reprieve from answering that question since Rose seemed uncomfortable with the subject. And Tiffany was still curious about how her mother managed to escape, especially since Tiffany now wondered if she might have to do the same thing.

"Isn't a horse faster than a stagecoach?" she asked.

"Yes, and I knew Frank would catch up to us, so in the next town I bought a stage ticket to the nearest train depot, but we didn't get on it. I hid us in that town instead."

"I have no memories of that trip, none at all."

"I'm not surprised, as young as you were."

"So he got ahead of us?"

"Yes. It was much less nerve-racking knowing where he was than constantly having to look over my shoulder. I telegraphed my mother so she knew to expect him and turn him away. I wasn't able to go directly home because of his stubbornness. For two days he didn't sleep, he just stood across the street from this house, waiting for us to show up. For three months he stayed in New York, banging on the door to this house daily. One day he even forced his way in."

"Were we here yet?"

"No, I wasn't about to go home until he actually left the city. You and I stayed with an old school friend nearby. Mama had Frank arrested, of course, for pushing past our butler and searching the house from top to bottom. She was furious with him by then because his persistence was keeping us from coming home. She let him rot in jail for a week before she dropped the charges at my request. He finally gave up after that and returned to Montana."

"Maybe he hasn't divorced you because he still hopes you'll come back to him," Tiffany said.

"Oh, I've no doubt of that. No matter what I said, no matter how nasty I got about it, he continues to think I'll return to him someday."

"Will you?"

Rose lowered her eyes to the table. "No."

"And you don't think that the fact that you haven't tried to get a divorce gives him false hope? Surely after this long he wouldn't still fight it, would he?"

"I don't know. He said he'd go to his grave married to me. He's a stubborn man. He just might. But like I said, I've never had incentive to find out."

"You two write to each other," Tiffany said incredulously. "Why haven't you simply asked him?"

Rose smiled wryly. "We don't write about 'us' in those letters, Tiff. We did for a while, at least he did. He was angry that I left without telling him, then he was heartbroken when I refused to go back, then he got angry again. He finally got the message that I would only write about you children and nothing else. The one time he wrote about our marriage, I didn't answer him for a year. When I finally did, I warned him you would be reading his letters from then on, so he confined himself to neutral subjects."

All those letters Tiffany got to read were friendly in tone. Some were even funny, indicating that her father had a sense of humor. But all he ever wrote about were the ranch, her brothers, and people she didn't know, friends of his and her mother's in Montana, people she'd probably meet once she got there. Never in those letters did he address Tiffany directly, other than to say, *Give Tiffany my love.* But she also got to read Rose's letters to him, and her mother always asked her if she wanted to add anything to the letters. She used to. She told him about learning to ice-skate with her best friend, Margery, and that Tiffany thought it was fun when she fell through the ice, but no one else did. She told him about David, a boy who lived on her block, and how she felt so bad for accidentally breaking his nose, but that he forgave her, so they were still friends. She told him about the kitten she found and lost and how she and Rose searched for it for weeks. She shared a lot in those letters—until she began to resent that he never visited her, not even once.

That resentment got worse, especially when her brothers would arrive at the town house alone. She used to stand at the door, staring at the coach that dropped them off, waiting for her father to step out of it, too. He never did. The coach would drive off. Empty. After the second time that happened, that's how her heart felt anytime she thought of Franklin Warren. Empty.

She stopped standing at the front door with hope in her

heart and tears in her eyes, and she stopped reading Frank's letters, or adding anything to Rose's. She'd been nine or ten at the time, she couldn't remember exactly. She only pretended to read them after that, so her mother wouldn't know how painful she found her father's rejection of her. It was the only way she could shield herself from something that hurt that much. She tried to put her father so far out of her mind that he didn't exist—until she got a letter from one of her brothers that mentioned their father and clearly conveyed how much they loved him. Then the tears would stream down her cheeks before she finished reading it.

Her brothers didn't know how she really felt either. The boys still talked about their father when they visited. *They* loved him. Of course they did, he hadn't abandoned them as he'd abandoned her. They just didn't notice that she wasn't listening to them, or that she interrupted them to get them to talk about something less painful. She hated it when they had to leave to return to Frank. She had so much fun with them when they were here—playing with them, riding with them in the park, being teased by them. It felt as if they were a real family. Their departure always proved they weren't.

"Did you lie to me, Mama? Do you actually hate him?"

"That's a strong word that isn't at all appropriate. He's an infuriating man. His stubbornness rivals my own. He had the sort of arrogance that I suppose comes with carving an empire out of nothing. He was at war with his neighbors. Sometimes I think he actually enjoyed the conflict. Some days I was afraid to even leave the ranch, but his attitude was for me not to worry my pretty head about it. You can't imagine how exasperating that was. I got so angry I could have ridden over to the Callahans' and shot the lot of them. I might even have tried it if I actually knew how to use a rifle. No, I didn't hate him, I just couldn't live with him anymore."

"And you're not going to tell me why, are you?"

"I did—"

"You didn't! He cheated on you, didn't he?" she guessed.

"Tiffany!"

"Just tell me yes. It's the only thing that makes any sense."

"It was simply two people who couldn't live compatibly in the same house anymore. I cared enough about him to leave, so he could find someone else."

Nearly in the same breath alluding to fighting then just the opposite, that Rose cared too much? What was so horrible about the truth that Rose was making up so many excuses, none of them with the ring of truth to them?

And then Tiffany threw out another guess, "Or you found someone else and it just didn't work out?"

"Tiffany, stop it. There was no other man. There was no other woman. It was a tragedy, it still is. Why are you making me relive it?"

That was the one question her mother knew would make her back off. And Tiffany did just that. She loved her mother so much. But she'd lived too long with the hurt of her father abandoning both of them. And now that she was finally going to meet him, she was afraid that all that hurt would spill out in recriminations when she got there, because while her mother might not hate Frank Warren, Tiffany was sure that what she felt for him had to be hate. It was too strong to be anything else.

Oh, God, she'd managed to put ice around her heart and pretend to be indifferent to her father's rejection. Now all that pain was suddenly back, welling in her chest, and she felt like the little girl standing at the door again, staring at an empty coach.

"I'm sorry," she said to her mother. "I was actually hoping you could give me a reason not to hate my father and you haven't done that. I'll go to Montana to honor the commitment you made, but I don't want to see him any more than you do."

She wasn't shouting it this time, which warned her mother it wasn't just an emotional statement, she actually meant it. And she added, "Callahan can court me from town, can't he? I don't actually have to stay at Papa's ranch, do I?"

"And how will it look to the Callahans if you're at war with your father? Not exactly reassuring that the feud will come to an end, is it?"

"Fine," Tiffany grumbled ungraciously. "I'll tolerate him."

Rose actually burst out laughing. "Baby, you'll be gracious and polite. You've been raised to be a lady. Now we're changing the damn subject," she added, quite unladylike herself. "Eat your fish. It's probably the last you'll be having for a while. Cattlemen eat beef and nothing else."

Tiffany nodded, but she wasn't used to feeling so frustrated. Despite everything her mother had just said, she *still* didn't know why her parents had separated. But if her mother wouldn't tell her, maybe her father would. . . .

Chapter Three

"AND I WAS SO sure I could get used to traveling," Anna huffed indignantly on Tiffany's behalf. "Your mama should have warned us that fancy Pullman car she rented wouldn't be coming with us on the last leg of the trip."

Tiffany grinned at her maid across the table in the dining car. "Mama spoiled us with the Pullman car. This is how most people travel across the country."

Anna Weston had been Tiffany's maid for four years now. Blond, brown-eyed, she was only five years older than Tiffany, though her cherubic looks made people think she was much younger. Despite being only twenty-three, Anna had more accomplishments under her belt than most women who had to work for a living. In addition to her being well read and having beautiful penmanship, one of her brothers had taught her how to lay wallpaper seamlessly, her father had taught her how to build and repair furniture, and her mother had taught her to play four different musical instruments. The agency that had placed Anna with the Warrens had gotten her two other job offers: one as a governess and another as a teacher. So Anna had her choice of employment.

Tiffany didn't know that until after Anna had come to work for them. She didn't know either that Anna had almost turned down the job because Tiffany had made her laugh during the interview. It wasn't that Anna didn't have a sense of humor, only that she did not think it appropriate to reveal it to her employer. But Anna was practical, too. In the end, she accepted the job in the Warren household because it paid much more than the other two choices she'd had at the time. But the maid prided herself on being strictly professional at all times, even to the point that she refused to call Tiffany anything other than Miss Tiffany. But that didn't stop Tiffany from trying to break down Anna's stiff formality. She saw no reason why she and Anna couldn't be friends as well as employer and employee. Only on rare occasions did Tiffany think her efforts might be working.

But while Anna wouldn't call herself Tiffany's friend and probably never would, she was fiercely loyal to Tiffany. And protective, which made her a fine chaperone. If a man even looked sideways at Tiffany, Anna gave him her hell-hath-no-fury look. And thankfully she was adventurous—well, until they left Chicago she had been. She'd agreed to travel to the "Wild West" because she'd admitted that she'd always wanted to see more of the world. Tiffany wanted to travel, too. She wanted to go on a grand tour of Europe like other young ladies her age, or even up to her friend Margery's cottage in Newport, where she'd spent a good deal of time last summer. But she certainly didn't want to go to uncivilized Montana Territory.

"The seats on this train aren't that uncomfortable, just not as lushly padded as those in the Pullman. At least this train has a dining car," Tiffany pointed out.

Anna's expression turned even more sour, telling Tiffany the seats weren't the problem. Of course they weren't. Anna's real complaint was how crowded the train was, and the heat and the stench that came with such overcrowding. The long seats in the passenger cars were designed for two to three people, but they were now occupied by four or even five, including children and screaming infants. Tiffany would have been complaining if Anna hadn't beaten her to it, which made it quite difficult for her to see the bright side of their situation. This was such a far cry from having that fancy private Pullman all to themselves, which had been like riding in a small parlor!

Rose certainly wouldn't have let them get on this train if she'd known they'd be traveling in such deplorable conditions. But then the long line of farmers hadn't boarded in Chicago but after they'd crossed the border into Wisconsin. The conductor had apologized to Tiffany and Anna, explaining that the high number of passengers was quite out of the ordinary, but nonetheless, they were now operating as an immigrant express train. It was just their rotten luck that a new tract of farmland had opened up in Montana and had been advertised in the East, causing hundreds if not thousands of immigrants to pour into the territory to start new lives. While the influx of farmers was good for Montana's growing population, which needed more food crops, it made the train ride into the territory uncomfortable.

"Look on the bright side," Tiffany said to Anna as their lunch was served. "We're actually going to arrive a few days early because the train is no longer stopping at every depot to pick up more passengers, merely to refuel and resupply as needed. And Mama said the ranch house is big and finely furnished, thanks to her. She's sure we'll feel right at home when we get there."

After reading Frank's last letter, Rose had also said, "They've already started building your house on the contested land—and come to blows. It was a mistake to think they could work together before the marriage takes place. But that's your father for you, quite the optimist."

Her mother had said that with such a fond expression on her face it sparked all sorts of new possibilities in Tiffany's mind, including one she used to think about often when she was little, before she'd turned bitter—getting her parents back together.

Before the waiter finished setting their plates down, he leaned slightly toward Tiffany and whispered, "I'm sorry, miss, but due to the long line, we won't be able to finish serving before the dinner hour is over if we don't fill every seat at the tables now."

It wasn't the first time Tiffany and Anna would have to dine with strangers. If the train hadn't turned into an express line to deal with the land giveaway, they could have taken advantage of restaurants at the station stops. As it was now, they were barely given twenty minutes to stretch their legs when the train stopped, sometimes not even that. But at least they still had the dining car, crowded though it was.

Tiffany nodded her understanding to the waiter. Anna sighed. A young woman named Jennifer, whom they had met the day before, sat down with a chuckle. Blond, rather pretty, she was dressed similarly to Tiffany, just without the high-fashioned bustle and in much less expensive material. Still, she was obviously a city girl, not one of the farmers' wives dressed in faded calico dresses. Jennifer also seemed to be traveling alone, which Tiffany thought was quite brave of her.

A moment later, a young farmer joined them, too, wearing overalls and a misshapen hat that he didn't remove. The harried waiter set down two more plates for him and Jennifer before rushing back to the kitchen. The farmer didn't say a word, just gave them the briefest of nods before he lowered his head bashfully and started eating. He was probably embarrassed to be seated with women he didn't know, or afraid they might be offended if a strange man spoke to them. Anna probably would have been, so it was just as well he didn't try.

Jennifer, on the other hand, was gregarious. "We meet again," she said to Tiffany. "Now that we're making a habit of this, I should probably introduce myself properly. Jennifer Fleming of Chicago. I'm a housekeeper by trade. My agency is sending me to Nashart for a year—or longer if I find I like it there."

Tiffany's eyes widened, recalling what her mother had told her while helping her pack for the trip. Tiffany had asked Rose, "Why the new clothes, Mama? I'll have no use for them on a ranch."

"You *will* use them. You will not change your routines just because you will be in Montana. I citified your father while I was there. He became used to a house full of servants, formal dinners, and the finer things in life. He may have regressed after I left, but you need only remind him of what you are accustomed to and I have no doubt he will adjust accordingly, if he hasn't already. He wrote that he's hiring a housekeeper from Chicago to make you feel more at home."

Tiffany hadn't read that in his last letter, so it must have been in an earlier one that Rose hadn't let her read. Could this young woman sitting next to her be that housekeeper? How many housekeepers from Chicago could be going to a small town like Nashart?

Tiffany laughed. "This could be quite a coincidence. I wonder if it is my father who has hired you. Franklin Warren?"

"Indeed!"

"I was under the impression you were already at the ranch," Tiffany said.

"I should have been. I had to placate my family, and my fiancé, who wanted me to wait until he could come with me. It was his idea that we start our lives together on this side of the continent. Though he favors California, he's willing to give Montana a try if I like it there. He's still quite annoyed at me for not waiting for him, but I couldn't pass up this opportunity when my agency offered it to me because it pays so well. Your father must be quite rich."

Tiffany had no idea if her father was rich, so she merely smiled in reply. Anna was giving Jennifer a disapproving look. Anna had met her fair share of housekeepers; so had Tiffany for that matter. Neither had met one who was such a chatterbox, or as young as Jennifer. But these were unusual circumstances, their traveling together on a hot, crowded train into a part of the country that was barely civilized. It could just be nervous chatter. Besides, Jennifer wasn't working yet, so maybe she didn't think she had to adopt a formal, professional manner with the daughter of her new employer until she reported for duty.

Jennifer continued to chatter about the trip. The farmer never said a word, didn't even introduce himself, just kept his head down the whole while. It was highly inappropriate that he even be sitting at their table, but understandable considering more men than women were on the train. Anna made her disapproval known though, at least to Tiffany, giving her all sorts of glances and nods directed at her plate. Tiffany almost laughed at the maid's facial contortions, but she got the message: to finish eating quickly so they could leave. She did, and after they said good-bye to Jennifer, who said she'd walk up to their car for a visit later that afternoon, they returned to their seats, where they found Thomas Gibbons, their well-armed escort.

The retired US marshal was on the back end of middle-age and not very friendly. The little that Rose had said about him before he joined them in Chicago was that he'd been recommended by the Pinkerton Agency, which she'd contacted. He worked for them occasionally if a job led anywhere near the Rocky Mountains, where he used to be stationed. He ate only twice a day, breakfast and dinner, so he hadn't joined them for lunch. While he took his job seriously, he let them walk around the train on their own. Anytime they left the train, though, at watering holes or depots, he was right beside them, his hand never far from the gun he wore on his hip.

They were a long way between towns, weren't due to reach the next one until evening, and Tiffany hadn't heard yet if they would even be stopping there. The farmers were supposed to disembark tomorrow morning, which would give her and Anna some peace and quiet for the last few hours of their trip.

"We should have waited until the line for the dining car was gone," Anna said, getting in one more complaint as Mr. Gibbons stood up and stepped into the aisle to allow Tiffany and Anna to reach their seats closer to the window.

He had gallantly taken the aisle seat, where he had to put up with a good deal of jostling as people walked down the aisle unsteadily while the train was moving. Since their car was pretty much in the middle of a long line of cars, many people walked through it on their way to and from the dining car.

"And risk their running out of food again?" Tiffany replied as she waited for Anna to take the seat closest to the window. "I didn't mind sharing the table."

Watching the countryside pass by was the highlight of the trip for both young women, so they were taking turns in the window seat. The view from the middle seat wasn't obstructed, but the window seat provided a more panoramic view.

The train had cut through the southern part of Wisconsin where wheat fields abounded, but Tiffany had heard the farmers talking about how the land there was becoming less fertile, which was why so many of them were excited about starting fresh in Montana. Well, the men were. She'd caught some of the wives crying over having to leave homes that had been in their families for generations.

The terrain in Minnesota had been more interesting, with many pretty lakes and prairies, though it, too, had its fair share of farms. The Dakota Territory, in comparison, was sparsely settled and was still mostly wilderness and open plains. She'd seen a few settlers near their small sod houses. She'd seen her first buffalo! But what she'd seen that morning when she'd had her turn at the window had been a little unnerving: two men, sitting on horses with no saddles on a bluff, just staring at the train as it passed. The men were bare-chested and wore their long, black hair in braids. She'd craned her neck to continue watching them until they were out of sight.

Anna had been napping at the time, her head resting on Tiffany's shoulder. Tiffany hadn't woken her to show her the Indians and had decided not to mention it to her, either. Rose had assured her the Indian wars were over in Montana, the last major battle having occurred six years ago. The cavalry had lost, but a year later the soldiers had chased down the tribes and forced them to move to reservations outside the territory.

As Tiffany settled into her middle seat, the train lurched to a stop and Mr. Gibbons was almost thrown off his feet before he could resume his. Tiffany was confused by his worried expression as he sat down slowly.

Anna didn't notice and was saying in exasperation, "*Now* what? I'll warrant the train has broken down due to all this extra weight."

"Nonsense," Tiffany said. "It's probably just something on . . . the . . . track."

It was neither. Tiffany's words died off at the sight of the man who entered the car with a gun in his hand and a bandanna wrapped over the lower half of his face.

Chapter Four

"Don't be making no sudden moves now, hear?"

The marshal started swearing foully under his breath. Tiffany's mouth had dropped open. Anna was frozen and silent—for the moment.

Jennifer was dragged into the car by another train robber who came in behind the first. Tiffany thought the second man looked somewhat familiar, though she was too alarmed to figure out why. Jennifer must have been passing between the cars when she ran into him. The housekeeper was in tears as she hurried to an empty seat where she crouched down. She looked terrified, poor woman.

Tiffany didn't feel too brave herself. The feelings that overcame her as soon as the surprise wore off were like nothing she'd ever before felt, almost like a wave of heat that left a slight trembling behind. Her palms began to sweat, her heart was racing. She wanted to slide down in her seat as Jennifer had done, but she couldn't move!

Anna gripped Tiffany's hand—to gain courage for herself,

or to give some to Tiffany? Were train robbers violent, leaving no witnesses alive? No, the robbers wouldn't have covered their faces if they intended to kill people—would they? The thought didn't give Tiffany much comfort, didn't end her paralysis either. She couldn't even close her eyes. She just watched in helpless, fearful fascination as the scene unfolded.

With her eyes riveted on the pair of robbers at the front of the car, it finally dawned on her why the second man looked familiar. She recognized his clothes and that misshapen hat. He was the farmer who had sat at her table in the dining car! But obviously he'd merely been disguised as a farmer so he would blend in with the other men on this train. No wonder he'd kept his head down during the entire meal and hadn't said a single word that would draw her or Anna's eyes to him. He didn't want them to be able to describe him to the authorities. Tiffany clung to that hopeful thought, that they'd survive this terrifying experience and be able to give an account of it.

"Just hand over all valuables, then we'll leave, and you'll get where you're going in one piece," the first robber instructed in a gruff tone. "Something from everyone, and don't try to pretend you don't have any money or jewels. If we think you're holding back, we'll just take your clothes as well. So if you don't want to arrive buck naked in the next town, fill the sack and do it quickly. But first, place all your weapons on the floor and slide them into the aisle. Now!"

With a few thuds and the sound of metal skittering across the wood floor, guns started landing in the aisle. Thomas wore two, but he only offered up one. The other he tucked under the edge of Tiffany's wide skirt on the seat. She was too terrified to think about what he was doing. The passengers in front of her were turning their heads, looking at the back of the car. Tiffany turned, too, and saw a third robber coming down the aisle holding a sack out to each passenger he passed. He held the sack in one hand and a gun in the other to make sure the passengers complied. Tiffany noticed a fourth man, gun in hand, too, who was guarding the back door. Purses, watches, rings, money clips, all were hastily being dropped into the sack. More women were crying loudly and more passengers were hiding low in their seats, out of the line of fire in case any shooting started. At least one baby had started screaming.

When the robber with the sack had reached them, the marshal dropped a money clip and a watch in it, but Tiffany could still barely move and her eyes got rounder as the thief looked at her directly, waiting for her to contribute her share to the sack. It wasn't that she didn't want to oblige. She didn't have much of value on her, wasn't even wearing jewelry for the trip. She had a little traveling money in her purse and a little more pinned to her petticoat, but not much since her mother had transferred all she might need to the Nashart bank long before they'd left home. She simply couldn't move!

Thomas took charge, lifting the purse from her lap and dropping it in the sack. Anna was another matter; her purse wasn't visible and she wasn't moving either. She was scrunched tightly against the window, as far from the outlaw as she could get. But the robber hadn't seemed to have even noticed Anna yet; his eyes were still on Tiffany.

"I've a mind to take you with us," he said to Tiffany. "I'd say you're the most valuable thing on this train, fancy piece like you."

Tiffany was sure her heart stopped beating, she was so scared. Oh, God, he was serious! She could see it in his dark eyes and feared he wasn't talking about taking her for ransom. . . .

"Get on with your business," the marshal growled at the man. "She's not—"

"Shut up, old man," the outlaw said, but that wasn't enough, he actually raised his hand holding the gun to hit Thomas with it.

Horrified, Tiffany shot to her feet without thinking. "Stop it!"

She was desperate to keep the man from hurting the marshal. He was the only one who could keep these robbers from dragging her off the train, and he wouldn't be able to help her if he was unconscious! But while she got the outlaw's eyes back on her, she had no idea what to say or do, now that she'd stopped him. But she didn't have to do anything else.

The moment she stood up, the gun her skirt had concealed on the seat was left in plain view, so she pretty much forced Thomas into action. He snatched the weapon up with one hand, yanked her down with the other, and shot the robber holding the sack in the belly. Almost in the same breath, he shot the man at the back door, too.

With no robbers behind him now, he ducked down behind the back of the seat in front of them, taking cover from the bullets that immediately came his way. Anna had already pushed Tiffany to the floor and fallen on top of her to protect her, screaming, "You're crazy, you're crazy, you're absolutely crazy!"

Yes, she was. If she had thought about it even for a moment, she would never have deliberately drawn the robber's attention back to herself. She would castigate herself later for doing something so impulsive—if they survived this ordeal.

There was more gunfire, quite a bit of it. Some of the other passengers had grabbed their guns back from the floor, inspired by Marshal Gibbons to join in the fight. As Tiffany lay with her face pressed against the floor and Anna wailing hysterically on top of her, she prayed for the deafening gunfire to end. She didn't want to die! Suddenly, there was silence, although she heard shots in the distance.

Then she heard a short bark of laughter and a man say, "Good work, men, but this isn't over yet. The engineer caught sight of one of them robbers racing toward the train, leading eight horses. He got off a lucky shot so the horses scattered, leaving the thieves with just the wagon they brought to cart away their loot. The horse count suggests there's four more outlaws at the back of the train needing to be dealt with. I'll welcome volunteers."

Tiffany had no doubt that the marshal would be one of those volunteers. In fact, he leaned down and told her, "This won't take long, I reckon. Just stay where you are and you'll be safe."

With the immediate danger over, Tiffany sighed with relief. And she could move again . . . well, not exactly. After a moment when Anna's weight didn't budge from her back, Tiffany said, "I'm sure he didn't mean that literally. You *can* get off of me, you know. I'll be the first to hug the floor again if those criminals come back this way."

"I'm not sure what came over me," Anna said as she got back into her seat and helped Tiffany up. "But what on earth came over you, to confront that man like that?"

Tiffany wanted to say it had been a good plan since she knew what Thomas was going to do, but of course that would be a lie. So all she said was "I was protecting our protection."

"You could have been shot instead!"

Tiffany was distracted for a moment by the sight of several of the male passengers and train attendants removing the dead bodies of the four outlaws from the car. She couldn't help shivering and then turned back to Anna.

"Didn't you hear what that outlaw said? He was going to cart me off with the rest of the valuables as if I were a bauble! I was desperate to prevent that from happening. So I panicked. And since it worked out rather well, stop fussing about it."

Anna sighed at that point, confessing, "I was so scared. I've had my purse snatched before. I've been pickpocketed twice. My father's house was robbed while we were sleeping in it! So it's not as if I haven't experienced my fair share of robberies. I've just never had a gun pointed at me before."

Tiffany knew exactly what Anna meant. There was a lot of crime in New York City, but Tiffany had always been sheltered from it. This was the first time she'd come face-to-face with a robber holding a gun. They'd been in serious danger. She refused to think about what could have happened if the marshal and those other brave passengers had lost the gunfight.

But the makeshift posse ended up winning the day with the help of the railroad employees, who were used to dealing with train robbers and traveled armed. The passengers in Tiffany's car cheered when the train started moving again. Some of them were laughing and some of them were jeering as they crowded around the windows on the side of the car that afforded a view of two robbers who had just jumped off the moving train and were racing to catch up with the wagon full of stolen trunks and valises that was speeding away.

Tiffany kept looking at the back door expecting Marshal Gibbons to return. The passengers quieted down when one of the train attendants announced that several of the passengers who had fought back were injured. Tiffany's heart sank when she learned that Marshal Gibbons was one of them.

Chapter Five

THE MARSHAL DIDN'T REGAIN consciousness before the train reached the next town. Tiffany was beside herself with worry because one of the train attendants who was attempting to treat the wounded passengers told her the marshal might not make it. She didn't know him well, he'd barely spoken with her, but he'd guarded her life admirably today. She would feel horrible if he didn't recover. His critical condition made the loss of all but one of her trunks in that robbery seem inconsequential.

With the help of the stronger male passengers, the three wounded men were carried straight to the local doctor. The marshal's wound was the most serious, so he was treated first. Tiffany and Anna waited anxiously to hear the doctor's verdict. They paced up and down the entrance hall of the doctor's home office for almost half an hour before the doctor approached them and said, "He's starting to come to, so you can see Mr. Gibbons now, but only for a few minutes. I'm sorry if this isn't your final destination because Mr. Gibbons isn't going anywhere for a while. I'm confident he'll recover, but he won't be on his feet anytime soon."

"Are we going to stay and wait for him?" Anna asked after the doctor walked back into the ward.

"We can't when we don't know how long that will be," Tiffany replied. "But we'll be fine. This is the last stop in the Dakota Territory. We'll be in Nashart tomorrow. I'll visit with the marshal while you go find out how much time we have before the train pulls out."

Anna didn't budge and gave her a pointed look. "Are you *sure* you want to go on alone?"

Tiffany tsked. "What are the odds of another train robbery happening?"

"Probably higher than we'd like."

"Nonsense."

Anna hesitated another moment before she nodded and left the building. If they hadn't been so close to their destination, Tiffany knew Anna would never have given in.

Tiffany found Thomas with his eyes open and on her as she approached his cot in the doctor's one-room ward. "You're a hero," she said softly as she sat in the chair beside him. "Thanks to you and a few other brave men, those farmers can go on to their promised land and still afford to start their farms. The doctor says you'll be fine, but you won't be leaving this bed for a while."

"I'm sorry, Miss Warren. I know your father is expecting you on time and will raise hell if you—"

"I've already telegraphed him," she said, interrupting Thomas. "He has a friend in town who will escort me the rest of the way. So you can rest easy."

Thank God Anna wasn't there to hear that lie, Tiffany

thought, but still she couldn't help blushing. She didn't make a habit of lying, yet this was the second time she'd lied to the good marshal. The first time had been when the farmers boarded the train and the conductor had told them that because of the unusual circumstances and the train's going express to Montana, they'd actually arrive at her destination three days early. Thomas had suggested she telegraph her father to let him know. She'd told him she would, but she hadn't informed her father. She had blushed then, too.

She might have agreed to two months of purgatory in the wilds of the West, but she knew the worst part of it wasn't going to be being courted by a man she didn't know, it was going to be living under her father's roof. She didn't want him to meet her at the train depot, where she was afraid she might cause a scene. She honestly didn't know if she'd start screaming at him for not visiting her while she was growing up . . . or cry and hug him. Considering the resentment that had built up in her over the years, it was likely to be the former. But either way, she'd prefer not to meet her father in public, so she was glad he didn't know that she'd be arriving early.

And Marshal Gibbons didn't seem to suspect her of lying this time either. He said with a sigh, "I had a feeling there'd be trouble after the farmers boarded. It was just too convenient, that many people crowded in one place, most of them bringing their life savings with them to buy the materials they'd need to start their farms. This land giveaway has been big news in the territory. Figured it might draw outlaws out of their holes to take advantage of it."

Tiffany nodded and patted the marshal's hand, glad the ordeal was over. Now she knew firsthand how dangerous the West really was. Had she *really* told her mother that she would view this trip as a holiday? She'd hated every minute of it since she'd parted from Rose. She just wanted to go home!

Tiffany stayed with Marshal Gibbons until Anna returned and told her they had to leave now or else they would miss the train. Tiffany had thought there would be a longer delay, considering what had happened. But the dead outlaws had been removed from the train, the wounded had been taken to the local doctor, the train's engineer and head conductor had informed the local sheriff of the robbery, and now the train was ready to go on its way.

Tiffany hesitated over leaving the marshal's bedside. She felt so guilty about his painful injuries, which she was responsible for since he wouldn't have been on that train if not for her. She almost decided to remain there to nurse him back to health. Almost. But saner thoughts prevailed, mainly that she didn't know much about nursing, so how much good could she do? And she couldn't bear staying in this primitive territory a day longer than she had to. She might get stuck in this tiny town if more express trains that wouldn't take on new passengers were going to come through.

Sixty days and no more she'd promised her mother, then she could return to the civilized part of the world. Well, she'd promised to be open-minded about Hunter Callahan, too, but really, how long would that take? Mere minutes, she didn't doubt.

She and Anna rushed back to the depot and got there with moments to spare. But they nearly missed the train anyway because of the Warrens' new housekeeper. Anna had already stepped on board. Tiffany had one foot on the step herself when Jennifer yelled at her to wait as she ran toward her and shoved a piece of paper in Tiffany's hand.

Tiffany didn't try to read it, there wasn't time, so she just asked, "What's wrong?"

"Give that to your father, please," Jennifer said anxiously, her expression full of misery—or was it guilt? "Tell him I'm sorry!"

The whistle blew, the train started to move, and Tiffany got her other foot off the ground before she was left behind. Jennifer was waving good-bye to her, but the housekeeper looked relieved now. Tiffany wondered why and glanced at the note before she took the last step up to join Anna.

"What was that about?" the maid asked.

Tiffany handed the note to her. "See for yourself. Meeting up with Western outlaws was too much for her. She's running back to her fiancé."

"Why do you look like you envy her?"

"Maybe because I wish I had the option of turning tail like that," Tiffany grumbled.

"The time to refuse to go to Montana was before you agreed to do it, not now when we're almost there."

Tiffany sighed. "I know. You just should have seen how relieved Jennifer looked, probably because she anticipated that I'd try to talk her out of going home and I didn't."

"Would you have?"

Tiffany's lack of options suddenly overwhelmed her. "No!" she said vehemently. "*She's* the lucky one right now. I don't blame her one little bit for going home when I don't want to be visiting this part of the country either. Even if my father had succeeded in hiring a housekeeper for me, I'm going to hate visiting him anyway."

"Then let's go home!" Anna said, sounding exasperated.

Tiffany looked at the maid. Of course Anna wanted to go

back East. She wasn't obligated to stay. *She* hadn't promised she would!

Stiffly Tiffany said, "You can, I can't. Honestly, Anna, I wouldn't blame you for going back where *we* belong."

Anna actually turned a little indignant over the offer. "I won't deny I thought about it while those bullets were flying. But the robbery is over and it is probably the worst thing we'll encounter. I'm staying—if you are."

Tiffany would have hugged the maid if Anna wouldn't have gotten all stiff and huffy about it. Instead she laughed and shook her head. "I hate to think of what type of servants they have out here if the good ones have to be hired from back East—and quit before they even arrive!"

Chapter Six

TIFFANY AND ANNA WERE the only passengers who disembarked in Nashart, Montana Territory, and they were still arguing when they stepped off the train. Tiffany's stubbornness had kicked in, and although she knew deep down that Anna was right, she was in the grip of the emotions that were clamoring inside her—fear, resentment, even anger—all because she was supposed to come face-to-face with her father, Franklin Warren, today.

But early that morning an idea had occurred to her of how she might put off that reunion a little longer. The dream she woke up to gave her the idea. In it she'd been standing in front of a door that was slowly opening to her, seeing a man on the other side of it who didn't actually have a face since she had no idea what he looked like. But she knew it was her father, and she started screaming until Jennifer was suddenly there, urging Tiffany to escape with her. Then she was running away from him with Jennifer beside her, holding her hand. They ran all the way back to New York, which was impossible, silly even, but it was just a dream, after all. Yet her fears had come to the surface in that dream, and before it started to fade from her mind, she realized she now had the means to avoid facing those fears—for a few days more.

She just needed her maid to go along with her plan because it wasn't going to work if Anna didn't agree to help her. She wasn't really asking for much, just a day or two of anonymity when she could talk to her father and observe him without his knowing who she was. They were three days early, so he wasn't even expecting her yet! It wasn't as if she weren't going to show up at the Warren ranch or intended to hide in town for three days. But Anna had balked and was proving to be quite stubborn about it.

"This will give me some time to talk to my brothers first before I introduce myself to Papa," Tiffany explained. "It's been five years since I saw Roy, longer since Sam and Carl visited. They were all still boys then. They're men now. I want to know how they feel about Papa, now that they're grown."

"You could ask them that in private, without pretending to be the housekeeper they are expecting."

Trust Anna to be forthright *and* logical. "Damnit, I'm not ready to be Frank Warren's daughter when I don't know anything about him and don't even know why Mama left him. I thought she would tell me the truth when I came of age, but she didn't. She gave me a bunch of excuses instead. I know she wouldn't have let me come here no matter the reason if she believed he was a bad man. But he must have done something bad to make her leave him, and I'm not as forgiving as she is. I don't know if I can reunite with him without accusing him of all sorts of things that might not even be true, and that's a horrible way for us to get acquainted, isn't it?"

Anna pursed her lips. "You haven't thought this through. He'll know you. He'll know——"

Finally sensing victory, Tiffany cut in, "But he won't! He hasn't seen me since I was three years old. He sent the boys to New York, but not once in all these years did he ever come with them to see me. And I don't really look enough like Mama—do I?—for him to think I'm his daughter. This *will* work. My brothers might recognize me, but I'll convince them to play along. Two days, that's all I'm asking for."

"You didn't let me finish," Anna admonished. "It's your hair he'll recognize. There's no way anyone can forget the color of hair like yours."

"Then we'll——"

Tiffany paused as a porter carried a few crates off the train and set them down next to them, forcing them to move out of the way. Her only remaining trunk was set down, too. She hadn't cried when she'd been told that most of her belongings had been stolen by the train robbers. They could be replaced. It was just one more thing to add to the list of complaints she was going to send off to her mother as soon as she had a chance to write her. Anna had been luckier. Her luggage, which she'd borrowed from her family, was so old and tattered that the robbers had ignored it.

Tiffany responded to Anna's remark about her hair, saying, "Then we'll dye it."

Anna was horrified. "No . . . we . . . will . . . not!"

"If you won't help, I'll do it myself. With black hair, my brothers might not even recognize me, but my father certainly won't. Black hair will throw him off completely, so no suspicion will enter his mind. Please, Anna. I don't know him at all, and he's disappointed me most of my life by refusing to be a part of it. I would as soon stay in town for this courtship I'm not interested in and not lay eyes on my father at all. But since my mama shot that idea down, I'd like a few days at least to find out what he's really like."

Anna tried a different tack to talk Tiffany out of her scheme. "You won't find hair dye in a town this small. Look over there, there's only one general store on the street and, by the looks of it, only one street!"

Tiffany finally turned around and looked at the town of Nashart, Montana. Anna had exaggerated. Several streets led off the wide main one, though they appeared to be mostly residential. And the one main street, which was lined with stores and businesses, was at least long. The town had obviously doubled in size since the time Rose had lived there, no doubt due to the arrival of the railroad.

"Well, that's a surprise," Tiffany said. "Nashart is bigger than I expected based on my mother's description of it. We can't even see to the end of the street. There could be all sorts of other stores down there—oh, my, they have a theater!" Tiffany said excitedly when she saw it. "And a restaurant next to it!"

Anna wasn't impressed. "One is open, the other is closed according to the sign on the door, so don't get your hopes up, Miss Tiffany, in that regard. Actors live in cities. They only travel to a small town for a few performances and then move on to the next small town."

"Yes, but we still might get lucky and see a troupe pass through in the two months we'll be here. Now, since it looks like Nashart does have a hotel, I'll get us a room while you find some dye. If the general store doesn't have any, you can try the barbershop."

"If they have one," Anna grumbled. "You know you will be

stuck with dyed hair for many months to come, and you will look silly with hair that is two different colors until your hair grows out—or you cut it all off."

Tiffany was horrified at the notion of cutting her hair and threw up her hands in defeat on that score. "I concede. I'll wrap it in a scarf or hide it some other way. We'll think of something."

Anna shook her head. "You're not considering all the consequences of this deception. Your father will be pleased to have you show up at his door early, surprising him. He will not be pleased when you show up at his door deceiving him. And what reason will you give him when you're done with the charade and admit who you are?"

"The truth. I'll try to present it without rancor, but I *will* tell him the truth. I've been harboring too much resentment not to."

"Fair enough. Just remember you said *without* rancor. I suppose you want me to remain in town while you carry out this trickery?"

"Why?"

"Because housekeepers don't travel with personal maids," Anna replied.

Tiffany frowned. "That won't do."

"It would for one day. I won't agree to more than that because anything longer and it becomes a deception rather than a surprise."

Having won, Tiffany couldn't keep the grin off her face. One day was long enough for her to find out how she would respond when she first clapped eyes on Franklin Warren.

Chapter Seven

"That's got to be her," Cole told his older brother, John.

"Like hell," John blustered. "She's dressed far too fancy."

"She's an Easterner. Did you think she'd show up in calico?"

"Too pretty, too," John mumbled. "You want to take the chance of bringing home the wrong gal?"

Cole chuckled, pointing out, "We're not going to just grab her and run, so maybe you should just let me do the talking. Better yet, why don't you go borrow us a wagon while I sweet-talk the lady. Damned inconvenient time for our good one to break down when we got more'n one thing to pick up that came in on the train today."

"No."

Cole sighed at that adamant response. "Can you be reasonable for *once*? You're too intimidating when you get in a surly mood, and you're *never* diplomatic. First sign of opposition and you start throwing punches! What are you so all-fired grumpy about today anyway?"

"Pa might think this is hilarious, I sure as hell don't," John said.

Neither did Cole, and he was the one who'd been shot at recently. Roy Warren swore he didn't do it, but Cole wasn't going to just take a Warren at his word. John was hot-tempered even on the best of days, so he should never have come along to carry out this task. They both took after their pa with brown eyes, but John had Pa's height, too, being well over six feet, while Cole was considered the runt in the family at only six feet. Cole got his smaller stature from their ma, as well as her brown hair, while the rest of the men in the family had black hair.

"We should hurry this up," John added as he glanced down both sides of the street. "I don't see any Warrens yet, but that could change at any moment. And I can't promise you I won't push back hard if they show up and start pushing."

Cole nodded, but he was starting to get worried, and not about the Warrens. "They might not've been told about the train's early arrival like we were," he said, then voiced his sudden unease: "What happens if she don't agree?"

"Why wouldn't she?"

"Yeah, but what if she don't?" Cole repeated.

"Pa said one way or the other, she comes home with us. We'll do what we have to do."

"Pa didn't figure on every eye in town being on her when he said that. You want to end up in jail?"

"How 'bout we just talk to her first 'fore you try to jump over all these obstacles we ain't run into yet?"

In the middle of the street, Tiffany finally managed to stop sneezing long enough to glare at the two cowboys who'd stirred up the cloud of dust she was choking on. But it wasn't really their fault, they'd merely ridden past her rather quickly, then come to a tearing halt nearby, which could well have been *her* fault.

Anna had already pointed out that they were causing something of a sensation in the town, which was why they'd been hurrying across the street to get out of sight inside the hotel. People had been coming out of stores to look at them, leaning over balconies, pointing fingers. Tiffany was a little surprised to see so many women dressed plainly in homespun clothes and so many men in work clothes wearing guns. High fashion had obviously not traveled this far west, but did Nashart get so few visitors that the sight of two strangers would cause such a stir?

Tiffany put a handkerchief to her nose and kept it there. One more thing to hate about the West. Dust. It settled on her clothes, discoloring them, and it made her sneeze. It was controllable in the city, but how did they control it here with their dirt streets?

"I only wanted to change out of these clothes we've been wearing for days, but now I need a bath, too," she complained to Anna.

"You actually think you'll find one here?"

Tiffany turned to stare at the maid aghast, only to find Anna pointing at a sign farther down the street: TIDWELL'S BATHHOUSE, HOT WATER AND SOAP.

"Wonderful," Tiffany groaned. "Boasting that they have soap, as if no one else in town does. I think we should get back on the train before it leaves."

"The bathhouse is next to a tavern, which, by the way, this town appears to have too many of, so it's probably for men who don't plan to reside in the hotel."

After that dust cloud they had both just endured, Tiffany

wasn't in a mood to hear tepid encouragement. Nothing short of a hot, steaming bath in a private room was going to appease her right now. "They call them saloons here, and if you were trying to relieve me, it didn't work."

"You'll get a bath at the hotel. I would wager a week's salary on it."

Tiffany finally noticed the slight grin on Anna's face. The maid was teasing her and trying not to laugh. "You're just full of surprises today, Anna Weston. You're lucky I didn't fire you for arguing with me over my decision. I still might. Now let's get out of the sun, and the dust."

Anna put her head down because she really couldn't hide that grin anymore. "Yes, Miss Tiffany."

Tiffany snorted indelicately and finished the trek across the wide street. She was just about to open the door to the hotel when a deep voice behind her said, "Are you the housekeeper, ma'am?"

She wasn't surprised that someone from the Warren Ranch had been sent to town to meet Jennifer. The housekeeper had probably sent word ahead to her new employer as soon as they'd been told how much sooner they would be arriving because of the farmers. Tiffany turned around, expecting to see one of her brothers standing there. Well, she could hope, since this would be a perfect opportunity to warn them she'd like her secret kept for a day, even if they didn't recognize her right off. Despite the years that had passed since she'd seen the three boys and the chance she might not recognize them either, she knew that blond and red hair wouldn't turn black or brown, and none of her brothers had brown eyes.

It was those two cowboys who had just stirred up the dust cloud she'd almost choked on, both of them now tipping wide-brimmed hats to her. Well, she reminded herself, she was just a servant, or about to pretend to be one. So she shouldn't be surprised that her father would merely send a couple of hired hands to collect a new employee.

Tiffany answered, "Yes, I've been hired by—"

"We know who sent for you, ma'am," the brown-haired young man cut in. "We're here to talk you into working for us instead."

Tiffany frowned, glancing between them. They were both young, tall, and actually rather handsome. They even bore a slight facial resemblance to each other, suggesting they were brothers. But why had they approached her if they weren't her father's men?

Just to make sure of that, she asked, "You're not from the Warren Ranch?"

"No, but can we step inside the hotel to finish this deal? Please, before any Warrens show up?"

"We don't have a deal—"

"We will."

"No, we will not," Tiffany said with finality, turning her back on them, and entered the hotel.

Anna barricaded the door with her body when the men started to follow Tiffany inside, her arms spread out to either side of the doorway. Her message was clear. They were not to bother Tiffany any further. The two men actually pushed right past her as if they didn't even see her there!

"Ma'am, you *really* need to hear us out."

Tiffany swung around, amazed the two cowboys had followed her into the hotel. Anna, behind them now, looked angry enough to start swinging her purse at them, which probably wasn't a good idea with both men wearing gun holsters.

Tiffany was exasperated. This was ridiculous. She was in dire need of a bath, and she didn't want to have to scream for help to get rid of two obnoxious young men. The hotel lobby was empty, except for an elderly man sweeping the floor at the back of the large room. She held up her hand to stop Anna from becoming aggressive in her defense of Tiffany and turned to the brown-haired cowboy, who had been doing all the talking.

"As briefly as possible, say what you have to say, then leave."

"You're awful uppity for a servant, ain't you?" the other man suddenly said.

Tiffany's mouth nearly dropped open. Her eyes flared wide for a moment. *He* was getting annoyed with *her*? But before she could lambaste him, his companion took off his hat and hit his friend with it.

"What part of *fancy Easterner* didn't you understand?" he growled.

"She's still just a servant—"

"A *fancy* servant, as fancy as they get. And when Pa hears you messed this up by shooting off your mouth, he'll tan your hide."

The black-haired cowboy who'd just got upbraided turned red in the face, but Tiffany didn't think it was from embarrassment. He was furious, possibly because he looked older than the other man and didn't like being reprimanded by a younger man. She hoped she wasn't blushing as well, having just had it spelled out rather plainly that she had no business sounding so imperious with them after going along with their assumption that she was the expected housekeeper.

Hat still in hand and looking conciliatory, the brown-haired man said to her, "Beg pardon, ma'am. Name's Cole Callahan. This here's my brother John. That ornery old cuss who hired you ain't the least bit friendly with us, but we're his closest neighbors."

Tiffany was reeling from the knowledge that these two men were her fiancé's brothers. Anna immediately looked contrite. Tiffany guessed Anna had indeed been about to swing her purse at them and would have regretted it because these were two of Tiffany's possible future in-laws.

Tiffany was also surprised to hear them refer to her father as an ornery old cuss. Was *that* why her mother had left Frank? He simply turned out to be too unpleasant and high-handed to live with? Rose did have a bit of a temper. She wouldn't have put up with orneriness for long. But old? Well, these two young men might consider anyone over forty old.

Highly curious now, Tiffany took a closer look at the men, wondering if Hunter looked like either of them. She had dozens of questions, none of which she could ask since she wasn't supposed to know about the Callahan family!

In a much milder tone she said, "I'm pleased to make the acquaintance of my employer's neighbors, even if you aren't the best of friends with each other."

"That's an understatement," John mumbled. "Thieves and liars who can't be trusted, the lot of them. You're lucky we aim to rescue you."

Tiffany stiffened indignantly on her brothers' behalf, so her tone was sharp when she replied, "And why would I take *your* word for that?"

"Now, John," Cole cautioned his bigger, older brother.

Tiffany didn't care if the older Callahan didn't like her questioning him. If he was going to hand out insults to *her* family, he had to expect some back. Oh, good grief, was this how feuds got out of hand?

But all John did was yell at someone behind her. "Hey, Billy, vouch for me. Am I or am I not an honest man?"

Tiffany looked behind her and realized John Callahan had called out to the skinny, old man who was sweeping the lobby floor. "Except when you're playing poker," Billy snickered.

"Answer the damn question," John said impatiently.

"Honest as the day is long in the summer, you betcha— except when you're playing poker," Billy said again, but with another snicker he quickly walked away, disappearing into the back of the hotel.

She noticed John hadn't asked the hotel worker to confirm that the Warrens weren't honest, because they were, but she wasn't supposed to know that yet. And considering John's size and intimidating manner, she wouldn't be at all surprised if he got the same affirmative response, true or not, no matter whom he asked to vouch for him.

So she went along with what he was trying to assert and simply said, "Thank you for the warning, gentlemen, but I am committed, so if that was your only reason for detaining me, I'll be on my way. Good day."

"How 'bout a rescue?" John snapped. "Seems like a damn good reason—"

Cole elbowed his brother to silence this time before saying, "What you probably don't know, ma'am, is the Warrens don't need a housekeeper, but we do. We even just lost our cook. So we figured to kill two birds with one stone and steal you out from under Frank's nose and get us some extra help to boot."

"Steal?" Tiffany gasped in alarm.

John actually shoved his brother halfway across the lobby just to have his say without any more interruptions. "What my brother means is, we'll pay you double what old Frank offered if you come work for us instead."

Chapter Eight

Tiffany could barely keep from laughing. Positively priceless. What servant would turn down a double salary? Jennifer certainly wouldn't, not when money had been her motive for coming here. She'd mentioned that she and her fiancé wanted to accumulate a nest egg before they got married. Logically, Tiffany had to accept the Callahans' offer, didn't she?

Two birds indeed, but the Callahan brothers didn't know they were *her* birds. Tiffany could now avoid meeting her father altogether, but still abide by the promise she'd made to her mother. A huge weight was lifted from her shoulders with that realization. She could also find out what kind of man Hunter Callahan was without his knowing she was his fiancée. She felt so relieved that she barely noticed how tense the brothers were, waiting for her answer. She avoided meeting Anna's eyes because she wasn't going to discuss *this* decision with the maid.

But she still had to put herself in Jennifer's shoes. While she already knew that the Callahans were a prominent family of ranchers, the housekeeper didn't. And wouldn't Jennifer present some conditions first?

She thought of one. "I was assured I would have my own room—"

John cut in, "Don't see why you'd need to share one when we've got extra."

"With a lock on the door."

"Pretty sure they've all got locks."

"And I will expect my wages to be paid promptly each week," she added.

"Pa pays the help. I'll mention it to him."

"Very well, I accept your offer."

John smiled at her for the first time. His relief was unmistakable, making her wonder what might have happened if she had turned them down. "You won't regret it," he assured her.

Anna had started to sputter. Tiffany quickly added, "Just give me a few minutes to say good-bye to the friend I made on the train, then I'll join you outside."

The Callahan brothers glanced around to find her "friend," then tipped their hats at Anna. The door had no sooner closed behind them than Anna lit into her.

"Have you lost your mind?"

Tiffany took Anna's arm and led her away from the hotel's entrance. "Keep your voice down!"

The maid glared at her. "Your charade was only supposed to last a day!" she pointed out in a softer though no less exasperated tone. "And it was only your father you wanted to fool, not the entire town."

"Yes, but who would have expected an opportunity like *this* to fall into my lap," Tiffany said excitedly. "Anna, don't ruin this for me. It's already set in motion. I'm going to be

Jennifer—*what* was her last name? I can't remember after only hearing it once."

"Fleming."

"You're sure it was Fleming? This won't work if I give the wrong name."

"Yes, I'm sure, and, no, it still won't work. You don't have a wardrobe suitable for a housekeeper for an *extended* time."

Tiffany laughed, relieved that was the only objection Anna could come up with this time. "They aren't going to know what I should or shouldn't wear, I doubt they even know what the duties of a housekeeper are. Besides, most of my wardrobe is littering the countryside, including all of my evening gowns. I can use the excuse that my work clothes were stolen in the train robbery if they think my few remaining day dresses are too fancy."

"Are you forgetting that your father expects you?"

"Not for another few days he doesn't, which is long enough for my mother to let him know I've been delayed."

"And how is she going to know to do that, or even agree to do that?"

"Anna, I never promised Mama that I'd meet my father, just that I'd give Hunter Callahan a minimum of two months. I'll let Mama know what I'm doing. I'll telegraph her before I leave town so she can arrange a 'delay' for my arrival at my father's ranch."

"And that will have her catching the next train here, I don't doubt."

Tiffany sighed. "I wish it would, but it won't. But I'll get a letter off to her tomorrow with a full explanation. Unlike you, she'll understand this is a much better way for me to handle this horrid situation."

"Or she'll be furious because now she's going to have to lie to your father to give him a reason for you not showing up."

Tiffany winced. "It won't be the first time. She lied to him before to get him out of her life. She admitted it to me. So now she can do the same for me."

"I simply don't understand why you would even want to do this."

That struck such an emotional chord Tiffany almost blurted out the truth, that she was terrified of coming face-to-face with Franklin Warren. Years ago all she wanted was to meet this faceless father of hers. Now she had no desire to know him. Her being in Nashart, Montana, had nothing to do with him. The engagement wasn't even his idea. He obviously couldn't care less if he ever met her. He just wanted to end the feud with the Callahans. That was the *only* reason he wanted her to show up.

But Anna didn't need to know all that. "Have I let on even once that I'm pleased with this situation?" Tiffany demanded. "No, I haven't. I've been viewing this trip to Montana as a two-month prison sentence, and the very moment the cell opens, we'll be back on a train going home."

Anna frowned. "I thought you told your mother you'd be open-minded about your young man."

"He's not my young man. And, yes, I'm going to be open-minded for all of one minute when I meet him. That's all the time it will take me to decide he won't do. He's a cowboy, Anna. Can you really see me married to a *cowboy*?"

Anna tsked. "You do realize that is not the definition of *open-minded*?"

"Two months and not a day more," Tiffany gritted out adamantly.

"You make this sound like a punishment, but I certainly don't see it that way."

"You're not the one being asked to marry a stranger."

"True, but then neither are you. You're not going to be rushed straight to the altar. He won't be a stranger for very long. And you could view this from a different perspective, you know. I agreed to come along because, unlike you, I thought I'd enjoy such an interesting new experience. New sights, new people, away from the hustle and bustle of the city. And other than that train robbery, I have been enjoying it. You've lived in the city your whole life, too. Aren't you the least bit curious about how people live in this part of the country?"

No, she wasn't, but Tiffany was tired of butting heads with Anna. For someone who hadn't wanted to be her friend, Anna was sure overstepping herself on this trip. Yet the maid could ruin everything if she refused to go along with this, so Tiffany did need to give her a reasonable explanation.

"You haven't considered all the ramifications, have you?" Tiffany said. "What if I do like my fiancé and think I can stomach it here for love's sake, but after the marriage I find out he's a horrible man? Then what? Run away like my mama did? And how will I know what he's really like if he has to come to the enemy camp to court me? He's either going to be extremely wary and not himself, or out to impress me with artificial behavior, so again, not really himself. But suddenly I have this perfect opportunity to find out what he's really like before he puts his best foot forward. I don't want to find out what the other foot is like after the wedding, when it will be too late to back out. So let me get to know these people before I have to deal with their insincerities." Tiffany raised her chin stubbornly. "And if you don't think that's a good reason, well, too bad."

Anna seemed to think about that for a few moments before she pointed out, "Sounded to me like they assume a house-keeper is also a cook."

Not expecting that simple reminder but a torrent of objections and disapproval, Tiffany realized that Anna was conceding and burst out laughing. "So? I'll set them straight on the duties of a housekeeper. Now, you still have the money Mama gave you, right?" Anna nodded. "So you should go ahead and get yourself a room as we planned, but just plan for a longer stay. *You* can consider this a holiday for the duration. I'll visit you tomorrow when I come back to mail Mama's letter and let you know how wonderfully this is going to work out."

Tiffany gave Anna a hug and walked out of the hotel before Anna could change her mind and voice any more objections. Only one of the brothers was waiting for her outside the hotel. She was glad it wasn't the grouchy one.

"I'll need a coach for my trunk," she told Cole. "It's rather heavy."

He stared at her blankly for a moment. Tiffany sighed to herself. She probably shouldn't be giving him orders. She was going to have to be more careful about that if she hoped to fool them into believing she was a servant.

Cole laughed, explaining, "No coaches round here, ma'am. John's gone to borrow a wagon and pick up the new wheels for our broken one. He'll meet us at the train station."

"Excellent. And if you could point me toward the telegraph office in the meantime? I need to let my family know I've arrived safely."

"Don't have a telegraph office, but we do have a telegraph. I'll show you to it."

"Thank you."

It was a short walk back across the street. At least no other riders went by just then to stir up any more dust clouds. He was taking her to the Nashart Stage Depot. Scribbled on the lower half of the large sign above it were the words AND TELEGRAPH.

"I'm surprised the railroad didn't put the stage line out of business," Tiffany remarked.

"Still towns north and south of here that the tracks don't reach. If you don't mind, I'm gonna wait out here to keep an eye out for any Warrens. Rather not get in a shoot-out over snatching you out from under them."

That was an alarming statement, but since he grinned as he said it, Tiffany decided he wasn't serious and went into the office without him.

She marched up to the counter to send the telegram, but paused when she realized the man she was giving it to might warn her father. Didn't everyone know everyone else in a small town? So she arranged to have the message, which she didn't sign, delivered to R.W. at the hotel in Chicago where Rose was staying. How many guests could they have with those initials?

The telegram read, "Change of plans. Give Papa excuse for extended delay. Letter explaining to follow."

Chapter Nine

TIFFANY SAID NOTHING TO the Callahan brothers about the vehicle they were forcing her to ride in, but she was highly indignant about having to travel anywhere in a freight wagon! The driver's bench she sat on had no backrest, and no canopy either to protect her from the June sun, which was getting hotter as the day progressed. She had the appalling thought that she might start sweating by the time they reached the ranch or, even worse, get sunburned!

If she knew whether her parasols were in her remaining trunk, she'd ask the brothers to stop so she could take one out, but she hadn't done the packing so she didn't know, and she'd be embarrassed if she made them wait while she dug through that trunk and then came up empty-handed. Her fancy bonnet was a fashionable wardrobe accessory and was of little use in protecting her from the sun, so she settled for using her hand to shield her face. It was obvious now why men in the West wore hats with such wide brims. She'd even seen a couple of women in town wearing hats like that.

As Cole drove the wagon and John rode alongside, Tiffany sat stiffly erect as was proper, but her back was already getting sore from the effort. Her mother would cry if she could see the discomfort Tiffany was suffering because of a promise Rose had made. No, actually, Rose would probably just say something encouraging like "You can laugh and tell your grandchildren about this someday." Tiffany would have scoffed because her grandchildren were going to be proper New Yorkers who would be horrified that she had to endure this. But she heard Rose whispering in reply, "Or a pack of little cowboys who would be horrified that you would even mention it."

This truly was absurd. She should be at home enjoying the social whirl in New York City with her friends, going to wonderful parties, meeting proper young gentlemen who'd never heard of outlaws, much less Indians! She shouldn't be *here*! And for what? Because two neighbors couldn't get along and be neighborly?

"Any riders come toward us, you drop down in the back and hide," Cole said.

That was a rude awakening from her miserable thoughts. "Why?" she gasped.

"Could be a Warren."

She bit her tongue to keep herself from answering immediately. What would Jennifer say? Wouldn't the housekeeper welcome the opportunity to tell the Warrens that she'd decided to work for the Callahans instead because they'd offered her double the wages? How ignoble, yet that was probably what the real Jennifer would have done if she had gotten the offer. But Jennifer was on her way back East.

While Tiffany didn't want to risk running into her father or any of her brothers yet, she had to reply the way Jennifer would. "I should let them know I've decided to work for your family instead. It's the honorable thing do to."

Cole snorted. "Warrens don't know the meaning of honor, so don't you worry your pretty head about that. 'Sides, this was our pa's idea, poking this little thorn in old Frank's side by luring you away from him, so you let Pa do the gloating when he's ready to."

That remark made her realize she couldn't send Frank Jennifer's note about deciding to return to Chicago, not if the Callahans intended to let him know Jennifer was with them. It could make him suspicious, might even bring him straight to her, demanding an explanation about why she would lie to him. But she was beginning to wonder if Frank had been honest with Rose in the letters he had written her. It sounded as if the feud had heated up again and was worse than he'd led Rose to believe. The way these Callahans spoke of her family with such derision made her wonder if even a wedding could end the feud. Maybe the Callahans had already called it off and she didn't need to be here at all!

That was something she needed to know *right* now. "You said you weren't friendly with your neighbors, but it sounds more like I'm walking into the middle of a war. Am I?"

Cole chuckled. "No, ma'am. A man can hate his neighbors without killing them."

So much for a quick excuse to go home. Nor had he mentioned the feud, so she couldn't ask specifically about that, either, when Jennifer wouldn't know about it. But she could find out more about his family. The housekeeper would be curious about the people she was working for.

Cole had glanced at her a few times while they were talking, but he finally noticed her difficulty with the sun and added,

"Here, change sides with me." He stopped the wagon and took her hand to help her get around him to the right without losing her balance. "I reckon I can give you some shade."

As tall as he was, he actually did somewhat block the sun, but he wasn't done. He also plopped his wide-brimmed hat down on her head, right over her bonnet, which kept it from sliding down over her eyes. She almost laughed at the image of what she must look like. Almost. But the hat did get the sun off her face as soon as she tilted it a little in that direction. She was more than a little grateful for Cole's thoughtfulness. It made her think a little more kindly of the Callahans, at least this one.

"Thank you," she said, giving him a smile as he resumed driving the wagon. "By the way, how did you know I was coming to town?"

"Heard it from one of Warrens' disgruntled employees."

"But how did you know I'd be there today, when the train is three days early?"

"Didn't. We had an order to pick up at the depot for our brother." He gestured to the back of the wagon. Tiffany turned around and saw a couple of crates that looked like the ones she'd seen unloaded from the train. "They let us know to expect it today. We hoped you might be on that train, too, but we didn't think we'd get this lucky."

Her father should have been there, though, for her! Tiffany thought. But obviously he didn't care enough to check on the train's schedule to find out she'd be arriving early.

She shook off the hurt that caused her and asked, "What sort of household will I be running? How many servants?"

"Two maids. Probably could use more, but they're hard to come by."

She was incredulous. Why did they hire a housekeeper

when they didn't have a staff large enough to warrant one? But since they had given her this opportunity to fulfill her promise to her mother to at least meet Hunter Callahan and yet avoid her father, she wasn't going to point that out.

Instead she said, "Can you tell me a little about your family and where you're taking me?"

"We're cattlemen, same as the Warrens. We own the Triple C Ranch, which comprises five hundred acres, and over a thousand head of cattle."

She was impressed, but wondered aloud, "Is that enough land for that many cows?"

He chuckled. "Course it ain't, we don't keep the herds on the ranch. This is open-range country in all directions."

"What does that mean exactly?"

"Free grazing for the herds."

So the two families obviously weren't fighting over land, just water, but she hadn't seen any bodies of water yet. They had taken the north road out of town. Tiffany gazed at the green, grassy fields that flowed on either side of the road and the huge snowcapped mountains in the distance. She'd never seen mountains that impressive except in paintings and picture books. They passed a forest with a logging camp nestled in the center of it. They passed a New England–style house sitting all by itself, an odd reminder of home. It was built of stone, so there must be a stone quarry nearby. She'd heard that industry was moving into the territory, but with so much open land it didn't intrude on the beauty of the wilderness.

She had to admit it was pretty country, though she would never admit that to Anna. But Cole still hadn't said anything about his family or Hunter, in particular, whom she was most interested in.

Hoping to get him to mention her fiancé, she asked next, "How big is your family?"

"I have three brothers. I'm the youngest, Hunter's the oldest. Morgan, that fool, got gold fever and took off on us last year when yet another gold strike was found over near Butte, one of the bigger mining towns in the territory. Pa had a fit, but Morgan's stubborn, and he did find some gold, not enough to get rich over, but enough to keep him from coming home."

"And why does that make him a fool?"

Cole snorted. "We're cattlemen, and there's already more miners in Montana than you can count. Hell, copper was discovered on our land this year. Pa figured *that* might get Morgan back. Told him if he's going to disgrace us by being a miner, he can do it at home. That hasn't worked either—yet."

There was no opening in what he'd just said to question him specifically about Hunter. She'd have to wait until she actually met him to find out what he was like.

Up ahead she saw a large pond—or was it a small lake?— surrounded by meadows of blue and gold flowers. Even a few shade trees were near the lake. This lovely, peaceful setting was the sort of place one might search for to have a picnic.

The road led straight to the little lake and forked to either side of it. The stream that fed it was quite wide and looked too deep to cross right now, probably still swollen from the winter melt. Farther north along the left side of the meandering stream was a long, dark-brownish mass that stirred her curiosity.

"What is that?"

Cole followed her gaze. "The Warrens' herd. It's their time of the day."

"Their time?"

"To bring their cattle to water. Morning for them, afternoon for us. The families decided long ago not to tempt fate by meeting up across the stream at watering time."

"Why?"

"No point in spurring tempers—or tempting someone to take a shot at the other side. Even one shot fired could cause a stampede. Used to happen a lot."

She barely heard his answer, her eyes caught by the riders in the stream who were keeping the herd from crossing it. When she realized those riders could be her brothers, that she could be this close to them, her breath quickened. But the cowboys were too far away for her to tell. Then the wagon turned and she lost sight of the herd and the cowboys, but caught sight of a building under construction. It was a ways back from the lake and had no walls yet, just framing. It was going to have an incredible view. . . .

Oh, my, Tiffany thought, this had to be the strip of land under contention that both ranches were claiming as theirs. And that had to be the house the two families had been building for her and Hunter that they'd stopped working on because they couldn't get along. Just as well, she thought, since she didn't intend to live in it.

The thought made her uncomfortable. The people here expected her to end their feud. That house would sit empty when she didn't marry Hunter. In all likelihood, it would probably never be finished. A weight settled on her shoulders. She shook it off in annoyance. It wasn't her responsibility to bring peace to the area, it really wasn't!

Before long they turned off the road and were driving up to a large house with a long, covered porch. Two stories high, built of smoothly cut boards, the Callahans' house wasn't the little log cabin she had half expected. There was nothing rustic about this house. Well, not on the outside anyway, as long as you didn't notice the spittoon placed between two chairs at one end of the porch or the mud tracks leading right up to the door.

John dismounted, and after she handed Cole's hat back to him, she let John help her down from the wagon. The moment her feet were on the ground she said, "I would like to get settled and have a bath before I meet the head of your household. Is there a butler who can—"

"A what?" Cole interrupted as he came around the wagon. "There's no shortage of rooms. Pa expected more'n four children, so he built the house bigger than it needed to be when he first expanded it. The bedrooms downstairs are taken, but there's plenty more upstairs. Help yourself to one you find empty. The bath is downstairs, though, next to the kitchen. And you don't have to go out to the well for water, we've got pumps."

That was more information than Tiffany needed to hear. The part about the bath had her groaning to herself. It was going to be intolerable if everyone in the household used the same bath. Almost too intolerable. Perhaps her charade wasn't such a good idea after all.

Cole suddenly looked over her head and yelled, "Could use some help here, Hunter."

"Hell no." Laughter rumbled behind her. "It wasn't my idea to get the Warrens riled up again. You kidnapped their fancy servant, you deal with her."

Tiffany swung around to catch her first glimpse of her fiancé. But two men were riding past the wagon, not one, and she had no idea which was Hunter Callahan. The men didn't stop so she didn't get a good look at them.

Then Hunter's words struck her forcefully and she turned her wide eyes to Cole. "Kidnapped?"

Chapter Ten

COLE CALLAHAN DIDN'T ANSWER Tiffany immediately, but he was certainly red-faced. He tried to take her arm to escort her up to the door, but she jerked it away. He finally said in a contrite tone, "Didn't come to that, now did it?"

"But it might have?"

"Settle down. Pa said to get you here one way or the other. We wouldn't have kept you long, just long enough to frustrate the Warrens."

That despicable feud. But it was just as well that she and the Callahans had the same agenda, sort of, or this opportunity wouldn't have presented itself to her. But she was sure she wouldn't have liked being held hostage here. That would have forced her hand to say who she really was, and they would have taken her straight to her father, which was *not* going to happen if she could help it.

So she merely gave Cole a baleful look and asked cuttingly, "Are you ranchers, or outlaws? I really would like to know before I step into your—lair."

"We abide by the law, ma'am," he said in a defensive tone.

"It sounds more like you skirt it."

"Wouldn't be paying you twice what you're worth if we were trying to skirt anything, now would we?"

She got a little pink-cheeked over that answer herself, so she left him with a curt nod and crossed the threshold into her temporary home. And stopped short. And sneezed. And sneezed again. The Callahans didn't need a housekeeper, they needed a new house. This one had gone to hell.

Dried mud was tracked halfway down the short foyer that opened into a large main room where several couches and chairs were scattered about. Obviously they'd been shipped in from the East and had once been handsome pieces of furniture, but they were so old that the upholstery had faded to a dingy gray. Smoke from a soot-blackened fireplace had probably backed up into the room too many times. The paintings on the walls were crooked, some very crooked. The hardwood floor was covered with a layer of dust so thick that footsteps were actually outlined in it. Were there no servants at all in this house?

Tiffany turned to ask Cole that question, but shrieked instead when she caught sight of herself in an oval mirror hanging on the foyer wall. Her complexion was a pasty gray riddled with streaks! She hardly recognized herself. She immediately took out her handkerchief and scrubbed at her face, but without water all she was doing was moving the dust and the dirt around.

"See a mouse?" Cole asked, coming in the front door carrying her large trunk with John's help. "Sounded like it." When she just stared at him blankly, he added, "You screamed."

"I did nothing of the sort," she corrected him indignantly.

"I merely squeaked delicately." But then she warned, "I won't tolerate mice. If you tell me you are infested with them, I'll tell you to put my trunk back in the wagon."

He chuckled. "No mice, not that I've ever noticed. Now run along upstairs and figure out which room you want us to put this heavy thing in."

"You may put it down where you are. There is only one priority right now: that you show me where I can bathe. I can't abide for another moment this veil of dirt you and your brother—"

"Take it on upstairs, Cole. I can show the lady where she wants to go."

Cole looked beyond her to say, "I thought you—"

"Curiosity got the better of me," the newcomer interrupted, and headed back the way he'd just come, so by the time Tiffany turned toward him, she merely saw a broad back. "Come along, Red. The bath is this way."

She wouldn't have budged an inch under normal circumstances. Did he *really* just give her a nickname based on the color of her hair? But she was starting to feel itchy from all the dust that must have gotten into her clothes.

She hurried after the tall man. He had unfashionably long, black hair. She would have thought him a household servant if he weren't wearing a gun belt, or did even servants wear them in Montana?

The hall had narrowed and dimmed once they passed the stairs to the upper floor, but at the end of it light came from a door that had been left open. Which was where the man led her, into the kitchen. Tiffany took one look and closed her eyes tight. And started counting to ten in her mind. And prayed she wouldn't start screaming. Whoever had last cooked here had left the kitchen strewn with dirty pans and dishes.

"I agree with you, you're in dire need of a scrubbing," a deep voice said with a laugh.

Her eyes flew open. She located her amused escort standing in front of another door he'd opened. Only vaguely did she see a porcelain tub beyond him because her eyes locked on his face and stayed there. Powder-blue eyes contrasted with his black hair and darkly tanned skin. A twinkle of laughter was still in those blue eyes, suggesting he was good-humored. With a strong nose and a wide brow, his was a masculine face and much more handsome than she was accustomed to. Tall, lean, and muscular, he wore a long-sleeved, black shirt and a blue bandanna tied around his neck, dark-blue pants, and muddy black boots.

He nodded toward the room behind him. "The tub actually drains. The pipes lead out to the garden Old Ed tended behind the house. It keeps the ground moist if occasionally soapy."

He had to be joking about the soapy garden so she ignored that and asked, "Who is Old Ed?"

"The cook we sorely miss. He couldn't be talked into staying. Ornery cuss just said it was time to move on to see more of the world."

"Not too old to do that?"

"Not old at all, midthirties maybe."

"Then why was he called Old Ed?"

"His hair turned gray years ago after he had a run-in with a grizzly. He was out hunting for his supper, so was the bear. Ed was sure the bear was going to go home happy that night when it startled him into dropping his rifle."

Definitely not a subject for delicate ears, yet her curiosity kicked in. "But he got away?"

"Ran like hell and even faster when he heard the bear shooting at him."

She stared hard at the man. "That's absurd—isn't it?"

He laughed, she was sure at her, which had her back stiffening indignantly. For a cowboy, he was too friendly *and* too impertinent. But she supposed a man this attractive was in the habit of flirting with the ladies.

"Course it is," he answered. "Old Ed was just scared enough at the time to have that crazy notion. He went back the next day to find his rifle on the ground and one bloody pawprint by the barrel. The bear probably swiped at the shiny thing that had been left for him and shot himself in the foot. But Ed did wake up with gray hair that morning."

Which reminded her. "My hair isn't red."

"Close enough," he disagreed with a grin. "If you want some hot water added to that tub, light up the stove. If not, you're all set. A pump was added for the tub a few years back at Ed's insistence. He got annoyed with everyone filling buckets at his sink when he was trying to cook dinner. Real annoyed. Wouldn't cook another meal until he got his way. That second pump went in pretty darn fast."

"I can't wait that long. I fear I will be screaming any moment now if I don't get this grime off me."

He shrugged and stepped away from the door so it no longer appeared that he was blocking her way from the little bathing room. "Suit yourself."

Suit herself? She realized she'd been doing just that. She'd been having a conversation with a perfect stranger when she knew very well how improper that was, at least before introductions! This was so unlike her. She blamed him, of course. She'd simply never encountered a man this handsome before.

Annoyed now, more with herself for allowing him to fluster her like this, she started forward. "Who are you? Do you work here?"

"Everyone here works. Speaking of which, aren't you a bit young to be a housekeeper? I have a feeling you're gonna wash up pretty—and young."

"Not at all. I'm much older than I look, likely as old as you are. How old are you?"

He chuckled. "If I answer that, will you?"

Why was she still talking to one of the hired hands? "Never mind."

He grinned back. "That's what I thought. I'll guard the door for you. On second thought, maybe you better lock it—so you'll be safe from me."

Chapter Eleven

TIFFANY WAS SITTING IN the tub of cold water shivering, but she was barely aware of it. She was still thinking about the fellow who'd teased her about locking the door. Was he still out there, waiting to see her "cleaned up," as he'd put it? She was a bit bothered that the thought pleased her—no, it excited her.

She wished he'd told her who he was . . . oh, good God, could he be Hunter Callahan? No, of course not, not with those light-blue eyes, when the two brothers she'd met both had brown eyes. Besides, Hunter had left the ranch. She'd seen him ride off herself.

She tsked at herself and got out of the tub, then groaned when she realized she had nothing clean to wear. She was so used to having a maid anticipate her needs that she hadn't thought that far ahead. But she was *not* going to put those dusty clothes back on. She wrapped herself in a towel and opened the door a crack to call for help and saw her trunk sitting there. Cole, bless him. He was thoughtful enough to have realized she'd need it.

A while later she glanced in the oval mirror above the shaving stand to make sure she was finally presentable. Clean, yes, but hardly presentable, at least not to her standards. She hadn't taken the time to carefully sort through the clothing in her trunk when someone might walk into the kitchen at any time, but she did get a yellow day dress in the armful she grabbed. She wasn't sure she'd managed to secure all the buttons up the back, though, nor could she twist around enough to tell. And the best she could do with her damp hair was to tie it back. It was dawning on her how much she depended on a maid because she couldn't even pin up her own hair!

Sighing, she opened the door and saw Cole standing there about to knock. He just stared at her though without saying a word, so she said, "Well, I've finished making use of your pretty tub."

Cole managed to tear his eyes away from her fresh-scrubbed face and glanced at the tub. "Ma ordered that contraption from a fancy catalog she got from St. Louis. You should've heard the laughter when it arrived, but I gotta admit, it beats the hell out of getting splinters in your ass."

She made no comment about his improper language because she'd heard worse from her own mother. Rose had picked up a colorful vocabulary from her years in the West.

"Thank you for bringing my trunk in here. I'll choose a room now so it can be—"

"Wasn't me who brought it in. And my pa—"

That was as far as he got before he was simply gazing at her again. It wasn't an unusual reaction. She'd had men stare at her like this before, but not men she'd already met. She was tempted to tell him to close his mouth, but that would, of course, embarrass him, and she'd rather not. Although it was his fault that her appearance had been so distorted by dirt and dust.

Tiffany tried not to grin when she prompted him to continue, "Your father?"

"Wants to—" he started, but, apparently still amazed by how she looked, he said, "Never seen a gal as pretty as you." Then he blushed profusely. "Sorry. Pa wants to meet you now. He sent me to fetch you."

"By all means. Lead the way."

Cole nodded, though his cheeks were still red.

Tiffany didn't try to keep up with his long-legged stride. But he didn't get too far ahead of her and stopped at the front door, holding it open for her. He was taking her outside? She started to frown until he pointed toward the end of the porch where an older cowboy sat—well, probably not a cowboy, but a man dressed like one. This had to be the owner of the ranch, her fiancé's father.

"Just got home," the older man said to Tiffany as she slowly approached him. "Was surprised to hear my boys were successful. Name's Zachary Callahan. What's yours?"

She was suddenly so nervous she couldn't recall the name she was going to use! This was her father's worst enemy, and, she realized, *her* enemy, too. She might not love her father, but she loved the rest of her family. And this man could actually end the feud with them if he wanted to. He must be somewhat open to the idea, or he would never have agreed to end it through marriage, would he? What was that housekeeper's name?

"Jennifer Fleming," she finally blurted out.

He didn't seem to notice her nervousness. He pointed to the seat next to him. He didn't stand up. He might have stood up for a lady, but obviously not for an employee. Tiffany ignored the chair since it was covered with dust and Zachary was smoking a cigar, the smoke blowing right across the second chair.

He appeared to be in his midforties, though his hair was still coal black. Dark brown eyes with lots of lines fanning out at the sides of them. Laughter lines, Rose called them. They did usually hint at a good-natured temperament. And he was quite a handsome man, which wasn't surprising. Rose had said he was. And Tiffany had seen the evidence in two of his sons.

She shook off her unease, reminding herself she had a role to play. "Why did your last housekeeper leave, if you don't mind my asking?"

"Never had one, and we just lost our cook, so we're plumb tickled you're here. You're not going to sit?"

She was going to have to address his assumption that she would be his cook, too, but she didn't quite have the nerve to do that yet, so she merely said, "No offense, sir, but I can't abide the smell of smoke."

"None taken. My wife won't let me smoke in the house. I abide by that rule even though she don't come downstairs anymore."

Tiffany was incredulous. He had a wife? With the condition of the house, she'd naturally assumed his spouse must be deceased.

"Why am I not speaking to Mrs. Callahan then? My job would fall into her domain."

"We don't bother Mary with trifles. She took a bad fall some months back and is confined to bed until her bones mend. If you need anything or got questions, you see me or my oldest boy, Hunter."

Ask her fiancé for help with her job? She pictured the two of them scrubbing floors together, side by side, on their knees, and had to quickly tamp down a hysterical laugh. And it would take too long for just two people to tackle a house this size. It would take an army to put this place to rights.

She didn't mince words on that account. "The condition of your house is atrocious. I was told you have maids, but I see no evidence of that."

Zachary started to frown. She'd undoubtedly offended him. She stiffened, waiting for him to put her in her place and afraid she might lose her temper over it and quit, before she'd even begun.

But he suddenly laughed instead. "Mighty assertive for a servant, ain't you?" That amused him? He added, "Don't know what that *atrocious* means, but I reckon it ain't good. I've got eyes, gal. I know the place is messy, but we've been a might shorthanded the last few days. When Old Ed left us without warning, he took his kitchen helper with him. Pearl cleans downstairs, but her sister took sick, so she asked for a week off to help with her sister's younguns. And Luella, who sees to the upstairs, said she'd quit if she had to do Pearl's job, too. Couldn't have that when we're in the middle of this damn quitting spree. But now you're here to get us cleaned up." He ended that with a grin.

Tiffany was even more aghast. It was bad enough he was down to only one servant, albeit temporarily, but even the four he'd had weren't enough for a house this size, and certainly not enough to require a housekeeper to supervise them.

"Are you aware, sir, what a housekeeper actually does?"

"Never had one, never even heard of one till we heard

Frank was bringing you in from Chicago and I got the idea to deprive him of your talents, whatever they are."

He chuckled when he said that. Apparently he saw it as a one up on the Warrens. Had both sides resorted to pranks like this during the truce? Anything to discomfit the other side was permissible? But she wouldn't remark on that. After all, it was better than bloodshed.

"As the name implies, I keep a house in order," Tiffany explained. "However, I don't actually clean a house. I am what might be considered a luxury for the lady of the house, allowing her to devote her time to her children or other pursuits. I make sure her house runs smoothly, that it's spotless, that all the servants are doing what they are supposed to be doing. A housekeeper is rarely needed unless there is a large staff of servants, since it would be my duty to oversee them. I would also look after your valuables personally, things like your good china, silverware, whatever you wouldn't trust to the hands of an ordinary maid."

Zachary mulled that over for a moment. "Well, we ain't got no good china. Mary had some fancy cutlery, but she considered it too fancy to actually use, so it rusts up in the attic. Ain't gonna have a passel of servants for you to rule, but since you'll have to do the cooking, I reckon you'll be kept busy enough."

"I don't cook," she said firmly.

"Yeah, I heard. It ain't in that description you just gave. But since I'm paying you double, and you don't intend to lift a broom, you're gonna be our new cook, too."

"You misunder—"

" 'Sides, Frank Warren ain't got a passel of servants either. He would've been asking you to pitch in on some other tasks as well, without paying you double for it like I am. So why ain't you sounding more grateful, huh?"

Tiffany's cheeks turned red. Was she about to be fired? But how was she supposed to do something she didn't know *how* to do? This wasn't going to work out. She'd been insane to think it would. A housekeeper's job wasn't so difficult that she couldn't have done it for a couple of months. A cook's job was much more hands-on and required knowledge she didn't possess. She didn't even need more than one hand to count the number of times she'd stepped into a kitchen before today. Her mother employed more than one chef and a half dozen helpers to assist them. The food they prepared was exquisite, always interesting, but she'd never been curious enough about how it was prepared to venture into their domain, which was the hottest, messiest room in the house.

She could learn to cook, she supposed, but not without instruction or—a cookbook! She wondered if the general store in town even sold books, much less a specific kind, or for that matter if the owner could even read. Besides, even if she could miraculously find a cookbook in a town as small as Nashart, that wouldn't help her tonight if these people expected her to feed them. And it was already late in the afternoon. Dinner should probably already have been started!

"Why ain't you married, pretty gal like you?"

The question cut into her thoughts and brought her eyes back to Zachary. She almost smiled when she answered, "I'm engaged to be." Only she would find that amusing since it was true for Jennifer and herself, Tiffany.

But to go by his sour expression he didn't like that answer and was quick to say why. "You ain't gonna up and leave us when you get hitched, are you?"

"I—I agreed to a two-month trial period here. If I like the area and the job, then my fiancé has agreed we can start our marriage here, instead of in California, which is his preference."

"He actually let you come here alone?"

She told him what Jennifer would probably have said. "It was a matter of necessity. We're both saving toward a nest egg, so we can buy our own house once we're married."

He chuckled. "So I'm actually helping you to get hitched all the sooner? Well, don't you worry, you'll earn every penny and then some. We're even expecting a visitor from the East sometime this summer, and Mary's been worrying about having fancy food on hand and some new curtains sewn for the parlor, but you'll have time to get all that figured out."

Tiffany groaned inwardly, afraid the visitor he was talking about was *her*. He actually wanted to impress Hunter's fiancée? Or was it just his wife who did?

She decided to find out, asking carefully, "Do you often get visitors from so far away?"

"Ain't a damn thing ordinary 'bout this visit," he said in a grouchy tone.

She knew she was overstepping her bounds, that a housekeeper wouldn't be so bold, but she couldn't keep herself from asking, "Who is it?"

"That's a sore subject, gal. Gives me indigestion just thinking 'bout it," he said with a grimace. But when he saw her staring at him with such wide eyes, he amended, if evasively, "It's just someone involved in an old business arrangement. You just worry 'bout getting the house in order."

He *was* talking about her. She was sure of it. And he obviously found the marriage arrangement as distasteful as she did. Was he regretting that he'd agreed to it so long ago? Why didn't he just call it off then? Was it a matter of honor? Or maybe these Callahans had been hoping she wouldn't survive to adulthood to marry their heir. She wished she could ask, but without Zachary's actually mentioning her name or the betrothal, she couldn't. But the lack of staff in his household was still a major problem and she could most definitely mention that.

"What I saw while walking through your house was much more than the accumulation of dust and dirt due to one servant's absence for a few days. Your downstairs maid obviously hasn't been doing her job."

Zachary's eyes narrowed. "Don't even think of firing her, gal. Maids don't grow on trees out here."

"Firing and hiring would of course be at your discretion. I would merely make suggestions."

"And expect me to agree to them?"

He didn't look pleased. But at least he didn't look angry either. Flustered was more like it. He was a rancher unfamiliar with the hierarchy of servants. And considering how few household servants he actually employed, that wasn't surprising.

"We can address this issue after I've met your downstairs maid and find out if she's lazy or simply ill trained. But since it sounds as if she won't be returning soon enough for the job that needs immediate attention, I'm requesting the use of some of your hired hands to help get this house into a manageable condition."

Zachary burst into laugher. "They won't clean a house! They're cattlemen, not maids. Actually, they might if *you* asked 'em." He laughed again at that notion.

"You won't insist that they help me?"

"Hell no. I ain't risking good cowhands up and quitting on me 'cause you don't know how to swing a broom."

There came the blush again. It wasn't a matter of knowing how, she thought indignantly, it was a matter of drawing the line, and this was where she drew hers. She'd hire and pay the maids herself if there were any to be had, but it sounded as if there weren't. Obviously, he didn't care that he was risking *her* up and quitting on him. She almost did. This was intolerable. His house was a pigsty!

It was on the tip of her tongue to confess who she really was and demand to be taken back to town when he looked over her shoulder and said, "Hunter, take our fancy housekeeper to the bunkhouse. Let her find out the hard way that cowboys ain't gonna scrub floors for her."

Chapter Twelve

IFFANY HAD ACTUALLY SEEN out of the corner of her eye a group of men riding from the open range toward the house. They'd been too far off for her to tell if they were cowboys, then they were gone from view toward the back of the house. And while she'd thought she heard footsteps behind her a little later, she'd been too involved in her conversation with Zachary to turn around and confirm it.

Swinging around now to finally see who her fiancé was, she once again saw two men, not one. The teasing charmer was one of them. He was half sitting on the porch rail, wrists crossed over his bent knee, hat tipped low to shade his face. The other man was leaning against the wall next to the door, arms crossed over his chest. He was almost as tall as the charmer, which was probably still over six feet, and surprisingly, just as handsome. Something unsettling about him caused her to stare for a moment. A distinct air of . . . danger? Surely not, yet for some reason he made her think of an outlaw. The Callahans wouldn't harbor criminals, would they? Yet she couldn't help imagining this was what an outlaw would look like when he wasn't trying to disguise himself for a robbery.

Like the charmer, he also had black hair, though his was a little shorter and a lot neater. His boots weren't scuffed, they were almost shining. The spurs certainly were. And he wore a black jacket more suited to a city street than a Montana ranch, a white shirt under it, and a thin cravat at his neck rather than a bandanna. His gun belt was much fancier, too, the black leather etched with a swirling design and adorned with silver studs. He didn't dress like a cowboy, so why was he on a ranch? Was he a visitor from town? Or—was *he* Hunter? The thought nearly paralyzed her.

Not once, in all her musings about the man she was to marry, had she considered the possibility that she would be *afraid* of her husband. That was the "something" she sensed about this other man. He was clearly dangerous. And that settled that. If he was Hunter Callahan, she was leaving.

Neither man had yet moved. They both simply stared at her, not quite the way Cole had stared, but it was staring nonetheless. Powder-blue eyes roved over her in a lazy, appreciative manner. Stormy-gray eyes locked on hers and moved no farther. Both men were unnerving her. And she still didn't know which one was Hunter!

The son should at least have said something to his father when he arrived, but he was probably more interested in listening to his father's conversation with her. Or had they even heard it? It was a long porch, so maybe not.

Then both men straightened at once, leaving her still glancing expectantly between them, holding her breath.

"Come along, Red. This will be amusing."

Her breath whooshed out. Hunter was the charmer and her relief was immediate, but only because the dark, dangerous one wasn't her fiancé. As for Hunter, she wasn't sure whether she was glad he was the charmer. But she couldn't think about it now, when he wasn't waiting for her and was already heading down the steps. The other man didn't budge, at least not until she rushed past him to catch up with her fiancé.

Hunter glanced back and stopped before he rounded the corner of the house, but it wasn't her he was looking at or talking to when he said, "Thought you were going to beat me to a bath, Degan?"

"That was before something occurred to break the tedium," the dark, dangerous man replied in cultured tones.

"You're just going to make the boys nervous," Hunter warned.

"So?"

Hunter chuckled. "Suit yourself."

Hunter didn't seem to fear him, although implying that the hired hands did confirmed her suspicions that the man standing too close behind her was as dangerous as she'd guessed. She wanted to move away from him. She actually had an urge to run back to the house. Irrational fears, she chided herself. Then she realized Hunter was glancing down at her.

He tipped his hat back with a finger and said in low tones, "I had a feeling there was a butterfly inside that cocoon of dust, but, damn, woman, you are one hell of a surprise. I suppose you're married?"

The way he was looking at her was more than a little disturbing, as if she were a meal and he were famished. "Not yet, I mean, I *do* have a fiancé."

He gave her a slow grin that set her pulse to racing. "*Not yet* works for me."

Tiffany blushed. Was he actually flirting with her? That would be more than just the charming nature she'd guessed at, that would be highly inappropriate, particularly since he'd just been told she had a fiancé and she knew he did, too. *Her.* Was Hunter Callahan the Western equivalent of a ladies' man? She didn't like the thought and pushed it aside and focused on her mission.

"You heard what I require, Mr. Callahan?"

He continued along the path but took her arm gently to make sure she kept up with him this time. "Sure did. And call me Hunter."

"You may call me Miss Fleming—*not* Red."

He actually laughed before he asked, "What goes with Fleming?"

"Jennifer, but—"

"Jenny might do," he allowed with a grin. "And keep in mind, this ain't the city. We're a lot less formal out here, but you'll get used to it."

Less formal was an understatement. But she had to admit he had a point. She wasn't just pretending to be a different person, she was assuming a role, that of an employee. She had to adjust to the Callahans, do things their way, not the other way around. At least, when they insisted, as Hunter seemed to be doing with the annoying nicknames he kept giving her.

When they reached the back of the house, she saw the ranch spread out before her—stables, corrals and holding pens, the bunkhouse where they were heading, the vegetable garden that Old Ed had apparently planted and fenced in before he left. There were other outbuildings, storage sheds, even a wash-house for laundry and lines spread with bedding and male apparel. She wondered if her father's ranch looked like this, almost a self-sufficient community.

"How many cowboys are available?" she asked, hoping for the small army she was going to need.

"There's seven hands who just rode in with me from the range. Three other men stay out with the herd at night."

She was expecting a much larger number. "That's enough men for a herd as large as Cole said you have?"

"More'n enough when my brothers and I work, too."

"Does their day usually end this early?"

"It ain't early, but we do start early. Now are you ready to be disappointed?" Hunter asked with a grin.

Tiffany grit her teeth. His humor, in this case, was annoying. "You said this will be amusing?" she remarked as he reached for the door to the bunkhouse. "That implies you don't think it's possible?"

"Sure don't."

"You like living in a pigsty?"

"Stop exaggerating. We work outdoors. Can't help tracking a little mud in the house after a rainy day."

Yet one word from him would correct the matter before the sun set. He was the owner's oldest son, after all. The cowboys might complain, but they'd do as he ordered. It was actually Hunter she needed to convince. . . .

"It's far more than—"

She didn't get a chance to clarify her point. The moment Hunter opened the door, he pulled her inside and said to the room at large, "Listen up. The lady here has something to say to you."

He might as well have added, "Don't laugh too hard." The

curve of his lips said it clearly. But the cowboys weren't laughing yet. Some were lying on their cots, some were playing cards in the back of the long building, and some were filling plates from a cauldron hung in the fireplace. There *was* a cook on the premises? But suddenly all of the cowboys were simply staring at Tiffany. She just needed to be concise—and maybe smile.

She started with the smile. "This may seem like an odd request to you, but I need some volunteers to work briefly at the big house. If everyone pitches in, we could be finished in a few hours."

"What sort o' work?" someone asked.

Encouraged, she said, "A lot. The furniture will need to be taken outside, scrubbed with soap and water, and the cushions aired out. The chimney is going to have to be cleaned and then the resulting soot removed from the room. The floors need to be scrubbed until they shine. The kitchen won't be used until it's thoroughly cleaned from top to bottom. I haven't even seen the other rooms yet, but they can't be in worse condition than the kitchen and the parlor."

No one else said a word. She glanced at Hunter to help, but he obviously wouldn't. He seemed to find it too funny that she wanted to put cowboys to work doing a maid's job. The men pretty much all took their cue from him. The blatant amusement on his face finally started them all laughing.

"I'll help."

The laughter stopped immediately. Tiffany was stunned. That had been Degan's voice. She glanced back and saw him leaning against the wall just inside the door, arms crossed over his chest, just as he'd been standing on the porch. Those stormy-gray eyes were slowly roving over the room, and not a man there didn't suddenly appear afraid for his life—with the exception of Hunter and the cook in the back of the room, who simply wasn't paying attention to anything other than the meat he was chopping.

The cowhands rose up in mass and started filing out of the bunkhouse. There were numerous comments, some polite, some complaining.

A short, bowlegged cowboy with a mustache so long the tips of it reached his chin, yelled toward the back of the room, "Jakes, keep the pot hot!"

Another stocky fellow growled at the man behind him, "You tell anyone I did housework and you're a dead man."

Tiffany was blushing and smiling in turn. She had her small army—no thanks to Hunter.

She knew very well their fear of Degan had swayed the men, but she still gave Hunter a smug look and whispered, "I'm glad you were wrong."

He gave her a long, appreciative look. "Not wrong, just outmaneuvered by a pretty smile. You do have persuasive powers, Red. It will be more fun if you turn them on me the next time you need something."

He was talking about seduction! The way his eyes were roving over her left no doubt about that at all and had her blushing furiously even as she bristled. *Her* fiancé was flirting with Jennifer!

When the last cowboy had left the bunkhouse, Degan said to Hunter, "You coming?"

"Hell no, I'm going to grab some of Jakes's stew. I have a feeling Miss Fancy won't be doing any cooking tonight. Don't worry, I'll bring the rest of it to the house later."

Tiffany glared at Hunter before she marched stiffly out of

the building, wanting to get as far away as possible from that infuriating man. Unfortunately, Degan followed her and kept step with her on the way back to the house. Nonetheless, she hurried. It felt strange to be frightened of this man and yet grateful to him at the same time.

Chapter Thirteen

"THANK YOU."

Tiffany felt compelled to say it. She'd waited until they'd reached the house so she could hurry inside before Degan could reply. She didn't make it inside the house though before Zachary's laughter drew her attention.

"Damn, gal, I really didn't think you'd pull this off. If you can turn cowmen into maids, I reckon you can accomplish anything. I'll let my Mary know she can stop worrying 'bout that fancy party of hers."

Tiffany didn't expect to feel so good about receiving a compliment from Zachary Callahan. A bit embarrassed because of it, she asked him, "Where might I find the cleaning supplies for the house?"

"There's a closet near the kitchen. Think the brooms and buckets are kept there."

She went inside to distribute the cleaning supplies and assign tasks before she started on one herself. She would have liked the walls scrubbed down, too, but that would probably be asking too much. Nor would she ask the men to polish the floors. That could be done later by the maid whose job it was. The hired hands were being nice enough to help, she wasn't going to overburden them. And she couldn't not pitch in herself. She'd already realized that. Much as she deplored the thought of getting dirty, how could she not do what she was asking the cowboys to do? Cleaning a house was as strange and repugnant a task to them as it was to her.

She started with the long-mustached cowboy. "Please take all the rugs outside and beat them with a broom to get all the dust off them. I suppose you can hang them over the porch rails to do that—on the opposite side of the porch from your boss, though. Let's not annoy him any more than we have to."

The cowboy laughed. "He's letting you get away with this, hell, don't bother me none if we annoy him a little."

She handed another man a broom and then gave a mop and bucket to the man standing next to him, saying, "The entire lower floor, please. Soon as one room is swept, mop it. And I'll need a volunteer to clean the fireplace and the chimney, which will be the hardest job." That request was met by silence. "Please?"

"I'll do it," a skinny cowboy spoke up. "My ma made me clean the chimney when I was this high, so I know how."

He'd put his hand down to his knee to show how small he'd been at the time, obviously an exaggeration, but it got the other men laughing. Tiffany even grinned before she tasked the last three men with carrying out the furniture for scrubbing and handed one of them a jar of beeswax for polishing the tables.

With all the cowboys busy now, she decided to tackle the kitchen herself. It was *apt* since they *expected* her to work in it.

She just had to count to ten first. And get up the nerve to pick up the first dirty dish.

"You might want to fill the sink with water first," said a deep voice behind her.

She swung around in the doorway, but Degan was already stepping around her and entering the kitchen. She was still glued to the spot. He'd said he'd help, but somehow she didn't think he'd meant that literally, which was why she hadn't dared to assign him any tasks. Besides, he'd already helped by getting the hired hands to do the heavy cleaning.

He started pumping water into the sink, then threw in a handful of soap chips from a box sitting on the windowsill above the work area.

"Some of this will wash up easier with a little soaking first."

Dirty dishes were piled high on the worktable in the center of the room. She shuddered at the thought of touching them and didn't reply to his suggestion. Although she had dozens of questions she'd like to ask him, she just couldn't get up the nerve to talk to him. All she could do was picture him robbing trains or a stagecoach or even a bank. Were outlaws that versatile?

Degan took off his jacket and hat and hung them on a hook by the back door. Then he rolled up his sleeves. The man looked so out of place in the kitchen with his wide shoulders, bare, muscular forearms, and the gun still on his hip. He started scraping what was left on the dishes into a large pot and slid the dishes into the soapy water. Seeing him do menial kitchen work made him seem less intimidating—for the moment—and loosened her tongue.

"Mr. Degan—"

"It's Degan Grant."

"Mr. Grant—"

"Degan's fine."

"Humor me, please. I can't abandon the etiquette of a life-time overnight. *Mr.* Grant, I know this is a long shot, but do you know anything about cooking?"

He almost smiled, she could have sworn he was about to, but he didn't. "I know once water boils, you should do something with it. I know that bread requires yeast, but I have no clue what else."

"Neither do I," she said with a sigh. "When I told Zachary Callahan that I don't cook, I wasn't just pointing out that it's not part of my housekeeping job, I meant it literally. I'm not sure if he heard me or if he just chose not to hear me, more likely the latter."

She took the hint that he didn't really want to talk when he filled another bucket with water and set it on the wide work board next to the sink, then told her, "You wash and rinse, I'll dry."

She pushed up her own sleeves as far as they would go, which wasn't far with her tight cuffs. Her yellow dress was going to be ruined. She already knew it.

If Rose could see her now, she'd think Tiffany had lost her mind. Was getting to know Hunter on the sly worth this drudgery? Maybe not, but not knowing the man who'd caused her so many pointless tears did make it worthwhile. Two months. Just two months and she'd go home *without* meeting her father.

Gritting her teeth over what she was about to do, she came forward to accept the cloth Degan was holding out to her. Out of the corner of her eye she saw a wooden box—a bread box—on the table in the corner. That gave her an idea of how to solve the cooking problem. "Bread! There was a bakery in town. I can have bread delivered!"

She didn't realize she'd said it aloud until Degan replied, "I highly doubt the Callahans are going to buy something they expect you to make. Besides, you can't just feed them bread."

Cringing at his response, she stuck her hands in the water and lifted a dish to scrub before saying, "I'll look for a cookbook tomorrow in town."

"Good luck with that."

She didn't think he was being sarcastic. She glanced at him to be sure, only to find him standing much too close to her. She wanted to put a little more space between them, but she was afraid he'd notice and be insulted. Heaven forbid she insult an outlaw!

But at the moment, he didn't look like an outlaw. In fact, his expression was simply inscrutable. And when he took the plate out of her hand to begin drying it, she almost let out a nervous giggle. What had he said? Oh, yes, she wasn't likely to find a cookbook in town. Anna had already pointed out that the general store probably only carried essentials. But where did *that* leave her?

Desperately she said, "The man named Jakes can't cook for the Callahans?"

"Was already asked and refused. He cooks for the hands, on the range and in the bunkhouse. Besides, his plain fare might be filling, but it's generally tasteless."

She was reaching her wit's end on how she was going to cook for these people without some sort of instruction.

She handed him another plate. Their shoulders touched that time. Her stomach flip-flopped with fear. Yet it appeared he didn't even notice. But she inched away from him so it wouldn't happen again.

Scrubbing the next dish a little harder, she said, "I'm posting a letter to my mother tomorrow. I can ask her to send me a cookbook."

"And in the meantime?"

Nearly every word Degan Grant said was pointing her toward the door. And his proximity to her was shoving her in that direction. Leave, she told herself, dilemma solved—the cooking dilemma anyway.

One last option occurred to her. "I'll talk to Mrs. Callahan. She must have some old family recipes she can impart. I'll explain to her how unreasonable her husband has been."

"The woman is probably partial to her husband. You might not want to say things like *unreasonable* in reference to him."

True. And she didn't really want to consult Mary Callahan. The woman would end up telling her husband, then Zachary would have to face that he was paying Tiffany double for nothing. His lack of staff had already negated the job of housekeeper. Cook was all that was left. And if she couldn't succeed at that job, she might just get fired. What an appalling thought. Not once since she'd come up with this scheme had she imagined that could happen.

Blatant failure—that possibility was more unsettling than giving up. Maybe she could spend more time in town tomorrow than she'd planned on. *Someone* there should be able to help her.

"I'll figure something out."

"Other than quitting?"

She glanced up at him again. He was looking directly at her

this time, which was more than a little disconcerting, though surprisingly, not actually frightening. The man was obviously dangerous, but good grief, he really was handsome in a dark sort of way.

She blushed at the thought and handed him the last dish to dry. "Yes, other than that." She moved to the table to gather up two pots to bring to the sink. They'd barely made a dent, which prompted her to add, "Why is this room such an appalling mess? Did one of the Callahans try to cook in here?"

An image of Hunter came to mind, standing in front of the cast-iron stove stirring pots, and her lips turned up slightly in a smirk. Degan didn't notice because he was stacking the cleaned plates in a cupboard.

"No, Ed left angry. He made one of his fancier meals, to soften the blow that he was quitting. It had the opposite effect. He made his announcement while we were still eating. Zach got furious. They had words, loud ones. Ed took off without cleaning up that night."

"Mr. Callahan should have controlled his temper better," she mumbled to herself.

Degan returned in time to take the first pot from her. Feeling a little more comfortable with him, she said, "What do you do here, Mr. Grant, if you don't mind my asking?"

"I don't herd cattle."

He said nothing more. And suddenly he looked dangerous again. She shouldn't have asked. What was she thinking!? She started scrubbing the remaining pots with a vengeance. She didn't look up until she heard someone behind her say, "You have *got* to be kidding!"

Chapter Fourteen

DEGAN MUST HAVE RECOGNIZED the voice behind them because he didn't turn around. Tiffany thought it might be Hunter sounding so incredulous, but she wasn't sure, so she glanced over her shoulder. Hunter was standing in the kitchen doorway, staring at Degan's back as Degan dried dishes.

Tiffany looked back at Degan. He was completely unperturbed, not the least embarrassed to be found working in a kitchen. Still without turning, Degan said, "Seemed the thing to do if we ever want to get a decent meal around here again."

"You're just not used to trail food," Hunter pointed out.

"Thankfully," Degan replied drily.

Tiffany moved to get the last pot that had been left on the stove, which drew Hunter's attention to her. "Didn't actually expect to see you pitching in, Red," he said in a lazy drawl. "Figured you'd just be cracking the whip."

She stiffened over that snide remark. "If you aren't going to help, Mr. Callahan, then I suggest you leave."

"Hell no. This is where the entertain—"

Fed up with his teasing, she tossed a wet rag in his direction. It landed short of his feet. She wished it had hit his chest, though she would probably have ended up regretting it if it did. "Then you help. And you can start by scrubbing down that table."

He didn't refuse. In fact, he was smiling as he came farther into the room, rag in hand. Did he find everything amusing? Then it occurred to her that she had reacted as Tiffany, not as Jennifer. The new housekeeper would *never* have given the owner's son an order like that.

Degan finally turned around and leaned back against the work board while he finished drying a pot. Tiffany guessed he just wanted to see for himself if Hunter would really help. To be fair, she knew she wouldn't if she were in Hunter's place. It's what hired help was for, even if the Callahans didn't have the right sort of help right now.

But Hunter surprised her. He started scrubbing the table. And serious for the moment, he nodded toward the door before he told Degan, "The boys are slacking off. They'll never get any sleep tonight at this rate. They need incentive. You're incentive."

Degan didn't argue with that reasoning. He set the pot down and left the room.

Tiffany didn't pretend not to know what Hunter had meant by *incentive.* "Why are they afraid of him?"

"Why are you whispering?"

She didn't realize she was. Louder she said, "Would you answer, please?"

"He's a killer. They know it."

She gasped. "So he *is* an outlaw?"

Back came Hunter's amusement. He laughed. "No, he's just fast enough with a gun that he makes his living at it. Outlaws

live outside the law. Degan doesn't go around shooting people just for the fun of it—well, not that I've ever seen. Around here, he abides by the law."

"What is his profession actually called?"

Hunter shrugged. "Gunslinger, hired gun, peacemaker, take your pick."

Tiffany was intrigued by the last description. "How does he go about making peace?"

Hunter chuckled. "By scaring off the opposition."

"You aren't afraid of him?"

Hunter seemed genuinely surprised by that question. "Why would I be? He works for us, not the Warrens."

She didn't like the sound of that. "So if he worked for them instead, you'd be worried?"

"Maybe—if I didn't know him. He's not a bushwhacker. He doesn't start fights. He's too fast for that. Simply wouldn't be fair."

"You actually know this, or it's just your opinion?"

Hunter was suddenly frowning. "Why so many questions about Degan?"

"If I'm going to work here—"

"*If*?"

"Yes, *if* I am, I need to know that it's safe to do so. So why did your father hire him?"

"There was an altercation a few months ago that put a dent in the truce we have with our neighbors. My brother Cole gave Roy Warren a shiner when they were working on my house together. A few days later, Cole's ear was nearly shot off. We've no doubt it was Roy trying to get even. But sending Sheriff Ross over to talk to Roy set off the Warren brothers' tempers."

"Something else occurred?"

"The oldest boy, Sam, came looking for a fight because of it. Damn obvious, too, with him showing up at the Blue Ribbon Saloon. We frequent that watering hole, Warrens usually stay away from it. He sat in on a poker game with my brother John and accused him of cheating. John won't take that from anyone, much less a Warren. They went outside to square off in the street. One of them would've died that night if the sheriff didn't arrive to break it up and toss them both in jail for the rest of the night. Sam apologized in the morning, said he was so drunk he couldn't see straight."

"And your brother's excuse?"

Hunter raised a brow. "John's a might hot-tempered, but he didn't need an excuse. Cheating at cards isn't taken lightly in these parts, and being accused of it when it ain't so—the surprise was that John didn't shoot Sam right there at the table for an insult like that. If that wasn't enough to start up the war again, someone took a potshot at me when I was in town one morning picking up a new saddle. I'd just left the saddle shop when the shot was fired and knocked me back through the shop window."

Tiffany gasped. "You actually took a bullet?"

Hunter started to laugh. "My new saddle did. I just came away with a few scratches from the broken glass."

"Who shot at you?"

"Never did find out. There were a few drifters in town that morning, but the train was also in the station and a handful of passengers were roaming about town, too. But Carl Warren was also in town that day."

Tiffany had to bite her tongue to keep from defending her brothers—when she wasn't supposed to even know them.

Nonetheless, she pointed out, "It sounds like a lot of assumptions without much proof."

"Maybe not much proof, but they're assumptions based on reason. When Pa heard that Degan Grant was in the area, he tracked him down and hired him."

"To kill the Warrens!?"

Hunter snorted at her guess. "No, to keep them from killing any of us. Pa would rather it didn't come to bloodshed, when we're so close to a permanent truce through marriage."

She didn't need to ask, but Jennifer probably would have. "Who's getting married?"

"The Warrens have a daughter."

She waited for him to elaborate. She hoped to find out what he thought of being engaged to a stranger all these years. Did he hate the idea as much as she did? If he did, they could be allies! Two heads would be better than one at figuring out how to keep the truce without sacrificing anyone at the altar. But he obviously wasn't going to discuss it. His eyes had been on her all this time, rather than on the job he was supposed to be doing. *Now* his eyes were on the table and he went back to scrubbing it. While she was getting some of her curiosity about these people satisfied, it wasn't proper to ask him his personal feelings—not yet anyway.

She got back to the gunslinger, whom Hunter apparently didn't mind talking about. "So in this case, Mr. Grant is acting as a guard?"

"You could say that. Pretty damn annoying though. Ain't like we can't take care of ourselves."

So Degan was just a deterrent. She could see how he was suited for that task, she just didn't see why he was needed. Roy would never do what Hunter had just claimed, and neither would Carl. Sam, on the other hand . . .

She didn't know her brothers as well as she'd like, she hadn't seen any of them for the last five years, but they'd continued to write to her. She was fairly certain none of them would take potshots at someone, heated temper or no. Least of all Roy, whom they were accusing of starting these altercations. He was a dreamer. He wrote poetry. He was only ten and a half months younger than she was. But she could see Sam getting so angry at the Callahans' accusing Roy of something he didn't do that he'd want to take the fight to the Callahans. As the oldest of the four, Sam saw himself as their protector. But even Sam was only nineteen! And she couldn't imagine any Warren siblings trying to shoot someone on the sly, and not just once but twice!

Which was why it occurred to her to ask, "What did your sheriff have to say about those shootings?"

"Ross deals in facts, not speculations. Whatever his opinion is, he won't share it until he has proof one way or the other."

It was too bad Hunter's family wasn't of a like mind, but she wasn't going to insult him by saying so. Instead she asked, "Is your family at odds with any of the other ranchers in the area?"

"Everyone in and around Nashart, with the exception of the Callahans and the Warrens, has always gotten along just fine. There's even common ground these days, with everyone banding together against the miners who moved into the area recently. A lot of the townsfolk are worried Nashart is going to turn into another Virginia City, Helena, or Butte, big mining towns west of here that lure in a bad element."

She was surprised. "This is the first I'm hearing that Nashart is a mining town."

"One mine doesn't constitute a mining town, at least not

yet. Earlier in the year, copper was found in a gulch just east of us, a bit too close for comfort. Butte is one of the biggest mining towns in the territory. One of the mine owners there by the name of Harding sent one of his crews here. A mine was in operation pretty much overnight before anyone in Nashart even heard of the find."

"And?"

"Two veins were found. One of them runs under our property. We didn't even know they were digging under us until one of their tunnels collapsed and left a damn big hole that a few of our cattle got injured in. Pa was furious, but Harding's foreman claimed they didn't know they'd trespassed. So they tried to buy that strip of land from us, tried to lease the mining rights, even offered to make us partners. Pa said no on all counts. He's a cattleman through and through. He could care less that we're sitting on a rich copper vein. And, yes, it's already occurred to me that Harding wouldn't mind if we up and moved—or died."

Tiffany felt anger rising and her tone with it. "So you've got a mine owner who wants your land, but you naturally assumed it was young boys who took those shots at you and Cole? When it could have been a miner instead?"

"What makes you think the Warren boys are young?"

"I just assumed, since Cole is and he and Roy had that first altercation."

"After those two fought, yeah, it was natural to assume that. Still is. Harding was told no. The sheriff was called in. Ain't nothing they can do but finish off the vein they got and move on. Gold, silver, copper, it's all been found in Montana, too much to kill for it."

"Maybe Mr. Harding doesn't see it that way."

"Then he'd be a fool!"

"Who says he isn't?" she shot back angrily.

"Is it my turn to say, 'You've *got* to be kidding'?"

Degan was back, leaning against the doorframe. He didn't look amused, merely curious. Hunter threw down his rag and walked out of the room without another word. Tiffany faced the sink again to hide her blush. Did she really just participate in a shouting match with the owner's son?

Stiffly she said to the man behind her, "Are you going to inform Callahan senior that I should be fired?"

"You want to be fired?"

She swung around. "You don't think I should be? I'm sure Hunter does now."

There it was again, that slight turning up of the lips that could have been a smile but wasn't. "Because you had an opinion?"

"It was an inappropriate disagreement. I should have kept my thoughts to myself."

"If Hunter wants to fire you, he'll do it himself—but I guarantee that's not what he wants."

Chapter Fifteen

Tiffany retired early that night to the bedroom she'd picked out earlier, a rather nice room, if spartan and small. A tall bureau, a standing wardrobe with a narrow mirror on the inside of one door, a double bed with a side table and lamp, an unlit brazier for the winter. So maybe it was a little too spartan. She might ask Anna to build her some extra furniture since at least *she* was going to have a lot of spare time in the coming weeks. She smiled tiredly with the thought. While Anna might have confessed she could do things like that, Tiffany just couldn't picture the petite maid sawing boards and swinging hammers. But then she couldn't really picture herself cooking, either.

This corner bedroom at the back of the house was directly over the kitchen. She'd selected it because it had three windows, which would let in more breeze if needed. She stood at one of the two windows that faced east. It was so dark outside she could hardly see anything, except the moon and the stars. How different from the nighttime view she was used to from her bedroom at home. There she could see streetlamps, elegant town houses, large coaches plodding down the street, even late at night. Here she saw a few flickering lights from the bunkhouse and more stars than she'd ever seen in her life. And heard an animal howling in the distance. A dog? Surely not a wolf.

At least she was satisfied that the house, while not spotless, was clean enough to live in. She was grateful to the cowhands. Now she could walk down the hall without sneezing. They'd done as she'd asked and in only a few hours. While they'd complained when they'd started cleaning the house, they'd actually looked worried about having done it right while she inspected the rooms.

One of them even surprised her. Slim, the cowboy with the exceptionally long mustache, had rushed into the main room carrying a jar of wildflowers. She'd been inspecting the furniture, running her fingers along the backs of the chairs and the dining table, when he'd handed her the flowers, saying, "My ma liked flowers in the house. Didn't see any here, not even dried-up dead ones."

She'd been so touched her eyes got a little misty. But she definitely got a little carried away with her role when she promised that the first cake she made would be for them. The cowboys were thrilled, hooting and calling out their favorite kinds of cake. She'd groaned over her impulsiveness, remembering that she had to learn how to cook first!

She still didn't know how she was going to do that, but after eating Jakes's stew that night, which Hunter had brought to the house as promised, it became her third goal, along with ending the feud and going home. The stew had been tasteless, the bread stale. At least the butter hadn't been rancid. But then she'd had to wash dishes again!

Hunter actually came in to help her this time. She wished he hadn't. Standing close to him at the sink was worse than standing near Degan, though she wasn't sure why and was too tired to give it much thought.

"You look a little overwhelmed," he said by way of explanation for his help.

What a polite way to say she looked as exhausted as she felt! She agreed, "It was more than I expected, when I accepted the job."

"Did I mention this is my favorite room in the house?" She gave him a sharp, skeptical look. He chuckled. "Let me rephrase that. It's *now* my favorite room. You do brighten up the place, Red, you surely do. I have a feeling you're going to find me underfoot—a lot."

Was he flirting with her *again*, or just being friendly? It was hard to tell with a man who laughed as much as he did. "Then you can hope I don't step on you too hard."

He'd grinned at that rejoinder. She was too exhausted to care. She wasn't just tired when she got upstairs, she ached from doing things she'd never before done. She would have liked to just drop into the bed, but she still had to write to her mother, and it was going to be a difficult letter to write.

Tiffany knew if Rose were there, she would never have allowed Tiffany to undertake this deception. Yet Tiffany still felt she needed her mother's permission—after the fact. Not for a moment did she consider lying to Rose, though she might leave out the part about Zachary's insisting she cook, simply because she knew her mother would be indignant about it on her behalf.

She would probably have cried if her stationery hadn't been in her only surviving trunk, but it was. She was too tired to unpack, but a quick rummage through her trunk indicated that she'd lost all but one of her evening gowns, many of her dresses, and all of her nightgowns, which meant she'd have to sleep in her drawers and camisole. But she still had her jewelry box, not that she could wear any of her expensive jewels in her new guise. But she allowed herself a tired smirk that the most valuable trunk on that train hadn't become a prize for the outlaws, probably because the robber who'd emptied most of the baggage car was saving the heaviest baggage for last, then ran out of time.

With no desk or even a vanity surface to write on, she had to write on the top of her stationery box while sitting on the bed.

Dear Mama,

I miss you so much! I just heard a wolf howling outside my window. Someone told me about a grizzly bear that scared a young man so bad it turned his hair gray. Wild animals, Mama—I'm finding out firsthand that Montana isn't as civilized as you told me it was. I feel so frightened and out of place, but I know you're worried about that telegram I sent, so let me explain.

It was so unexpected! There I was, so nervous about meeting my father that I almost didn't get off the train, and who should show up but two members of the very family you want me to marry into. They mistook me for the housekeeper their father hired, who did happen to be on my train. But the West overwhelmed her, too. She'd already done what I wanted to do, go back home. I didn't. I'm not forgetting my promise. But the opportunity that the Callahans presented me with was just too intriguing to ignore.

They hired me to be their housekeeper. They don't know who I really am. And don't laugh, despite how amusing you might find their mistake to be, but I think this presents an ideal situation, however unconventional, for me to get to know my fiancé, the <u>real</u> Hunter Callahan, not some artificial, cleaned-up version of himself that he'd pretend to be when he courts me at my father's house. It was your idea for me to give him a chance. But how can I if I don't trust him to be honest and forthcoming about what he thinks about this marriage? Here, in his house, I can find out what he's really like and what <u>his</u> real feelings are. And by the way, you were right. He did turn out quite handsome and he appears to be good-natured, too.

And annoying. And too quick to jump to conclusions, but she didn't add that. If her mother thought she might like him, then she'd be much more amenable to Tiffany's staying right where she was for a while.

I'm not asking to stay here the whole two months, Mama, just long enough to form an opinion of my fiancé. I don't know how long that will take, but I don't feel I'm ready to meet my father yet, anyway. He's waited fifteen years to meet me, so a few more weeks won't make a difference to him. But it will to me. I promise I won't keep up the charade too long, not when I'm dying to see my brothers again. But this will give me a chance to get to know these people and acclimate myself to Montana as well, before I have to deal with meeting my father for the first time. And you already know how I feel about that. It was too much all at once—this frightening place, a fiancé I don't know, a father I don't know. Let me get through half of that at my own pace. I know what I'm doing. So please find an excuse to delay my arrival a little longer. Be vague. And, so I don't starve in the meantime, would you please send me a few cookbooks that I can give to the Callahans' cook? Yes, I'm exaggerating about starving, but not about needing the books. He's a trail cook. I'm sure you can imagine how unappetizing his meals are.

Love,
Tiffany

Satisfied that she'd stated all the pertinent reasons in making her case, Tiffany knew she was still going to be anxious until she heard back from her mother. The trouble was, if her mother was really against what she'd decided to do, Rose might just come to Nashart, despite her own obscure reasons for not wanting to, and drag Tiffany out of there—and straight to Franklin. Or worse, she'd simply telegraph Frank where to find her. But she was too tired to worry about that tonight. Too tired to undress, too. With her letter ready to go, she simply lay back on the bed and was asleep within minutes.

Chapter Sixteen

TIFFANY WOKE UP TO the sound of a cock crowing and sunshine streaming in through the bedroom windows. She felt refreshed and rested. After washing, she unpacked the few dresses she had left, her riding habit, which she doubted she'd have enough leisure time to use, all her shoes and boots, and plenty of parasols. She was relieved to find her underwear, which was made of the softest spun silk and likely irreplaceable in Nashart. She donned a pale-blue walking dress, which, thankfully, had a tailored jacket that covered up the gaps in the dress's back that she couldn't button up herself. The jacket flared and ended just above the bustle, which had come back into fashion recently, though not in a style as pronounced as it had once been.

While she'd thought her day dresses would suffice for her role as a housekeeper, they wouldn't really do in her role as a cook and dishwasher. She would have to look for a seamstress today. What if Nashart didn't have one! But she definitely needed more serviceable dresses, ones she could don without a maid's assistance.

She found a blue ribbon for her hair and simply tied it back again. Maybe she could ask Anna to show her how to pin it up today when she visited her. If there was time. Her list of errands for town today was getting pretty long.

She debated whether to knock on Mary Callahan's door before she went downstairs. She should introduce herself to the lady of the house before she was summoned to do so. But that wasn't going to be an easy meeting, especially if Tiffany had to tell the woman who was worried about impressing her, the *real* her, that the new cook didn't know how to cook. She decided to put off that meeting until later in the day. Her only hope was to find help in town today. Someone there had to have a cookbook, and she'd be willing to pay a fortune to borrow it!

Last night at dinner Tiffany had told Zachary she needed to go to town this morning, and Cole had said he would take her. So she was unpleasantly surprised to see Degan waiting on the porch for her instead of Cole, the borrowed wagon hitched out front.

"Zachary wants me to accompany you," Degan informed her. "He's worried you'll run into a Warren or two and they'll figure out who you are and try to steal you back."

Sound reasoning, she supposed, but she didn't want to be alone with him again! She didn't budge. Being alone with him in the kitchen yesterday had been nerve-racking enough. She did *not* want to experience it again. "What happened to Cole?"

"I told him I'd take you," Hunter said from behind her as he stepped out of the house. "My brothers might fight amongst themselves, but they tend to defer to the eldest without question."

She turned to catch his grin—no, it was a definite smirk.

He enjoyed his role as oldest brother and the advantages that gave him. She wouldn't know how that felt. She'd grown up without her siblings. But she was relieved that he was taking her. With Degan she would have been nervous the whole trip. With Hunter, she just had to worry about getting into another shouting match.

"Then Mr. Grant doesn't need to—"

"Degan tags along," Hunter cut in. "Didn't I mention I can't go anywhere without the guard dog?"

Such a derogatory term, and said with the same disgust she'd heard in his voice when he'd used it last night. She glanced quickly at the gunslinger to see if he was insulted. He didn't appear to be. Without expression, he sauntered down the steps and mounted a palomino horse with a flaxen mane and tail, a color not often seen in the East. It had been tied to the hitching post in front of the porch.

The one horse hitched to the wagon had a distinctive coloring. She'd only seen it once before, in a painting her mother owned of a herd of Western horses. Rose had called it a pinto, a two-colored horse with large patches of brown and white that Tiffany found quite beautiful. But with just one horse, she wondered how she was supposed to get back to the ranch.

She could rent a horse just for today. She'd noticed at least one stable in town yesterday. But then the horse would need to be returned to Nashart, too. She could have bought one or rented one for her entire stay if she weren't pretending to be a woman who was pinching every penny so she could get married. She enjoyed riding, had learned in Central Park before it had even been completed, though as big as that project had been, the huge park had been opened to pedestrians and riders long before the extensive landscaping was finally completed.

She sighed to herself. In her guise of servant, she probably wouldn't find time to ride anyway.

Holding a folded parasol and a reticule containing her letter to her mother, Tiffany went down to the wagon to climb aboard. The step leading to the long wooden seat was rather high, though, designed for a man's long legs, but she could reach it if she stretched a little. She'd just got one foot on it when she felt hands reach through her bustle to her arse and push. She gasped, "Mr. Callahan!"

"Be quiet, Red. How else did you think you were getting up there?"

She was standing on the step now and maneuvered herself onto the wooden perch. Hot-cheeked and her posture stiff, she gazed straight ahead, ignoring Hunter.

"You need to unbend a little," he said as he climbed up and sat next to her. "You're in Montana now."

Oh, God, one more reason why she didn't want to remain here. Had the hardy settlers who'd moved West left all propriety behind? Little had survived as far as she could see. Kidnapping housekeepers—very well, *possible* kidnapping—banditry, private wars, ruthless mine owners.

"Why exactly are you returning to town so soon? Our pantry is well stocked."

He wanted to converse after what he'd just done? He'd already cracked the reins to get them moving, and now she felt his light-blue eyes on her. Lovely eyes, though she couldn't seem to keep from getting annoyed with him long enough to gaze into them for any length of time. Nor did she try now.

Stiffly she answered, "For a number of reasons. I have a letter to post. I need to see a seamstress since my wardrobe isn't suited for dishwashing. I need to buy some other essentials I seem to be missing. Your father mentioned that the person who previously helped your cook quit when Ed did, so I'm going to hire a replacement if I can find one. Oh, and I'm going to have a decent meal while I'm there, breakfast or lunch, which is why we're leaving early. I shudder to think of what Jakes served up this morning. And I'm going to visit a friend I made on the train."

He was looking at her incredulously. She didn't know that until she heard, "Hellfire, woman, that's going to take all day!"

She turned a frown on him and tsked. "No, it won't. I'm very efficient."

He snorted at her confidence. "I can take one thing off that long list. The only people looking for jobs around here are cowboys, miners, and drifters. Women tend to get snatched up real fast."

"You mean hired for work?"

"Work, wife, amounts to the same thing, doesn't it?"

She disagreed, "Out here, possibly, but not where I come from."

"Now that simply ain't true, unless you're talking about rich folks."

Although she was gazing straight ahead at the dirt road, she could feel his eyes on her again. That was a blunder she shouldn't have walked into. "Yes, of course," she agreed. "I've known several cooks who told me their husbands married them for their skills in the kitchen." Which wasn't true either, but he wouldn't know that.

He chuckled. "A common motivator for a man. How are you at those skills?"

She tensed. Talking about wives and cooking in the same breath, was he suddenly viewing her as a prospective wife?

When he had a fiancée? Was he too impatient to wait for his fiancée to arrive? Or totally opposed to the marriage as she was? She wished she could discuss that with him, but she couldn't until someone actually told her that Hunter was engaged.

But he was waiting for her to answer his question. Briefly she repeated what she'd told Degan last night about his father refusing to believe she couldn't cook. All Hunter did was laugh.

Gritting her teeth, she returned to the subject of finding help for the kitchen. "So what you're saying is, there is a shortage of women in the territory?"

"You got that right. Always has been. And if you keep sashaying around town, we're going to end up with an army of wife-hunting men beating down our door. You're about as prime a catch as it gets."

Compliments didn't usually make her blush. She wasn't sure why that one did, unless it was because his tone got a little sharp as he said it, as if she should apologize for being pretty. But she didn't like the damper he was putting on her finding help when she'd been counting on it. Then it occurred to her that Hunter might be basing his negative opinion on the likelihood that a woman out here would probably opt to marry rather than work for the low wages of a kitchen maid. And no doubt he was right. He just didn't know that she would pay whatever it took to get that help. Nor could he know. Tiffany had deep pockets, Jennifer didn't.

But to prepare him ahead of time for her success, she drew on Jennifer's probable experience, telling him, "I have been tasked with hiring before. I can be very persuasive."

"I bet you can. You could probably talk me into anything— if you tried." Then he leaned closer to whisper, "Want to try?"

Shivers ran down her back because of his warm breath on

her neck. It wasn't because of what he'd said to her, of course it wasn't. But why wasn't she outraged over what he was implying? She should be!

She responded much more primly and properly than she guessed Jennifer would have. "I will assume that you are accustomed to indulging in meaningless flirtation. I am not. Please keep in mind that I have a fiancé."

"But he's in Chicago, which might as well be on the other side of the world, while I'm here. And what sort of man would let you get away from him like this?"

"You make it sound as if I've escaped him, when that isn't the case at all. We thoroughly discussed my coming here. It was a mutual decision. We both want to save up a nest egg before we marry."

"You didn't answer my question. What's he like?"

Jennifer hadn't told her anything about the man she was going to marry! All Tiffany could think to do was to describe the sort of man she hoped to marry one day. "He's noble-hearted. Kind and sensitive. Brave and very loyal. He's been devoted to me since the day we first met. *He* wouldn't think of being unfaithful."

Hunter raised a brow at her. Well, she shouldn't have mentioned that last part or made it sound like a reference—to him. But he wasn't done criticizing her choice in men.

"His first mistake was wanting to wait to marry you, no matter the reason. His second mistake was letting you come here alone. I'd never let my fiancée leave me. In fact, I'd marry any woman I want to stake my claim on right away, not come up with excuses to wait."

She was a little indignant—on Jennifer's behalf. Hunter's family was rich, even if they didn't exactly live like it. He didn't know what it was like to be of the servant class that worried constantly about money. Neither did she, but he'd finally given her an opening to ask about his own engagement, and she wasn't passing that up to point out his opinion was biased.

"You're talking as if you have a fiancée. Do you?"

Hunter mumbled something under his breath before he said, "I've had enough conversation for this morning. Let's get to town. Hold on to your hat, Red."

He cracked the reins so hard that the horse and wagon suddenly sped up. Tiffany gritted her teeth. *Why* wouldn't he admit he was engaged to her?

Chapter Seventeen

JUMPING DOWN FROM THE wagon the very moment he stopped it behind the freight company in town, Hunter snarled at Degan, "I need a drink. You stick to her like glue. Well, not that close, but make sure no one bothers her."

Then Hunter just walked off and disappeared around the corner of the building. Tiffany sighed, but managed to get down from the wagon on her own before Degan could dismount to help her. If she hadn't gotten Hunter angry, she wouldn't be stuck with Degan again. It was her own fault.

But she wasn't sure why Hunter was angry. Because she didn't agree with his point of view about her fiancé? Or because he had one and hated it so much he refused to talk about it at all? She didn't know him well enough to guess. She realized too late that she never would if she kept being offended by his brand of friendliness. And disturbed by his husky whispers. She had to get better control of her reactions to him. She didn't *want* to like him. She wanted to go home to New York. And she didn't want to be excited by words he shouldn't even have said to her!

Degan fell into step beside her as she walked in the direction Hunter had gone to reach the main street. Degan led the two horses and tied them to the first hitching rail they passed.

"I'd like to post my letter first," she said when he joined her on the long, boarded walkway that fronted all the buildings along the street.

"This way."

She followed him past a few businesses, but stopped at the one where delicious aromas were wafting out its open door. Without telling Degan, she entered the small bakery. The single-room kitchen had ovens lining the back wall and a few tables in the front laden with long loaves of bread and pastries.

The owner closed one oven and smiled at her. "What I help you with, eh?"

She didn't really expect the businesses in Nashart to provide the services she was accustomed to in the city, but she still had to ask, "Do you deliver?"

"No."

"I'll pay you handsomely."

"No, no time to deliver. You want bread, you come here to buy it."

Disappointed that she couldn't get what she wanted even if she paid extra for it, she said, "Then can you at least give me a recipe to make bread? I'll pay you for that."

His smile vanished. "Give away my secret? No!"

Her exasperation was rising. "Not your special bread, just plain, everyday bread."

He raised a brow. "You really don't know how?" He started to laugh. "What sort of wife will you make, eh?"

"One who hires a baker like you," she snapped, and marched out of his shop.

Degan didn't say a word about her failure. However, he did caution her about any more detours, brief or not. "I wouldn't be doing my job if I didn't encourage you to take care of your business quickly and leave any extra errands for another day. I want you out of town before the trouble starts."

Tiffany halted abruptly. "What trouble?"

"It's Saturday. There's always trouble of one sort or another on Saturdays, but it's gotten worse since the Harding mine opened. And cowboys will be riding in later today to raise some hell like they always do. The miners don't get paid much, which makes for frayed tempers, and cowboys and miners don't mix well because they have nothing in common."

At Degan's mention of trouble, Tiffany thought of the gunfight on the train. "The sheriff should outlaw guns in town."

The slight change in Degan's inscrutable expression told her he would have laughed at her remark—if he ever laughed. "Why? No one's been murdered, no one's been shot unfairly. Trouble around here isn't usually at the point of a gun unless some braggart rides in looking to make a name for himself. The miners don't carry guns; the cowboys who do are mostly decent men. They won't draw on an unarmed man. But that gives the miners an advantage. They're damn good with their fists. Like those two across the street there with their eyes on Hunter."

Tiffany followed his gaze to the two men he'd just mentioned. They were not tall, but were quite muscular and broad-chested. And they definitely looked disgruntled.

"Hunter told me a little about the miners," she said. "I think it's absurd that some of them might be carrying a grudge against his family when the Callahans were here first."

Degan shook his head. "Not absurd when it's nearly un-heard of for someone to turn down what amounts to free money, like Zachary did. Harding even offered to give him a percentage of what the mine earned, but Zachary turned that down, too. If you ride out that way, you'll see soot coating the range from their smelters. Zachary wants them gone, not to be partners with them. And they think I was hired to see to it, which just got them even more angry."

"I know why you *were* hired," she said in a disagreeable tone.

"You object to me keeping the peace?"

She was positive this time that she heard a note of amuse-ment in his voice. He might think he was keeping the peace, and maybe he was for now, but she suspected that peacekeep-ing could lead to bloodshed in too many ways. And those two miners were still deliberately provoking Hunter by staring at him.

She saw that Hunter had stopped in front of the general store, which was in the opposite direction she was headed. He seemed not to have noticed the miners because he was talking to a dark-haired woman with a voluptuous figure. Her low-cut blouse was nearly indecent, it showed so much cleavage, and her red skirt was guaranteed to draw every man's eye. The skirt had no bustle and wasn't the least bit fashionable, though come to think of it, Tiffany still hadn't yet seen a single woman in town wearing one, so she was actually the one standing out like a sore thumb.

Hunter was definitely engrossed in his conversation, no doubt a flirtatious one. He had the woman trapped there with his palms flat against the wall on either side of her, preventing her from walking off, not that it appeared she wanted to leave him when she had one arm draped loosely over his shoulder. Tiffany was sure that they were about to kiss. Whose idea it was she couldn't tell. Their faces were too close. Tiffany was holding her breath, watching as her fiancé was about to be unfaithful to her, and she couldn't take her eyes away. . . .

Chapter Eighteen

TIFFANY BARELY HEARD DEGAN as he continued explaining why she shouldn't have come to town today of all days. "The miners have been warned not to start anything, so they won't approach Hunter, but they're hoping he'll come their way so they can trip him or say something nasty that will provoke him. As long as he lands the first punch, they won't get tossed in jail. And those miners are strong. Comes from wielding a pick all day. Hunter could take one, but not two at a time."

"His ladylove?" she asked, still gazing across the street at Hunter and the dark-haired woman.

She realized she'd just asked Degan a question completely unrelated to what he'd been talking about. She didn't blush though. She was feeling too—she didn't know, but it certainly wasn't embarrassment.

"That's Pearl, the missing Callahan maid," Degan said. "But don't read anything into that. Hunter's engaged to someone else."

Finally someone had mentioned that pertinent fact to her.

She planned to use it as ammunition to keep Hunter from making any more inappropriate overtures to her. "Who is he engaged to?"

Degan took her arm to continue them on their way. "Someone he's never met, which is why Pearl doesn't think anything will come of it and tempts the hell out of him."

Now Tiffany blushed. She should never have broached the subject of Hunter's love life, and certainly not with the gunslinger. To get quickly off that subject, she recalled she had something else she wanted to ask Degan.

"What happens when the Warrens and the Callahans come to town at the same time?"

"They don't frequent the same saloon—at the sheriff's insistence—but it can get loud if they cross paths here or near the lake. The truce they had has been falling apart for months now."

"Do *you* think the Warrens have been shooting at the Callahans recently, like Hunter does?"

"No."

"Why not?"

"Roy, he wasn't afraid to fight. So he got a shiner. What man hasn't? That's no cause to break out a rifle. As for the shot at Hunter, there were too many strangers in town that day to hazard a guess, but whoever it was, he was either a lousy shot, so not from around here, or he wasn't shooting to kill."

Her thoughts exactly. "So you don't think it was the Warrens either."

"I don't think the Warrens are taking potshots, but I do think they're out to cause trouble. There was no doubt about Sam Warren's motives when he called John a cheat. That boy was looking for a fight."

"But why?"

"John had been the loudest in accusing Roy, and Sam was damn mad about it. But it was John who picked guns for that fight. Sam probably only wanted to beat the hell out of John. Those two might still have another go at it, the next time they cross paths."

What an alarming thought. "It sounds like there's no longer any sort of truce."

Degan shrugged. "The elders still like to think so. This started up when it became clear the Warren boys don't want to see that house by the lake finished."

"Why not?"

"Because the house is for Hunter and his fiancée, the Warren boys' sister."

Tiffany had to force herself to appear surprised, now that she was finally hearing whom Hunter was to marry. "Star-crossed lovers then?"

"They haven't even met yet."

"Oh, well, that sounds—awkward."

"By all accounts, the Warren boys would like to keep it that way. It's obvious they think their sister, a fancy Easterner, is too good for Hunter. Mr. Warren might want to abide by the marriage agreement to secure a permanent truce, but his boys are more concerned about their sister."

Tiffany was so touched by her brothers' protectiveness toward her that tears welled in her eyes. Her father didn't care about her happiness, but her brothers did.

Without thinking she gushed, "That's so sweet!" Degan gave her an odd look, making her realize Jennifer had just disappeared, leaving only Tiffany standing there. She tried to quickly salvage her mistake, adding, "I mean, I wish I had brothers like that. How does Hunter feel about this arranged marriage?"

"I don't know, but I suspect that as the eldest son, he will feel obligated to do what's best for the family and the ranch, even if it means sacrificing his heart."

Tiffany stiffened indignantly. How dare he refer to Hunter's having to marry her as a sacrifice. She almost marched off in high dudgeon until she heard Degan add with a shake of his head, "Nonetheless, there's no mistaking it, the Warren boys aren't going to let their sister become a Callahan without putting up a fight. But don't worry. It's my job to make sure it doesn't get too bloody."

Did he have to say that?! Tiffany groaned to herself, wishing she'd never broached the subject, at least not with *him*. Don't worry? She was even *more* worried now about the situation between the two families. While the older generation saw the betrothal as a means to secure a longer-lasting truce, the second generation, at least her brothers, viewed it as another source of conflict between the families.

She was going to give herself away completely if she didn't get her reactions under control, so she said no more to Degan and hurried off to do her errands as he'd suggested. After posting her letter, she headed to the hotel to see Anna, but they had to pass by the general store again to get to the hotel. Now that Hunter was no longer seducing women in front of it, she could go in. Even though she had no hope of finding what she needed, she knew it would bother her later if she didn't at least ask.

"*One* minute," she told Degan, and slipped inside the store before he could complain about another detour.

She didn't waste time looking around the large, cluttered

room for what she wanted. She went straight to the owner and asked, "Do you have any cookbooks for sale?"

"Sorry, miss, but I don't stock books." Hearing what she'd feared she would hear, she tried not to appear as disappointed as she actually was, but the owner must have remembered something because he stopped her from leaving. "Wait a minute." He opened a drawer behind him and handed her a thin book. "My wife ordered this a while ago, but no one ever bought it. Glad I didn't throw it away."

Tiffany read the book's title: *The Basics of Cooking*. She could have kissed the man! She quickly paid for the book and was so excited that she showed it to Degan when she left the store.

"Basics?" he said, clearly not impressed. "Let's hope that's not where Jakes learned his cooking skills. Are you about done?" He was glancing up and down the street. "More miners have shown up and I've lost sight of Hunter, though he's probably in the Blue Ribbon Saloon for that drink he mentioned."

Degan actually sounded a little concerned, which prompted her to suggest, "Go ahead and find him. I still have a lot to do." She gave him her agenda, ending with "And I need to hire a woman to help me in the kitchen, though Hunter doesn't think I'll have any luck finding one."

He didn't budge from her side as she walked to the hotel, but he did agree with Hunter. "He's right."

Tiffany frowned. Old Ed had had help. Why couldn't she? She considered asking Anna to take the job, but quickly discarded that idea. It was too lowly a job for Anna, who would likely complain and argue with her. The maid might even blurt out the truth to the Callahans, and Tiffany couldn't risk that. The look of disappointment on her face was probably what

made Degan add, "You said a woman. Why aren't you considering a man instead? Plenty of them around looking for jobs."

She skeptically raised a brow. "To wash dishes? I really
can't see—"

"That restaurant you plan to eat at is completely staffed by
men. Ed's helper was a man, too."

A little more encouraged, Tiffany said, "Well then, if you
know of anyone looking for work whom you would consider
trustworthy, do point him out. Oh, and I should have said this
sooner, but please tell me if you see any of the Warrens in town
today. I would be so embarrassed if I were to come face-to-face
with any of them after I abandoned my job with them."

"Why did you?"

Trying not to show that he had flustered her, she said, "My
intended and I agreed we should delay our marriage until we
save up enough money to buy our own house."

"So the more money you make, the sooner you get to the
altar. I get it. What I don't get is how your young man would
be willing to wait—for any reason. Whose idea was that?"

"Mr. Grant! Really, you—"

Degan's stormy-gray eyes met hers. "If he really exists and
you love him, I'll warn Hunter to back off. Just say the word."

"*If* he exists? You think I'm lying?"

"Wouldn't be the first time a woman claims she's spoken for
to avoid unwanted attention. Which is what Hunter thinks. So
maybe you better set him straight."

Chapter Nineteen

TIFFANY HAD NO IDEA what the gunfighter was insinuating about Hunter, but she had no trouble recognizing that he suspected she was lying about having a fiancé. She felt like laughing because, ironically, she was being completely truthful in that regard. Jennifer had a fiancé and so did she! She pretended to take offense at his even broaching a matter this personal with her. Quickening her step and walking away from him sufficed to let him know that. She hoped. While she'd have no difficulty upbraiding anyone else for such impertinence, she wouldn't tempt fate and do so with a man who reeked of danger.

But there was no getting rid of Degan Grant. He followed close behind her, though he did wait outside when she entered the hotel. After she asked the clerk where she could find her friend Anna Weston, she got her annoyance under control before she knocked on Anna's door. Unfortunately, it came right back with the first thing Anna said to her.

"You've come to your senses? I knew you would."

"I'm just visiting to let you know how wonderfully my plan is going."

"You're being sarcastic, aren't you?"

Of course she was, but she didn't intend to complain to Anna, so she avoided answering and said, "I've already learned a lot. There's still bad blood between the Callahans and my family. That truce they have is tenuous at best. I have a feeling it won't take much at all to break it. And there are some miners who might be trying to stir things up in that regard."

"From the Harding Mine?"

"How did you know?"

"I met a Harding executive last night in the hotel's dining room, a Mr. Harris. He seemed like a nice gentleman. His boss owns mines in Montana and elsewhere. It's Mr. Harris's job to travel between them to solve problems and make sure each mine is producing as expected."

"I doubt the Nashart mine has turned out as expected for them." Tiffany explained briefly what she knew about it. "If you should see Mr. Harris again, maybe you can find out what his boss plans to do, now that they aren't getting access to all of the copper they came here for. But I don't have much time in town today, so let's talk while I look for a local seamstress."

"That would be Mrs. Martin. I asked the clerk downstairs. You wouldn't have found her otherwise because she doesn't have a shop, just works out of her home. I can show you where it is."

When they left the hotel, Degan was waiting for them. Tiffany knew it would be rude not to introduce Anna to Degan, but when she made the introductions, she only referred to Anna as a friend from the train trip and Degan as a worker at the Callahan ranch. She hurried Anna along when she saw how uncomfortable the gunslinger made Anna.

"Who *is* he?"

"I told you, he works at the ranch and he's my escort today. You don't have to whisper, he's not following us that closely."

Anna glanced back to make sure of that before she said, "Why haven't you said anything about your fiancé yet? You have met him, haven't you? Oh, and were they very annoyed when you told them you wouldn't cook for them?"

Tiffany mumbled, "I'm going to cook."

"You? In a kitchen?"

"Don't make it sound so ridiculous."

"But you don't know how!"

"I intend to learn."

Tiffany held up the book she'd purchased, then quickly stuffed it back into her reticule before Anna could see how thin it was. She couldn't help wondering how much information it could contain if she could fit it in her purse. But she'd definitely surprised Anna.

"You're really going to do this? I was sure you would have given up this notion of impersonating a housekeeper by now and demand to be taken to your father's ranch."

Anna might view her as a spoiled, pampered rich girl who'd never lifted a hand to help herself, but she was failing to take into account Tiffany's stubbornness. "I'm not quitting and I *will* learn to cook. Besides, whether I hate my job or not, it's still better than meeting my father."

Anna shook her head sadly. "Is it really?"

Oh, God, Tiffany suddenly felt the urge to cry. She'd thought she was done with tears on *his* account. She glanced away without answering, concentrating on keeping the tears at bay. They had already turned onto a side street with small houses on both sides, yet another stable farther down, and a quaint church at the end of the street.

Anna opened the fence gate at the second house they came to, then glanced behind them once more, apparently to make sure Degan was still maintaining a discreet distance, before she said, "You still haven't mentioned Hunter Callahan."

This subject definitely quelled the urge to cry. "Because I've already found out that he's a philanderer. He's even trying to seduce me."

"That's a good thing, isn't it? It means he likes you."

"You're missing the point. He doesn't know I'm Tiffany Warren, so it means he's cheating on me! And I also saw him flirting with one of the Callahan maids today in town."

"Why do you sound so indignant about it? You haven't 'officially' arrived yet. Did you really think he would remain celibate all these years? It's what happens after the marriage that counts, not before—well, not before the couple even meets."

Tiffany could see the logic in what Anna was saying, but logic had no place in the welter of emotions she was experiencing. It was almost as if she considered Hunter to be hers, when she didn't want that at all!

"I wonder if your two months in Montana have even begun yet," Anna added. "As long as you're pretending to be someone other than yourself, no courtship can commence."

"My mother stipulated that time period for *me* to decide if I want to marry Hunter, not for him to decide if he wants to marry me."

"But how is he going to woo you if he doesn't know it's you?"

Tiffany didn't want to answer that because her answer

would be she didn't want to be wooed, at least not in Montana. Her goal was to go home to New York so she could live a normal life, the life she'd been raised to expect. But she did have one other goal she hadn't completely thought through yet, so she didn't want to mention that either. She wanted to hear both families' views of the feud to see if she could find a way to defuse it without having to marry a cowboy. In that she was thinking of her brothers' safety, not just the promise she'd made to her mother.

When she didn't answer, Anna pointed out, "You don't have to pretend with these people, you know. So you don't want to stay with a father you don't know. Fine. But the Callahans are expecting you, too. They'll be pleased to have you under their roof. Having been betrothed to the eldest son your whole life, you're practically like family already."

Tiffany rolled her eyes. "That negates my plan of getting to know what they are really like."

Tiffany put an end to the irritating conversation by knocking on the seamstress's door. Agnes Martin was a sweet old lady who led them into her parlor and offered them tea. Tiffany was surprised to find that she already knew Anna.

"Have you decided to work for my husband, Miss Weston?" was the first thing Agnes said.

"I'm still thinking about it, ma'am," Anna replied, then blushed when Tiffany gave her a questioning look.

"Good, he could really use the help and—"

A gasp from the hall drew their eyes to a young man holding a broom. He was a little taller than Tiffany, but she could tell from his face and his scrawny physique that he was a few years younger than she was.

The seamstress was immediately contrite. "I'm sorry, Andy,

I know you wanted that job, but my husband is too old to teach someone his trade. Miss Weston is already an experienced carpenter."

Embarrassed, Agnes excused herself and left the room to get the tea. Tiffany, incredulous, asked the maid, "How did *that* come about? You've only been here a day!"

Anna grinned. "I explored the town yesterday after you left. I was passing the furniture store and heard the hammering inside. I love the smell of fresh-cut wood and couldn't resist going in. The Martins were both there and we started talking. The moment I mentioned my father is a carpenter and that he taught me a thing or two, the owner offered me a job."

"You're not actually considering it, are you?"

"Do you know how rare it is for a woman to get offered a job like that? It would never happen back East. So, yes, I am thinking about it. It would give me something to do until you come to your senses."

As Agnes was returning with a tea tray, Tiffany heard her say to her helper as she passed him in the hallway, "I don't have anything else for you to do today, Andy, after you finish up the sweeping. You can check with me again next week."

Tiffany, mindful that Degan was waiting for her outside, told the seamstress what she needed and was taken to the back room where Agnes worked. Although she only wanted a few skirts and blouses, and nightgowns, measurements still had to be taken and materials selected. She was too impatient to look through Agnes's design books though and simply told her to make something suitable for kitchen work and offered to pay her extra if she could finish the order in just a few days.

Then it occurred to her to ask, "Does that boy need a job?"

Agnes nodded. "Indeed he does. He even mucks out the

stable in exchange for feed for his horse and a bale of hay to sleep on. He's tried to obtain more gainful employment everywhere in town, but he's not experienced in anything other than odd jobs, and there aren't even many of those around here. I've been letting him do some of my own chores because I feel sorry for him."

"Is he reliable? Trustworthy?"

"Yes, and polite, too. He arrived in town a few weeks ago. Hails from Wisconsin. He's not a drifter, but I expect he won't be around any longer than it takes him to earn enough to move on. He's just not having any luck with that. Do *you* have a job for him?"

"I might, for a couple of months at least—but not if he's going to leave before he barely gets started."

Agnes shrugged. "Ask him. He came West to find his father, has been going from town to town looking for him, but some steady work might convince him that earning more'n his next meal for a while might help him achieve his goal. Let me fetch him for you before he leaves, and you two can figure it out. Oh, and if you're interested in marriage, keep our sheriff in mind. He's a good man. We'd hate to lose him just because he's hankering for a wife and can't find one here."

Tiffany was *not* going to reply to that gossipy tidbit, but Agnes didn't seem to expect her to, and a few moments later the lanky teenage boy, broom still in hand, came in to meet her. He had freckles, sandy-brown hair, and brown eyes. Tiffany understood now why he was so skinny—he probably wasn't getting a meal every day, much less three. But he was presentable, clean, and Agnes must have told him he was going to be offered a job because he looked so eager.

Tiffany smiled at him. "I'm Jennifer Fleming."

"Andrew Buffalo, ma'am," he offered bashfully.

"Well, Andrew, I've been hired to cook at a ranch near here and I need a kitchen helper. The job doesn't require experience, just hard work and diligence. Are you interested?"

"Yes, ma'am!"

Tiffany was nearly as excited as the boy appeared. She had accomplished all of her errands after all. So much for Degan's and Hunter's both scoffing at her intention to find a helper.

But before she celebrated a victory she had to learn more about Andrew. "I do require that you keep the job for two months at least—or as long as I do." When the boy nodded, she continued, "So tell me a little about yourself. Mrs. Martin said you came West to look for your father. Do you have reason to think he's in Montana Territory?"

"Well, the last place he wrote from is a ghost town now. But that was several years ago. Heard the land up here is rich with ore. Figured he would have heard it, too, so I thought I should at least check some of the bigger mining towns like Butte and Helena. Just haven't earned my way that far West yet."

"He stopped writing?"

"Yeah, after the last of us kids were grown. I finally figured out he wasn't coming home. Him and my ma never did get along. She never expected him to come back."

"So you don't know if he struck it rich, or—or if he's even still alive?"

Andrew shook his head. "I don't think he's dead, but I don't think he's trying to strike it rich anymore either. His last letter was full of despair, said he got claim-jumped, that it was too dangerous to go it alone anymore, so he was going to mine for someone else."

That was so sad, and Andrew's mission seemed next to impossible. The West was just too big a place to find his father if he had no trail to follow.

"You haven't thought of giving up and going home?"

He grinned. "Yeah, I think of it each time my belly growls. I take work when I can find it, long enough to save up enough to hit the next town. I'd really like to at least see my pa once more before I go home, maybe beat the tar out of him for leaving us for something that never did pan out. I don't know. Each time I think I've had enough, I get the gumption to go on. It's not as if I'm needed back home. My sisters are married and my ma is fine, she's a hatmaker with her own shop. But maybe my pa needs me."

"You're a good son, Andrew," Tiffany said with a smile. "If you're agreeable to my terms, gather your belongings and meet me at the restaurant for lunch. It's my last stop before we return to the ranch."

He gave her a big smile and rushed out of there so fast she nearly laughed. She rejoined Anna in the parlor, so pleased with her success she had to share it. But mindful that Degan might soon be banging on the door, she invited the maid to lunch.

Anna declined. "Agnes already asked me to share hers. Besides, do you really want your employers asking me questions over lunch?"

Tiffany winced. "No, I'll see you in a few days then when I pick up my work clothes."

"No wincing and no complaints. *You* can end this charade at any time."

Tiffany walked away in a huff, and when she stepped outside, it wasn't Degan sitting on the porch steps waiting for her. Hunter had taken his place.

Chapter Twenty

"DID MR. GRANT RETURN TO the ranch?" Tiffany asked as Hunter stood up.

"No, he had a few errands of his own, and since you've already taken up half the day with yours, I told him to go ahead. He'll be meeting us at the restaurant. I hear you're still determined to stop there for a meal."

His tone sounded aggrieved, but she was feeling too good about her accomplishment not to share it. "I've hired a boy named Andrew Buffalo to help in the kitchen. You may have seen him running out of here."

"Yeah, couldn't help noticing when he nearly tripped over me. But what do you mean you hired him? Didn't think you'd find anyone, but since you did, you should've just let Pa know so he could decide whether to hire him."

"I wasn't asking for permission. Your father can pay him or I will. But your previous cook had a helper. If you think I won't insist on the same, think again."

Since she was pretty much butting heads with him, the last thing she expected to hear at that moment was his laugh.

"You're damned bossy—for an employee," he said with an engaging grin.

"Thankfully I don't work for you, but for your father," she retorted.

"Do you really see a difference? Around here, a Callahan is a Callahan."

"Where I come from, a housekeeper *isn't* a cook."

"Yeah, but I definitely like the idea of you working for me," he said with another laugh.

Why would that remark so amuse him? Or were they even still talking about the same thing? Feeling suddenly out of her depth, Tiffany headed back toward the restaurant and what would hopefully not be her one and only good meal for the next two months.

"You said his name is Buffalo, huh?" Hunter said as they returned to the boardwalk on the main street. "You know that's a fake name, right?"

"Is it? Does it matter?"

"No, as long as he's not running from the law."

"Don't be absurd. He's just a boy."

"So? I've seen them younger than him in gunfights. You'd be amazed at how many boys come West looking for excitement and, when they don't find any, create some of their own. But it's usually only the ones that run into trouble that change their names."

"If he were an outlaw, he'd likely be well fed, don't you think?"

"Not necessarily."

"Mrs. Martin has vouched for him," she gritted out.

"Agnes did? Well, hell, why didn't you just say that to begin with? I'll trust her judgment."

His approval came too late. Whether he'd meant to or not, he'd put a damper on how good she'd been feeling about hiring Andrew, and now she was annoyed with Hunter. So when he tried to take her arm to cross the street, she pulled her arm back and kept walking down the boardwalk. The restaurant was still nearly a block away, and someone had just ridden by, stirring up dust, so she was *not* crossing the street just yet. Then she realized they were approaching one of the town's saloons, where a few men were loitering out front. Miners by the looks of them. They'd just passed two other hefty men leaning against a storefront who made her think of the two miners she'd seen earlier who'd been trying to provoke Hunter with their stares. They might even be the same two. . . .

She heard Hunter's exasperated sigh. "I haven't killed anyone lately. I guess I'm due."

Tiffany immediately did an about-face, even though she was sure he was exaggerating. He had to be! But she was willing to concede the point he was making with that alarming statement. "Let's cross the street now."

"You're sure you don't want to walk us straight into trouble?"

She finally noticed his grin. She could have hit him for deliberately frightening her like that.

"I'm glad to see you haven't left town yet, Mr. Callahan. Might I have a few moments of your time?"

They both turned and saw a middle-aged man who had come up behind them. His stiff-crowned hat with the short brim and his expensive business suit were more suitable for the city than a small ranching town. Dressed in fashionable,

Eastern-style clothes, the man stood out as much as she did. Then it occurred to her, could this be the mining executive Anna had mentioned?

"I don't think so," Hunter replied curtly. He obviously knew the man and didn't like him. The two hefty miners who had been leaning against the storefront walked over and stood a few paces behind the well-dressed man. "If you have anything else to say, you know where to find my pa."

"Your father hasn't been a reasonable man. As his eldest son, your opinion could sway him."

"What makes you think my opinion isn't the same as his? Your smelters are spitting out a crazy amount of soot. There's no way to prevent it from floating across the range."

"The range is vast, you certainly don't need it all. You're being offered a fortune to concede that point."

"Our answer isn't going to change, Harris. Why don't you just cut your losses and move on?"

"We could ask you the same question."

The man no longer looked so affable as he turned and walked away. Executive? More like a strong-arm for the mine owner. But the moment he left, those other two men who had been close enough to hear what had been said both stepped forward to confront Hunter. One, the taller of the two, actually tried to shove him!

Hunter must have expected something because he quickly knocked the man's hand aside. Without taking his eyes off the man, he told Tiffany, "Go on to the restaurant while I take care of this. I won't be long behind you."

She stepped out into the street to get out of the way, but she didn't go far. He might be confident that he could defuse their aggression, but she wasn't so sure, especially when more miners were at the saloon down the street and two of them, obviously drunk, were weaving their way over to see what was going on.

"You're making a big mistake, boy," the shorter man said. "We got no work, thanks to you and your family."

"Then why haven't you left town?"

"We been told to stick around, that there—"

"Shut up, Earl," the other cut in, then said to Hunter, "We got a message for your pa. Not for you to deliver, mind you," he added with a snicker. "He'll figure it out when they carry you home."

Tiffany winced when Hunter doubled over. He'd blocked the first punch, but both men swung at him at the same time! What happened to the miners just baiting and not throwing first punches as Degan had said? Because a porchful of witnesses in front of the saloon would back them up that Hunter started it? Were they forgetting that she was there to say otherwise? Or didn't they care? But Hunter's having to fight two at a time was ridiculous. Her hand gripped her parasol a little tighter, for what purpose she wasn't sure, but she wasn't going to let these two brutes beat him senseless. *Where* was the town sheriff?

She'd been holding her breath, but let it out a little when she saw how fast Hunter was. He kicked one man back, which gave him a little leeway to deal with the one named Earl, and quickly landed some punches to Earl's face and belly, and then an uppercut that sent Earl to the ground. Hunter now had some time to lay into the other man. But then Earl was back on his feet, furiously charging at Hunter. She gasped. If they got Hunter down, he wasn't likely to get back up! Incredibly, Hunter shoved the other man into Earl's path instead, so both miners went sprawling. And were even more angry now. But managing to keep the men staggering back or falling to the ground, Hunter somehow kept the advantage. It looked as if he was actually going to win!

Then she saw the flash of sunlight on metal. One of the drunks had drawn a little gun from his pocket and was pointing it at Hunter's back.

"Hunter, behind you!" She threw her parasol at the man even as she yelled the warning. And missed. But instinct must have made Hunter drop to the ground and pull his gun before he even looked back. Almost in the same breath he fired a single shot. The little gun fell to the ground and the man started screaming and gripping his upper arm, which was turning red with blood. Either Hunter's aim was off or it was really accurate and he'd only meant to disarm the man.

"I wouldn't," Hunter warned when the other drunk bent down to pick up the gun on the ground.

That miner raised his arms and backed off immediately. With a roll, Hunter got to his feet. He didn't holster his own gun yet, just aimed it at the two men who'd attacked him. They started stepping backward, but didn't get far with the sheriff finally showing up, drawn by the gunfire. Hunter had a few words with the lawman before picking up Tiffany's parasol and joining her in the street. She watched the sheriff, who was only leading the wounded man away.

"Why isn't he arresting them all?" she wanted to know.

"Because the jail is already overflowing with troublemakers, and I don't feel like lodging a complaint today."

"Why not?" she demanded indignantly. "That was two against one, *and* they started it."

He grinned. "Were you worried about me?"

"Certainly not," she quickly denied.

"Well, thanks for the warning, Jenny. Those Deringers might be tiny, but they can still kill a man." He laughed as he handed her the parasol. "Did you really throw this at a man with a gun in his hand?"

An insane moment on her part! Was this how Hunter was when Degan wasn't around to caution restraint? Up for any challenge? She was exasperated that he hadn't drawn his gun sooner to make the two miners back off, before the drunk drew his gun. Had the whole thing been a setup arranged by Mr. Harris? She was beginning to think the Callahans had a lot more to worry about than her family. . . .

Chapter Twenty-One

"**D**ID YOU SEND ME off just so you could get shot at?"
Degan said drily as he came up behind them.

Hunter chuckled. "How'd you guess?"

Degan wasn't any more amused than Tiffany was and asked
her pointedly, "Are you ready to go home now?"

To her real home, absolutely, but she still had fifty-nine
days to spend in this purgatory. Just an ordinary day in
Nashart, she supposed. For them. If she had any intention of
staying, she might try to convince herself to get used to it. Not
a chance. Yet these men seemed much too nonchalant about
the fight she'd just witnessed.

Stiffly she said, "I'm not leaving yet. I'm going to *pretend*
this is a civilized town and still have lunch in it." And to
Hunter: "If you tell me it isn't safe to do that, then I will go
to the train station instead and buy a ticket home. *Is* it safe,
Mr. Callahan?"

"Yes, for now. But do us all a favor and don't ask to come to
town on a Saturday again."

"Oh, believe me, I've already figured that out. But your answer wasn't the least bit reassuring." She marched off in the direction of the restaurant.

He fell into step beside her. "I won't let anything happen to you, Red, I swear."

She heard confidence in his tone, and a sincere desire to keep her safe. Did Hunter have a bit of a chivalrous nature? That would have been quite reassuring—if she had any intention of marrying him, which she didn't. So besides his engaging humor, his incredible good looks, his courage, which she'd just witnessed, he had this good quality, too? She had hoped that while carrying out her charade as Jennifer she would discover more bad qualities than good ones. Of course, the possibility that he was trying to cheat on her by seducing Jennifer was bad enough. But that hadn't been proved yet.

Andrew Buffalo was waiting for Tiffany outside Sal's Restaurant. She introduced him to her escorts. The boy was so happy about getting a real job that he wasn't even leery of Degan. Tiffany had been a little worried that the restaurant might be too rustic for her tastes, but she was pleasantly surprised by the decor inside. White, embroidered tablecloths, even little bouquets of daisies on each table, though they were stuck in jars instead of vases. And the dining room was crowded, but then it was around lunchtime and there were only ten tables.

They were shown to the last one available. Hunter was stopped a number of times on the way, with friends asking after his mother. He might have introduced Tiffany if she had stopped with him. Then again, he might not have because she was just a servant in his household. She wouldn't introduce a servant to her mother's friends, so Jennifer would understand even if Tiffany might get huffy about it. But Degan didn't give her the chance to find out which side of her would have re-acted, taking her directly to their table instead. She needed to get a better handle on the part she was playing. She was behaving and speaking up too quickly without forethought, as herself instead of the housekeeper.

But some reactions just weren't controllable. Her reaction to Hunter after he sat down was one of them. It was by far one of the most uncomfortable meals she'd ever had, when it shouldn't have been. Hunter grilled Andrew while they ate. She'd expected that and couldn't object to it, since Andrew would be living at the ranch. And at least Hunter did it in a friendly manner. But Tiffany was only half listening.

She had been doing her best all day to ignore how handsome Hunter was. It was fairly easy to do when she wasn't looking directly at him, but in the restaurant, sitting across the table from him, it stopped being easy. She knew why. Because he was looking at her even while he was talking to Andrew. It made her nervous. It made her blush. While she wanted to tell him to stop it, she *didn't* want him to know how much it was bothering her.

As she'd been finding out lately, she chattered a little too much when she got nervous. When the "interview" paused briefly, she jumped in, saying, "When I first saw the sign outside the restaurant, I thought *Sal* would be short for *Sally*, but Degan mentioned today that only men work here."

"You were right about the name." When her eyes widened, Hunter laughed. "No, the man's name isn't Sally. Sally was Tom's wife. He owns the place. He named it for her and didn't change it after she died. The whole town was saddened by the loss because Sally was a wonderful woman. We were afraid Tom might pack up and head back East, but Sarah Wilson offered to help. She spits out kids like chewing tobacco, so she had milk to nurse Tom's newborn."

"You're confusing even me," Degan said, "so I can't imagine what Miss Fleming is thinking."

"Sorry," Hunter said, his eyes back on Tiffany. "Sally died in childbirth their second year here."

"Nashart doesn't have a doctor?" Tiffany asked.

"We do, but men with that type of learning are pretty rare out here. For as far back as I can remember, we've had the only doc for miles around. But he frequently gets called away to other nearby towns, so he isn't always on hand for our own emergencies. Like complications in childbirth, which is what happened with Sally."

The remark made her realize she was hearing about another danger in the West, for women specifically. Had her mother had help with the births of her four children? How brave Rose was to face that, knowing she might have to do it alone and could die because of it!

Hunter had been right to begin with, the tale was sad, so Tiffany tried changing the subject. "Sarah Wilson, how many children does she actually have for you to have described it so—colorfully? Five? Six?"

"Twelve by last count."

"And she hasn't shot her husband yet?"

Hunter burst out laughing. Tiffany almost grinned herself, but she hadn't been joking. That poor woman!

"You don't like kids?" he asked curiously.

"I—I don't actually know. I haven't had occasion to be around them very often."

"No, I guess I was getting at, how many do you hope to have someday?"

"A *much* more moderate number."

"You'd make some beautiful kids," Hunter said with an admiring look, then leaned closer to whisper, "Want to make some?" She gasped. He laughed. "Figure out when you're being teased, Red. You take things much too seriously, even for an Easterner."

She decided to tell him the truth. "I don't—usually. I actually have a nice, even temperament."

"Where've you been hiding it?"

She blushed. He was probably teasing again, though maybe not this time. But then, she couldn't exactly discuss with him the debacle her life had become—when he was the cause of that.

She quickly changed the topic of conversation again. "Well, I'm glad Tom decided to stay and raise his child here. This chicken dish is exquisite."

It was, but the creamy sauce was what made it special. If she hadn't had such a bad experience with the town baker, she might have asked Tom for the recipe. But as she gazed around the restaurant, watching Tom move from one table to another, accepting compliments on the food and money from happy diners, she belatedly realized that a baker or a cook wouldn't want to share his recipes because the food those recipes helped them produce was their source of income. She noticed that all three men had ordered beef in some form, though Degan's steak was different, accompanied with a dark sauce. She had a feeling that he was as accustomed to refined food as she was. If her thoughts went down that path, she'd be crying, because she didn't think she'd ever be able to cook anything as delicious as this.

Hunter somehow read her mind! "Don't worry, we don't

expect you to start with anything this fancy. You have to get the hang of it first."

She gave him a slight smile. It did relieve her a little to hear him say that. But then he added, "Tom came from Chicago. Does his food make you feel homesick?"

Yes! She'd been homesick since the day she'd left New York City. But she didn't say so. Instead she asked, "Why did Tom leave Chicago and travel this far west to open a restaurant?"

Hunter shrugged. "Money, or the lack of it, brings a lot of people out this way. Tom couldn't afford to open his own restaurant back East. Here, it cost him next to nothing; in fact, just the building materials, and even half of those were donated. The folks in town were so pleased to get a real restaurant in Nashart, they all pitched in and this place went up in a day."

They were about finished. If they had stood up a few moments sooner, they would have run into disaster at the door, because the worst thing that could happen did happen: one of her brothers walked in. Tiffany froze, paralyzed with indecision. She should bolt out of there, but she had no excuse to do that! She wasn't supposed to know that was Sam Warren standing by the door with two other young men she didn't recognize. She could be wrong. It had been six years since she'd seen her oldest brother. He'd changed so much in that time. . . .

But as she gazed at the man, she knew it was Sam. His face was more masculine now, he even sported a mustache, but that was her brother—his blond hair, his green eyes. And, oh, God, she wanted to hug him so badly it almost brought tears to her eyes!

Then she heard Degan say to Hunter, "I'll distract him while you get her out of here the back way."

So she wasn't the only one who had noticed a Warren had

entered the restaurant. Hunter stood up as Degan did and came around the table to take her arm, saying quietly, "Don't make a fuss, but a Warren just walked in. Pa wants them to find out. That was the point, after all, of winning you to our side. But Pa wants to savor this victory for a spell, so we'd prefer they not find out this soon."

"I would prefer it never happen," she whispered back. "I'll feel terrible if I have to explain my decision to them in person."

Hunter put his arm around her neck and held her close to shield her from Sam's view. She didn't object. She didn't *want* to be found out. Thankfully, she was out the back door without hearing anyone call her name—her real name.

Chapter Twenty-Two

Hunter hurried Tiffany down the street to the hitching post where Degan had left their horses, but he didn't wait for the others to join them. He mounted his pinto and leaned down to offer her a hand up. She didn't protest because the only thing on her mind was escaping. She was still too upset over such a close call, and they weren't out of town yet. If Sam had recognized her, she'd be facing her father—today. But a small voice reminded her, "And be reunited with your brothers." Could she stomach Franklin for that? No, not even for that. The hurt that man had caused her ran too deep. She'd have to figure out some other way to visit with her brothers before she left the territory.

"We need to do this more often."

It took a few moments for Hunter's remark to break through and make sense to her. Was he talking about her practically sitting on his lap? Oh, good grief, why was she?

"Wait! I thought you were taking me to the stable in town. I was going to rent a horse for the ride home."

"You're already riding home."

"But this is highly improper."

"Me taking you home is improper? You sure get some silly notions, Red."

She snapped her mouth shut and gritted her teeth. They were out of town already, so she wasn't surprised he'd say that. Yet he had to know what she was talking about. Etiquette in the West couldn't be *that* different from the rules of social decorum she'd been taught. But even worse, the position he'd put her in was far too intimate. He hadn't placed her behind him or astride in front of him, he'd set her down sideways, right across his lap, so she couldn't miss his gazing down at her. And grinning.

He was mighty pleased with himself, the cad, while she was distinctly uncomfortable. She turned her head away from his glance and looked at the road ahead. The long mane of his pinto blew across her hand. Such a beautiful animal. She wanted one just like it. Before she left the territory, she was going to purchase one to ship home. She'd be the envy of all her friends as they rode around Central Park. Most of her friends didn't know about her dilemma. She'd been too ashamed to tell them where she was going. They would have been so shocked.

Oh, good grief, she couldn't think about home now, or having seen Sam, because she'd start crying, and she couldn't let Hunter and her proximity to him fluster her. She had to focus on being Jennifer, the housekeeper, and engage in normal conversation. That would calm her down.

Keeping her eyes off him, she said, "This is a pretty horse."

Hunter's snort made her glance back at him. He grimaced as he told the horse, "Don't listen to her, Patches, she didn't really just call you pretty." He then leaned down to her and whispered, "Don't insult him again, he's damn touchy."

She didn't believe a word he'd said, but she couldn't help laughing. Until she realized Hunter was just creating an excuse to bring his face down close to hers. With those lovely powder-blue eyes so close now, she stopped breathing. If he kissed her—oh, God, she didn't know what she'd do.

She blurted out, "I like riding, but I like holding my own reins. You should have taken me to the stable in town so I could rent a mount for myself."

He leaned back, the moment he might have kissed her gone. She could breathe again. Relief should have rushed in, yet she felt disappointed instead. What was wrong with her! It would be better for her if she didn't know what it was like to be kissed by Hunter Callahan.

But he was still looking down at her. "Wouldn't have taken you for a rider. I thought all you city folks just travel around in carriages."

Finally a distracting topic that should compose her. "Not at all. I lived near a big park, possibly the biggest in the world. I was quite young when I was taught to ride. Perhaps you might let me borrow your Patches sometime?"

He shook his head. "A man bonds with his horse, it's like family."

She burst out laughing, but cut it off when she realized he might actually be serious.

He was quick to remark, "That's a beautiful laugh you've got, Jenny. Why don't I hear it more often?"

Because she was in constant turmoil, anxiety, worry, but worse, the man she'd come here to disdain was proving to be likable. Occasionally. When she didn't catch him seducing women, including herself. But of course she couldn't say any of that.

Primly she said, "A housekeeper must be reserved at all times."

"Stop it." He chuckled. "That might have been the case in those fancy homes you worked in back East, but you're in Montana now."

Did he have to keep pointing that out? She got back to the subject that had briefly calmed her, and his silly—or not—remark about his horse. She asked, "Were you joking about Patches? I've only owned two horses. I confess I never considered either one a pet."

His expression turned curious. "Horses ain't cheap. How'd you even afford one?"

She groaned to herself, but quickly thought of a reasonable excuse. "A good friend of my father's was a horse breeder. The man he worked for wasn't very nice. Any horses that didn't meet his standards, he ordered put down. Our friend didn't like doing that and gave them away instead whenever he could."

"Easterners," Hunter said with some disdain. "Out here, we'd just set them free. We've got a few extra horses at the ranch. You can ride one of them. Just let me know when you feel like riding and I'll take you out."

She frowned. "I would prefer not to be restricted to your schedule. I'd like to ride out when I feel like it—alone."

"Can you shoot a gun?"

"No."

"A rifle?"

"Of course not."

"Then you don't ride alone."

She would have argued if his tone hadn't suggested it would

be pointless. Perhaps she could learn to shoot a weapon. No, why bother when she wouldn't be here that long.

Then it occurred to her: "If you have extra mounts, why didn't you bring one for me today?"

He chuckled. "And miss you sitting in my lap for the trip back? Hell no."

So he'd planned this uncomfortable situation she found herself in? He was grinning at her, obviously patting himself on the back for arranging this intimacy. Why? *Was* he like this with every young woman who crossed his path? More to the point, was he enjoying some innocent flirtation or was he actually bent on seducing her—Jennifer, she corrected herself. She ought to find out, but how could she if she kept taking offense at his style of friendliness. She could be nicer to him, she supposed, perhaps even go along with his flirting just to see where it would go. No, that smacked of tempting him to be unfaithful. She couldn't in good conscience use that against him to get out of this arranged marriage, not if she provoked it. It had to be his idea and serve as proof of *his* philandering nature that she could present to her mother.

Lost in her thoughts, she realized she'd absently been gazing at Hunter all the while, long enough evidently to make him think she might welcome an overture from him now because he was slowly leaning down toward her, his eyes locked on hers, so blue, so sensual. Her stomach flipped over, her breath caught, and she couldn't stop what was happening, couldn't even move. She inhaled his masculine scent—a mixture of leather, pine trees, and something she couldn't identify. But she liked it and wondered what he would taste like. Her world would change drastically if she let him kiss her because she might like it. He might like it . . . and he might want more. It would be business as usual for him, a daily seduction or two. And she was probably right on the mark with that number because she remembered Pearl's arm wrapped around his shoulder in town. . . .

That memory ended the alarmingly hypnotic state she'd been in the grip of. "Stop!"

She meant to stop him from kissing her, but he must have thought she wanted him to stop the horse! Patches did stop. Tiffany was too frazzled to upbraid Hunter yet for trying to kiss her. She looked around and saw that they were near the lake and not far from the abandoned house.

After taking a deep, calming breath, she said, "I saw that house yesterday. Could I take a closer look?"

"Jenny."

That's all he said, yet she *knew* he was still thinking about kissing her. Now that she'd gathered her wits, she had to nip that idea in the bud.

"Don't mention what shouldn't have happened—and don't let it happen again. I may work for your family, but that doesn't mean you can take advantage of me."

"I wouldn't."

Every word she'd said had been building up steam and she couldn't seem to stop the tirade now. "And never mind my curiosity about the house. Just take me back to the ranch. You and I shouldn't be keeping company like this—alone. It's beyond improper and do you see why? It gives *you* the wrong idea!"

"It must be the red hair," he said under his breath, and slid her off his lap to the ground before he dismounted. "Come on."

With the reins in one hand, he grabbed her hand with the other and he led her through the trees toward the water, and the building that was no longer being built. She tried to get her hand back. Twice.

He must have noticed she was still annoyed because he actually said, "Shake it off. There's no call to get in a snit over a harmless kiss—that didn't happen."

Did he see it that way? Harmless? Without meaning? Maybe she did overreact. She needed to have a care about how she dealt with this man. Mindful of who she really was tempered with who *he* thought she was, she needed to juggle the two identities so she didn't lose her job—or a possible ally. Because it occurred to her that if Hunter Callahan was as carefree and generous with his affections as it was beginning to appear he was, then if anyone could help her avoid this marriage, it would be him.

They'd reached the house, or rather, the framing. Its layout indicated it was going to be much bigger than it appeared from a distance. She was going to ask him about his engagement and what he thought about it, now that Degan had mentioned it to her, which is why she'd asked to see this house. Discussing the house and whom it was for was a perfect opportunity to get him to talk about that betrothal, without her own anger getting in the way. But if she couldn't calm down, then maybe this wasn't such a good time, after all. No, anger or no, she had to learn his thoughts on the matter.

"I've heard this house is being built for you and your fiancée. That's another reason why I don't want you trying to kiss me."

He let go of her hand and gave her a sharp look. "Who told you about that?"

"Degan mentioned it, when I asked him about the feud this morning while we were in town. It's true then? You *are* engaged to a Warren?"

"So? I'm supposed to stop living while waiting for that

woman to show up? I've never met her, Red. There's no attachment."

"But you're going to marry her."

"Now *that* remains to be seen. My pa hopes I'll like her, but he won't force me to marry her if I don't."

"It sounds like you've always known it would be your choice in the end. And what? That everyone expects it to happen is just too damn bad?"

"Exactly," he snapped. "And I sure as hell won't pretend I'm married before I actually am!"

His attitude amazed her. She hadn't expected this. He was talking about the impending marriage as if it were a noose around his neck.

But he must have noticed how surprised she was because he continued in a calmer tone, "I've had this burden all my life. The day I started noticing girls, Pa pulled me aside to tell me, 'You can touch, just don't get attached, you got a wife handpicked for you.' What the hell, this is the nineteenth century. Who the hell gets stuck with a handpicked wife these days? And for what? Because two men can't sit down and say this ain't our fight, why the hell are we still shooting each other? And why are you smiling now? You think this is funny?"

She was surprised she wasn't laughing, because what he'd just said echoed her own thoughts, but she couldn't say that. "Not at all. I was just wondering, what if your intended feels the same way you do?"

"I can sure hope," he mumbled.

"But have you never considered that?"

"No, can't say that I have. I figured she'd do as she's told."

"Maybe you figured wrong," she snapped, and started to turn away.

He stopped her. "What's your hurry? Do you really think she won't like me?"

"If she's anything like me, she's used to refined city gentlemen, not brash, overconfident cowboys who don't know when to give up."

He gave her a half grin. "Overconfident with reason." He stepped inside the framing. He stood there, his hands on his hips, gazing around at the beginnings of a house that might never be finished. She started to follow until she noticed how dark his expression had turned. She'd never seen him look like this. Angry. Very angry. Not at her—well, actually, maybe at the *real* her. This might not have been the right place to discuss the betrothal, when the house was such a blatant reminder of it.

That thought was reinforced when he suddenly raised his leg and kicked at a corner post. It took two more kicks before it cracked in two. He got out of the way as framing from overhead started coming down, though nails kept it from falling all the way to the floor. It just hung there now, misshapen. Ruined.

Incredulous, she asked, "Why'd you do that?"

"Because the damn thing never should have been started when it might never be lived in. I've been meaning to tear it down." Then he grabbed her hand again. "Come on, it was a mistake stopping here. Let me get you back to the ranch."

She didn't object. He didn't know it, but he'd just given her the best news she'd heard since arriving in Montana. He hated the betrothal as much as she did. Then why wasn't she ecstatic? Was she so vain that she could be annoyed that he *didn't* want her?

Chapter Twenty-Three

HUNTER'S MOOD DIDN'T IMPROVE in the short distance they had to travel to reach the ranch. Tiffany's feet were on the ground in front of the porch before she noticed Zachary leaning against a post there. Glancing back and forth between Hunter and her, the older man didn't seem too pleased that they had ridden in alone. Did at least *someone* here besides her realize how improper it was?

"My Mary's been asking after you, gal," Zachary said gruffly to Tiffany. "Go on up and make her acquaintance."

"Certainly."

"I'll introduce you," Hunter offered.

"She can manage," Zachary disagreed. "I want a word with you, boy."

"I'll be back in a minute, Pa," Hunter said, and ushered Tiffany inside and straight upstairs.

"Wait!" Tiffany said when he was about to knock on Mary's door. "I need to at least make sure I'm presentable before I meet your mother."

He smiled. "You're beautiful. Relax, she isn't going to bite you."

"I didn't think she was, but first impressions—"

He lifted her chin to examine her face, then pretended to wipe a few smudges of dirt from her cheeks. She knew he was pretending because he did it too slowly, too gently, his hands practically cupping her face, his fingers caressing her rather than wiping. Heat spread all over her. Caught by his eyes, so intense, Tiffany sucked in her breath.

She heard Hunter groan as he pulled his hands away from her. He turned and opened the door to his parents' bedroom, mumbling, "Trust me next time I say you look fine."

That wasn't what he'd said at all! He'd thrown her off-balance by telling her she was beautiful. Abruptly, she was escorted into the large corner bedroom. So much light flooded into the room from the two walls of windows, all of which were open and had their curtains drawn, that it took a moment for her eyes to adjust to it. The room was big but was cluttered with furniture. Tiffany was delighted to see that vanities weren't foreign to the West after all. Mary had a frilly one, *and* a writing desk, and a small, round dining table where she and her husband probably shared meals on occasion while she was recuperating. The room also contained bookcases, several straight-back chairs, and one comfortable-looking stuffed chair that had been drawn up next to the bed, no doubt for Mary's visitors.

Hunter's mother was sitting propped up in the big four-poster bed, a half dozen pillows at her back. Her long brown hair was braided, one braid on each side. She was wearing a long, plain white, short-sleeved nightgown designed for comfort. It was too warm to be under the covers. Even her feet were bare. Rose had said Zachary had a pretty wife. She was still a handsome woman, sturdy, not delicate at all, with keen blue eyes. Hunter's eyes.

Hunter went straight to the bed and leaned over to kiss his mother on the cheek. "I've brought you Jenny, Ma. If she seems a little stiff, remember she's an Easterner."

He said it in his usual teasing tone, accompanied by a grin, so Tiffany didn't take offense. Mary grinned, too. "Run along and let us get acquainted. She's not going to be reserved with me."

He was no sooner out the door than Mary said, "I heard what you did." Tiffany's heart skipped a beat until Mary added with a smile, "Zach says you did an amazing job, getting the downstairs back into shape. I didn't know it had gotten so bad, though I should've expected as much, with Pearl away so long. To be honest, I never would have thought to ask the hired hands to help. Sit and tell me how you managed that."

Tiffany was amazed at how quickly her nervousness vanished with Mary's friendly manner and smile. She even chuckled before admitting, "I don't think it had anything to do with me. I asked the cowboys if they would help and they were about to laugh, but then Degan Grant said he'd help. Suddenly they were all willing to help, too."

"Well, that explains that. That man can be a powerful motivator. Polite, can't deny that, but I'm glad he won't be needed after the wedding and will be moving on."

"Your son's wedding?"

"Yes. You and I will have a lot to do to smarten up the place before then. That Warren gal is rich, was raised in the lap of luxury. We just hope she hasn't been so pampered and spoiled she can't settle in here—well, I do. My menfolk expect the worst, but they've never had a kind thing to say about her family, so that's to be expected. Her father sure is looking forward to seeing her again, though."

Tiffany managed not to sound incredulous. "He told you that?"

Mary tsked. "Haven't spoken to him in years. Heard it from the town gossips who visit me from time to time. It's all he's been talking about for months now."

"You're—worried about impressing her?"

"Hell yes, I am. I'll be treating her with kid gloves. A lot rests on this wedding, gal. A lot. Which is why I'm so glad you're here to help with it. So tell me why someone who looks like you isn't married yet?"

No beating around the bush for Mary Callahan, obviously. Tiffany suddenly felt uncomfortable about deceiving the Callahans because Mary had just sounded so pleased about the wedding. Nonetheless, she once more repeated Jennifer's story, though it was beginning to sound a little trite to her own ears by now. She was even inclined to agree with Hunter's assessment of Jennifer's relationship with her fiancé. If they really loved each other, wouldn't they have opted to marry first and save up for a house later?

But Mary surprised her with a new take on it. "I remember what it was like back East, how things could be thought out and worried to death before decided on. Too many choices were the problem. Here in Montana it's just the opposite. There aren't enough choices, so a man has to be impulsive when he sees what he wants or risk someone else snatching it up."

It sounded as if Mary was describing Franklin Warren's situation. Was that all her parents' romance had been? Impulsiveness on Frank's part because of the scarcity of women out here?

Impulsiveness that didn't work out, she reminded herself. But she hadn't expected Mary Callahan to be an Easterner, too.

"I somehow assumed you grew up around here like your husband," Tiffany said.

"Goodness, no, but Zach wasn't born here either. No one but trappers and Indians lived around here back then. Zachary's father, Elijah Callahan, was a rancher in Florida; mine was a butcher who did business with him, which is how we met."

Tiffany was surprised. Why had she thought these people had been here so much longer? Was the feud not that old either?

"So you actually moved here with your husband?"

"Yes, and with his father, with whom we lived. Elijah's wife had just died. Elijah had no reason to stay in Florida after that, and every reason to leave. Bad blood with his neighbor was what really drove him away."

Mary had almost whispered that last part, yet Mary couldn't be talking about Warrens, so why would she add that so quietly, as if it were a secret Tiffany shouldn't know about? But she wanted to ask Mary about the feud, and this was somewhat of an opening to do so.

Carefully she said, "How . . . ironic, since your son Cole said your neighbors here aren't friendly either. It would seem it's the bane of your family to have—"

"Oh, it's worse than that, but we're hopeful that it will be over soon. Well, *I'm* hopeful. Zach is more skeptical. Seeing is believing, you know? But who can blame him when it was she who followed us here and instilled that hatred of hers into the rest of her family."

"Who did?"

"Mariah Warren. Has no one told you about the feud?"

Tiffany choked out, "I was going to ask, since I seem to have landed in the middle of it. Who is Mariah Warren?"

"Elijah Callahan's one true love. She was Mariah Evans back then when they lived in Florida. Elijah and Mariah were to marry."

"But they didn't?"

"No, they surely did not." Mary sighed. "The night before the wedding, Elijah's best friend got him drunk and thought it a fine joke to dump him in a whore's bed so he'd wake up there and think the worst. But Mariah wanted to talk to him that night. Some people think she was having wedding jitters, others think she didn't want to wait for the wedding night. She spent hours at Elijah's ranch, waiting for him to come home. Finally, she went to town to find out what was keeping him. When she entered his favorite tavern, looking for him, everyone got quiet. At the point of her musket she demanded to know where Elijah was, and someone told her he was upstairs."

Tiffany gasped. "She shot him?"

"Not that night. That night she was just in shock. But she shot him the next day when he came to explain. She didn't believe he didn't have relations with the tavern floozy. She meant to kill him; she just wasn't a good shot and left him with a permanent limp instead. But that jealous rage that took hold of her that night never did let go. Within the week she married an old suitor, Richard Warren, just to spite Elijah. That's when Elijah got jealous, too. It took him longer to find a wife, yet he married for the same reason, just to spite Mariah."

"Why couldn't they both just let it go?"

"You'd think, wouldn't you? That would have been the sensible thing to do. But their love for each other was powerful. That's why it turned into such powerful hatred. Jealousy can do that to a person, you know, when it festers like that, and hers festered for the rest of her life."

"How did both families end up here?"

"Elijah was trying to get us as far from Mariah as it was possible to get. Mariah's husband, Richard Warren, had died early in their marriage. He gave her three children, but only Frank survived to adulthood, and she raised him to hate us, too. They followed us here . . . well, she did. To be fair, Frank didn't know that's what his mother was doing. She was a little crazy by then, she had to be, to come all this way just to finally have it out with Elijah."

"An actual confrontation? How did that turn out?"

"As might be expected. They couldn't live together but they died together."

"Indians?"

"Goodness, no, the Indians in the area weren't at war with the white man yet. They were mostly friendly or we never would have built here when there was only a fur-trading post nearby."

"Then how did Elijah and Mariah die?"

"They shot each other."

Chapter Twenty-Four

THE STORY OF MARIAH and Elijah might be old news to Mary Callahan, but it was a fresh tragedy to Tiffany. She had trouble getting the tale out of her head. *They shot each other.* How could anyone get so angry they'd want to shoot—well, obviously, that happened all the time. Duels, war, gunfights here in the West. But to leave that legacy to your children and their children? How dumb was that? And now she was supposed to pay for her grandmother's lunacy?

She felt bad now, since it sounded as if her family was ultimately to blame. Or was it? She'd only heard one side of the feud today, the Callahans' side. Yet to hear the other side, she'd have to talk to her father. *No* thank you. Besides, what else could he add? That Elijah wasn't eloquent enough to make Mariah see reason? Or that Mariah was a little crazy to begin with to keep that fury alive for so many years?

Tiffany hadn't expected to like Mary Callahan. She didn't want to disappoint the woman by admitting she couldn't cook and asking for help. She decided to give it a try on her own first. So she spent the rest of the afternoon reading her little cookbook, which didn't take long as thin as it was, and making a list of the ingredients she would need. She went through the pantry thoroughly and discovered the ice cellar next to it. It was packed with large chunks of pond ice and a lot of salted meat. None of the ice was melting yet, with summer only just beginning.

She couldn't find a few of the ingredients mentioned in the cookbook.

"What's wrong?" Andrew asked as he came in the back door.

Tiffany realized she must have been frowning. She held up the cookbook she was reading. "Several of these recipes call for eggs and I can't find any in the ice cellar."

"I think I heard some chickens when Jakes was getting me settled in the bunkhouse."

"Really? Let's go find out."

They found the henhouse behind the barn. It held quite a few adult birds, but she didn't see any eggs lying around. There were also dozens of chicks, some perched on the planks where the nests were lined up, others picking at seeds on the ground. She was fascinated. She'd never seen live farm animals before, or dead ones ready for cooking either.

"Get away from there!" Jakes barked at her, coming around the corner of the barn with a basket on his arm. "Those gals belong to me."

"I wasn't going to disturb them," she assured the trail cook with a smile, while she was thinking, such a grouch!

Jakes wore a full beard, brown streaked with gray, but he wasn't that old, maybe in his forties. He was skinny, bandy-legged, short, and obviously cantankerous. But he could probably give her tips on cooking, so she didn't want to get on his bad side.

"I was just curious about eggs," she said.

"I bring two dozen to the house each day. If you need more, just tell me. But by no means do you *ever* bother my hens. They don't like strangers. Upsets them. Then they don't produce."

That was fine with her, since she didn't know how to get an egg out of a hen anyway. "What about cows for milk?"

"Two dairy cows are kept in the barn. The hens and Myrtle are mine, the cows ain't, so you're on your own with them."

Oh, no, she wasn't! "Andrew?"

"Be glad to, ma'am."

She beamed at the boy for reading her mind. He was already earning his keep, but his quick reply made her wonder, "How are you acquainted with farm animals?"

"My oldest sister married a farmer. I got to spend one summer with her in the country before I came West. I liked it. Even thought about taking up farming myself, till I got the notion to find my pa. So here I am instead."

"If you're done admiring my gals, take your jabbering elsewhere," Jakes grumbled.

Tiffany grit her teeth to keep from berating the fellow for his rudeness. "Are there any other cooking resources I should know about?"

"The lake's got fish, but cattlemen don't fish. If you want any, you'll have to do the fishing yourself like Old Ed did."

That actually sounded interesting. She wouldn't mind visiting that pretty lake again, so she didn't delegate that chore to Andrew yet. But with the ice cellar so well stocked, she didn't need to try fishing right away.

However, she did want to make sure she didn't trespass

on Jakes's domain, so she said, "You mentioned Myrtle was yours?"

"Her you can meet. Come along, I'll introduce you."

She blushed. She'd misunderstood and thought Myrtle was an animal! Did the man have a wife? If he did, the woman must have the temperament of a saint to put up with him. But it made her wonder if any of the cowboys had wives, too. Were there other houses on the property for employees' families?

Jakes wasn't waiting for her to follow him, so she had to hurry to catch up. But he stopped next to the pigsty on the back side of one of the sheds.

"Myrtle's the sow," he said proudly. "Won her in a poker game. Kept her to dispose of food scraps. Beats the heck out of digging daily holes to bury the stuff so it don't lure in wild animals. Mrs. Callahan figured to make even better use of her and bought her a mate. This new batch of piglets will taste good later this year."

Now Tiffany was blushing for thinking Myrtle might be Jakes's wife! The two adult pigs were huge in comparison to the little piglets running about. So Myrtle was a pet . . . well, maybe not, since Jakes was practically smacking his lips over the thought of eating her young when they were grown. She tried not to feel disgusted at the thought, reminding herself the piglets had been bred to end up on the dinner table—at Mary's suggestion, too! But they looked so cute! One piglet had even squeezed under the lowest plank on the pen fencing and was sniffing at her boots.

She was not going to think about their being dinner someday and said to Jakes, "Shouldn't they be better contained?"

"They don't wander far, and don't be throwing them no rotten food, neither, just fresh scraps. You can pick him up and set him back inside if you're worried 'bout it."

Pick up a pig? She stared at him aghast. "I wasn't worried, and thank you for giving me the information I needed."

She hurried back to the house with Andrew, who was full of surprises. He couldn't cook other than to roast meat over a campfire, but he did know how to grow vegetables. The garden behind the house was already fully planted, but she assigned the task of tending it to him and thought she might ask him to teach her about gardens until she saw him dig his hands into the dirt. She was willing to cook food but not to grow it.

She was sitting at the table reading when Degan came in the back door of the kitchen and dropped a large sack next to her on the table. "Start with something simple to go with this," he suggested.

The word FLOUR was stamped on the front of the sack, yet she knew from the delicious aroma what was inside it and gave him a delighted smile. "You brought bread from the bakery!"

"Sorry about the sack, but most people who go to the bakery bring their own baskets. Just dust the extra flour off the loaves."

She was so pleased she actually teased him with a grin. "You expected my first meal to fail?"

"I wasn't going to bet on it. But there's one thing I do know about bread. If you want any, you have to start it the night before you eat it. Maybe you've already learned that from your cookbook."

She shook her head. She hadn't, but she had selected a recipe for a simple meal for that night, chicken soup—she'd just have to substitute beef for chicken—which would go quite well with the bread he'd brought.

He continued on to the bathing room. "I'll clean up now before the brothers show up. We'll be heading back to town tonight."

She was surprised. He'd told her today that the cowboys rode to town for hell-raising, but she hadn't expected the Callahans to be included in that group. Maybe they weren't. Maybe just Degan was.

She asked, "Who is *we*?"

He paused before closing the door. "All the men who aren't married. That would include the brothers."

"To raise hell, as you put it? What exactly does that mean?"

"Drinking, poker . . ." He started to add something else, but finished with merely, "More drinking. Drunks tend to get in fights, and saloons get busted up. Just ordinary Western fun."

"So you're babysitting again? Keep a better eye on Hunter then. It looked, and sounded, as if those miners wanted to kill him today."

"Sounded?"

"They said he'd be carried home. I think they meant dead— as a message for Zachary to give in and give them what they want."

"Are you sure you haven't let your anxiety over what you witnessed spark your imagination?"

"You said the miners don't carry guns, but one of them pulled a gun on Hunter. Or maybe he wasn't really a miner, only pretending to be one. That would be one way to get rid of the Callahans, to kill them off one by one in gun challenges."

"An interesting conclusion."

She had a feeling he would have laughed if he ever laughed. But at least she'd stated her concern. "Will you keep it in mind?"

"I keep all possibilities in mind, Miss Fleming. It's my job. But please don't let Hunter hear you call me a babysitter. He already dislikes my tagging along."

"Then why does his father feel it's necessary?"

"Because he's actually trying to keep the peace with the Warrens until the wedding. And while Hunter might be a charmer with the ladies, he can get a bit aggressive when it comes to the Warrens. I temper that."

"You hold him back?"

"No, my presence stays his hand."

"How?"

"I was hired to protect the Callahans. He won't start any fights with the Warrens if he thinks I'll draw my gun and start shooting them. He enjoys a good fistfight but he's not out to kill anyone."

She didn't like the sound of that. "Would you shoot the Warrens?"

"Hasn't come to that."

"But would you?"

He closed the door instead of answering. She hoped he simply hadn't heard her repeat the question rather than refusing to give a direct answer. Then she got so busy making her soup that she didn't even notice when Degan finished his bath and left the room.

Fortunately, she did notice when Hunter showed up for his bath, or else she might have burned herself when he pressed himself against her back as he leaned over her shoulder to sniff what she was stirring. She stiffened her posture in an effort to push him away.

"Smells like I'll be eating in town tonight," he teased.

"Would you have gotten this close to your previous cook?" she demanded.

"I couldn't lean over Old Ed. He was too tall."

"*Don't* do that again."

Unrepentant, he said, "Don't take away my excuse to do this."

This was his placing a kiss on the side of her neck. Then another, and one more even lower. She gasped and tried to ignore the gooseflesh his kisses were causing but couldn't, since now her skin tingled so deliciously all the way down her back. She closed her eyes, fighting the pleasurable sensations rising inside her that she'd never before felt. It would be so easy to turn around and . . . oh, God, what? Put her arms around him? Encourage him? Was she insane?! That was no way to deal with a fiancé she wanted to get rid of.

Instead, she swung around with her spoon raised like a weapon, but he'd already jumped backward, his grin wide.

"Besides," he added before he disappeared into the bathing room, "you smell better than what's in the pot!"

She didn't smile, but she didn't get angry either. She simply picked up her cookbook and walked out of the kitchen to the porch, where she intended to stay long enough to avoid seeing Hunter when he came out of the bathing room. The incident made her realize she had to do or say something to make him stop treating her in such a cavalier, playful manner. Innocent flirtation or not, not only was it inappropriate for the son of the house to be taking advantage of one of the servants, but he was so charming and handsome that she was beginning to worry he might succeed. Did he even care how many hearts were going to be broken when he married his intended?

Her plan was working better and more quickly than she'd expected. She was finding out what kind of man Hunter was—and not liking it one bit. All signs indicated he would make a lousy husband.

Chapter Twenty-Five

HER FIRST ATTEMPT AT making dinner, and no one was going to be there to eat it. Tiffany was surprised that she felt disappointed about that—until she actually tasted her soup. It was watery and the meat she'd added was too tough to chew. She almost threw the cookbook away until Andrew suggested she might have missed something in the recipe. She read it again and found the part about letting soup cook all day. A few hours simply wasn't enough.

But at least she could serve Zachary and Mary, who were staying home for dinner, some of the best bread she'd ever tasted, thanks to Degan. Andrew brought out some canned beans to go with it and carried the large pot of soup down to the ice cellar, where it would keep overnight so she could continue cooking it tomorrow. Thank goodness for Andrew. She would have just thrown the cookbook away if he hadn't suggested she reread the recipe. She mentally patted herself on the back again for hiring the boy. He'd even offered to get the bread started for her tonight after she'd read in the cookbook that you had to let bread dough rise overnight. Degan had been right about that. It was supposed to magically puff up and be ready to bake come morning. She'd believe it when she saw it.

She went out to the front porch for a break before she finished cleaning up the kitchen. She was so surprised by what she saw that she stood transfixed for a moment. The sky nearly made her gasp. The tree line was far enough back from the house that she had an unobstructed view of bright oranges and reds filling the sky. Now this was something she'd never see in a city of tall buildings.

She sat down on the long swing that hung from the porch roof. She didn't even think to dust off a spot first before she did. She was going to have to make a habit of coming out to enjoy the sunset each evening—while she was there. She wouldn't be seeing things like this when she went home.

A group of the hired hands rode past the house on the way to town. She didn't see Hunter with them. Another group came around the other side of the house. Degan and Hunter's brothers. He wasn't with them, either, but they had his horse, Patches. They stopped to wait for him, and in unison they tipped their hats her way. Then the door opened next to her and she turned to see Hunter looking at her with his powder-blue eyes.

"Wait up for me, Red?"

She stiffened at the sensual tone he'd just used, a clear indication of what he wanted her to wait up for. More teasing or was he serious this time?

"No."

"I promise to make it worth your while."

"No."

He shrugged and was soon riding off with his brothers. She

wished she could follow them to see how cowboys truly raised hell, since she was sure Degan had left out a few particulars. No, that wasn't entirely true. She wanted to spy on Hunter. She had no doubt he was heading straight back to Pearl.

"Am I really supposed to take bread and beans up to Mary for dinner?"

Tiffany winced. She'd forgotten about serving dinner to the owners of the ranch. Zachary was standing in the front doorway. He didn't look disappointed, but he certainly sounded it.

"Mr. Callahan, I warned you. I know as much about cooking as you do. Actually, you probably know more. I am determined now to learn, but today's effort failed because I didn't read the fine print. I'll prepare a tray—the bread is delicious, by the way—for you and Mrs. Callahan. If I can't do better by the end of next week, I'll fire myself so you won't have to."

His lower lip quirked upward a little. "I saw the book you left on the table. You'll figure it out."

Famous last words, she mumbled as she went to the kitchen, where she served up the Callahans' meager dinner and handed the tray to Zachary.

She went back to the porch for a few more minutes, enjoying the last of the bright colors on the horizon before they all faded to dusk. But she nearly screamed when she felt something move against the back of her ankle, just above her shoe. Thinking of snakes, she yanked her legs up so fast the swing swayed under her. It took a moment for her to get up the nerve to bend over to look under the seat. Then she laughed when she saw the little, chubby, white body with the flat, pink nose and big ears.

"So you don't wander far, huh?" she said aloud, remembering Jakes's earlier remark. "And I bet you missed your dinner, too. Jakes would have already gotten rid of his slops, and we didn't exactly have any today. Come on, I'll get you a bowl of beans, but you can't have any of that delicious bread when we're going to be eating every last crumb of that."

She was halfway down the hall before she realized the little pig wouldn't have understood a word she'd said to it. She started to turn around, deciding to just take it back to its pen instead, only to hear the patter of little, cloven feet on the hardwood floor behind her. It might not have understood her, but for some reason it still wanted to follow her. Then she realized it was probably tracking dirt into the house and immediately scooped it up in her arms. The pig held itself stiff for a moment before it melted against her. She glanced down and saw that it had even closed its eyes. It looked so content it would probably be purring if it were a cat! It made her laugh again. It had been so long since she'd had anything to laugh about, she was actually grateful to a pig. Even that made her laugh!

Holding the piglet with one arm in case its little feet were dirty, she scooped out the last of the beans onto a plate and set them both just outside the kitchen door. It wasn't a lot of food, but probably enough for such a small animal. She had no idea how old it might be, but it wasn't even a foot long yet. She left the door open to let in a little extra breeze while she finished cleaning up the kitchen, but a few minutes later a strong gust of warm wind blew it shut. She quickly closed the window on that side of the room, too, wondering if a storm was brewing. She hoped the pig would go home.

She turned away from the window, only to find the animal at her feet again, looking up at her expectantly. She shook her head, scooped it up once more, and walked it back to its pen. It wasn't full dark yet and she could see that most of the piglets were nursing from their mama. She chuckled at herself for thinking the wandering one would go hungry tonight when the sow was still feeding her young.

Tiffany didn't stay long to watch. The wind wasn't steady, but from time to time it gusted from the north, strong enough to whip her tied-back hair over her shoulders and play havoc with the hem of her dress. She hurried back to the house. At least the clouds hadn't blown in before sunset.

Chapter Twenty-Six

TIFFANY COULDN'T SLEEP, EVEN though she was tired. She stood at the open window for a while, which faced the back of the house and all the outbuildings, not that she could see any of them in the darkness other than the bunkhouse, where a lantern was still burning. Her room was uncomfortably warm tonight because, as she'd done in the kitchen, she'd had to close the two windows on the north wall of the bedroom when a gust of wind came in so strong it knocked an old painting off the wall. She was hoping to catch a little breeze at the back window, the only one she'd left open, but the wind was blowing in the other direction.

The rain hadn't started yet, but thick clouds were racing past the moon, obscuring it. She wouldn't see the men when they returned unless they lit a lamp at the stable, and she doubted that she'd hear them either with the wind howling occasionally. But as late as it was, it didn't look as if they would come back tonight. Women and booze. The booze probably made it unsafe for them to ride home until they sobered up. Or the threatening storm would make them decide to stay inside where it was dry. She could just imagine where Hunter was keeping dry tonight.

He was the reason she felt so unsettled tonight, and knowing that he'd gone to town to see his paramour. He was probably with Pearl at that very moment. He'd asked *her* to wait up for him when he was on his way to see another woman!

Anna might be right, that what he did prior to the wedding was irrelevant, yet he was cheating on her right before he was supposed to start courting her! He should be wrapping up his casual affairs instead of trying to start a new one with Jennifer. But was he really doing that? He'd almost kissed her today, yes, but he might consider that nothing to raise a brow over. And he'd obviously just been teasing her with those kisses on her neck in the kitchen. He couldn't know the powerful effect they had had on her.

Even though she didn't care for his behavior, she hoped Hunter could help her defuse the feud without her having to sacrifice herself to do so. His cavalier, seductive behavior and what he'd told her at the unfinished house by the lake actually suggested that he did not want to honor the arranged marriage either. Once she stopped impersonating Jennifer, she needed to discuss that with him without letting her anger get in the way. And why the devil *was* she even angry at him when he was supplying her with the perfect reason for why she wouldn't marry him. She ought to let him prove it beyond a doubt. He was certainly trying to—if it wasn't all innocent play with him.

She went back to bed and started counting sheep. She was still tossing and turning a little while later when she heard a voice in the hallway.

"Jenny, did you wait up?"

Oh my God, Hunter wasn't really knocking on her door in the middle of the night, was he? He had to be seriously intoxicated. She put her pillow over her head until she couldn't hear him anymore. So he didn't spend the night with Pearl? That didn't mean he didn't bed her though. But so much for hearing him ride in or enter the house. That annoying wind was blocking out all other sounds.

But he was back. She smiled for some reason and suddenly her exhaustion caught up with her. She turned over with a yawn, sure she'd fall asleep now. She didn't. This was ridiculous. She'd never had such trouble sleeping before. Of course, she'd never experienced such an eventful day before, either. Sensual excitement, that jolt of fear when she saw the gun pointed at Hunter, getting so emotional when she saw her brother Sam, hearing Hunter talk resentfully about his fiancée—her! And listening to Mary Callahan's version of the tragic story that started the feud and the lies about her father's being excited to see her. All combined, it was much too much.

She started counting, numbers now instead of sheep, to calm herself. She was only up to ten when she smelled smoke. It had to be Hunter having a cigar before bed. Not very wise of him if he was as drunk as she thought he was. Nor had she known her room was close enough to his for her to smell the smoke wafting from his window to hers.

She got up to close the last window. It had been pointless leaving it open, with no breeze coming in tonight from the east. She'd have to move to a different room tomorrow. There were still a few empty ones upstairs she could pick from, where Hunter's bedtime habits wouldn't bother her like this.

She immediately saw the light. It wasn't bright, but it was definitely illuminating the backyard directly below her room. It was coming from the kitchen. So was the smell of smoke. Had someone lit the stove again?

Her first thought was that it had to be Andrew trying to surprise her. He was so grateful for the steady job she'd given him that he felt he had to do more than she was asking of him. He would consider baking the bread tonight so it would be ready for her in the morning, a delightful surprise. Was it that close to dawn already? Not according to the sky it wasn't, and her window did face east so she'd be able to tell, though those thick clouds might extend to that horizon, too. Then she actually *saw* the smoke billowing past her window, far too much for the stove to account for it.

She blanched and ran out of the room, screaming, "Fire!" She raced along the hall and down the stairs. For a split second, every instinct she had urged her to go out the front door to safety. She resisted. She wasn't even sure if anyone had heard her yell. The fire might not be as bad as the smoke indicated. A simple bucket of water might put it out before it got out of control. If not, she had to go back upstairs to make sure no one was sleeping through this. She nearly cried at the thought.

She pushed open the hallway door to the kitchen. Its having been closed was the only reason no smoke was in the hall yet. She started coughing as soon as she opened it. The room was so full of acrid smoke her eyes stung.

The smoke eliminated even the thinnest sliver of moonlight at the window. It was so thick she couldn't tell where the fire was. But she looked toward the stove, where she assumed it would be. On top of the stove she saw flames flickering out of a black pot that hadn't been there when she went to bed. So someone did light up the stove again to cook something, then just left the pot there to catch fire? Who would do something so dangerous and irresponsible? The flame in the pot was rising higher. She prayed it wouldn't reach the wall or the ceiling.

She ducked into the bathing room and closed the door to keep the smoke out while she filled a bucket with water. She heard someone else in the kitchen before she opened the door again. She headed straight for the stove, glad that someone had brought a lantern so she could see.

"Hell, don't do that!" Hunter yelled at her, startling her into dropping the bucket. Water splashed over her feet and halfway up her bare calves.

He was bent over the cupboard and rose with a lid in hand that he slammed over the pot. The flame simply disappeared under it.

Amazed, she asked, "How does that put it out?"

"Smothers it. Learned that from Jakes out at the range camp after a few trees caught fire when we used water to put out a lard fire. If there's any fat involved, water just splashes the fire around."

He grabbed her arm as he explained that, dragging her out the back door. More smoke followed them out.

"Are you all right?" Hunter asked as he grasped her chin to examine her face.

She swatted his hand away. "My feet are wet."

"Then you're all right."

He glanced back at the kitchen. Most of the smoke had cleared out with the door left open. When he looked back at her, his eyes didn't stay on her face, but traveled slowly down her body. Until that moment, she hadn't realized she was wearing only her underclothes.

"You could have grabbed a robe," he said, his tone suddenly surly.

Blushing, she said defensively, "I thought the house was burning down!"

She noted indignantly that he was a fine one to talk. His shirt was completely unbuttoned, his feet were bare, and without a belt to hold them up his pants were slipping down his hips! But she didn't point that out as he reentered the kitchen. She followed behind him. There wasn't any actual damage, just a lot of soot on the walls and a large puddle of water on the floor, thanks to her. It could have been so much worse.

"Go back to bed," he said as he found a couple of cloths and lifted the hot pot off the stove. After he placed it outside on the flagstone walkway, he said, "We'll get it cleaned up in the morning."

As she walked slowly to the door to the hallway, it dawned on her that no one else had come to help. "You're the only one who heard me yell?"

"I wasn't asleep yet, and you only yelled once, outside my door, so I doubt my parents heard you at the other end of the hall." He'd glanced her way when he'd said that. Again, his eyes stayed on her and moved slowly up and down her body before he added, "Scream louder next time."

Mortified that he kept reminding her of her lack of proper attire with the direction of his gaze, she said, "There better not be a next time. Do I need to put a lock on the kitchen when I leave it?"

He shook his head. "No, you just need to make sure the stove top is cold or at least don't leave anything on it, not even the coffeepot."

She was about to say it had been cold *and* empty when she retired for the night, but she thought of Andrew again. If he had carelessly caused this fire, he would lose his job, so until she found out if he was responsible, she'd rather not mention that the stove had been refueled after she'd gone to bed. It probably had been Andrew, just a careless accident. She'd have to shoulder the blame instead. Apparently, Hunter already thought it was her fault.

He followed her out to the hall. "Good thing I came home tonight. If you had used that water, the walls would've caught fire."

She shuddered at the thought, but it also reminded her of those hours she'd spent sleepless tonight—and why. He'd fallen into step beside her. She suddenly leaned a little closer to sniff him for evidence of where he'd been. He wouldn't notice.

He did! "What? Do I smell like smoke?"

Tight-lipped, she said, "I was seeing if you smelled like Pearl."

He burst out laughing. "Jealous, Jenny? I spent the night playing poker. Won, too."

She wasn't going to dignify that with a response. As she walked away from him a little too quickly, her wet, bare feet nearly slipped on the smooth wooden floor.

He grabbed her arm to prevent it. "You need me to carry you upstairs?"

Detecting concern in his voice, she thought he was serious, so she simply said, "No."

"Be happy to."

That wasn't serious. The humor was back in his voice. If she glanced back, she knew exactly where she'd find his eyes, too. Where they shouldn't be.

"No! And get your eyes off me."

"Hell no."

His laughter followed her up the stairs.

Chapter Twenty-Seven

THE KITCHEN WAS FILLED with Callahans when Tiffany came downstairs the next morning. Andrew was there, too, and he didn't look at all guilty when he met her glance and smiled in greeting. The Callahan brothers and Andrew were washing the soot off the walls while Zachary sat at the table supervising. They were nearly done and were even joshing around. Cole threw a wet rag at John and was laughing as she walked into the room.

Hunter noticed her immediately. "Coffee's hot." His light-blue eyes lingered on her, slowly sweeping down the length of her cream morning dress and back up. The grin that followed said clearly that he was remembering her scanty attire from the night before.

She managed not to blush. It wasn't as if she'd chosen to let him find her in her lacy chemise and drawers.

The younger men greeted her. Zachary didn't. As he stood up to leave, he put on his wide-brimmed hat that he'd been holding. His nod in her direction was rather curt. "Accidents happen, but this one could have been very serious. Make sure it doesn't happen again, Miss Fleming."

He blamed *her*? She waited for someone else to take responsibility, but no one did. Yet she knew the stove had been down to embers behind its iron grate last night, the surface no longer warm to the touch. She knew that since she'd wiped the stove down before retiring. Yet someone had restarted the fire after everyone else had gone to bed.

"It wasn't me, Mr. Callahan," Tiffany said stiffly. "I wiped down a cold *and* empty stove before I turned out the lanterns and went up to bed."

"Then who would have been in the kitchen in the middle of the night?" Zachary asked.

All the Callahans were suddenly looking at Andrew.

The boy blanched. "I didn't, I wouldn't, I love it here! After Miss Fleming and I finished making the bread dough, I spent the evening in the bunkhouse with Mr. Jakes. You can ask him. He called me a new audience. Talked my ears off a good part of the night, he had so many stories to tell. He was still at it when the first of the cowboys wandered in."

"That would have been Billy, who rode back with me," Hunter remarked.

Zachary said to Andrew, "His first name is Jakes, and we aren't blaming you, boy. If someone wanted to burn us down, they'd just throw a lit torch through a window. It's summer and we keep most of them open at night. So why bother to make it look like an accident?"

He addressed that question to Tiffany, evidently still believing she was responsible.

But Hunter answered, "Because whoever set the fire wanted it to look like an accident, not arson. Most of us were in town last night, including the hired hands, so chances were no one would discover there was a fire in a deserted part of the house in time to put it out before it burned out of control. And in case one of us did get to it in time, it could be chalked up to carelessness in the kitchen. And you know who might want to do this without getting blamed for it."

Tiffany's eyes flared wide. Oh, good grief, they weren't really going to accuse her family of this, were they?

But John confirmed that they were. "A Warren," he said, looking quite angry.

Tiffany groaned to herself, aware that this could get out of hand real quick. "Have your neighbors ever tried to burn your house down before? In all these years?"

"No, they're more straightforward than that," Zachary answered. "And after it rained at dawn, we aren't going to have any tracks to follow. So I'll pay Frank Warren a visit. If he wants the shooting to start again right before the wedding—"

"Then there won't be a wedding," Hunter finished the thought.

"Maybe a funeral instead," John growled.

Tiffany was horrified to see how angry they all looked now, even Zachary. Desperately she offered an alternative: "It could have been one or both of the two men Hunter fought with yesterday."

Zachary stared at his son. "When were you going to get around to mentioning you were in a fight?"

Hunter shrugged. "It was nothing, just a couple out-of-work miners blaming me for their woes."

"Ah, so you failed to mention it because their woes are my fault, not yours. What happened?"

Hunter simply said, "They lost."

Zachary snorted. Tiffany stared in disbelief at Hunter. Really? That was all he was going to say about that altercation? What about the shooter? And no one was taking into consideration her view of who might have set the fire?

"We're going with you, Pa," John said. Hunter and Cole nodded.

Zachary looked grim. His eyes moved from Hunter to John, and finally to Cole. "Okay, boys, let's go."

Tiffany stared in disbelief as they all filed out the back door. "Wait! Don't do anything rash. You don't know that the Warrens did this!"

All the Callahan men, even Hunter, ignored her and continued to head to the stable. Tiffany leaned back against the counter.

"I don't know these people, but—but it sounds like they have enemies. Is it safe to work here?"

Tiffany glanced sharply at Andrew. He looked as frightened as he sounded, but she couldn't blame him after he'd heard the Callahans angrily talking about getting justice. And how could she reassure Andrew when she couldn't reassure herself?

She still tried. "They'll probably have one of their men stand guard now just to make sure no one is sneaking around late at night." If they didn't, she'd suggest it herself—if anyone came back alive today. . . .

She blanched with that thought, but the boy had turned so he didn't see it. "I'll fetch the soup pot from the cellar to get it simmering again."

Such an ordinary thing to do when she was so frantic with

worry for her family that she couldn't think straight. Was there no way to stop the Callahans?

She suddenly heard the sound of horses galloping past the kitchen. She ran down the hall to the front porch to see four men with rifles riding away. She sat down on the porch swing and put her head in her hands. "I hate this damn feud!"

Chapter Twenty-Eight

Rose's expression was bleak as her coach moved along the streets of Chicago. She felt the same way she'd felt the first time she had gone to the grand mansion fourteen years ago. Nervous, afraid, desperate. She didn't have much hope that she would succeed this time when she had failed so miserably before.

The hatred this man harbored was crazy. Every time she had gone to his home over the years to try to make Parker see reason, she'd been turned away. He refused to hear her pleas a second time. He refused to give her back her life. She had hoped time would make this go away, but it never did. The threat still hung over Frank's head—and hers. God, wasn't fifteen years long enough for the bastard to savor his twisted revenge?

She was still the only one who knew. That had been Parker's stipulation for letting her husband live. Frank could never be told the real reason she'd left him. She guessed that Parker had hoped Frank would die of a broken heart—history repeating itself. But Frank was too strong for that.

Every time she came here, she ended up reliving Parker's first act of vengeance and how Franklin almost died because of it. She'd blamed herself for so long, but was it really her fault?

She'd raced to Nashart to get the doctor herself that night. She'd screamed at him to hurry. She was in shock. Frank's wound had looked so serious. The doctor ran to get his horse at the stable. Before she could remount hers, she was stopped and dragged to the side of the house, a hand over her mouth. The man didn't take her far, just into the shadows. She didn't recognize his voice. She never saw his face.

"This was a warning," he told her. "Leave your husband or he dies."

She didn't understand. She'd thought one of the Callahans had shot Frank. Everyone was going to assume that. But what the man had just said had nothing to do with that damn feud.

"You're not a Callahan?"

"No."

"Then what do you have against my husband?"

"Nothing personally. I work for Parker—"

"My old neighbor from New York?" she interrupted incredulously. But she realized that was a crazy conclusion on her part even as she said it.

Only it wasn't. "I see you understand."

"No, I don't. I was engaged to his son Mark!"

"An engagement you should have honored instead of breaking. The boy is dead—because of you. His father wants revenge."

"That makes no sense. I broke that engagement five years ago. If Mark just died, I'm sorry, but how could his father possibly blame me for that?"

"You don't know?"

"Know what? I haven't seen that family for years. I know they sold their house and left New York not long after I married Franklin, but I don't know where they moved and I never saw Mark again after I told him I couldn't marry him."

"Parker moved his family to another state because he thought it would help his son get over you. It didn't. The boy turned to drink to forget you, then recklessness when that didn't work. He finally killed himself. The note said he couldn't bear the heartache anymore. Parker sent me to kill your husband. He's in a grief-stricken rage."

If she wasn't already horrified, that last statement tipped the scale. "You said it was a warning! Now you're saying you were paid to kill him?!"

"Not paid. I've worked for Parker for years. He did everything he could think of to pull Mark out of the despair you left him in. So did I, for that matter. Nothing worked. And now he's dead. But I'm not a cold-blooded killer. Neither is Parker—usually. Wanting to kill the man who stole you from his son was his first reaction, but I managed to talk him into a less bloody revenge."

She struggled in that moment, rage finding her. "You call what you did tonight less bloody!?"

He swung her around. The gun that had been pressed deeply into her back to keep her from screaming was now pressed to her belly. She still couldn't see his face in the shadows, not that it mattered when it sounded as if he was just Parker's lackey.

"Would you rather he be dead?" he hissed at her. "Make no mistake, Parker didn't get where he is today without having a ruthless streak, and he blames you *and* your husband for his loss. He *will* have revenge. I couldn't dissuade him from it. It's just a very simple one now. If Mark couldn't have you, no man will. So are you willing to save your husband's life?"

"By leaving him?" She started crying. "Please don't ask me to do this."

"Someone has to pay, Mrs. Warren, by death or despair. The choice is yours."

She couldn't stop crying, but it got even worse. "There is one stipulation," the man added.

"This isn't enough?!"

"No, the pain of your desertion has to cut deep. So you can't tell your husband the real reason you're leaving him."

"Then I'll need a little time. If I go while he's recovering from that wound, he'll never believe it's what I want."

"Three weeks, not a day more."

She'd hoped in that time she could find some way out of that nefarious bargain, but she didn't. Every time she saw Frank favor his side where he'd been shot, she was reminded that his life was in her hands. She left. She didn't have a choice. But at least she'd taken a part of Frank with her, their little daughter, and she'd protected her sons before she snuck off, arranging that truce with their neighbors. She would have gone insane with worry if she still had to worry about the Callahans, too.

Rose stared out the coach window. Such an interesting city, one she could have enjoyed if she didn't hate it so much because her tormentor lived here. And her view was blurred. Tears again. Every single time the memories surfaced, she cried.

It had taken her nearly a year to find out where Parker had moved. He had so many interests and businesses across the country and was constantly traveling between them. She wasn't surprised he'd picked a more central location in Chicago. And she was going to kill him. She'd thought about it long and hard. He was causing too much pain and suffering. He wasn't the only one who could enact revenge.

She hadn't been sure he'd even see her when she'd called on him. A butler had shown her to his study. He was sitting behind his desk, his arms crossed. His short, brown hair was starting to gray, but that was to be expected of a man in his late forties. Rose was disappointed to see that he still looked quite robust. If he was sickly, she might have considered waiting for him to die naturally. But she wanted her husband back! She wanted her family to be whole again.

He didn't offer her a chair. "Still calling yourself Mrs. Warren?"

"I haven't divorced him."

"It doesn't matter. Him, some other man—you do understand you're to have none? Ever."

"You've had your revenge. Let it go."

"I'm curious," he said. "Did you really never tell him the truth?"

"No, I protected him with lies. He was devastated!"

"You say that with such anger when all of this points to you."

"You're insane to blame me for your son's weakness."

"You dare! He loved you! He'd always loved you! You gave him hope, then ripped it away."

"Mark and I were childhood friends, nothing more. I shouldn't have let him talk me into marrying him. I had doubts from the start, but he was so sure we'd be happy, I didn't have the heart to turn him down. I did care about him, I didn't want to hurt him. Finding real love showed me the difference. Mark even agreed with my decision to end our engagement!"

"No, he didn't, he only pretended to. It was a lie! He never stopped loving you, and that love destroyed him. So how do you think it isn't your fault, when you *did* say you'd marry him and then dropped him for another man?"

"I think I've suffered enough. This has to end. Now."

She pulled the pistol from her pocket and pointed it at him. She didn't get the reaction she'd hoped for. He actually laughed at her.

"Go ahead. My life lost all meaning when my only child died. But my death doesn't end this for you, Rose Warren. The men I pay to follow you now will continue to follow you after I'm gone. It's in my will. And the very day you try to live with your husband again, or take another, is the day your line ends, just as you ended mine."

Oh, God, it was worse than she'd thought. She'd hoped that his death would be the end of it.

Nonetheless, over the years, she'd still tried to make him see reason. She'd come back here so many times, but all uselessly. She'd never been let back into the house again. He'd only agreed to see her that one time to ascertain for himself whether his vengeance was successful.

As the coach drew up to the Harding mansion, Rose steeled herself for disappointment. She had to try again to convince Parker to give up his vengeful bargain. She would keep trying until the day she or Parker Harding died. As she stepped down to the street, she saw that she was still being followed. . . .

Chapter Twenty-Nine

T IFFANY SOMEHOW MANAGED TO bake bread that morning and make lunch for the household when most of the household wasn't there to eat it. She barely remembered doing anything she was so preoccupied and worried about what was happening between the Callahans and her family. The men hadn't yet returned, or maybe they had and were out on the range. She was dying to know what had happened. Were her brothers all right? Had anyone been wounded? She wished she could ride over to her father's ranch and find out. But all she could do was hope that no one would shoot before any questions could be asked.

As if she weren't already fretting enough, she nearly had a crisis with the upstairs maid that afternoon. She had merely wanted to make sure Luella was doing her job properly, but the moment Tiffany mentioned changing the bedding daily, Luella threw up her hands. "I quit!"

"Wait!" Tiffany quickly followed the maid out of the bedroom she had been cleaning. "Why?"

Luella swung around. Short, chubby, possibly twice Tiffany's age, the woman was bristling. "It already takes a full day to wash all the bedding from up here. A full day! Then I have clothes to wash, too. All these rooms to clean, beds to make, and Mrs. Callahan to see to. You will *not* give me even more to do!"

Good grief, that was three separate jobs the woman had just described. Tiffany had never heard of one servant doing two of them, much less three!

Appalled, Tiffany said sympathetically, "I quite agree. I had *no* idea."

Yet she should have. She'd already seen that servants were far too scarce in the territory. She wouldn't be in this house enacting this charade if they weren't.

But her response had the maid giving her a suspicious look now. "My sister told me about you housekeepers. She said you just stand around cracking whips all day, and you even get paid for it."

Tiffany had to bite back the urge to laugh. "That's not true, really it isn't. But as you may have heard, without a large staff to manage here, I've been given other tasks myself, same as you."

But she was suddenly reminded that she was going to have extra time on her hands, now that she had a kitchen helper. Aside from an occasional ride, she had thought she might try fishing for the family's dinner, so she could provide something other than beef and more beef. Cowboys might not expect anything other than that meat since it was what their jobs were all about, but she did. Yet riding and fishing wouldn't be daily outings.

Impulsively, she offered some of that extra time to this overburdened woman. She couldn't dust, not when the slightest stirring of it made her sneeze, but how hard would it be to make up some of the beds, straighten up some of the rooms, even help carry the dirty laundry to the washing shed? She said as much. And left the maid incredulous.

Luella admitted, "Pearl does share half the wash load—when she's here," but then she added in disgust, "and when she's not cleaning her nails instead of getting them dirty."

A bit of rivalry there? Tiffany wondered. Or had she just been warned to expect some trouble from the downstairs maid when she returned to work?

"For now, I'll finish the room you were in," Tiffany offered. "And in the morning, I can make the beds on this side of the stairs."

Luella gave her a brilliant smile. "Hunter was due fresh sheets. I brought them. I really appreciate this, Miss Fleming."

Hunter's room? But Luella had already hurried off before Tiffany could take back her offer. She made a face. Going into *his* bedroom probably wasn't a good idea. But as long as he wasn't in it, what harm could come from it?

It was a masculine room. A rack of rifles hung on one wall. The three paintings on the other walls each depicted a Western scene—a herd of cows, a cowboy trying to ride a bull, a group of cowboys sitting around a campfire. An ornately carved wood chest, quite lovely, was at the foot of the large bed. With the clean bedding left on top of it, she guessed it contained more bedding and peeked inside. She was wrong. It was filled with cowboy gear, ropes, chaps, spurs, some extra long-barreled guns, another gun holster much more fancy looking than the plain one Hunter usually wore.

Two wide-brimmed hats were hung on pegs next to a dark-wood wardrobe, one black, one cream colored. She resisted opening the wardrobe. A brown stuffed chair sat with its back to one of the two windows, faded, worn in the seat; it looked entirely too comfortable. She pictured Hunter sitting in it reading and eventually nodding off. Had he taken naps in it? Had this always been his room? If it was, no evidence of his childhood was left in it.

She recognized the two medium-size crates stacked in a corner as the ones John and Cole had picked up at the train station the day she'd arrived. So it was something Hunter had ordered shipped in? Then why hadn't he opened the crates yet? But she'd snooped enough, too much. She shouldn't be so curious about the man.

Luella had already stripped the bed and tucked in the bottom sheet. Tiffany grabbed the folded top sheet. A lovely knitted coverlet in dark browns and blues, thin for summer, was to go on last. She wondered if Mary had made it and decided to ask her when she saw her next.

She was opening the top sheet and letting it flutter across the bed when she heard Hunter remark, "I'd wondered where you'd gone off to. Never expected to find you waiting for me in my room."

Tiffany jumped. He'd startled her enough that she'd let go of the sheet. It floated across the bed and landed on the floor on the other side. It should have been obvious what she was doing there, so he was just being him with a remark like that. She glanced behind her to tell him that her being there had nothing to do with him. She gasped instead and looked away immediately. He was standing in the doorway wearing nothing but a towel!

"Good God, why aren't you dressed!?"

"Got knocked on my ass and I was a little too muddy to wait for a bath. That rain came down hard this morning. It will take a few days to dry up."

She hadn't been outside to notice—did he get muddy fighting with her brothers? "What happened when you went to the Warrens' ranch?"

"Don't know. We ran into Degan coming home from town while we were riding over there. Pa decided to just take the guard dog with him and sent the rest of us back to check on the herd. If the Warrens *are* on the offensive, rustling would be another kind of attack."

"Are you missing any cattle?"

"Doesn't look like it. We'll have to wait until dinnertime to learn what Pa found out today. If you didn't start that fire, and a Warren didn't, that just leaves our new neighbors to the east."

"Once again, we are in complete agreement. I am becoming quite amazed by it."

"Surprise and sarcasm in the same breath, Red?" He chuckled, but then asked curiously, "When was the first time you agreed with me?"

Why did it sound as if his voice was getting closer to her? Nervously she said, "Never mind that, I'd like to know why you didn't say that to your father this morning? After everything I've heard about the miners, and what I witnessed yesterday for myself, they were certainly my *first* guess, not my second. It's not just the owner of that mine who would benefit from driving your family off, but every miner who works there. Doesn't your father know that?"

"He knows, but we got a judge involved who made a ruling. They have to clear out as soon as that lesser vein is gone, which won't be long now. So while they might be angry enough to start something, they don't stand to gain from it."

"Anger was enough to drive your family over to the Warren ranch this morning, wasn't it?"

He chuckled. "Point made."

"There are a lot of variables to consider. Which is why you might want to post a watch here at night."

"Intended to," he said. "But no need for you to get worried about it."

After the worry she'd gone through today, that statement just annoyed the heck out of her. "Don't be obtuse. I work here. So what happens here *does* affect me."

"But I told you I wouldn't let anything happen to you. Did you think I didn't mean it?"

"What I think is you concern yourself too much with me. I'm not yours to protect, Hunter."

"Do you want to be?"

He said it so softly she wasn't sure she'd heard him correctly. But she finally remembered why she was keeping her eyes off him and got even more red-faced, mortified that she was still in a room with a half-naked man! She should have bolted out of there immediately. She should have waited until he'd put on some clothes to ask her questions. He must think by now that she didn't mind his undress.

Belatedly she said, "I'll only be a few minutes if you can wait."

"Wait for what?"

"Wait outside for me to finish."

"You've got some really silly notions, Red. It's my room. I need my clothes."

She turned to say, "Then I'll come back later to—"

She didn't get to finish, couldn't. He was standing right in front of her now, so close she might have collided if instinct hadn't made her back up instead. Too quickly. The bed was in the way and her balance deserted her. She fell back.

A slow grin turned his lips. "When you put it like that . . ."

Her hands shot up to keep him from leaning in close, which he started to do. Such a paltry defense and it didn't stop him. He merely leaned slowly into her hands. When she realized it might appear to him that she was caressing his chest, she yanked her hands back as if burned. That's when he got really close.

"I know kissing you is a bad idea. I'm probably going to regret it till the day I die, because *I'll* never forget it. What about you?"

Words wouldn't come out of her mouth. A gasp did when his lips actually touched hers. She turned her head to the side, she couldn't let this happen! Across her cheek, his lips followed her. A tingling sensation spread along her neck, down her shoulders. Her heart started to pound.

"Hunter . . ."

"When you whisper my name, it ties me in knots. How do you do that, Jenny?"

His breath was hot on her cheek. He put a hand under her head to guide her mouth back to his. It was such a gentle kiss, yet what it did to her was anything but gentle—more like a maelstrom bursting inside her. She felt it in places that were nowhere near her mouth! She felt urges that were not in her nature! She wanted to put her arms around his neck and pull him in even closer. That's when she knew she was in trouble.

"I'm going to smack you if you don't let me up!"

Hunter rolled off her with a sigh. "I thought I left the cold water downstairs."

She didn't answer him. Keeping her eyes closed until she was off the bed, she did what she should have done sooner and bolted straight out of the room.

Chapter Thirty

S HE WAS FURIOUS WHEN she returned to the kitchen. She banged more than one door, including the oven door when she shoved the bread in for dinner. This might be Hunter's house, he might be used to walking around in it like that after a bath, but, good grief, she wasn't! The kitchen was run by a woman now, not Old Ed, who wouldn't blink an eye over such a display. She was going to have to insist on some house rules. Leaving that bathing room in just a towel had better never happen again. Kissing her better never happen again. Oh, God, that's what she was really angry about. She'd let him get to her. She hadn't ended it instantly as she should have. And she knew he would have let her. It was all a game for him, the teasing, the risqué remarks, even the playful kissing.

She was suspicious, too, of his excuse for that scandalous display of bare skin. The man probably wanted to show off his muscles to her. Hadn't he mentioned wondering where she was at? Because he'd expected her to be in the kitchen to ogle him!

Did he think she'd fly into his arms, unable to resist his amazing physique, if she saw him half-naked?

No mud was on the kitchen floor to support his claim that he'd gotten muddy. She glanced in the bathroom. Very well, the pile of clothes he'd left on the floor looked muddy. No boots though. Was he actually thoughtful enough to take them off outside so he wouldn't track mud on her floor? She peeked outside, then opened the back door wider. His muddy boots were there. So was the little piglet, who was currently rolling all over the boots and seemed to be in ecstasy. At least someone around here was happy.

Tiffany rolled her eyes and, without really thinking about it, picked up the pig, held it as far away from her as she could, and carried it inside to set it in the sink. It squealed when she pumped water over it, but quieted when she rubbed the mud off him.

"Like petting, do you? We are *not* making a habit of this," she warned.

She dried it off with a kitchen towel, then set it back outside and pushed his rump in the direction of the pigpen. Once again the little animal had lightened her mood. All the anger was gone—for now. But it would probably return if she clapped eyes on Hunter again today.

It didn't. And he was already in the room. She didn't know how long he'd been standing by the other door watching her, but it was long enough for him to have seen her carrying the pig outside.

"Dinner visits us now?" he asked with a chuckle.

"Don't *even* think it."

His brow shot up. "Don't tell me you've made friends with a pig?"

The notion was absurd, yet her chin rose defiantly. "Of course not, but what if I did?"

"You're about as standoffish as it gets, Red, all Eastern prim and proper, so making a pet out of an animal that's going to get big, really *really* big, more'n six hundred pounds big, it just . . ."

What it did was make him laugh so hard he couldn't even finish. It was almost contagious, so she couldn't quite manage to get annoyed over his assessment. The man truly enjoyed life and could find humor in the smallest things. But she'd looked at him too long. The image of his wide, bare chest came back into her mind somehow. She lowered her eyes, remembering it—and what had come after it. Her heart beat a little faster.

She hurried to the stove and picked up a large spoon to start stirring the soup vigorously, so vigorously the soup was sloshing out of the pot. Laughter gone, he was suddenly standing next to her, but just to pour himself a cup of coffee. Yet he didn't walk away with it after he set the coffeepot back on the stove.

She kept her eyes off him, but could feel his on her. Was he always going to make her this nervous? Was it even nervousness he made her feel? Whatever it was, it was disturbing. Maybe talking would take her mind off the image of his naked chest.

"How did you get so muddy?"

"One of our older hands, Caleb, caught a wild mustang near his place. He wasn't part of your broom-pushing crew, so you haven't met him yet. We don't have many married cowboys working here, but we built a few houses on the north end of the property for the ones that get hitched and still want to stay on with us. Caleb is one of them. He's expecting his second kid anytime now. Anyway, he brought the mustang in today and I had a go at breaking it in. Could have picked a better day for it.

Knew I'd get tossed off him a few times before he gave up the fight."

"So why didn't you wait?"

He grinned. "Because I'm still trying to break Sam Warren's record."

She went still at the mention of her brother and asked carefully, "What record would that be?"

"Sam challenged me to a horse-breaking contest a couple years ago in town. He brought in a string of six wild ones he'd caught. Even suggested the sheriff do the timing, since we wouldn't trust anyone in either family to be impartial about it."

"Timing of what?"

"How long it took us to break one of them. Best two out of three would win. We never got to the tie point. He beat me in half the time on the first two. I should've known I was being set up to lose since he claimed to have caught all six of them. I found out later he's been breaking wild ones for years. Does it just for fun, so he's damn good at it."

She actually recalled Sam's telling her about that unusual hobby of his. He tracked wild herds. The challenge he enjoyed so much was catching one of the mares without alerting the stallion that guarded them. He also rescued new mustangs before the herd stallion got aggressive enough to fight them or run them off.

But what Hunter had just described Sam as doing sounded so much like what Zachary was doing in depriving Franklin of his housekeeper. A prank. So both sides enjoyed pranks? That didn't sound like a killing feud to her. It made her wonder if the feud might have petered out on its own if the approaching marriage hadn't riled up her brothers. Had it just simmered down to distrust, name-calling, and pranks until this year? Was the very thing that had brought about the truce all those years ago going to be its downfall? But she was forgetting the water under contention, the damn water they didn't want to share. And how angry the Callahans had been this morning when they rode off to confront her family. No, it wasn't over, and it wasn't harmless.

"If you do manage to beat his record, do you intend to challenge him again?"

"Depends how this year plays out. I could be challenging him in other ways instead."

Tiffany blanched, seeing him put his hand on his gun as he said that. A shoot-out? *With her brother!?*

Chapter Thirty-One

"**W**ORRIED ABOUT ME, RED? Don't be. You saw for your-self I'm handy with my fists. Sam might be nearly as tall as me and fast, but it'll only take one good punch to knock him out, as skinny as he is."

Color flew back into Tiffany's cheeks. Fists, not guns. She should have remembered she'd seen Hunter rest his hand on his gun before, so it was probably just habit for him to do that. Now she was embarrassed because he'd seen her look so hor-rified and he had assumed it was on his account. She could at least correct that impression.

"I wasn't worried. I just don't like violence of any sort." Then she snapped, "If you aren't going to marry Sam Warren's sister, you should let his father know it."

He gave her a long, sweeping look that ended with a slow grin. "Yeah, I probably should."

Oh, God, he'd do it for the wrong reason, because he was attracted to *her*! That wasn't going to end the feud, it would just end the truce!

"I'm sorry," she said quickly. "I have no business making suggestions like that. And logically, you should make peace with the Warrens before you do something that rash."

He snorted. "That ain't going to happen. But you were right, this isn't your business, so why are we even discussing it?"

She stiffened. "I agree. We should be discussing your lack of decorum instead. Perhaps some pegs are needed in the bathroom so you men can hang your robes there?"

He chuckled. "I don't own one."

"Then buy one."

"And we're supposed to change our habits why?"

Was she being unreasonable in making such a simple request? Oh, God, she was because once again she was reacting like Tiffany, not Jennifer. Jennifer would never ask her employers to change their ways!

She was forced to compromise. "I will simply go outside when you men bathe and stay outside until you're done."

"Why is this a problem for you?"

"Are you joking? It's beyond inappropriate, it's scandalous for you to parade yourself naked in—"

"I wasn't naked. You're complaining about a bare chest? When a man doesn't think twice about taking his shirt off on a hot day?"

"Where I come from—"

"Isn't here. It was the kiss, wasn't it? That's what's got you riled up. Got you thinking you've been unfaithful to your far-off beau? Or maybe you've figured out you made a bad choice there and should be thinking about new choices—here?"

She wasn't going to dignify that with an answer, but she had a feeling it was all just teasing when he changed his tack and sniffed the air over the stove before he added, "Do I need to eat in town again?"

"It's not done yet," she lied in a grumbling tone.

Hunter turned to leave. Finally.

His crack about eating elsewhere hurt though. The soup had thickened and she'd had high hopes for it, until now. Why would he suggest it wasn't edible? She'd been afraid to actually taste it yet, but she sniffed it now as he'd done. Then sighed. It had no aroma. That's why he'd said that.

The recipe called for two spices, but since she knew absolutely nothing about spices, she'd thought she'd play it safe by not adding them. She decided now to try adding one, so she tossed in a handful. Steeling herself, she tasted the soup and bit into something that made her eyes water. It was too spicy now, spicy hot! She lost track of the time as she picked out all of the peppercorns she'd added.

Cole showed up at the door to point out the hour had gotten late. "Dinner's not ready yet?"

The bread! She'd forgotten it was in the oven. Afraid to look, she squinted as she opened the oven door, then sighed in relief. The bread looked fine. The crust was a little darker than she would have liked, but otherwise it was fine. She took out the six loaves and put three in a basket to take to the dining room, along with a crock of butter.

The men were sitting there waiting, all five of them, Hunter and his brothers, Zachary, even Degan. She'd already set the table with soup bowls. She slowed her step though when she heard the topic they were discussing.

"And you believed Frank?" John was asking his father.

"I did. Told you, it ain't their style."

"So what'd he say when you told him we have Miss Fleming working for us?" Cole asked, his eyes on Tiffany. He was grinning. His brothers were, too. They were all enjoying this prank they were playing on her father . . . with her help.

But Zachary surprised them all with his answer. "Decided to wait. I could almost see him squirming when I asked how his new housekeeper is working out. Had a hell of a time not laughing when he mumbled that she hadn't got here yet. I was about to tell him why when he said his daughter's arrival is going to be delayed. He didn't even try to hide how disappointed he is. Almost had me feeling sorry for him. Seems she sprained her ankle on the trip from New York City and will be staying in Chicago to recover."

Tiffany couldn't help looking down at her ankle and wiggling it. But Zachary wasn't finished. "But that delay could give Frank time to bring in a new housekeeper before his daughter gets here, and he might try that if I tell him too soon that we got the first one here. So I need to time my confession closer to when his daughter is expected."

Tiffany was surprised that she felt a little guilty about deceiving everyone until John snidely remarked, "The daughter seems a might delicate if a simple sprained ankle put the brakes on her getting here."

That annoyed Tiffany. She got even more annoyed when Hunter said, "Any delay suits me just fine, but what do you expect from an Eastern lady? A pinprick would probably make her swoon."

She stared at him incredulously. He didn't notice because Zachary held his attention, telling him, "Be nice, Son. Frank says she's looking forward to meeting you. Bringing a fancy wedding dress with her, too. I'm afraid to mention that to your ma. She's gonna get all upset that you haven't got yourself a fancy suit yet for the wedding."

Tiffany nearly slammed the basket of bread down, she was so angry now. Her father was lying about her? Rose would never have told him that she was looking forward to meeting Hunter when it was anything but true. How dare he lie about her! She did have a wedding dress. She'd wanted nothing to do with it, but Rose had had it made for her anyway. She'd refused to bring it with her and had told Anna not to pack it. Too bad. If she'd brought it, the outlaws would have it now. She turned to go back to the kitchen to get the soup pot with the ladle in it so they could serve themselves. They'd be lucky if she didn't pour it on them instead.

Someone yelled, "Hey," at her before she left the room. She turned to see John holding up one of the loaves to show her it was solid black underneath. Hunter was chuckling as he pounded his knuckles on another loaf. It sounded as hard as rock.

She glared accusingly at Zachary. "I warned you I wasn't a cook!"

"You're a woman, all women can cook," he said matter-of-factly. "You're just nervous. It's understandable. You'll do better with the next meal."

She sputtered. This *was* the next meal. Somehow she didn't cry, but now misery was mixed in with her anger. She hurried back to the kitchen to get the soup. The pot was so heavy she almost dropped it before she got it to the dining table. Hunter was still grinning at her. Was he amused at her failure? That's when she turned her anger on herself for even thinking she could master cooking. She had no skills, no work experience. All she'd been raised to do was to dress fashionably, converse properly with people of her own social class, and conduct herself as a lady. Feeling frustrated and defeated, she picked up one of the loaves of bread and hit it hard on the edge of the table. It took three more tries before the loaf finally cracked. Then she tore out chunks of the soft bread inside the rock-hard crust and tossed them into the soup pot.

"We get the idea," Cole said. "Don't drown it all. Leave some for us to dip in butter."

"Don't be discouraged," Degan offered. "Keep reading that cookbook. You'll figure it out."

He might as well have added, "Because you're a woman." She had no doubt he was thinking it. But what sort of logic was that!? All she'd figured out was that getting angry and eschewing table manners had enabled her to salvage some of the bread!

As she turned to go back into the kitchen, Zachary asked, "This is just the first course, right? What else are you serving us tonight?"

First course? That's when she cried.

Chapter Thirty-Two

TIFFANY'S SOUP TURNED OUT not to be so bad after all. It didn't have much flavor, but it was definitely filling. And Hunter, Cole, and Degan had second helpings. So it wasn't anger or disappointment that was keeping her awake tonight. She simply couldn't get out of her mind that image of Hunter standing in his room wearing just a towel around his hips. She hit her pillow and shook her head, trying to rid her mind of him. But there he was, hair wet, chest damp, long legs and bare feet, and that broad, muscular chest.

He was the most attractive man she'd ever met, and she got these strange flutterings in her stomach and felt a little nervous—no, not nervous really, just more aware of everything when he was around. *He* would never know that, not if she could help it. But, good grief, when he was smiling, which was usually the case, he was too handsome, far too handsome. She didn't want to feel this attracted to him, but she couldn't figure out how to change her feelings. But it wasn't changing her mind. She still wasn't going to marry him. Be stuck here with gunfights, outlaws, too much dust to tolerate, and no servants to hire? And never seeing her mother again? No!

Besides, Hunter wouldn't like her when he found out who she really was, saw how she really behaved and lived her life. She'd heard him and his brothers' scorn when they'd talked about Tiffany Warren at the dinner table. Hunter liked more down-to-earth working women such as Pearl and Jennifer. It was too bad she couldn't just enjoy her time here and *really* be more like Jennifer. Would Miss Fleming be able to resist Hunter's attractiveness? Would she even want to? The real housekeeper probably wouldn't have turned away from him today when he showed up wearing only a towel around his hips. She probably wouldn't have run from his kisses, either, not when they made her feel so . . .

Oh, God, her thoughts were going down a dangerous path. She brought them back under control by picturing cows jumping over a fence and counting them, which eventually put her to sleep. But not for long. Sometime later a noise woke her. No, it wasn't a noise, it was a voice quietly whispering, and right next to her bed!

"Miss Fleming, I'm here to help you. Miss Fleming, please wake up!"

She would probably have screamed immediately if sleep hadn't been clogging her mind. Someone was kneeling beside her bed. The offer of help made her think there was another fire and one of the Callahans was trying to get her out of the house. Then why was he whispering?

"What's wrong? Who are you?" she asked warily, trying to make out the man's features in the darkness.

"Sam Warren, ma'am."

She sucked in her breath. Oh, God, her oldest brother here

in her room? He shouldn't be here! How had he found out? She wanted to hug him but she couldn't! He'd called her Miss Fleming so he didn't know it was *her*, his sister.

"I finally figured it out," Sam said. "That it had to be you I saw at Sally's place. I only saw you from behind, but it was your dress that got me thinking. No one wears clothes like that around here. And it looked like you were being coerced out of the restaurant. This is just like the Callahans, to pull a stunt like this. But I'm here to help you."

Every word out of his mouth just made her want to hug him even more. Sam to the rescue. That was so sweet of him. And lying now, to make him go away, was probably going to make her cry.

"Are they keeping you prisoner here? With the downstairs doors locked, I was afraid your room might be locked, too, but I guess they figured that guard circling the house is enough to make sure you don't leave."

"That guard is there because someone set a fire here last night."

"I heard about that, but I swear my family didn't set it."

"How did you get past the guard?"

She imagined he was grinning, he sounded so proud when he said, "I'm fast. Left my horse off by some trees and snuck my way closer, then dashed for the back door only to find it locked. But with the guard at the other side of the house I made it to the front to climb up to the porch roof. The windows above it are wide-open, including the one at the end of your corridor. 'Sides, it's good and dark tonight, dark enough that the guard's patrolling with a lantern so he's easy to see."

"But if they find you here, they'll think your family set that fire and you're here to try it again."

"No, they won't. My pa already told Zachary he was full of it, to even think we'd do something like that."

"How did you know which room was mine? You didn't enter them all to find me, did you?"

"Course not, didn't need to. Saw you at your window before you turned out the light. There aren't any other women in this house on the upper floor, least that can stand at a window, so it had to be you up here."

"How would you even know the sleeping arrangements in this house?"

Sam chuckled low. "My brothers and I used to dare each other to come here to spy on the Callahans when we were younger."

Tiffany rolled her eyes toward the ceiling. He couldn't see that because he wasn't exaggerating about how dark it was. There was no moonlight tonight with yet another storm rolling in.

She mustered the determination to say what she had to. "You need to leave. I'm here by choice. I'm not proud of it, but I was swayed by money. The Callahans offered me much more than my job is worth to work here instead. I was too embarrassed to explain that to your father."

"Well, hell, if it's just a matter of money, we can better whatever they offered."

She sighed. "No. This is starting to feel like a tug-a-war. I have to draw the line somewhere."

"But you don't understand," he persisted. "They probably just did this to be ornery, while my family actually needs you. My sister is coming here for the first time since she was a tyke. You were hired to make her feel at home. She's used to butlers and housekeepers and more maids than you can count. It's really important to my father that she feel comfortable here. That's why he sent for you."

And that's when the tears started. She hoped she could keep them silent. No such luck. He quickly struck a match when he heard the sounds she was making. With a gasp she yanked the covers over her head. She wasn't quick enough.

"Tiffany? What the hell?!"

Chapter Thirty-Three

Tiffany slowly lowered the covers. Sam was staring at her incredulously—until the match started to burn his fingers. He dropped it, lit another, then lit the lamp next to her bed. Ignoring the frown on his face, she gave in to the urge she'd had since he woke her. She threw her arms around his neck and hugged him.

"I can explain," she whispered.

Sam set her back from him. She feasted her eyes on him, feeling so happy to see him after so many years. Blond, green-eyed, and so handsome now. She'd asked him once why he didn't look like her. He'd proudly said he took after their pa. That was back when she'd craved any and all knowledge about her father, and she'd childishly envied Sam that day because he looked like Frank and she didn't

The expression on his face had darkened. "So they did kidnap you. Why didn't you just say so?"

"Because they didn't. They thought the same thing you

did—that I'm Jennifer Fleming. And what I told you is true, they think they've lured me to work here with a double salary."

"But why didn't you set them straight?"

"Because this is where I want to be."

"Tiff . . ."

"Sit down." She patted the bed beside her. "Just listen to me, please. I didn't want to come to Montana at all. I definitely don't want to marry a cowboy. But Mama arranged this betrothal, and while she won't insist that I go through with it, she did make me promise I'd stay here two months to give Hunter a chance. This is where I want to do it."

"Me and the boys don't want you to marry Hunter either. It's just the elders that want the marriage to secure the truce. But that's ridiculous. It ain't like we can't take care of ourselves—hell, we can kick the Callahans' butts any day." Sam laughed scornfully. "They must think so, to bring in a notorious gunslinger like Degan Grant to protect them. Old Zachary even dragged him along this morning to accuse us of setting a fire. We're not afraid of hired guns, Tiff."

In this case his confidence scared the heck out of her. "You *should* be afraid! That man is dangerous—"

"Never mind him. You can't imagine how much we've all been looking forward to your arrival, and now to find you *here*."

She winced. "And I've wanted to see you just as badly. But more than that—" She bit back the words. She couldn't tell him how she felt about Frank, that she'd taken on this charade just so she could put off having to come face-to-face with their father. Sam simply wouldn't understand because he loved Frank.

"What?" he said, waiting for her to go on.

"I've been here a few days, long enough to know this life isn't for me."

"A few days is nothing, and"—he suddenly seemed to realize—"you're spending them as a servant, so of course you'd hate it!"

She grinned and pointed out, "A housekeeper's duties are minimal." She was *not* going to mention cooking. "And besides, I'm talking about this part of the country. I've already met train robbers, been shot at, saw dead men carried off the train, lost most of my luggage, saw Hunter almost shot in the back . . . that's actually more than enough. Out here"—she waved a hand—"this is your life, it's not mine."

He sighed. "I do know what you're talking about, Tiff. Every time we visited you and Ma we felt so out of place. We didn't belong, we knew that, it was blatant everywhere we went. But you know Roy, who visited the most? When he came back that last time, he said he actually missed the city, that it was growing on him. Just takes time to get used to a new place."

"Maybe for a man, but every time I turn around I witness violence of some sort."

"Sounds like you just had a rotten run of luck. Really, we can go months without hearing a gunshot, and then it's mostly just someone shooting a snake." Tiffany made a face. "Outlaws are a dying breed. US marshals show up to hunt them down these days. We're becoming more and more lawful every year thanks to the railroads."

She patted his hand. No reassurance he offered could change what she'd already seen. *Becoming* wasn't *being*.

He must have figured that out because he looked so frustrated. "That's why you should come home to us. We'll show you a grand time. We'll go fishing and riding, take you out to see some real mountains, show you what it's really like here. And Pa is longing to see you." Tiffany raised a skeptical brow, but Sam misunderstood, saying, "Yeah, he wants to marry you off to a Callahan, but don't worry, we won't let him. And maybe Ma will come out and visit, too, if she hears you're enjoying yourself here."

Her brothers had obviously anticipated quite a different kind of visit than she had if they expected her to have fun in Montana and for their mother to join them. None of that was going to happen. Tiffany suddenly felt furious with her parents and their secrets. Their strange relationship was still hurting her brothers, even now when they were grown men.

But she didn't mention her frustration to Sam. Instead she asked him, "Why did you all stop coming to New York? It's been five years since any of you visited us."

He actually looked surprised by the question. "I mentioned that in my letters, didn't I? We grew into more responsibilities. We started going on trail drives to get the cattle to market. I got to go on my first one when I was thirteen. Of course, the railroads arriving in the territory last year have almost put an end to that. We still have small drives from nearby towns that aren't connected to the rails yet, but just a couple men can handle those. And then there was school."

"But that didn't stop you before."

"Because we didn't actually have school before. Pa used to teach us when he had time. But then Nashart actually got its own teacher, a real bona fide teacher, and they built a schoolroom for him. We weren't forced to attend, but Pa figured it would please Ma if we did, so we went. Every darn day."

"I loved school, you didn't?"

"The learning was okay, but being stuck in a room with John and Cole Callahan every day was hell."

"Oh." She tried not to laugh. Then she realized that wasn't a laughing subject, though it *should* have been. But *her* brothers hadn't grown up with normal childhood difficulties. They'd had real enemies living nearby, and mostly all older than them. If they got into a scuffle with a Callahan, they probably never won. How horrible.

"Like I said," Sam was saying, "things are rapidly changing in the West now. Nashart has even doubled in size in just the last couple years."

She winced again. He was still trying to convince her to like it here. But she suddenly realized she needed to do some convincing of her own, just not about that.

"Sam, I have to figure out a way to end the feud without being part of the solution. I'll have a better chance of doing that here in this house with these people. Mary Callahan is probably the key. If anyone can talk some sense into this family, it would be her. I just need time to work her around to that way of thinking. And I don't want Papa shoving me down the aisle to the altar with Hunter just because he's impatient to end the feud. So—so I want you to keep it a secret that I'm here, from Frank, even from our brothers."

Sam shot to his feet. "You can't ask me to lie to Pa. You just can't!"

"Not lie, just don't say you saw me."

"That's the same as—"

"Sam, this is *my* life, not yours. I need some time to figure this out. If you tell anyone I'm here, anyone in our family or even this one, I swear I'll get on the next train home, promise or not. Then there won't be a truce anymore. Do you even know what it was like before the truce? Of course you don't, you were too young, same as I was. But Mama knows. She lived here then. She told me about it. And she hated it!"

He looked stricken. "Is that why she left?"

Tiffany blinked. "You don't know why?"

"I asked Pa. I even asked her. Do you know how much it hurts when you *know* your parents are lying to you? They aren't very good at it, you know. But I never had the heart to press. Pa always got so sad looking. Ma just got angry, though I swear it was fake, just to cover up that she was sad, too. Which doesn't make a damn lick o' sense."

"No, it doesn't." Tiffany vowed again to make her parents come clean about their separation. She wasn't a child any longer. She had a right to know. She'd had enough of their lies. But for now she had to get Sam to agree to her plan. "So will you keep my secret?"

His lips thinned out. He was obviously wrestling with his decision. She held her breath.

Then he said, "We were so hoping you'd loathe Hunter but love Montana so much that you'd stay here anyway and live with us. Just think, we could see each other all the time."

Fighting back tears, Tiffany shook her head. "Sam—"

He looked angry as he stood up. "This isn't over, Tiff. It's not right you lying to Pa and impersonating a housekeeper for the Callahans. *You* think about that. But I won't say anything—for now."

Chapter Thirty-Four

TIFFANY WAS TOO NERVOUS to stay in bed after her brother slipped out of her room. She should have escorted him out of the house to make sure he made it safely. But she'd realized that too late, so she walked back and forth between her two corner windows instead even though she couldn't see a darn thing out in the yard other than the guard walking by with his lantern.

The sudden light coming from the kitchen below made her blanch, it was so similar to what she'd seen the night of the fire. But no one would dare try that again with the house being guarded now. It could just be the guard, but she hadn't thought he was patrolling inside the house, too. . . . Oh, God, had Sam been caught? She had to find out!

Tiffany threw on her petticoat and grabbed her traveling jacket—why hadn't she thought of telling Mrs. Martin to make her a robe, too!? She looked ridiculous. She didn't care. At least she wasn't flying downstairs in her underwear again.

She burst into the kitchen just as Hunter was stepping out

the back door. He must have heard her because he turned and asked, "What are you doing down here?"

"I heard a noise."

"Yeah, so did I. It was nothing, go back to bed." He didn't look as if he thought it was nothing. He looked tense, and he'd been going out to investigate—where he might run into her brother. . . .

She had to give Sam time to get away! Desperate to keep Hunter from going outside, she ran across the room and threw her arms around his neck. "Don't leave me alone!"

He put his arms around her, not hesitating even a moment. But she was obviously confusing him and he asked, "What's wrong?"

"You—that is, the light you brought into the kitchen. I could see it from my window. It made me think we were on fire again."

He choked out a laugh. "We just might be." At her gasp he said, "I didn't mean that literally—never mind. Come here."

He led her to a kitchen chair, sat down on it, and pulled her onto his lap. He kept one arm around her back while he began to rub her shoulder and arm soothingly with his other hand. He wasn't exactly caressing her, but it seemed as if his touch could easily become a caress, and she was leaning against his chest—his very bare chest. He'd come downstairs in just his pants tonight. She was beginning to feel embarrassed for having thrown herself at him, no matter the reason. Or was she just too shy to admit she was glad to have had an excuse to do that?

"I'm surprised you were scared, considering how brave you were last night."

"That was different."

"How?"

"That fire was already burning. I reacted without thinking. I just wanted to put it out before it got any bigger." She took a deep breath, inhaling his distinctive scent of leather and pine trees. She loved the way he smelled.

"You're braver than you think—but I kind of like you coming to me when you think you aren't."

She didn't have to see his smile to know it was there when he said that. She felt a little bad for deceiving him tonight. Not that she hadn't been frightened—for her brother. Sam should have made his escape by now. It was time to get up and go back to her room.

"I guess it will just take a little while to get over being jittery at every noise or unexpected light in the house," she said with a smile, leaning away from him.

That was probably her biggest mistake because now she could see just how attractive he was, and she wasn't hurrying to get off his lap. She gazed in fascination at his bare, muscular chest and arms, his strong, wide shoulders, the thick cords of his neck, and his handsome face. His blue eyes captured hers and wouldn't let go. Was that the heat of desire in his eyes or a reflection of the lantern light? It was a breathless moment. She reminded herself that he didn't know who she was and that he wouldn't like her if he did. But he liked Jennifer. Why couldn't she be the real Jennifer for just a little while tonight?

"Jenny," he said softly.

It was as if he'd just answered her question, given her permission to do as she pleased. She didn't stop him from drawing her closer to him again; no, she threaded her fingers through his long, dark hair and held on tight as his mouth claimed hers.

His kiss was gentle at first, then turned strong and probing as his tongue pressed against her lips until they parted. Passion exploded for both of them. For long moments it engulfed them and neither of them seemed able to get enough of the other. Hunter ran his hands up and down her back as he deepened the kiss. Her hands clutched his shoulders as every nerve in her body sizzled with each thrust of his tongue. He was the one who finally tempered it, probably because he didn't want to frighten her. He didn't know she was beyond that point. But she was too inexperienced to do anything other than let him be her guide.

He pushed back her jacket and the straps of her chemise with it, then put his mouth on her bare shoulder, kissing her and leaving a mark before he moved his lips to her neck. She was trembling inside as Hunter continued to kiss her and softly stroke and caress her. He excited her in ways she'd never dreamed of. He was so big, so strong, more handsome than any other man she'd ever encountered—and he wanted her.

She felt him pulling the ties to her chemise, loosening it, and then his large hand was cupping one of her breasts. She gasped. His fingers moved to her nipple, gently circling it, igniting hot sensations that skittered through her body and made her gasp even more loudly. They both heard the footsteps at the same time. She inhaled sharply and started to get up, but he pulled her closer to him to cover her bare breasts as the guard passed by the kitchen windows.

Her heart was pounding. She was still panting as the footsteps faded and she leaned back again.

Hunter gave her a regretful smile. "Probably just as well. I was getting a little carried away."

What an understatement—that's what she wanted to say but she couldn't get any words out. She simply clutched the edges of her chemise closed and hurried out of the room and back upstairs. Now she was assailed with a double dose of guilt, for asking Sam to keep her secret and for giving Hunter the wrong impression. For God's sake, she'd only met the man three days ago! And she had no intention of marrying him. How could she give in to forbidden urges? She'd even talked herself into allowing it! What was wrong with her? She was playing with fire.

This had to end, and sooner than fifty-seven days from now. She was going to write another letter to her mother tomorrow. This time she'd tell her everything, all the horrors she'd witnessed, the fear she'd suffered, and what she was having to endure, dishwashing and all, just to avoid Frank Warren and find a way to end the feud without marriage. She'd tried to spare her mother additional worry, but it was too much for her to bear alone anymore. If Rose heard it all, she would release Tiffany from her promise. Before she left, she'd set these people down at a table and get them to resolve what should never have become a feud in the first place. Then she'd go home without a single regret. . . .

Chapter Thirty-Five

Tiffany's second letter to her mother was long and had to be worded just right. She couldn't finish it all in one sitting because she had to prepare her first breakfast for the entire household. She served eggs, fresh-baked bread that came out perfect this time, and beef that Andrew offered to grill in the backyard so they wouldn't have to overheat the kitchen by lighting the fireplace. It turned out so well that not even Hunter's risqué remark that the eggs weren't the best thing he'd ever tasted in the kitchen, a reference to what she'd foolishly let happen last night, didn't ruin her good mood.

It did embarrass her, though. A little. What had embarrassed her even more was her first sight of Hunter that morning and realizing how eager she'd been for it. She'd played with fire last night, and that flame would burn out of control if she couldn't tamp down these inappropriate feelings he kept stirring in her.

But her day was full enough to keep those thoughts away. After breakfast she had to get dinner started early, since she was going to make a roast. Just to make sure it didn't turn into another disaster, she visited Mary again.

Tiffany was still trying to avoid telling Hunter's mother that she couldn't cook, but she'd figured out a way to get some help from her without directly asking for it.

"I'm going to make a roast tonight. There are many ways to do so, but I wondered if you had a favorite recipe of your own that I could try out?"

"I have many, but it'd be hard to explain them unless I was right there with you in the kitchen. I didn't actually cook for my family, you know. Zachary's father, Elijah, had his own cook, and she made the trip here with us. When she retired, I thought I might start cooking for the family. My mother did teach me how. But Zachary went and hired another cook, and, well—I'd actually rather be out on the range, anyway."

"You—work with cattle?" Tiffany asked incredulously.

Mary smiled. "Herding isn't hard work, dear. Lets me spend more time with Zach, and I love the outdoors. I don't get involved with the spring branding, but roping stray calves to bring them back to their mothers is fun. You should have one of the boys show you how sometime."

Tiffany decided this ludicrous idea didn't merit a comment, and she'd gotten sidetracked. She needed recipes, not tips on roping cattle. That cookbook she'd bought just gave her bare basics or too many choices to vary a dish by adding this, or this, or that, but never saying just how much of those ingredients to add. Of course the book did sort of stress up front the value of experimenting, but she didn't have time for experimenting. She wanted her dishes to come out right the first time around, not five ruined meals later.

"So you don't actually have any suggestions for the roast tonight?"

"My mother preferred to prepare her roasts in a Dutch oven, with just a bay leaf, garlic . . . oh, and she always poured in some red wine, about half a cup."

So *that's* why there was wine in the pantry! But Mary suddenly frowned thoughtfully, adding, "Old Ed had his own Dutch oven, but he probably took it with him. The one my mother left me is in the attic. You might want to fetch it, unless you traveled with your own?"

Tiffany stared at her blankly. Travel with an oven? Would she even know what a Dutch oven was if she saw it? Andrew might. She could send him up to the attic for it. But while she had a sort-of-recipe for tonight, that wasn't going to help her tomorrow.

So she shook her head in regard to having her own oven and said, "I'll try adding the wine tonight. Do you have any other recipes you'd care to share?"

"As I said, my mother taught me and she was a damn fine cook, but it's all up here." Mary pointed at her head.

"Perhaps you could write a few down for me?"

Mary chuckled. "It's hard to describe a pinch of this and a dash of that when it comes to spices. And it's all in the measurements, you know. Put in too much and you ruin a dish, put in too little and you also ruin it. But I'll be back on my feet before the wedding. I can show you then."

The damn wedding. And that wasn't going to help Tiffany now. Actually . . . "You might consider trying to sort out those dashes and pinches on paper," she remarked with a smile. "Imagine what a wonderful gift it would make for your future daughters-in-law."

She'd managed to surprise Mary. "I'll be damned, gal, that is a right fine idea. I'll see what I can figure out and then you can make copies for yourself, too."

Tiffany stood up to leave, pleased she *was* going to get what she came for—hopefully soon. But then she remembered the letter to her mother that she'd started. If it got her the desired result, which was permission to go home, Mary here was probably the only one who could make her trip home guilt-free.

To that end she impulsively said, "There's another gift that would be even better, Mary, at least for the daughter-in-law you're expecting soon. Well, if it was me, I'd certainly think so."

Mary perked up. "What?"

"End the feud with her family before the wedding. That would be a magnanimous gesture, don't you think?"

Mary slumped back against her pillows. "Indeed it would. It's such a shame. My boys should've been best of friends with Frank's. Heck, we practically live within shouting distance of each other."

"Then why depend on a marriage to end it? Why not just end it?"

"You think I haven't tried? Rose wanted the hostilities ended, too. We both did. It just ain't right, us carrying on something we had no part of starting."

"Rose?" Tiffany fought hard to keep the blush down, for asking something she already knew.

"Frank Warren's wife. I'd talk to her whenever we crossed paths in town. She was such a friendly young girl, never put on airs, coming from the big city like she did. She fit right in because she wanted to, but then she and Frank seemed so happy together, always touching, laughing"—and in a whisper—"even kissing in public. Then I heard she turned high-strung and started complaining about ranch life after Frank got shot. She just up and left one day, taking their little girl with her. Never understood that. To this day, I still don't. But at least the truce lasted, even with her gone."

"Perhaps—perhaps she missed city life too much."

Mary actually snorted. "No, that gal loved it here, really loved it, and her man. I wasn't surprised when she arranged the betrothal, *and* the truce, demanded it actually." Another whisper: "I think she scared Zach a little that night she came over here by herself. She was in such a rage she was crying. Least, she definitely confused him. But I seen it coming, her doing something like that. She wasn't afraid to butt heads with the menfolk over the water access. I knew it infuriated her that they couldn't just share it. Did me, too. I just never had the nerve to put my foot down the way she did that night. She had fire and gumption, that girl. Must've been that red hair . . . ," Mary said, gazing at Tiffany's long hair.

Chapter Thirty-Six

"Do you never stay in your pen anymore?" Tiffany asked when she felt the nudge on her shoes and glanced down to find the piglet on the porch with her again.

It stood still, staring up at her. She leaned down to pet it, but it continued to stare. She finally gave in with a roll of her eyes, picked it up, flipped it over on her lap, and began to rub its belly while she got back to watching the sunset.

No summer storm had showed up today to ruin the glorious details of this one, such bright streaks of pink and yellow. The trees along the skyline looked as if they were aflame, with so much red behind them. She had time to enjoy it while the bread baked.

"Don't mind me, gal," Zachary said as he stepped out of the house and headed down the porch to his favorite chair for his evening smoke.

He didn't comment on the piglet in her lap, which meant he hadn't really looked at her. She was just another servant to him. Invisible. Actually, he did vaguely know she was there, so she probably shouldn't tar him with her own brush. Her mother's house was full of servants, but how often did she actually notice any of them other than Anna? This role she was playing was giving her insight into herself that she wasn't all that comfortable with. But she could ignore Zachary as he, apparently, intended to ignore her. And she didn't mind sharing the porch with him. With the breeze blowing his way, she wouldn't notice the smoke either.

"Something smells damn good, coming from the kitchen," he yelled her way before he lit up his cigar and enjoyed the sunset, too.

Tiffany smiled. Dinner tonight was going to be a cause for celebration . . . well, for her, anyway. Mary's cast-iron Dutch oven turned out to be an amazing covered roasting dish. It was shallow enough to fit on the stove's baking shelf. It had handles so Tiffany could simply bring it to the table and serve from it. It even came with a platform it could rest on, so it could be used over a fire, too. It was on the kitchen table right now, the roast inside it simmering in its gravy while the bread baked.

She'd left a note on the lid that simply read, *Don't touch.* It was going to be her surprise, her first good meal, and she wanted to be the one who revealed it. Of course the aroma that had filled the kitchen for most of the afternoon was a good indication. Still, presentation was everything, and she'd arranged the vegetables that Andrew had brought in and washed for her just right, circling them around the huge roast. And timed them perfectly, not adding them too soon.

It had been a busy day, but it had gone smoothly—well, mostly. That unease she'd felt after leaving Mary's room was long gone now. She'd been foolish to think even for a moment that Mary had somehow guessed who she really was when she'd mentioned Rose's red hair and had stared at Tiffany's—red hair. But the shades weren't similar! It was absurd to think the woman might have made the connection. Even if it did occur to her, she would quickly have scoffed at the notion. Which is what Tiffany should have done sooner, instead of letting it make her uneasy for half the day. What really bothered her was what Mary had said about Tiffany's parents. . . .

Happy, so in love, and yet Rose just up and left. *Why?* Was no one ever going to answer that question for her? But this was the first she'd heard about how happy Rose had been here, which just made it all the more confusing. And made her realize for the first time, too, that she'd be a different person if Rose hadn't taken her away from here. Tiffany would have grown up knowing Hunter and would probably be looking forward to marrying him, would probably be head over heels in love with him by now. It wasn't such a horrible thought anymore; it was a bit sad because it hadn't been destined to happen.

"I'd like to see you hold him like that six months from now. Didn't hear my warning about size, did you?"

Thinking of the devil, she gave Hunter a smile. He was leaning in the doorway, a book in hand and freshly washed, by the look of his damp hair. He'd spoken quietly enough that Zachary hadn't noticed him yet.

"I don't fetch him," she said in her defense. "He seems to find me whenever a door is opened or I step outside."

"I know just how he feels."

She blushed and glanced back at the sunset. She should go back inside. He'd probably come out to talk to his father; he just wasn't moving in that direction yet. And she didn't move yet either.

She even delayed him by nodding at the book he was holding. "Where did you get your schooling—or did you get any?"

"Thinking I'm not up to your standards, Red?"

"No, I just wondered." Her talk with Sam last night had
got her curious about the boys from both families growing up
together, but she couldn't mention that. "Where I come from,
schools are plentiful. It occurred to me that isn't the case out
here."

"Ma taught us boys. She was going to be a teacher herself,
but got married instead. But Nashart did finally get a schoolroom. And I brought this out for you." He put the book down
on the swing next to her. "Figured you might enjoy some fic-
tion set west of the Rockies—if you find time to read."

She probably would since she didn't expect every day to be
as busy as today, but her curiosity wasn't satisfied yet. "A single
schoolroom implies you had to attend with your hated neighbors. Did you ever pick on them? Were you a bully growing up,
Hunter Callahan?"

He chuckled. "If I'm going to fight someone, he needs to be
my size or bigger. I don't mind bigger. The Warren boys never
fit the bill. Even with Sam full grown now, I've still got a lot of
weight on him."

Yes, he was definitely bigger, more muscular, broader in
the shoulders, stronger in the legs . . . she got her eyes off him
fast and shot to her feet. She started back into the house, but
stopped when she remembered the piglet in her arms. She
turned to take him back to his mama.

Hunter held out his hands. "I'll take him. I'm sure you've
got a table to set or other things to finish up before dinner."

She nodded and handed the animal over. She was just inside the door when she heard Zachary say, "What the hell is that doing here? Jakes needs to be more careful with the food stocks."

Tiffany yelled as she marched down the hall, "He is *not* going to be dinner! Ever!"

"Did I hear her right? She can't—"

She missed the rest of what Zachary said because his voice was drowned out by Hunter's laughter.

Chapter Thirty-Seven

HUNTER CONTINUED TO WATCH Jennifer as she marched down the hall, her bustle swaying, her copper hair tied at the neck, but still so thick it spread across her back all the way to her waist. Those emerald eyes were probably flashing right now, proving she'd do battle for a pig. She would, too. He didn't doubt it, and it kept the grin on his lips even after she'd disappeared into the kitchen.

He'd laughed when he'd read the note she'd left on top of the Dutch oven. She didn't even have to be in the room and she could make him laugh. . . .

"Stop it. *Stop it!*"

He turned toward his father to find Zachary sitting forward in his chair, glowering at him. Hunter moved to the end of the porch to half sit on the rail, one leg dangling, the pig tucked under his arm. "Stop what?"

"Looking at her like that."

Hunter wasn't abashed when it was something he seemed

to have no control over. He said as much with a shrug. "Can't help it."

"You sure as hell can."

Hunter chuckled. "I guess you don't remember what it was like, when you were young."

"I'm not that old," Zachary grumbled. "And this ain't amusing."

"Now that's where you're wrong, Pa. I've never laughed so much in my life as I have since Jenny got here. It's like when she walked in the house, joy walked in with her. Everything about her makes me want to smile."

"Damnit, Hunter, you need to nip that in the bud *right* now. You think I don't know where this is heading?"

Hunter put both feet back on the porch. "And what if it is?"

"She's already got a man, and you've got a gal coming across the whole country for you."

"You know how I feel about that, Pa."

"Yeah, I do. I hate it just as much as you do. But Rose Warren got me to agree to it . . . well, it was mostly your ma who did, taking Rose Warren's side in it. Now it's a matter of honor."

How many times had Hunter heard that? But no one else was the sacrificial offering here, just him. While he'd never done more than complain about having this all set up for him before he was old enough to have a say in it, he'd never had reason to simply refuse either—until now. Actually, he didn't have that reason yet, just hoped he would. He sighed.

"We give them back their steers that wander over," he reminded his father. "They do the same. It's been mostly peaceful around here for fifteen years other than those fights between Cole and Roy, and John and Sam, and simple squabbles before that. *Peaceful*, Pa. We don't need a marriage to keep it that way. Make a damn agreement with Franklin already. You're not Grandpa, who wouldn't even talk to one of them."

"Can't trust Frank to honor a mere agreement. It's got to be signed with a blood bond. His wife knew that. It's why she put that card on the table."

"You've got four sons. Any one of them will do."

"Well, Rose picked you. We agreed it'd be you because you're the oldest."

"So disagree on that point."

"We've had this discussion before, Hunter. I could've sworn we settled it. You meet her first, *then* you decide if you want her or not. In the meantime, keep your hands off the hired help. I raised you better than to trifle with a woman already spoken for."

Zachary had to pull out that card? Hunter threw up his hands in defeat or started to, until he nearly dropped the pig. "Fine," he snarled, and left the porch, heading around to the back of the house.

He should have gone the other way. Zachary leaned over the railing to say as Hunter passed by, "Maybe the Warren girl don't want to marry you either. Did you think of that? Maybe you're getting all riled up over nothing. But you two can figure that out when she gets here."

Hunter kept on going without replying. He didn't like arguing with his father. He *knew* the choice would still be his in the end. Zachary had made that clear. Hunter shouldn't even be trying to settle the matter before he met the Warren daughter. It would just have been nice to have peace without a time limit on it, so their neighbors didn't get up in arms when he did finally end that dumb betrothal.

He didn't find Jennifer in the kitchen when he got back to

the house. One look at her and this annoyance would go away, he was sure. It did when he entered the dining room and found her just setting the roast on the table and the rest of his family already seated. She passed him to head back to the kitchen. With Zachary raising a brow at him, he managed not to follow her with his eyes and took a seat instead.

So he was surprised to hear Zachary tell him as he stood up to cut the roast, "Fetch her back. Smells like she did good tonight. She can start sharing meals with us like Ed did. And she might teach you boys some table manners you've forgotten since your ma got laid up."

That was a concession on his father's part—for Hunter. He nodded before heading back into the kitchen. Jennifer was standing by the sink, her back to the room.

She heard his step and glanced over her shoulder. "I forgot to mention, save some for the rest of us. I didn't want to ruin the presentation by cutting into it yet."

He grinned. "I guess that *Don't touch* note was for yourself, then?"

She laughed. "No, I just . . . what?"

She'd rooted him to the spot with the merry sound she'd just made. Had he never heard her laugh before? If he had, it certainly hadn't affected him like this. How was it possible for her to get even more beautiful?

He found his voice. "Makes you sparkle, when you laugh. Lights you up like a candle. Give me a frown, Jenny, so I can move again."

She gave him another laugh instead, apparently thinking he was teasing. He wasn't sure he was. But she'd turned her back on him and was facing the sink as she said, "Go eat while it's hot."

He cleared his throat. "Well, then, you need to return to the dining room for that to happen. Come on, Red. Pa won't eat until you're seated."

She turned, even took a few steps before she stopped to point out, "It isn't appropriate for hired help to sit with the family. Do the maids eat with you?"

"No, but you're not exactly a maid. And Old Ed ate with us, so does Degan. 'Sides, Pa thinks you might teach us boys some table manners. So no arguing."

He returned to his seat, leaving the choice to follow up to her. Actually, he didn't trust himself to touch her right now, not even her hand. But she entered a moment later, not the least bit embarrassed as most servants would be to be included in the family dinner. She carried herself as if she owned the room. Come to think of it, there wasn't a subservient bone in that girl and had never been. He wasn't really surprised by that. Jennifer Fleming was aware of her own worth.

She stopped behind the empty chair directly across the table from Hunter. She didn't touch it. Lesson number one. Hunter started laughing, he simply couldn't help it. It got worse when Cole, Degan, even John, all started to get up to help seat her. But Cole was the quickest and the closest and pulled the chair out for her.

She gave him a brilliant smile of thanks, which started Cole blushing. Zachary was still cutting the roast, and taking so long at it, Hunter had a feeling his father was wary of messing it up, which would disappoint the cook. They started passing their plates down his way.

"Don't everyone talk at once," Zachary said.

A few nervous laughs and throat clearings ensued. Jennifer introduced a topic to put them at ease with her presence. She *was* causing their nervousness. It was her dress. She simply didn't look like a servant in her fancy duds, and with her sitting there so properlike, it was as if they had some rich lady at the table. None of them were used to that! Not even their father.

"Perhaps someone can tell me a little more about Nashart? Mrs. Callahan said the town didn't exist when your family moved here. It was merely a trading post?"

Zachary answered, "Yeah, that was all. For a long time, too."

"But didn't being so far from markets for your cattle make business difficult?"

"That actually wasn't a deciding factor, since we expected it would take quite a few years to build the herd back up. We only brought a hundred head of cattle with us and lost a quarter of them on the trip."

"The trip was that difficult?"

"Not really. We came most of the way by river, first on the Mississippi, then the Missouri to Fort Union. That's a ways northeast of here, but while the Missouri continues west and steamboats travel that route now, they didn't back then."

"Why didn't you settle near Fort Union?"

Zachary chuckled. "My pa wanted more isolation than that. We'd already made our fortune ranching in Florida, where some of the oldest ranches in the country are located. Truth is, cattle rustling got really out of hand down there. Too many ranches too close to each other. We aimed to get away from that—among other things. So we weren't looking for a well-settled area, just the opposite. Yet we couldn't go too far from water, either, so we followed the Yellowstone River. Couldn't raft it since it flowed north into the Missouri, but we never strayed too far from it or its spouts. The creek that flows by here almost year-round and feeds the lake is why we put down roots here, that and finding the trappers trail to the trading post in the area."

"Almost year-round?" she asked.

John answered as Zachary began to hand the plates back, "It dries up some late in the year; one year, it dried up all the way."

"It would freeze here in winter, wouldn't it?" she questioned. "How do your cattle get water then?"

Cole piped up, "We crack the ice at the edges of the lake for the cows that are too dumb to lick snow for their water."

Jennifer nodded. "So when did the town of Nashart actually come into being?"

"My boys can answer that. I'm going to share this fine dinner with Mary," Zachary said as he picked up two filled plates and started out of the room.

Jennifer looked around her, waiting for an answer, though Hunter noticed she was doing a good job of not looking at him. He spoke up anyway. "With our ranch springing up near the trading post, it didn't take long at all for a saloon to be built. Still, I hear it was just those two buildings for a few more years. There just wasn't enough traffic through here to warrant more—heck, none at all other than trappers and Indians back then."

"What changed that?"

"Gold. Before it was discovered in the western part of the territory, Nashart barely had a handful of buildings. Folks struck with gold fever came from all over the country and from all walks of life, most of them too late, with news traveling so slowly back then. Some from the East passed through here on their way to get rich because by then we'd delivered cows a few times to Fort Union, so there was a pretty good trail between here and there. And they came back through here on their way home when it didn't pan out for them."

"And stayed?"

"Some, yes. They'd see construction going on here. The trading post was already being converted to a general store to take advantage of the new traffic passing through. And progress, it can be as infectious as gold fever. Tiny shops went up fast, those that didn't take much to get going—barber, laundry, carpenter, to name a few."

"So that's when Nashart became a real town?"

"Yeah, but it was still not even a quarter the size it is now. It continued to grow, though, just more slowly until a stage line went in. Wasn't surprised to see that happen despite the rush being over. Butte, Helena, even Virginia City, they got so big, they were drawing in new businesses instead of new prospectors."

Hunter had talked so much, he was surprised to find only himself and Jennifer left at the table. He was about to turn the conversation in a more personal direction, now that they were alone, but she became aware of that, too, and stood up to leave.

She did so politely, though, ending their conversation with the thought "I wonder if this territory will ever see statehood, or be nothing but ghost towns after the ore runs out."

"You underestimate the power of the railroad. There are towns now that aren't mining towns, and more and more will spring up along the lines." He stood up to follow her. He felt a powerful urge not to lose her company just yet. "Let me help you clean up."

"No!" she said a little too quickly, amending, "I mean, Andrew is waiting to do that. And we have bread to get started for tomorrow. You'd just be in the way."

He raised a brow. "Help is help."

"Not when it's a distraction." Her tone was starting to turn annoyed. "I don't want to spend all night in the kitchen, thank you." She blushed as soon as she said it. She was obviously remembering last night. He'd barely been able to think of anything else today. "But if you want to be helpful, you could arrange for me to have a horse to use tomorrow."

He smiled. She considered him a distraction! "So you're ready for a ride with me?"

"No, I just need to go to town to pick up the clothes I ordered. Andrew can accompany—"

"I think we had this talk about you not going anywhere without me."

"Fine!" she huffed, and flounced off.

He started laughing to himself. Jennifer definitely had a problem with not getting her way. Life with her would never be simple. Life with her . . . was he really thinking that far ahead?

Chapter Thirty-Eight

TIFFANY WAS AMUSED THAT Hunter didn't get his way any more than she did about her outing to Nashart. He seemed quite disgruntled when Degan insisted on tagging along yet again. She enjoyed being back on a horse though, and she was dressed appropriately for the occasion in her one remaining riding habit. Made of emerald-green velvet, it was a bit warm for the weather and missing the splendid hat that went with it, but none of her hats had survived the train trip. This time she had no intention of staying in town any longer than she had to, so she wasn't even going to risk stopping to visit Anna. In and out, before she ran into any more of her brothers, was her plan today.

"Only two stops," she assured the men on either side of her as the three of them rode down the main street into town. "I have a letter to post first, but that will only take a moment."

"Another letter?" Degan said.

"To my fiancé," Tiffany lied.

"Figures," Hunter said, and did an about-face, heading in the other direction.

Degan sighed as he turned to gaze at Hunter. "You could have lied."

She did lie! And did again when she replied, "No, I couldn't. *He* needs to be reminded that I have one."

"Point taken."

She posted the letter to her mother and was back on the horse as quickly as she'd said she would be. And back off it just as quickly when she spotted her brother Roy across the street. Had he been looking directly at her? God, she hoped not. Hiding on the other side of the animal, head ducked low, she walked with it that way, trying to make it far enough up the street to an alley between two of the buildings so she could dash between them and skirt around the back way to Mrs. Martin's house.

"What are you doing?" Degan asked as he followed her, still mounted.

"Working off a cramp in my leg."

"I would have guessed the cramp was in your neck. Are you hiding from someone?"

"Of course not. I'm just watching where I'm walking."

She made the dash without incident, quickly remounted, and rode behind the buildings on the main street to reach Mrs. Martin's house. Her heart was still pounding, though. She was going to have to stop coming to town, she realized. It was too risky.

Degan waited out front with the horses. Agnes already had Tiffany's order bundled and ready to go, she just had to fetch it from the back. Tiffany paced, waiting for the seamstress to return. Roy obviously hadn't seen her, but that had been too close. And then she froze. It wasn't Agnes coming back down the hall toward her. Roy had noticed her after all, and he looked livid. And, oh, my, had he grown!

"I can explain!"

He wasn't interested. Roy grabbed her by the hand and dragged her out of the house the back way. He was almost her age, just ten and a half months younger, but he was already as tall as their older brother Sam, which was at least six feet. And he was strong. It was a wonder he hadn't won that fight with Cole. Maybe he had and had gotten a black eye to show for it. He was too strong! She had no chance of getting her hand back from him.

"You're hurting me," she said as they reached the backyard.

That actually worked. He let go, swung around, and demanded, "What the hell are you doing with that gunfighter? He works for the Callahans!"

He was shouting. She winced before whispering, "I know. So do I."

"Like hell you do."

"It's complicated, Roy. I don't have time to explain, but go find Sam. He knows what I'm doing and why. Just don't tell anyone else you saw me."

"Is this a joke?" He grabbed her hand again. "You're coming home with me."

She dug in her heels. "No, I am not!"

"She really isn't," a new voice said calmly in a deadly tone.

They both glanced to the side and saw Degan slowly walking toward them from the side yard. And he'd drawn his gun! Tiffany blanched and leapt in front of her brother, putting her back to Degan.

She told Roy in a desperate whisper, "He doesn't know who I am, but he *will* protect me. Don't ruin what I'm doing. Go. Find Sam. And don't talk to anyone else about this or—or I'll never forgive you."

For the briefest moment he looked hurt that she'd say that, but then he gave Degan a fulminating glare before he angrily walked off. She hoped he'd talk to Sam right away. But another layer of guilt settled on her shoulders because he was so angry with her and she hadn't been able to give him the explanation herself. But she was horrified when Degan stopped Roy from leaving. . . .

"Warren."

Roy turned back around slowly. His chin was jutted out defiantly by the time he faced Degan. Tiffany could have throttled her brother for his bravado when he said, "You going to shoot me into silence?"

She was about to jump back in front of Roy when Degan replied, "It's a thought . . . or I could just convince Pearl to stop seeing you. Tell me, which would you prefer?"

A number of emotions crossed Roy's face—anger, confusion, some definite frustration—before he said, "What's it to you?"

"Simple loyalty to my employer. Zachary has every intention of telling your father that Miss Fleming works for him. So we're going to let him do that in his own good time. Neither elder needs to know about this incident, which would only embarrass Miss Fleming."

Roy glanced at her again. Her entire expression was pleading with him. He might still say who she really was and was probably thinking about doing just that, he stared at her so long. She was going to have to see her father before she left the territory, whether she wanted to or not, but damnit, not like this, not dragged home by her angry brother.

But Roy finally eased his aggressive stance and told Degan, "She's already asked me to say nothing and I won't—for her, not because of your threats."

"Good enough," Degan replied. "Don't make me regret trusting you on this matter."

Roy just snorted before he left. Degan holstered his gun. Now that the danger was over, Tiffany glared at the gunman. "Would you really have shot him?"

"Over a prank and when it gets sprung? Of course not."

"Did you mean what you said, that you aren't going to tell Zachary about this, either?"

"I'll tell him the day he rides over to the Warren ranch to do his gloating. I'm not going to let him get egg on his face during that encounter. But for now, I don't see much point in mentioning it."

"You really are loyal, aren't you?"

He didn't answer, just led her to their horses. What a complex man he was. . . . He seemed to make his own rules.

The rest of the week passed slowly, with her waiting to hear back from her mother when she knew it was still too soon. Pearl returned to work that week and just in time, since Tiffany had started sneezing again that very morning. But it was an unpleasant first meeting.

Pearl sauntered into the kitchen, took one look at Tiffany in her new, appalling work clothes, and said accusingly, "You stole my clothes?"

Since they were wearing the same style of skirt and blouse,

Tiffany could certainly understand the woman's mistake. The maid was much more curvaceous than Tiffany and filled out the low-cut blouse provocatively. Tiffany didn't doubt that Pearl wore that type of blouse because it abetted her seductions. With black hair worn loose to her shoulders and gray eyes, she was pretty in an earthy sort of way. Now that Tiffany was seeing Pearl close up, why Hunter would be tempted by her was obvious.

Tiffany quickly explained, "When I ordered new work clothes from Mrs. Martin, I didn't specify the style. She obviously patterned mine after yours. Believe me, I would never wear anything this revealing if I had a choice."

Tiffany had filled in the ridiculously low neckline though. It had taken her several hours in Mary's sewing room to fashion an insert that covered her upper chest. It was fastened behind her neck and tucked into the low, loose bodice. She'd had to give up on wearing her chemise with the blouse because the straps would show due to the short, capped sleeves that hung off the shoulder.

But Pearl had picked up on the insult, intended or not, and angrily said, "Stay away from Hunter, he's mine!"

Where that came from, Tiffany wasn't at all sure, but she replied, "Yours?"

"He belongs in my bed."

Aghast that she was even discussing something so personal with a stranger, Tiffany told the maid stiffly, "I have a fiancé."

"Good, see that it stays that way."

Embarrassed, green eyes narrowed, Tiffany said, "I'm the new cook. I'll be making *your* food. You might want to keep that in mind."

As retaliatory threats went, that one had been quite weak. It infuriated her that she hadn't done better. That was the only reason she was so angry that day, she assured herself. But if Hunter had shown up before she'd calmed down, he would have gotten an earful about his paramour.

Degan did though, and Tiffany was still too angry at the time to realize she shouldn't mention it, even to him, especially to him. But he did shed some light on a question that had been bothering her.

"She doesn't really want Hunter, you know. What she wants is to be the lady of a house like this. That will never happen here while Mary Callahan lives, so Pearl would actually rather have a Warren for a husband. She wouldn't even be working here if they had hired her over there. It's Roy Warren she's got her matrimonial sites on."

Tiffany had feared her brother was somehow involved with the maid when Degan had used Pearl as leverage with him in town the other day. When she was out of this mess, she was going to have to warn Roy against that abrasive, conniving, two-timing woman. Would he listen, as angry as he was with Tiffany right now? Or was it already too late? It made her wonder just what Roy had been doing in town in the middle of the week, when Pearl had been there, too.

The next day, the piglet showed up at the house again, but in Jakes's arms this time, and the trail cook was angry about it. "You never should've made friends with him. He's been crying for you since he can't get out no more."

"You added more fence planking?"

"Had to," Jakes had grumbled. "Never had a dang problem with the babies wandering till they got a whiff of you. Here, he's yours now."

He shoved the animal at her and marched off. Tiffany was surprised, but not actually displeased. She'd never owned a pet before, and this one did seem to have a calming influence on her. Of course now that the piglet was her pet, she had to name it. She decided on Maximilian, a noble name to counter its mud-loving nature. But an even greater benefit of the unexpected gift was that the piglet's being underfoot in the kitchen all day kept Pearl out of it. The maid had some sort of aversion to the animal that had her hurrying in the opposite direction if the pig even looked as if it might approach her.

Tiffany's cooking continued to improve that week, though it was hard to outdo that roast she'd made that everyone had thanked her for the next day. But amazingly, she actually started having fun cooking—well, not the cooking part, since the days kept getting warmer and so did the kitchen. Sweating was such an appalling new experience! But she found that experimenting with spices was fun. She just reserved the results for lunches, which most of the household didn't ride in for. And she kept notes! Even that was fun. She was making her own recipes! And anything that tasted good got moved to the dinner menus.

Hunter didn't go to town that next Saturday night with the rest of the men. He stayed home to teach Tiffany how to play poker, which he could have done any night, but he used the excuse that Saturday was the only time he ever played poker, so it had to be that night or never.

She hadn't wanted to. Spending the evening with him didn't seem like a good idea when she already saw far too much of him every day. He'd even started joining her on the porch in the evening for the sunset, sitting companionably on the swing with her and Maximilian, not always talking, but, when he did, always making her laugh. But he cajoled her into the card game that night.

They used the poker table in the parlor. Just the two of them in that high-ceilinged room, their laughter echoing loudly, so loudly that Zachary yelled at them from the top of the stairs to quiet it down. But she couldn't win a game no matter what decisions she made about the cards in her hand. She began to suspect Hunter was cheating. Even that was funny!

She had to stop having fun with the man. She shouldn't be feeling so comfortable with him now that she constantly got roped in by his humor. Roped. That was another amusing memory now. She'd actually roped a cow!

It had happened the day he invited her out for a ride. He'd let her choose in which direction to ride. She wanted to see the damage the copper mine was doing to the range, so they rode east. The Callahans hadn't been exaggerating. The grass above the gulch where the mining camp was set up was blackened with soot. The cave-in had created a large hole in the ground. They didn't approach the edge of it until they heard the cow. Yet another one had gotten trapped in the deep hole. Luckily, this one had only fallen to a ledge about four feet down and was stuck there. It didn't look injured, but it wasn't getting out without help.

Hunter dismounted and grabbed the rope hooked on his saddle. When she saw that he was going to lasso the animal rather than just drop the loop down over its head, she remembered that Mary had told her she enjoyed roping stray calves, so she asked Hunter if she could try it. He was surprised she'd want to, but he showed her how. Mary had been right. It was fun once she got the hang of it and stopped wrapping the rope around herself instead of the cow's head.

But it definitely delayed their return to the ranch. Sunset had started, and she started drifting away from Hunter as she watched it.

"Pay attention," he told her, "or do I need to take your reins to lead you?"

She grinned at him. "I'm sorry, it's just so beautiful out here, and the sunsets are spectacular."

He'd laughed. "I already figured you liked them. When you've lived with them your whole life like me, you don't tend to notice them as much."

"Lucky you. In the city, with buildings all around, you never get to see the horizon. Maybe a little pale pink high in the sky before it sinks low, but nothing like this."

A perfect end to an enjoyable day. When she had that thought, it disturbed her a little. When had she started to enjoy spending time with Hunter? She hadn't even been here two weeks yet, though it was getting close to that. But she was no closer to finding a peaceful solution to the feud that didn't include marriage. Hunter could—if he would.

That stayed on her mind as they left the horses in the stable. As they strolled back to the house, she actually asked him, "Have you given any thought to arranging a permanent truce with your neighbors without marrying one of them—since you said you didn't want to?"

"Didn't say I didn't want to marry, just not her."

"Even if she's pretty? Er, that is, I've heard her mother is beautiful."

"The daughter probably is, too, but it won't matter, not when I've lived with this hate for that family all my life. I don't think anything's going to make that go away. It's always going to be deep down, under the surface. Anything she does wrong, it will probably burst out, and it won't even be her fault." He'd suddenly looked surprised. "I never mentioned that to anyone before, that particular fear."

Tiffany hurried inside the house. She wished he hadn't mentioned it to her, either.

Chapter Thirty-Nine

ANOTHER SUCCESSFUL MEAL HAD Tiffany climbing the stairs that night with a half smile on her lips. It was still early. She thought about writing letters to her friends back home. She could have someone else post them for her. She couldn't tell her friends what she'd been up to, but she could tell them some positive things about Montana—as long as they didn't tell her mother. Rose had to continue thinking her daughter abhorred everything about the territory.

Tiffany believed her mother had received her second letter by now. She'd half expected an immediate telegram saying simply, "Come home," but her mother probably wanted to express her thoughts more articulately in a letter. Rose would have self-recriminations to address, apologies to make, but hopefully not an "Are you certain?" Tiffany still worried that Rose would do what Sam had done—try to convince her that she'd merely had some bad luck in witnessing so much violence in such a short time. Maybe it was bad luck, but that wasn't changing her mind.

She untied her hair, shook it out, then laid out one of the new nightgowns to get comfortable in before she started her letters. At least Mrs. Martin had made her two normal night-gowns, one long-sleeved for winter, one short-sleeved for sum-mer. But she wasn't going to be here come winter, so she'd cut off the long sleeves so she could use both now.

She removed the insert from her blouse, then went over to the wardrobe mirror to have a look at herself without it. She shouldn't have. With her hair loose around her shoulders and that silly blouse, she didn't even recognize herself. The image made her blush and slam the wardrobe door closed.

This would never have happened if the men hadn't rushed her that Saturday she ordered the clothes. She should have spared a few more minutes to pick her own designs—no, that would have taken much longer than a few minutes, as par-ticular as she was. But she should really have taken the blouses right back to Mrs. Martin, and she would have if she weren't so afraid to venture into town again.

She moved back to the bed to finish undressing but stopped midway when someone pounded a bit too loudly on her door. Oh, God, now what? A number of disasters came to mind, in-cluding the thought that a member of her family was pounding on her door, which had her leaping toward the door to open it.

But it was just Hunter, who looked unusually harried. He didn't even say anything, just grabbed her hand and started pulling her down the hall. She smelled for smoke. None. She couldn't think what else would have him rushing like this.

Halfway down the stairs she asked, "Where are you tak-ing me?"

He didn't pause, didn't even glance back as he said, "Caleb

just rode in, and, my God, he's in a panic. He needs a woman and fast, and you're the closest one."

"What?!"

"For his wife, Shela. She's having her baby tonight, but our doctor isn't due back in town for another few days."

"She can't wait?"

As panicked as *he* seemed, he still managed to chuckle. "No, she really can't."

"But I know nothing about childbirth!"

"You don't have to. Shela does. This is her second. Didn't I mention that to you last week? You just need to be there to catch the baby when it comes out."

"Caleb knows his wife—intimately. So why can't he do that?"

"You'd think, wouldn't you? But he tried it with the first one and fainted before it came out. No, he's useless in that regard."

What made Hunter think she wouldn't faint, too? Just because she was a woman? Was this another of those situations these men believed a woman could handle due to her natural feminine instincts? Probably.

They'd reached the stable before Tiffany remembered what she was wearing and her cheeks lit up. "I'm not dressed to go anywhere. Let me go back and change."

"There's no time for proper tonight, Red."

"I at least need a jacket! Or your shirt. Yes, that will do nicely."

He tossed his jacket at her, then tossed her up on a horse. Someone had already saddled two for them. Caleb must have woken one of the hands to do so before he raced back home.

"I sent Cole to town, just in case the doc got back early,"

Hunter said. "But that isn't likely when he's more often late than on time."

She put the jacket on quickly before she grabbed her reins. She still wanted no part of this. "Why didn't you get Pearl or Luella instead? They probably know much more—"

"Couldn't," he cut in as he mounted. "Luella visits her folks twice a week. Tonight's one of those times. And Caleb won't let Pearl near his place after she tried to seduce him when Shela was eight months pregnant with the last kid. That leaves you."

That hussy! How many men was Pearl sleeping with? Tiffany had to warn Roy before he succumbed to her wiles.

They rode out. The moon on the unclouded horizon to the east provided light so they could see the narrow trail. She couldn't count the lightning flashes that rent the northwestern night sky. They were so far in the distance, the storm they heralded could easily dissipate and not affect the Triple C.

She kept asking Hunter how much longer, but he probably didn't hear her they were riding so fast. Yet her nervousness was building just as fast. She couldn't do this. It was so far out of her realm of experience, she was sure she'd faint just like Caleb, and then who would help the baby?

She was frozen with that fear when they reached Caleb's cabin. Hunter actually had to drag her off the horse and pull her inside. But the first thing they heard when they walked into the main room was the cry of a baby. Tiffany's relief was instantaneous!

"Looks like you're off the hook, Red." Hunter moved to one of two doors in the room and knocked on it.

Caleb opened the door. He wasn't tall, but he was a handsome man around Hunter's age—which explained why Pearl had tried to tempt him when she wouldn't get anything from him other than sex. He was holding a bundle in the crook of one arm and stepped out into the room with it, closing the door behind him.

"It's a boy this time," he said proudly, beaming at them. "I didn't know Shela was this close. She'd had one false go last week, when she thought the baby was coming, but the pains were gone before I got home, so she didn't even mention it, foolish woman. But she thought this one was false, too, since it's early, so she didn't tell me when I rode in for lunch today. It scares the heck out of me when I think it could have happened when I rode for help."

"Ma told me once, only the first one takes forever," Hunter remarked. "The rest pop out easier and much quicker. Usually. Least they did for her."

"And you couldn't mention that to me?" Caleb replied.

Hunter shrugged. "Figured Shela would know that."

There it was again, his assumption that women instinctively knew everything about home and family matters. Tiffany rolled her eyes. Hunter took a moment to introduce her properly to Caleb before she asked, "So the baby didn't need catching?"

Caleb grinned bashfully at them. "I managed not to faint this time I was so shocked when I walked in the door and she screamed at me, 'Get your ass over here!' " After he and Hunter enjoyed a good laugh, Caleb said, "Would you mind, ma'am?" and handed the bundle to Tiffany before she could reply. "I've cleaned him up, but I want to check on Shela. Poor thing, she's exhausted and is falling asleep."

He disappeared into the bedroom. Hunter was heading to

the front door, saying, "I reckon we'll be here a bit, so I need to put the horses away. Be back in a minute."

Suddenly she was alone with a baby. Oddly, she didn't panic this time. She walked slowly about the room. There wasn't much space to do so. This house was more what she'd expected the Callahans to be living in, minus logs for walls. It was just one big, open room with parlor furniture in one corner, a dining table in another, and a kitchen in yet another, with just two bedrooms tucked into the last corner. There was no stove for cooking, which was probably why the fireplace was still lit and made the room uncomfortably warm. But it was big enough for a small family, she supposed, and homey looking, with crocheted doilies everywhere, even little round ones under the knickknacks.

She finally sat down on the sofa and pulled back the blanket a little when the baby made a noise. It was so tiny! And funny looking with no hair and a face that was nearly red. His hands were moving, at least the one that was out of the blanket, though his eyes were closed. He was adorable and she started whispering silly things to it. Which is what Hunter caught her doing when he came back in.

"You're going to make a good mother," he whispered so he wouldn't disturb the baby. She grinned even as she blushed at the compliment. She guessed some things did come naturally to women after all.

"I think he's awake," she said. "I'm not really sure, since he won't open his eyes."

Hunter sat down next to her to have a look at the baby, so close that their shoulders touched. He was grinning, too. He liked babies?

Then he added, "Let me check on their little girl. Don't think she's much older than four. She might be lying in her room terrified, after all that screaming."

"What screaming?"

"Birthing can get pretty loud."

He disappeared again, but was back in a moment. "She must have slept through it, or she's back to sleep again now that it's quiet."

Tiffany nodded and stood up. "Can you hold him for a moment? With this jacket and a blanket in my arms, I feel like I'm going to melt, it's so hot in here."

"Of course," he said without hesitation, and took the infant from her.

She quickly shrugged out of the jacket and draped it over the back of the sofa, then held her arms out for the baby again. Hunter didn't immediately move, his eyes on her half-exposed breasts. She'd kept the jacket buttoned, so he hadn't seen what she was wearing until now.

She'd thought she could take off the jacket without blushing, but she was wrong. "I warned you I wasn't dressed to go out." She moved closer to him and took the baby from his arms. Holding the little bundle in such a way that it blocked Hunter's view of her breasts, she sat on the sofa again.

"Sorry, that was just—unexpected," he said, and moved over toward the fireplace. But when he turned to face her again, he actually drew in his breath. His eyes were on her face, so she didn't understand until he said, "Your hair lights up like a flame in the firelight. I'm glad I didn't have to wait until winter to see that."

"It's just—just your imagination."

"Is it?" he said huskily. "What about your eyes gleaming when you look at me? That's not my imagination, Jenny."

"A reflection—"

She was too tongue-tied to go on, with his looking at her like that. Fire was reflected in *his* eyes, and yet—the fire was behind him.

Chapter Forty

Tiffany didn't know what might have happened if the rain hadn't arrived with a vengeance. It sounded like a stampede of animals approaching before it pounded so loudly on the roof she thought for a moment that the house was coming down. The baby even started crying, though she was able to quickly quiet it with soothing assurances.

But she couldn't quiet her own panic, which had nothing to do with the summer storm. She was beginning to like this man, too much. And what she'd just felt with his looking at her so sensually, what *was* that? She was still a little breathless from it.

She needed to get out of here, not the house, but the territory, before her feelings for Hunter got even stronger and she started thinking it might not be so bad to actually marry him. But it was going to be another day or two before she heard back from her mother on her first letter, and another few days after that before she heard on the second letter. Before the end of the week, surely. Then she could jump on the next train out and put all this behind her.

"We'll have to sleep here tonight," Hunter said, looking a little exasperated now.

Where? she wondered. This house was too small to accommodate guests, and this room was still much too hot to sleep in. She'd just as soon ride home in the rain—no, she wouldn't. It had blown in fast and the trails were surely muddy. Maybe it would blow out just as fast and they could still get back to the Triple C tonight.

"Had a feeling that storm was heading our way," Caleb said as he rejoined them. "Least you didn't get caught in it."

Hunter shrugged. "To be expected at this time of the year."

"This is the rainy season?" Tiffany asked.

"Midspring to midsummer, so we're still smack in the middle of it," Hunter replied.

"You're welcome to sleep here for the night," Caleb offered.

He took the baby from Tiffany. She immediately crossed her arms high over her chest.

"It's too warm in here," Hunter declined. "The barn will do."

"Let me get you some blankets then."

It was easier to just turn her back on Hunter when Caleb left the room. Actually, if they were going outside, she ought to put his jacket back on. She did, but she almost took it back off again because the jacket smelled like him, that distinctive scent of leather and pine trees. That's what she smelled whenever she was close to him, and the idea of being close to him all night was giving her shivers all over!

Caleb returned with the blankets, even one pillow. Thanking them for coming, he promised breakfast in the morning. Hunter handed her the blankets, keeping one to flip over their backs. He held it up and spread it wide in front of them. "Stay next to me or you'll get drenched."

There were already puddles in the yard everywhere. Tiffany was stepping in them before she saw them, soaking her shoes. At least she took the precaution to bunch her skirt up to her knees with one hand so the hem wouldn't get wet, but they were both laughing like children by the time they reached the barn. Hunter tossed aside the wet blanket and lit a lantern, revealing that the barn also served as a stable, with four stalls, all of them filled now, one with a dairy cow.

"We'll get up high, away from the smell of the animals," he said, looking up. "There are some bales of hay in the loft. I'll open one to make us a soft bed."

"Two beds."

"We only have two dry blankets left, one to lie down on and one for a cover. So don't be a prude tonight, Red. I don't hanker catching a cold for this good deed."

It wasn't the least bit cold! Of course she was the one wearing his jacket, so she didn't argue about it. The temperature was likely to plummet during the night, rain or no, so he wasn't exaggerating. Each night she'd left her windows open at the ranch, she'd woken in the morning buried under her blankets, the room chilled.

He hooked the blankets around his neck before climbing the ladder, then had her toss him the pillow so she could follow him up. But throwing something wasn't as easy as it looked, at least not over her head. She missed five times getting the pillow to go in Hunter's direction, which had them both laughing before she made it.

Light from the lantern under the loft reached most of the

exposed rafters, but the loft itself was left in dim shadows, though it was certainly enough light to see by. She helped Hunter lay the blanket after he spread the hay. The remaining stacked bales enclosed the makeshift bed like a wraparound headboard.

He removed his gun holster first, then his belt, before he sat down on the blanket to take off his boots and socks and toss them aside. He then stretched out on his back on one side of the blanket. She'd been looking at him. She hadn't meant to, but she was getting a little nervous over this sleeping arrangement. When he opened the top button on his pants, her eyes flared wide.

She gasped. "What are you doing?!"

He chuckled. "Not what you think. Just getting a little more comfortable. I'm not exactly used to sleeping in my clothes, but don't worry, they're staying on."

She swung around to give him her back and hide her embarrassment. Had he deliberately planted that image of his undressing in her mind? It was definitely there, and she was suddenly sweltering from heat again.

She slid out of the jacket, but that didn't seem to help. She finally sat down and took off her shoes. She wasn't about to get under the blanket yet, as hot as she was now.

"You could share that pillow," he suggested idly behind her. "I'm told I have a soft arm you could use as one."

"No."

"My chest is even more comfortable."

"No!"

"Worth a try."

She couldn't see it but she could hear the grin in his tone.

She relented enough to toss him his jacket. "Use that for a pillow."

She caught his sigh as she lay down on her side of the blanket, as far away from him as she could get, barely an inch from the edge of the blanket. There had to be at least a foot or two between them. Then why did it feel as if they were touching?

"Snuggle if you get cold, Jenny. I promise I won't mind."

Humor was in his tone, but he'd turned away from her as he said it, so she didn't bother answering. She did try to sleep, she really did. But she simply couldn't get comfortable. Her nerves were frayed. Her skin felt so taut. Even her breathing wouldn't settle down. She was aware of and embarrassed by every sound she was making simply because he was making none.

It must have been an hour later that he said, "Get some sleep, Red. It will be morning before you know it, hopefully with some sun shining."

"I've never in my life had to share a bed," she whispered back. "I'm not doing it very well, I'm afraid."

"There's nothing to it. Cuddle if it's cold. Stay as far apart as possible if you're too hot. Kick me if I snore. I'll try not to do the same if you snore."

She almost laughed. She did relax a little, so she knew that was his intent and thanked him silently. But ten minutes later she was tossing again. She at least tried to do it more quietly now since she realized she'd been keeping him awake, too.

This was such a bad idea. If she knew how to saddle a horse, she'd ride back to the ranch house herself despite the rain. She had to resign herself to not getting any sleep tonight with this man so close to her.

Then she heard him snoring softly. She opened her eyes.

She was facing him. Big mistake. Having had her eyes closed for so long, that dim lantern light below seemed much too bright now. She could see Hunter too clearly. It was actually the first time she could look at him for any length of time without his knowing it and her feeling embarrassed. She took full advantage of that.

He was on his back again, an arm behind his head. His shirt was mostly unbuttoned. His body was so long! And hard, the muscles so clearly defined. He'd given her leave to snuggle, an excuse to touch him. No, no! She didn't dare. She remembered what had happened when she'd sat on his lap that night in the kitchen. If she got closer to him and started touching him, she had a feeling she might not stop, and then he'd wake and . . . and . . . She shied away from that thought, but it still spread heat all over her and turned her breathing heavy.

And she still couldn't take her eyes off him. She even looked where she'd never dared to before, at the bulge between his legs. She knew what it was. Her mother had been thorough in explaining the intimacy of the marriage bed to her, even describing the male body and the changes it would undergo in that bed. On Hunter it looked a little too big. That had to be uncomfortable for him. Then her eyes flared wide. Did it really just move?

Several minutes later she realized he wasn't snoring anymore. Her gaze shot up to his face to find his eyes open and staring at her.

"You weren't asleep?" she whispered.

He groaned before he admitted, "I faked it, so you could relax. Why aren't you asleep?"

She didn't answer. She didn't know! She was just so pent up with what he made her feel, and he hadn't even been trying to make her feel anything, just the opposite. But it was still there, the heat coursing through her, the high tempo of her pulse, the fraught tension, as if something inside her were going to explode if it didn't get out.

It must have been some yearning in her expression that made him groan again. "It was killing me, but I swore I wouldn't take advantage of you tonight."

"Swore to whom?"

"Myself."

"Unswear."

Did she really say that? She must have because she met him halfway in the middle of that blanket. The explosion did occur, all her inhibitions let go. She was kissing him, aggressively, passionately, and soaking in every nuance of his doing the same. But it wasn't enough. God, she couldn't get close enough to him.

He tore off his shirt, pulled her loose blouse off so quickly she barely noticed. His skin was so hot she was afraid to touch it, but she did anyway, had to, thought she would scream if she couldn't. Something was still building in her. Kissing him was immensely pleasant, deeply satisfying, but it still didn't stop the clamoring inside her for something else.

"How do you make me feel like I'm going to die if I don't taste you? All of you."

Even as he said it he began to do that. It was too much and yet she wouldn't have stopped him for the world. Down her neck and shoulders, to her breasts and beyond. He'd been serious, he intended to kiss and taste every inch of her. He even licked her palms and sucked on every finger! Everything tingled even as she was scalded by the heat of his mouth.

"Help me," she gasped when she could catch a breath. She couldn't catch many she was panting so hard.

"Anything. Just tell me—"

"Now!"

She didn't even know what she was begging for. An end certainly. It was too much pleasure all at once and yet, not enough. That didn't even make sense in her frazzled mind. But he knew, and an ecstatic cry was wrenched from her as he gave her what she needed, him, in the deepest part of her. She held on tightly to him, her arms wrapped around his neck as the throbbing waves were soon flowing through her clear to her curling toes. She could never have imagined something so beautiful and perfectly satisfying to burst from so much frantic yearning.

She continued to marvel at what he'd given her even as she heard him reach his own ecstasy. After a few more moments he moved to her side, pulling her with him. She felt his lips soft on her brow and then a final kiss, so tender, so—loving. She would probably have cried from the emotion it inspired if she weren't still surrounded by such lush languor she couldn't move, couldn't speak. She'd sort it out in the morning, but right then, she finally felt comfortable enough to snuggle against him and fall asleep.

Chapter Forty-One

Tiffany woke first but didn't move an inch. She was facing away from Hunter but could still feel the length of him pressed to her back and curled legs. Her head was on an arm he'd extended. His hand rested on the pillow she was staring at on the far side of the blanket. Neither of them had ended up using that pillow. That might have made her laugh if she wasn't feeling so—so—like tears were imminent.

She was going to have to lie to him, a lot. She'd have to tell him that what had happened was a mistake and that it couldn't happen again. Fiancé, honor of that commitment, she'd break out every excuse, even the truth if she had to. Because what they'd done *was* a mistake.

"Ready to go find a preacher?"

She blinked. That didn't sound like a philanderer talking. He was probably just teasing. Of course he was, that *was* his forte, after all. By the end of the week she would be gone with her mother's permission. Hunter would never have to find out who she really was. He would forget her completely—and why did she feel like crying?

He suddenly leaned up to kiss her bare shoulder, then her cheek. "You're going to be the prettiest bride the territory has ever seen."

Oh, God, he was serious? Tears filled her eyes, he sounded so happy! What had she done, giving herself to this incredible man she couldn't have? He didn't even know who she really was. If he did . . .

She stood up abruptly and started dressing. "I can't talk about this right now. I—I didn't expect this to happen."

"I understand. You're probably feeling bad because of that man you said you'd marry, but don't. He was a fool to let you get away. You have to know by now he wasn't right for you."

Every word he said was making her feel worse. He wanted to marry a woman who didn't exist.

She swiped at her cheeks to remove the wetness before she said, "I want to get back to the ranch before anyone discovers we were out all night."

"Yeah, I've got a lot of explaining to do to my pa, but I don't care, I'm telling him I'm marrying you, not Tiffany Warren."

The tears returned with a vengeance. She continued to swipe at them. He didn't notice since he was dressing.

"So you don't want Caleb's breakfast first?"

"I'm not hungry," she lied, praying her stomach wouldn't betray her. "If you could just saddle me a horse, I can probably find my way back easy enough."

"You know that's not happening, you riding alone. But we can head out now if you want. Come to think of it, I'd rather have your cooking anyway, as good as it's gotten."

She didn't get a chance to reply to that compliment. He suddenly swung her about, right into his arms, and kissed her lazily.

"Good morning, Red." He grinned down at her. "It is, ain't it? Best damn morning ever!"

He let her go with a gentle swat to her rump, shrugged into his shirt without buttoning it yet, and headed down the ladder. She dropped to her knees as soon as he was out of sight and let the tears flow freely. Why did he have to be a cowboy? Why couldn't she have met him in New York? Of course then everything she liked about him wouldn't be there. He wouldn't *be* Hunter, teasing, laughing, charming, carefree, courageous, gallant—Hunter.

It was a short ride back to the ranch. Not actually short, just much faster than last night's ride. He stopped at the front porch so she could go on inside before he put the horses away. She was off the horse before he could dismount to help her. But she didn't make it inside the house before he could detain her.

He did that with the suggestion "How about joining me on a picnic at the lake sometime this week?"

She groaned to herself. But she needed to act naturally, say what he expected to hear. She couldn't tell him yet why she wouldn't marry him. She would start crying again if she tried. Last night had been so beautiful! *Why* did she have to find that out?

So she turned and said, "If you'll fish for dinner." Then, realizing Jennifer wouldn't have said that, she added, "I suppose you expect me to fill a basket with food for it?"

"No, of course not!" He was lying, he'd obviously thought just that. "I can arrange for a basket from town."

It might have been a fun thing to do if she didn't have new

dilemmas to deal with now. But it might also be her last opportunity to talk *him* into doing something about the feud that didn't include violence. Obviously she couldn't do it now. She was simply going to slip away in a few days and be gone without any good-byes, and maybe without having to meet her father at all—which was the only bright spot in all this bleakness.

She nodded and slipped inside, but didn't get far enough away not to hear, "Red, get my pa. Looks like trouble is riding in."

She peeked back outside and looked in the direction Hunter was facing. A small army, still a few minutes away, was riding fast toward the ranch. She raced upstairs to pound on Mary's door. It was still early enough that Zachary might still be in there.

Mary bid her enter. Tiffany said immediately, "Your husband?"

"In the kitchen making me some breakfast. Is something wrong?"

"There's a very large group of men riding this way. Hunter called it trouble."

Mary threw back her covers. "Hand me that hobbler."

Tiffany was surprised, but did as requested. "You can get out of bed?"

"I'm almost mended. Still need support though, and still too soon to attempt the stairs. Go on and let Zach know. And you stay out of the way, gal. Don't want you getting hurt if this turns nasty."

Tiffany rushed back out of the room. *Violent* was what Mary had meant, and Tiffany immediately thought of the miners. Were they coming en masse to slaughter the Callahans? Total massacre, leaving no evidence behind to point the blame on them? And her family would probably end up getting blamed.

She glanced at the rifles hung on the parlor wall as she flew back downstairs. She wished she'd asked Hunter to teach her how to use one. But she'd grab one anyway and use it if she had to. But first she found Zachary, told him what Hunter had said, and followed him back toward the front porch, just more slowly. But the shouting had already started.

"Zachary! The gossip in town says you've got an Easterner under your roof that should be under mine. Get out here and prove me wrong!"

Tiffany froze. *His* roof? Oh, God, don't let that be her father!

But whoever it was, Zachary was amused. He was chuckling before he stepped out on the porch. "So you found out?"

"Then it's true?"

"We offered her more money than you did. She works here now, and this is where she's staying, so don't *even* think of topping my offer. She's needed here. She's not needed at your place."

"You expect me to believe that? You're holding her prisoner!"

Zachary snorted. "That's pure nonsense."

"Prove it!"

"You calling me a liar, Frank?" Zachary asked in an ominous tone.

He was standing at the top of the porch steps. Tiffany saw him draw his gun with that last question. She couldn't see much of the riders spread out in front of the house. There were too many of them. Frank had come to do battle. He'd brought his sons and all his hired hands with him, and he'd come here angry. Now Zachary was angry, too. And Tiffany couldn't move! That her father was out there had her rooted to the spot.

"You *are* a liar, Zach! You had your chance to say she was here when we last spoke. You didn't because—"

"I think what ya'll are going to do is get the hell off my property and right now, before Frank takes the first bullet!"

"You'll be dead before you fire," Frank countered.

A new voice intervened, somewhat angry, too, but not as angry as the voices of the two elder men. "We just need to hear it from her, that she's here by choice."

That was her brother Roy! She was going to kill him. He *knew* what would happen if they saw her. But would it? Frank had no idea of what his own daughter looked like. He'd never bothered to find out. So Roy must be trying to force her hand, so she'd go home with them. He wouldn't think it a betrayal of her confidence, but it was!

Then she heard Hunter say, "He's right. I'll fetch her."

Run! Run out the back, get a horse and ride to town. Now! Now!

She was still frozen in place when Hunter took her arm to escort her outside, saying softly, "Just tell them you're not here against your will, Jenny, and they'll go away."

She looked up at him frantically. "Don't make me go out there, please!"

"It'll be fine, I promise."

She dug in her heels. He still pulled her out on the porch anyway. He didn't understand. He figured he could protect her. He'd be throwing her to the wolves himself in a moment. This could make the feud escalate, if they all didn't kill each other right there. It could be history repeating itself!

"Tiffany?!"

It wasn't Sam or Roy or her father who said her name in utter amazement. It was her brother Carl, and every eye was on her now. It was easy to spot Franklin front and center in the group. The oldest of the riders, he was also a combination of her brothers in looks. Blond and broad shouldered. A handsome man. A furious man. No wonder her mother had left him. He looked as if he were going to kill someone, and that someone might even be her.

But it was Zachary he turned his heated green eyes on, accusing, "You son of a bitch, you knew all along, didn't you?"

"What the hell are you talking about?" Zachary demanded, then turned his gaze on Tiffany. "What's going on here, Miss Fleming?"

Tiffany couldn't have answered if she tried, she was so shocked by the anger and accusations, and then she heard Hunter's voice beside her: "Jenny? Tell them they're making a mistake." Oh, God . . .

"She's my daughter," Frank said furiously. "Stop pretending you didn't know. She looks too much like Rose for you not to!"

"Like hell," Zachary snarled back. "Rarely saw your wife to remember what *she* looked like. Bastard! You sent your girl here to spy on us? Like that ain't obvious. The wedding is off and that dumb truce with it!"

"Damned right it is! Should have known better than to trust a Cal—"

A single shot was fired. A half dozen hands reached for their own guns, but only in surprise. The sound had come from above. The riders were all looking at one of the windows upstairs. Zachary even stepped off the porch to stand next to Frank's horse so he could see above the porch roof himself.

"Now, Mary," he began in a conciliatory tone.

"It's my turn, Zach, so hush up," Mary said. "The men in our two families never did have a lick of sense where the old feud was concerned, but us women knew better. The wedding will go on, just as Rose and I arranged it years ago. And, Frank, since you're going to be depriving us of the best cook in the territory, we'll be coming to your place tomorrow night for dinner. We can get this sorted out then—peacefully, hear?"

Frank didn't agree or refuse, but he did put his shotgun away before he said to his sons, "Get your sister."

All three of her brothers started to dismount, but no one had to get her. Numbly, Tiffany walked to Sam's horse. He extended a hand and she got on it behind him. She didn't look at her father again, didn't care what he thought, didn't care how angry he was with her. Once she got over the shock of being discovered, she intended to tell him exactly why she'd done something this drastic—because of *him*!

The two main antagonists said nothing more to each other. Mary was still leaning out of a window upstairs, a rifle cradled in her arms, though she did wave at Tiffany as they rode off. Hunter was still on the porch. The last thing she saw was his expression. Along with the hurt in his eyes, he looked absolutely furious.

Chapter Forty-Two

THE WARREN RANCH LOOKED much like the Triple C. The house was just as big, but it was made of stone instead of wood. Tiffany knew it couldn't have been like this twenty years ago when Rose had come here as a bride, yet her mother had said Tiffany would feel right at home here. Frank must have built a bigger, more comfortable house just for Rose to give his new wife a home that was more like what she was accustomed to. Tiffany found it hard to believe that her sophisticated mother, who lived a luxurious life in New York City, had ever lived here. Tiffany had lived here, too. But she'd been so young then she had no memories of it. She sure didn't feel as if she was coming home.

Sam had tried to tell her on the ride to the ranch, "It wasn't me," but she hadn't responded. The hurt she felt was like a fist tightening around her heart. What had she expected? For Frank to gather her in his arms in front of all those Callahans and his own hired hands and tell her how much he loved her, missed her, wished Rose had never taken her away? Why not? He was her father! But he hadn't said one word to her!

When they arrived at the house, she hurried inside with Sam close on her heels. She was frantic. If Frank came in and said anything to her right then, all the pain and rage she was feeling would spew out, so she begged her brother, "Show me to my room and quickly. Please!"

The note of panic in her voice must have convinced him to go along with her plan, and he led the way upstairs. She was going to barricade herself until she heard from Rose, then just sneak off as her mother had done. Sam could do the explaining for her. There wouldn't be any dinner with the Callahans. There wouldn't be a confrontation with that heartless man who had sired her. And she certainly wasn't going to marry Hunter even if he could forgive her. Actually, she hoped he wouldn't. It would be so much easier to leave here if she didn't have to see him again.

Sam said it again as he followed her into the room he'd opened for her, "It wasn't me or Roy who told Pa, but Roy wanted to. He argued with me like crazy about it. I finally had to pound on him some to get him to agree to silence. But I think I would have told Pa anyway pretty soon. Guilt was eating me up, keeping silent. It just wasn't right, Tiff. You belong here with us."

"And now everyone's angry," she replied tonelessly.

"Pa sure was this morning," he agreed. "We were riding out to the range when Herb, one of the hands, got up the nerve to tell him what he heard in town over the weekend. You were seen more'n once with the Callahans. Doesn't take much to start townspeople to speculating and gossiping about new folks.

No one guessed it was you, but they did think you were the expected housekeeper lured to the wrong camp. I think Pa was more angry that Zachary didn't tell him about his one-up prank when he had the chance to. But Hunter looked hurt before it sunk in and he got angry, too. Understandable, when you'd been eavesdropping in plain sight over there. Was it worth it?"

Tiffany stiffened, her guilt showing up. She'd made such a mess of things. The Callahans already had a low opinion of her, and now? So very much worse.

But to answer his question, she said, "Yes, actually. They're no different than you are. They're nice people when you get to know them. But because of that old feud, neither side ever got the chance to. Because of it, they feel like you do. Hunter even admitted to me that he couldn't trust himself not to hate me if we married."

"You mean hate the woman he hadn't met yet?"

She blushed. "Yes, but he said no matter what he felt about her—me—the hate would always get in the way because he's lived with it all his life."

Sam mulled that over. "I never liked Hunter because of who he is, but I respected him. He never picked on me or my brothers when he could have. He was so much older and bigger than any of us. John now, that man seems to be angry at the world, and he was the same when he was a boy. He goaded us every chance he got, hoping for a fight. But one of his brothers always stopped him. Most often it was Hunter who did. I think their parents had a standing order going, to leave us alone—because of the truce."

"Some truce," she muttered, "when both sides still revile each other."

Sam actually grinned at that. "It's hard to let go of something that entertaining."

Her eyes narrowed on him. "What did you just say?"

He chuckled. "Don't know about our parents, but the boys on both sides have pulled our fair share of pranks."

"You don't remember the shootings, obviously, or you wouldn't say that."

He shrugged. "I grew up with the truce, Tiff, same as Hunter and his brothers. We never witnessed anyone getting killed. That was before we were born. Now I'll send one of the men back to fetch your belongings today. I assume Mary Callahan will let him do that. She's always been friendly when we'd run into her in town—not like her menfolk."

"I don't want to see anyone, Sam."

"You mean Pa?"

"Yes, I mean your father."

"He's yours, too."

That statement hit her hard. "He's *not* mine! When has he *ever* been mine?!"

"When I held you after you were born," Franklin said softly from the doorway. He nodded Sam out of the room before he continued, "When I fed you before you could hold a spoon. When I rocked you to sleep at night. When I sat by your bed all night long when you caught your first cold, because your mother was terrified you'd choke in your sleep. When I kept you from falling when you took your first wobbly steps. When—"

"Stop it!" Tiffany cried, the pain tightening, choking her. "You expect me to believe things I have no memory of? I have no memories of you! Not one! Where were you when it would

have mattered? Where were you when I needed you? And now it's too late. You want to know why I really pretended to be someone else? Because I'd rather live with your enemies than with a father who cared so little about me that he couldn't visit even once in all these years!"

She turned her back on him so he wouldn't see the tears she couldn't hold back any longer. They streamed down her cheeks, pouring out with the pain of his indifference, the pain of his absence, the pain . . .

"This was your room," he said in that same soft voice. "At the beginning of the year I had it readied for your return, but until then, it still had all your baby things in it. I would come in here every night before bed to tuck you in—in my mind. I knew you weren't here, but I could imagine you were. I missed you so much, Tiffany. It was a double blow, when Rose left me, taking you with her."

It sounded sincere, but she wasn't fooled. My God, did he really think she would believe his lies at this point? Why couldn't he just admit the truth? He might have doted on her as a baby, but he forgot about her as soon as she was gone. She would never believe otherwise because she had the proof, fifteen long years of proof.

She couldn't bear any more of this—of him. Barely getting the words out past the lump in her throat, she said, "I must ask you to leave my room. I'll stay here for the time being, but I would prefer that you and I dispense with the pretense. If you can't respect my wishes, then I will stay in town until I hear from my mother."

"Tiffany—"

"Please! Not another word!"

The door closed. She glanced back to make sure he was gone before she collapsed to her knees where she was. She put a hand over her mouth to silence the sobs. She didn't understand. This shouldn't still hurt so much after all these years. She should be rejoicing instead that she'd finally shown him that she didn't care either. . . .

Chapter Forty-Three

ZACHARY HAD WANTED TO talk. Hunter didn't. His horse was still hitched to the post in front of the house. As soon as the Warrens rode off, he did, too. Zachary yelled at him to stop. In moments Hunter couldn't hear him anymore.

He rode to town in a straight path that avoided the stretch of road where he'd seen the Warrens. At the Blue Ribbon Saloon he ordered a bottle of whiskey. Someone spoke to him at the bar, laughing and drunk. His fist flew. He didn't even know whom he'd hit, didn't care whom he'd have to apologize to later. He just grabbed the bottle and left. But he hoped he'd see a few of the miners on the street. He'd be happy to take out what he was feeling on them. He didn't get lucky, didn't spot a single one.

He left Nashart and rode all day, he couldn't even remember where. By noon half the bottle was empty. It hadn't done what he wanted. Her image stayed with him, riding off with her family, expressionless, not one bit of guilt or remorse on her face for what she'd done. He finished the rest of the bottle and continued to ride aimlessly.

The second half of the bottle worked, just not nearly long enough. But it opened a flood of other memories. Jenny roping a cow and laughing at herself over how long it took her. Jenny making beds, washing dishes, cooking for them. It was a wonder she hadn't poisoned their food. Jenny trying to put out a fire even when she didn't know how—or would the truth come out now, that she had started it?

Was this her idea of fun, snooping on his family? Had she been laughing at them all along for believing her housekeeper story? And what an idiot he was, telling her how he felt about his fiancée—her! He wouldn't put anything past that woman who'd tricked him into . . . There was no point in denying it. Her deception was killing him because he was in love with her. And it had happened so fast! He'd seen it coming and had tried to stop it. But seeing her with Caleb's newborn son had clinched it. He was in love with a woman who didn't exist!

He was sober again before he let Patches find their way home. The sun was setting. My God, he'd never see a sunset again without thinking of her and her enjoyment of them. That he could believe, but nothing else.

He entered through the kitchen. A mistake. He was going to have to avoid that room like the plague when he could see her everywhere in it. Andrew was the only one there now. He was reading Jenny's cookbook as he stirred whatever was in the pot on the stove. So he was going to take over her job?

Maximilian rushed into the room at the sound of the door's opening, then disappeared back down the hall when he saw it wasn't his mistress coming home. Hunter wanted to laugh every time he saw that pig following Jenny about. She hadn't taken it with her. No, course she wouldn't, it had all been an act, especially her affection for a pig

Warily, probably because of Hunter's expression, Andrew whispered, "I didn't know—"

"Shut up, kid" was all Hunter said as he passed through the kitchen.

He thought he could get away with slipping up to his room unnoticed and locking the door. But his parents were in the parlor, both of them. Both were staring at him the moment he came into view by the stairs.

He was surprised enough to stop. "How'd you get down here, Ma?"

"I carried her down," Zachary grumbled. "We've been waiting here all day for you! She refused to go back upstairs, afraid you'd try to sneak in without us noticing."

"I tried," Hunter admitted with a shrug. "I don't want to talk."

"Sit down," Mary said softly.

It was one thing to disobey Zachary. Hunter did that often enough, two males butting heads. But it was quite another thing not to comply with his mother's dictates. He sat down, but he immediately changed seats to sit next to his mother on the sofa so the poker table wouldn't be in his view. More damn memories of fun and laughter with Jenny that just made him even angrier now. Could she really have faked it all? He'd even thought that night that he'd never go to town on a Saturday night again if he could spend them all with her instead. What a fool he'd been!

"Don't pretend you're not going to be a happy groom now," Zachary began. "You were all over that gal from the moment she got here."

"All over Jenny, yeah," Hunter said coldly. "But that's not who rode off from here today."

"So what if she fooled us," Zachary replied. "We got to see what she's really like, and let me tell you, I'm damned glad she's not the snooty, high-muck-a-muck society gal I was expecting."

"Isn't she?" Hunter asked angrily. "You haven't figured out yet that she was *acting* a part? What you saw and heard wasn't the real girl, just a role she was playing."

The pig clip-clopped down the hall at the sound of their voices, apparently still hoping to find his mistress. Max stopped there at the bottom of the stairs staring at them, almost accusingly, as if he were blaming them for her absence. Zachary threw one of Mary's small, embroidered pillows at it, making it squeal and trot off upstairs.

"That damn pig," Zachary grumbled. "You need to take it to her tomorrow, Hunter."

"Why? She'll just send it to their kitchen for dinner. Do you really think she befriended a pig of all animals? It was just another part of her deception. In fact, I don't doubt she was meticulously deliberate in doing the exact opposite of what she'd really do, just so we wouldn't make the connection between Jennifer Fleming and Tiffany Warren."

"What connection?" Zachary demanded gruffly. "Them both arriving from the East at the same time? Them both having that pretty red hair? We would have just thought it was coincidence."

"Yeah—unless she behaved the way she usually behaves, then we would have guessed pretty damn quickly. It hasn't sunk in yet, Pa? She *is* that cold, snooty Easterner you were expecting her to be."

"Not exactly," Mary disagreed. "Keep in mind, your broth-

ers approached her, she didn't approach them. And for whatever reason she went along with it, she came to us expecting to
be just a housekeeper, which isn't a strenuous job in the least,
but we put her to work instead, real work. If she's the spoiled,
uppity rich gal you're both now thinking she is, she would have
quit right away. Society ladies don't get their hands dirty. They
always have a personal maid close to hand, too."

Hunter snorted. "Now you mention it, she's visited a
woman at the hotel in town. Said she was an acquaintance she
met on the train, but it's probably her maid. The real Tiffany
Warren wouldn't have traveled this far alone, would she?"

"No, she wouldn't," Mary agreed, but reminded him, "We
don't know why she did this yet."

"To spy for her pa, of course," Zachary reasserted his earlier
guess.

"To what purpose?" Mary interrupted. "We have nothing to hide. If anything, this smacks more of a prank and a
whopper, to top any her brothers ever pulled. The Warren boys
might even have talked her into it, but her father certainly
wouldn't have. Yet, I don't really believe that, either. It's just far
more likely than spying."

"Does it matter why?" Hunter said. "The fact remains, she's
a liar and a damn good one. We'll never be able to believe a
word she says now."

Mary patted his hand. "I know you're angry. You have every
right to be. You can even direct some of it at me because I
could see Rose in her, not clearly, but enough to make me wonder. Yet I said nothing."

"Why the hell not?" Zachary asked.

"Because you stubborn jackasses would have gotten all up
in arms about it," Mary replied, staring at her husband point-

edly. "And because I figured she had her reasons. And also because I sensed kindness in her. She'd have to be the best actress in the world to fake that."

Hunter stood up to leave. His head was starting to ache from all the possibilities, none of them good. "I'm going to bed."

"You're not going to eat first? Your pa talked that boy into taking over Jenny's, that is, Tiffany's job."

"I've got a bottle of rotgut in me; food doesn't have a chance of staying down tonight."

Mary nodded, promising, "This will look better in the morning, Hunter. And tomorrow night—"

"I'm not going with you."

"Of course you will," Mary said. "You'll probably even ride over sooner because you won't be able to stand it, not knowing what her motives were."

Hunter nodded for his mother's sake, but he didn't agree. He went upstairs and there was the pig again, standing outside Jenny's door, waiting, hoping she'd open it, probably feeling as bereft as he was. Without even thinking about why he did it, Hunter picked Max up and carried him to his room for the night.

Chapter Forty-Four

TIFFANY WAS ENJOYING A happy reunion with her brothers at least. That painful knot in her chest eased throughout the day as one by one her brothers visited her in her room, expressing their happiness at seeing her again. Sam must have told Carl and Roy her reasons for staying with the Callahans, the ones she'd told him anyway, because they didn't mention what she'd done, not once.

Carl was adorable. He was so bashful. He'd slicked back his blond hair to show her he was a man now, though he was only sixteen. But he'd always been shy, so it would probably take a few days for him to relax around her.

She'd expected Roy to be a little more vocal, but dreamer that he was, maybe he understood better than anyone else why she had done something so drastic. He slipped her a poem before he left her, his way of apologizing for being so angry at her in town that day.

By early afternoon one of the Warrens' hired hands had delivered her trunk of clothes. At Tiffany's request, Sam had gone to town and brought Anna to the Warren Ranch.

"About time," Anna had started to crow in an I-told-you-so tone until she noticed Tiffany's red eyes. Then she amended, "So it's not your choice to be here then?"

Tiffany had shaken her head. "And meeting my father was as horrible as I knew it would be. But I'm sure I'll only have to endure it for another few days."

"What's happening in a few days?"

"I'm going to get a reprieve and go home where I belong. Will you come with me, or do you prefer working with hammers and saws now?"

"I enjoyed it for a few days, but that's how quickly we ran out of work to do, so I was getting bored. This town is still too small for a full-time furniture maker, though it's something I could pitch in on occasionally if *you* were sticking around. But Mr. Martin didn't really need a helper, he was just lonely, spending every day in his shop by himself."

There was one other surprise. When Sam had gone to town to fetch Anna, he'd run into the postmaster, who told him a package for Tiffany had arrived on the train that morning. It was her mother's response to her first letter. Her mother's having addressed it to Tiffany at the Warren Ranch was indicative of how angry Rose was. Tiffany didn't think her mother had intended to expose her charade because in all likelihood Frank would merely have thought it was something they'd had shipped early to make sure it would be there when Tiffany arrived.

She was delighted to see it was the cookbooks she'd asked for, French, Italian, even New York favorites, thick volumes all three of them. But no letter was included with them. Tiffany was certain the letter had been addressed to Jennifer Fleming at the Triple C Ranch. How ingenious of her mother. She wanted to make sure Tiffany contacted at least one of her brothers to get the cookbooks. She'd probably been hoping they would make her see how foolish she was being. But Tiffany wasn't eager to read that first letter. Even on paper, Rose was quite capable of shouting. It was the next letter from her mother that she was anxiously awaiting because that was the one that would rescue her.

She was impatient to join her brothers for dinner and tried to rush Anna in preparing her, but then she laughed at herself. Had she gotten a little too used to how quickly this went without a maid dressing her and styling her hair? She took a deep breath and kept her mouth shut because the result would be worth it. Looking at her reflection in the mirror before she left the room, she was right. She looked like Tiffany again, the real Tiffany.

She was laughing with her brothers when Franklin walked in to join them. The boys continued to talk excitedly, telling her funny stories and more about what they'd done in the last years since she'd seen them. No one noticed that she'd stopped participating in the conversation. She knew then it had been a mistake to come down for dinner. She'd just been unable to resist her brothers' company.

"What do you think, Tiff?" Roy asked her. "Tiff?"

He finally got her attention, though she'd missed the original question. "Pardon? What did you say?"

"How about going for a swim in the lake sometime this week?"

That god-awful lake! It was the very reason she was here,

contention over water rights. She was bitter enough to say, "You don't think we'll get shot at?"

That definitely put a damper on the merry atmosphere at the dinner table. All three boys looked contrite, when it wasn't even their fault. It was Franklin's fault though, and he didn't look the least bit apologetic for his part in that feud. A little exasperated maybe over her remark. It was obvious now why Rose had married him. Blond, eyes as green as Tiffany's, apparently quiet in demeanor as opposed to tempestuous the way Rose was, and still incredibly handsome, even in his early forties.

"Can you at least give us one evening to enjoy your company without dredging up the past?" Frank asked.

She wished she could, she really did, but not with *him* sitting at the table. She almost asked him to leave. Almost. But her brothers would no doubt leap to his defense and be upset with her, so she didn't.

Instead, she reminded him, "It's the only reason I'm here. The past. A feud that none of you have had sense enough to end. I've heard the Callahans' side of it. I'd like to hear your side now."

"We can discuss that if we must." Frank even offered a slight smile. "Not exactly good for the digestion though. Can it wait until after we eat?"

Levity when his presence infuriated her? But a servant came in with a big bowl of salad that the girl started serving them as the first course. At least Frank had a decent cook, and many servants for that matter. Most of them appeared to be Indian or of Indian descent. After two servants who had looked more Indian than white had filled Tiffany's tub today, her *own* tub, she'd asked Sam about them. He'd explained that twenty years ago it hadn't been uncommon for Indians to trade their women to the first trappers in the area. The women couldn't go back to their tribes after that, and by the time the Indian wars began, they already had families of their own and weren't involved in the fighting. But because many white men had died in those wars, the prejudice against the Indians intensified, even after the tribes were driven out of the territory. The offspring of those interracial unions had had trouble finding work after the wars. Frank, apparently, didn't share that prejudice, but then he'd been trading with the tribes long before the animosity had started. Which was probably why the Warren Ranch had been spared during the hostilities.

Tiffany managed to hold her tongue for the meal. The main course arrived, a chicken casserole smothered in freshly churned cheese. It looked and smelled delicious and made her wonder what Hunter was eating tonight. She hoped it wasn't Jakes's cooking.

The boys continued talking and laughing. She smiled tepidly when they tried to include her. Frank watched her quietly. Every time she caught him at it, that pain in her chest got worse. It was a wonder she could get any food down, even the cherry cobbler that arrived for dessert. All it did was remind her that she hadn't yet made dessert for the Callahans, or that cake she'd promised the hired hands after they'd cleaned the house.

But when the last fork was set down, she was done waiting. Her brothers realized that. Sam nodded them out of the room to give her some privacy with her father. She hadn't counted on being alone with him and almost railed at him again, but there was no point. He'd had his chance this morning to mend their breach, but all he'd spoken of was "thinking" about her. A fat lot of good his *thoughts* had done her growing up.

So she stayed focused on her goal and said, "I want your feud to end without a marriage because I can't live here. I've led a genteel life. Not once, ever, was it marred by violence until I came here, where I've had guns pointed at me, seen men die in front of me, seen men fighting on the street. I'm going home just as soon as Mama agrees that she never should have sent me here. So before the Callahans come over tomorrow, I want to know why I had to get tangled up in this."

"I'm sorry you had to witness—"

"Please," she cut him off coldly. "Sam's already mentioned it was probably just bad luck. Whether that's so or not, the fact remains that a marriage isn't going to end what's gone on for three generations. It would stand no chance of succeeding if the only reason for it is to end this feud."

"I didn't think that would be the only reason," Frank said. "I was positive that you would like Hunter. You don't?"

She felt like groaning, she was so tired of hearing that question. "I do, but he's spent his whole life hating Warrens. That will always get in the way. So explain it to me. Why did he have to grow up hating you?"

"I suppose the Callahans blamed us when they told you about it?"

"I know your feud didn't start here, that it began with a practical joke on Elijah Callahan that went seriously wrong. And your mother, Mariah, shot him the day they were to marry." Tiffany recounted the full story Mary Callahan had told her.

Her father nodded. "She shot him because he cheated on

her, plain and simple. That's why she was so furious she married someone else so soon. My father, Richard, even suspected she still loved Elijah, but he still wanted her enough to marry her. However, he ended up hating the Callahans because of it. My God, she had a powerful hate."

"And infected you all with it?"

He nodded. "I think some of it was self-directed though, because she knew she was incapable of forgiving the man she loved. She loved him with all her heart. That's why she never let it go. . . ."

So her family wasn't entirely to blame? Had Mary purposely left out the part about Elijah's actually cheating on Mariah, or had Elijah been too ashamed to tell his family about his indiscretion? But that didn't explain why the feud moved to Montana.

"Elijah tried to get away from her," Tiffany said. "Moved his family across the whole continent. Why did she follow him here?"

"My mother was a strong, courageous, passionate woman who withstood a lot of heartache and loss in a short time. My father and two brothers died within five years, and she shouldered all the responsibility for our ranch while I was young. After so many deaths in our family, her obsession with Elijah intensified. She was furious when she learned he was moving away from Florida. I didn't know it at the time, but she hired a man to follow him and find out where he settled. Then she started complaining about Florida and suggested we move West to Montana. I was barely eighteen. I didn't suspect she was playing me, to get me to agree to pull up stakes and move up here, though it wasn't actually a bad idea."

"To follow them?"

"No, to leave Florida," Frank said. "There were too many ranches fighting over too little land and far too much rustling. Those were her excuses, which were accurate, but easier than telling me the truth, which I would never have agreed with. I was as surprised as the Callahans were to find us settling on land so close to theirs."

"You didn't confront her about it?"

"Of course I did. All she said was she needed resolution. Peace. I should have known her definition of peace wasn't the same as mine. Her peace meant killing him. She'd said it enough times over the years, that she should have killed him that fateful night before they were to marry."

"When did they shoot each other?"

"It was almost a year after we got here. Zachary came over one morning, demanding to be told where his father was. I didn't know until then that my mother was missing, too. It took us the whole day, but we finally found their trail. They were in an old trapper's cabin. They were lying in each others arms. Their weapons, both of which had been fired, were still in hand or close to it. Theirs were the only fresh tracks up there. We don't know exactly what happened. Maybe they hoped to find happiness together in the next life because they sure couldn't find it together in this one. I can only hope they were able to forgive each other in the end."

"So all you are fighting over now is the water?"

"Not exactly. The Callahans blamed my mother for everything, shooting Elijah instead of marrying him, following him here, killing him in the end. The water is just a side issue. I was only eighteen when we came here, Zach was a few years older. He and I couldn't get near each other without accusations flying. I was weaned on hate, Tiffany, we both were. It was hard to let that go even after our parents were gone."

"Do you still hate them?"

"More than ever."

"But why?"

"Because they drove your mother away."

Chapter Forty-Five

TIFFANY WAS SUDDENLY REELING. Her father had just given *her* a reason to hate the Callahans. How could she talk their families into a truce with *that* now on the table?

But a few moments later, she frowned. The feud couldn't be the reason her mother had left. That was something Rose could easily have admitted when Tiffany had asked her, but she hadn't—unless she'd kept it from Tiffany because she was afraid her daughter would use the same excuse not to marry Hunter.

But before Tiffany took up the gauntlet, she demanded, "Did she actually tell you that?"

"No, she wouldn't lay that guilt on me. She came up with so many other excuses instead. Each time I shot one down, she'd drop another on me. She said she hated it here, yet she'd never been happier than when she was designing this house. She said she missed her mother too much, yet we visited her every year and the old gal even came here once. She said her mother finally convinced her she'd made a mistake. She said she'd been told another child would kill her after having too many too quickly. She used that one to move out of my bed-room, yet she couldn't keep her hands off me. She even used *that* excuse after she was gone, for why she left. It was the only one I believed for a while. So many excuses—and anger, when I tried to talk her into coming back."

Tiffany shook her head at him. "So you now blame the Callahans for something you're not even sure they should be blamed for?"

"Nothing else makes sense. Fifteen years ago they nearly killed me. It was shortly after I took that bullet that Rose snuck off with you. I think she just realized she couldn't bear to live through something like that again."

"Or she was kind enough not to tell you she'd stopped lov-ing you."

"Don't say that, Tiffany. Please don't."

She sucked in her breath. He looked as if she'd just devas-tated him. She should be pleased, not feel that knot swell in her throat again for hurting him. She leapt to her feet and headed for the door before he noticed the tears gathering in her eyes. She only paused for a moment.

Without looking at him again she said, "I don't know why she left any more than you do. But I know why I want to leave. I'm going to suggest tomorrow that your truce with the Calla-hans become permanent immediately, that both families share the water from now on. Will you agree to it?"

"I won't agree to share it without establishing a blood tie between our families that will secure access to the water for future generations. Your mother had the right idea. I want my sons and grandsons to be able to raise cattle on this land we love well into the future."

Her cheeks already wet with tears of frustration, she ran

out of the dining room. She had to find somewhere private to let the pain out before she rejoined her brothers. She slipped into an empty room. She hoped it was empty. She shouldn't have asked Franklin that question when she already knew the answer. Because like everyone else, he expected her to marry Hunter. *How* was that going to end anyone's hatred? How could it not just make everything worse?

She'd only just managed to wipe the blurriness from her eyes and dry her cheeks when Franklin said behind her, "The Callahans are going to be here tomorrow. I need to know why you pretended to be their housekeeper before they get here." His tone was firm now.

"I'll give them my reasons."

"Letting them in my house is going to be difficult enough, Tiffany. I won't be dealt any more surprises. Why?"

"I wanted to see for myself what they're really like because I didn't think they'd behave normally with me due to the feud."

"That's all?"

She could have left it at that, but didn't. "No. Mainly I didn't want to meet you. I didn't think you'd mind, since you never wanted to meet me either."

"If I didn't think you'd tell Rose, I'd give you the whole of it," he said in frustration. "But she can't know."

"Know what?"

He didn't answer. As she'd thought. He just wouldn't own up to the truth, that he hadn't cared about her. "I gave you your answer, now leave me alone."

She didn't hear him leave. She made a point of ignoring him by gazing around the room. It was a study, lightly furnished in oak. A small lamp had been lit on the desk that held many picture frames. Pictures of what? She was curious enough to pick one up, but sucked in her breath when she saw it was a framed letter in a childish scrawl—a letter from her. She picked up another. Another of her letters to the father she'd loved, and missed. He'd framed them all and kept them in his office all these years? He must recently have taken them out of some musty, old box to impress her. With what? The idea that he cared, when it was so obvious that he didn't?

The tears were starting again. Oh, God, she couldn't cry now, not when she wasn't sure he'd left and was afraid to look! She concentrated fiercely on the room's decor to push back the emotion. Burgundy velvet drapes, her mother's favorite color. Had Rose picked them out? Were they that old? A few book-cases, a liquor cabinet, paintings of Western scenes on the wall, except for one that stood out oddly. Her eyes went back to it and slowly widened. It was a wintery city scene of a girl skat-ing on a frozen pond in a park. It was a painting of her. Her mother had never mentioned having it commissioned. But how else would Frank have it unless Rose had sent it to him?

"He was the best artist in New York," Franklin said quietly, having followed her gaze. "I found him my last trip there. It took him all winter to finish it. You didn't skate much that year."

"You were in New York?" she asked in a small voice. "Why didn't you tell me this earlier when I accused you of never visiting?"

"I shouldn't be telling you now, but this misconception you seem to be under can't continue. Your mother made me prom-ise never to return to New York again. I broke that promise, but I couldn't let her know that, or she would have stopped writing to me. So I couldn't even let you know, couldn't take the chance that you might mention it to her, even inadvertently. I lived for her letters, Tiffany. They were all I had left of her. Can you keep this secret for me?"

"You still love her?"

"Of course I do, I always will. Just as I love you. Yet I've been afraid to even hug you, you've been so angry since you got here. All these years, I never imagined you would think I didn't care, Tiffany. I poured out my love in my letters. You didn't believe me?"

"I stopped reading your letters. It hurt too much that you never came to visit when the boys did."

"But I did, every trip, and even a few other times. I just couldn't get close to your house. There was a man watching it, a guard your mother no doubt hired to keep me from approaching. So damned unfair of her to do that. But I yearned for the sight of you both, so I disguised myself, and once I did that, I realized I *could* see you, talk to you—I just couldn't tell you who I was. You don't remember Charlie?"

She had to sit down. Old memories flooded her mind of that friendly, old gentleman in the park she and her friend Margery frequented, never in the summer, only briefly in the winter—whenever her brothers would visit. Would he even have introduced himself if he hadn't had to rescue her when she was a child? It had been the first year she'd tried to ice-skate at the park. Rose was supposed to be there for it and had asked her to wait until she could be, but Margery wasn't waiting, so Tiffany couldn't bear to either.

It had been a disaster. Her mother was going to teach her how to skate. Without that instruction she'd promptly fallen and sprained her ankle. Charlie had seen the accident and rushed onto the ice to carry her to her servants. He'd seemed more upset than she was over that sprain. He'd asked after her injury the next time he saw her in the park with Margery and told them an amusing story about an injury of his own. There were many funny stories over the years. When Tiffany was older, she was sure none of them were real. Charlie just liked to make people laugh, but that's how he was, a kind, caring man, one who wouldn't hesitate to help someone in need—the kind of man she'd wished her father was. . . .

She looked up at him now, saw the tears in his own eyes, and burst into sobs as she flew into his open arms. "Oh, God, Papa, I wish you had told me! It was so painful, thinking you didn't care!"

"I'm so sorry, Tiffany," he said, hugging her tightly. "I wanted to tell you—I *would* have, if I'd known what you thought." Then: "Do you think I liked dyeing my hair gray for those trips and having to endure the wisecracks from the hired hands about it when we got back? They called me a grayhorn! Do you even know how insulting that is?"

She did know because years ago her brothers had explained to her what a greenhorn was. But she knew her father was just trying to introduce a little levity to ease her remorse for the horrible way she'd treated him since she'd got there. It worked. He could still make her laugh!

Chapter Forty-Six

TIFFANY HAD EXACTLY ONE evening gown, which she had Anna dress her in for what was likely to be an uncomfortable dinner. She hadn't even unpacked it at the Callahans since she couldn't wear it there. Even if there had been an occasion for it, it was far too expensive for Jennifer to afford. It was one of her older gowns, which is why it had ended up in her accessories trunk. Pale blue silk with pearl edging, silk shoes to match. Finally she could wear her jewelry again. Her fingers, wrists, neck, ears, even the pins in her elegant coiffure, sparkled with sapphires. The Callahans might think they knew her already, but they didn't. Tonight there would be no trace left of Jennifer Fleming.

She joined her brothers in the parlor before their guests arrived. Roy laughed when he saw her radiance. "Did you cast some spell to whisk us to New York? You know you don't have to dress up fancy here, don't you?"

"I know. My maid calls it 'armed for battle.'"

"Well, least Ma ain't here to make us wear them fancy duds,

too," Sam said. "That was pure hell, Tiff, having to dress up like that for *every* dinner in the city."

"You're expecting a battle?" Carl asked, picking up on that single word.

"Considering what I'm going to ask the Callahans to agree to, yes."

They already knew what she intended to do tonight. They knew, too, that her issue with their father had been resolved last night. Her brothers actually shouldered some guilt over her misconception, since they had kept it secret, that Frank had always traveled with them to the city. It all came out at breakfast that morning, which had been a wonderful family experience that could only have been more perfect if Rose had been there, too. Of course, that was never going to happen.

Frank walked in and stopped short when he saw her. "My God, you look like her done up like that."

Tiffany grinned. "Did Mama make you suffer formal dinners every night?"

"No, just a few times a week. She actually loved being more relaxed here. But you should have warned us you expected tonight to be formal."

"Not at all. If we all turned out elegant, then the Callahans would be embarrassed by it. This"—she waved a hand at her gown—"is merely the easiest way for me to show them that I'm not really the woman who was living in their house—in case they're actually thinking I'm anything like her."

Riders were suddenly heard arriving out front. Tiffany's nervousness arrived with them. Would Hunter even bother to come? Probably not, considering how angry he'd looked the last time she saw him. But it was only Zachary she needed to talk to tonight. And she wasn't alone. Her family was here. She didn't *have* to be nervous. She stood between Sam and Roy while their father went to let in—the enemy.

"Jesus, Frank, what's this shiny stuff on your floor?" Tiffany heard Zachary ask out in the hall.

"Marble."

"Your wife's doing, huh? It ain't going to crack if we walk on it, is it?"

Neighbors for more than twenty years and the Callahans had never stepped foot in this house before, not even once? But then, Frank probably hadn't been in theirs either. Such a *stupid* feud.

Zachary entered the parlor carrying his wife. The first thing Mary said when she saw Tiffany's elegant attire was "I take it you didn't cook dinner?"

Cole came in next with Mary's crutches in hand, but stopped cold when he saw Tiffany. John pushed him out of the way, then he, too, didn't move another inch.

Seeing the two brothers released some of Tiffany's tension—because Hunter wasn't with them. But maybe she shouldn't have worn the evening gown, after all. She hadn't meant to surprise them this much, merely to stress, without putting it into words, that she wasn't meant to live on a ranch in Montana.

Politely she said to Mary, "Welcome to the Warren Ranch. My father already has an excellent cook."

"That Buffalo kid is going to cook for us now," Zachary said as he set Mary down in the nearest chair.

"My mother sent me some cookbooks. Perhaps Andrew can make use of them."

"Right kind of you," Mary said.

"Not at all. And please, let me take a moment to apologize for—"

She stopped when she heard the pig squealing out front. They'd brought the piglet to her? What a generous gesture, after what she'd done! Smiling brilliantly, she excused herself and rushed out of the room. She found Maximilian tied to a rail on the porch and picked him up immediately to cuddle him, giving no thought to her attire.

"So Red's still here? She's not completely gone?"

She sucked in her breath at the sound of that deep voice and turned abruptly, smack into Hunter's kiss. Well, he helped it happen, his hand behind her neck pulling her head closer for it. She didn't stop him, too aware that this might well be her last taste of him. It made the kiss bittersweet!

Then Max squirmed when Hunter got a little too close. She leaned back, flustered. That shouldn't have happened, she shouldn't have *let* it happen. She was supposed to make an impression tonight, that Jenny—Red, whatever he'd called her—*was* gone. She wasn't real. If he expected to find her here, he was wrong!

"Thank you for bringing Max to me," she said politely.

"Had to. With you gone, he thought he could take over my room."

"Really?"

"I let him last night, but one night's enough. For some reason he thought he could sleep in my bed, too. Were you letting him do that?"

"I didn't mind." She rubbed Max behind one ear. "I've never had a pet before—well, I don't count the kitten I brought home once, since it ran off before I had a chance to get used to it. Can you untie him for me, please, so I can bring him inside?" She wasn't going to let the pig down yet, afraid that Hunter would try to get close again if she did.

He untied the pig. "Your pa won't mind him in the house?"

"No, he's not the uncaring man I was trying to avoid."

Hunter gave her a sharp look. "Is *that* why you did it?"

"Yes, no—mostly. I'll explain to you and your parents at dinner. You—you aren't coming inside?"

When he didn't say anything immediately, her heart skipped a beat. She didn't want him to leave. She had to admit to herself she felt happy to see him. He looked so handsome tonight in a clean, white, pressed shirt and dark trousers, and clean black boots. He leaned back against the wall next to the door, raising one knee and resting the sole of his boot on the wall. She was so used to that posture of his. She often saw it in her mind—when she wasn't picturing him wrapped in a towel or buck naked making love to her! She closed her eyes briefly to banish those images.

"Still thinking about it," he answered. "Figured I had time to make up my mind, that you'd be out back watching the sunset. Too bad this house faces east. You're going to miss sitting on a porch watching them."

She almost grinned but caught herself in time. It was too easy to fall back into the relaxed familiarity she'd had with him. That hadn't been her! But Jennifer had been from the East, too. And Jennifer *should* have stuck to her guns and given him proper at every encounter, instead of allowing him to give her nicknames and flirt with her and kiss her and . . .

She mustered a prim tone. "I won't miss the sunsets because there is a small porch out back. Papa said it was my mother's idea, to build it, that she loves the sunsets, too, and they spent every evening on it before dinner."

"Rumor was he beat her and that's why she left. Was that true?"

"Of course not!" she said sharply in her father's defense.

"Then why'd she leave him?"

"I was hoping he could tell me. He actually blamed your family for it—well, the feud. One more reason for him to hate Callahans."

"That would be—incredibly unfortunate if it's so." Hunter's powder-blue eyes were gazing at her intently.

"Why?"

"Because that's a dumb reason for a woman to abandon her husband *and* sons. Because you and I could have grown up together if she hadn't run off. Because we'd be married by now."

How dare he assume such a thing! Indignantly she said, "Do *not* presume that would have happened if I had grown up here. If I had, it's much more likely that I would have fallen in love with your brother Cole, since he's more my age."

She marched back into the house before he could reply to *that*.

Chapter Forty-Seven

Tiffany was sure Hunter had left after all, but he came inside a few minutes after they'd adjourned to the dining room. Hearing the sound of boots on the polished wood floor, she peeked over her shoulder and saw him standing behind her in the doorway. He was just in time to hear her apology.

"I assure you I didn't plan to impersonate a housekeeper," she was saying to Zachary and Mary, who were sitting next to each other. "When your sons assumed I was Miss Fleming and offered me the job, I realized it was an opportunity to get to know your family without the feud modifying your behavior in my presence."

"But your pa didn't even know," Zachary said, then turned to Frank. "Or did you?"

"No, she wasn't ready to meet me yet. But that's a private matter—"

"It's all right, Papa. They have a right to know. The fact is that I didn't know my father. I had no memory of him. My brothers would visit me in New York, but Frank never did."

"Now that ain't so," Zachary disagreed. "We know where he went when he took off with his boys. Came home every time with gray hair. We figured Rose was scaring the bejesus outta him," Zachary ended with a snicker.

"It was a damn disguise," Frank mumbled.

"So you *did* beat her while she was here? Threatened to shoot you if she ever saw you again, eh? Figured as much."

"Don't be an ass," Frank retorted.

Zachary didn't take offense. He was chuckling to himself over getting Frank's goat. Tiffany gave both of them pointed looks so she could get on with her apology.

She addressed the Callahans again. "Mama made me promise to come here, but I didn't promise to stay with my father. You gave me the means to avoid him, for which I was grateful at the time. I was certain he didn't care about me—and because I thought that, I had convinced myself that I didn't care about him either. I was wrong on both counts."

"So all patched up?" Mary said with a smile.

Tiffany smiled back. "Indeed."

"Apology accepted, gal," Zachary added gruffly. "No harm was done—"

Hunter cut in, "Depends on how you define *harm*."

No one wanted to address that remark, least of all Tiffany. They assumed he was referring to how angry he was over the deception, but she was afraid he was talking about compromising her. If he got all noble and told her father about it . . .

Standing behind Tiffany, he dropped a letter from her mother on her plate now before he took the seat across from her. She stared at it, tried to resist opening it, pretty much knew what it would say. She couldn't resist.

Have you taken leave of your senses? were the first words on several pages. *Do you realize how hurt your father is going to be if he finds out you'd rather stay in the enemy camp than with him?!*

Tiffany read no further and quickly stuffed the pages back in the envelope. "Bad news?" Hunter asked, watching her.

She glanced across at him. "No—it's just my mother has a bit of a temper."

"A bit?" Franklin said, and even grinned slightly.

"More like a volcano in britches," Zachary said, actually agreeing with Franklin.

Tiffany blinked at the oldest Callahan. "My mother wore britches here?"

Her father answered, "She did occasionally when she was in a hurry to go riding."

"She was wearing them when she came to my place to tell me I was going to give my boy to you in marriage," Zachary added. "Said she'd shoot me, too, if I didn't honor a truce till then."

"I wasn't aware she threatened you," Franklin said to Zachary.

"He's exaggerating," Mary put in. "Well, she did say that, but it was after he'd already agreed to the match."

"That was *your* doing," Zachary reminded his wife.

"It was a good idea," Mary insisted.

"But she must not have thought you'd honor it, or she wouldn't have left," Franklin said coldly.

"Now hold on," Zachary growled. "You ain't putting the blame for *that* on us!"

Tiffany intervened with marked disapproval, even tapping her fork against her empty wineglass in case someone didn't hear her. "*If* you please, a civil tone will be maintained at any table I sit at. And my father was mistaken. It is embarrassing to admit it, but we don't actually know why my mother left Montana." Then she abruptly changed the subject, telling Hunter, "There will likely be another letter from her in the next day or two delivered to your ranch. Papa already telegraphed her to let her know I'm with him now, but her second letter will have already been dispatched."

Tiffany was still eager for that second letter and Rose's permission to leave. As much as she'd like to spend more time with her father and brothers now, her feelings for Hunter were too powerful. She had to get away from them, away from him, and the sooner she did, the sooner she could start forgetting him. Because she still couldn't marry him. Her mind hadn't changed about that. Her own reasons paled in comparison to the one he'd given her himself. It didn't matter what she looked like, wouldn't even matter if he thought he loved her. Deep down, the hate he'd lived with all his life would always be between them.

Ironically, she would never have found that out if she hadn't impersonated Jennifer. But then that's who he was actually attracted to, a woman who'd done things for effect, for the role she'd been playing, a role that had allowed her to behave with abandon and do things Tiffany would never otherwise have done. She tried not to blush but she felt her cheeks growing warm. He wasn't going to like the real her, her sophistication and elegance, and her adherence to propriety. She hoped he'd figure that out before the night was done.

She had planned to introduce the dreaded subject of the feud with dessert, so as not to spoil the dinner, but no one was comfortable at the table after they had nearly just come to blows. She still tried to delay it, introducing a few neutral subjects, but only Hunter, or occasionally his mother, replied.

His brothers were still staring at her as if they'd never seen her before. Zachary was sitting there with a deep frown now. Frank was tight-lipped. Her brothers were, too, for that matter. Hunter—well, she tried to keep her eyes off him, even when he replied to something she said.

At least they were eating, if not talking. Frank must have told his cook to outdo himself tonight. Was it universal, the need to impress one's enemies? The appetizer was French, individual bowls of onion soup crusted with cheese. The main course was English, a large roast so pink it was nearly rare, with a half dozen baskets full of Yorkshire-pudding buns added to the table.

Tiffany's own stomach was tied in knots. What she said tonight could end the feud—or make it worse. With most of them almost done with the roast, she gave up trying to wait any longer.

"I would like to discuss the future—and the past," she said, glancing between Frank and Zachary. "There may be some things our two families aren't aware of. I've heard both sides of the story of the feud now. I wonder if anyone else here can say that."

"We lived it, gal," Zachary said with a snort. "What's not to know?"

"That facts may have gotten lost over the years or were never revealed. For instance, did you know that Elijah was actually unfaithful to Mariah that night? He did cheat on her, which was why she shot him the next morning."

Zachary didn't answer, but she could see in his expression that she'd surprised him. "So many people have suffered over this because those two couldn't work things out. They're dead, and their only legacy is to still cause suffering?"

"She never should have followed us here," Zachary finally spoke up. "Never seen my pa so furious. That wasn't an easy move, and he did it just to get away from her, but she shows up *here*? That was nuts!"

"I think even she knew it was," Frank chimed in. "I was as surprised as you were to find us neighbors again."

"Then why didn't you leave?" Zachary shot back.

"Because she convinced me she'd never find peace without some sort of resolution."

"Is that some fancy name for killing my pa?" Zachary nearly shouted.

Frank glowered. "They were intimate before they shot each other. You were there to see it. Who's to say she didn't intend to put an end to the animosity?"

"And changed her mind afterwards?"

"You never told me they made love, Zach," Mary piped in.

"Because I didn't believe it," Zachary mumbled.

"They were barely dressed, Zachary," Frank said.

"Doesn't matter, I don't doubt she shot him first."

"I don't doubt it either," Frank said.

"Stop agreeing with me, damnit. Ya'll tore down our fences!"

"No, actually, my herd did that with no help from me," Frank replied. "A cow wants water, it's going to damn well get to it. You know that."

"And which time are you talking about?" Zachary growled. "The first, or the fifth?"

Mary intervened, asking her husband, "Does it matter? That first fence went up just because Elijah had a point to make, that the Warrens shouldn't have followed us here. It continued to go up out of pure orneriness. But you and Frank finally had it out, as I recall. That was a nasty fight, but at least you two didn't bring your guns to the table." Then she glanced at Tiffany to explain, "Warrens tore down the fence, Callahans put it back up. That went on for nigh six months. It ended up that both sides would just keep any cattle that crossed over the creek. That didn't decimate either family's herd, just gave the cowboys something to brag about."

"Until the night Zachary had someone shoot me, and my wife left less than a month later," Frank said bitterly.

"I didn't tell anyone to shoot you!" Zachary denied hotly. "And if Rose was so all-fired upset about it, she would've mentioned it when she came to my ranch that night. She didn't say a single word about you being shot. She was *only* interested in getting a truce going. I'll warrant she already knew she was leaving and was just doing what she could to protect her boys."

Silence followed that particular speculation. Tiffany was actually inclined to agree with Zachary. But since only Rose could confirm or deny it, and she wasn't there to do that, it wasn't pertinent to what they needed to discuss tonight. And it was time to say it.

"I'm going to suggest a permanent end to a feud that never should have started," she began carefully.

"We've already agreed to an end," Zachary reminded her.

"With stipulations, because even with your parents dead, you still found something to fight over. But let me ask you, did your father really claim a whole lake as his? Wouldn't you have built closer to it if he did? Or did he only claim it after my grandmother arrived, so she'd know how furious he was that she'd followed him here?"

"We were here first," Zachary said.

"Yes, and in loyalty to your father, you weren't willing to

share a natural resource. You've both enjoyed a truce for fifteen years. You expect it to become permanent through a marriage. Go one better and just end your feud now. Because if you both can't admit you were wrong to let this go on for two more generations, no marriage is going to help that."

Zachary frowned. "You calling off the betrothal?"

Tiffany groaned to herself. Had he heard nothing she'd said? And why hadn't Hunter jumped in to agree with her? He'd hated the burden of their marriage all his life. It should not be a prerequisite for peace! So what if wars had been ended throughout history with marriage alliances. Were they ever happy marriages?

"I'm just asking you to think about what I said," Tiffany answered.

"What I'm thinking is we've overstayed our welcome," Zachary replied, and stood up.

No one disagreed with him. In fact, the exit was rather quick. Mary said a few polite things in parting, but she was obviously embarrassed. Had she thought they'd be discussing wedding plans tonight?

Chapter Forty-Eight

HUNTER WAS THE ONLY Callahan who didn't leave the dining room immediately. Tiffany glanced at him to discern what he thought of her suggestion, but the look she got back was pensive, a little curious, utterly lacking in humor. It told her nothing.

But he must have intended to share his thoughts because when he did stand up, he said, "Come out to the porch with me to say good night."

"Not if you're going to kiss me again."

"You strike a hard bargain, Red."

"I'm going to pretend I didn't hear that," Frank said, actually sounding amused as he left the room to see his guests out.

Hunter came around the table and held out his hand to her. She stared at it a long moment before she took it. They *did* need to talk. If it wasn't obvious to him yet, she had to make it clear to him that she wasn't Jennifer—and without making him angry, because his support was paramount to ending the feud. So she led him out of the room and started to follow her father to the front porch, but Hunter pulled her in the opposite direction.

"That one's too crowded. Show me where you'll be watching the sunset."

She nodded and led him down the hall, which branched to a T at the back, then down another short passage between a couple storage rooms at the left corner of the house, quite a different design from the Callahans' home. The outbuildings here were even on the right side of the house instead of behind it. The small porch at the end of that passage was private, with no windows looking out on it. It wasn't completely dark outside. The sun had set, but the moon was on the rise, looking quite beautiful since it was nearly full tonight.

Tiffany ignored the two comfortable, short chaise longues that were placed side by side. They were new. Her father had told her he'd had to replace them every few years due to weathering, but they were the exact same design Rose had picked out so long ago. Tiffany had pictured her parents leaning back in them as they watched the sunset, holding hands.

She moved to one of the corner posts and leaned against it, staring up at the moon.

"Your mother had good ideas," Hunter remarked as he moved to stand behind her. "You're going to want a porch like this, too, aren't you, Red?"

She would have if her future home were going to be in a place that had sunsets as spectacular as they were here, but it wasn't. "You *have* to stop calling me that. My name is Tiffany."

"That's the problem. In my mind, it's not. And maybe it's not in yours, either. Would the woman you're trying so hard to convince me you are have mentioned kissing me in front of her whole family?"

She tsked. "I know you're trying to make a point with that logic, but among family is the only time I don't have to watch what I say."

"But with everyone else you do?"

"Certainly, as is only proper."

"Do you *like* living that way?"

"It's ingrained in me. It's as natural to me as being blunt is to you. What wasn't natural was my trying to be Jennifer, the housekeeper. That was—difficult. That was wrong. I apologized to your family, Hunter, but that didn't express how sorry I am for deceiving you. I know you're angry. You have every right to be."

"I was," he said softly, and put his hands on her shoulders. "But do I sound angry now?"

She quickly stepped to the side to get out of his reach and turned to face him. "You sound like you still think I'm Jennifer Fleming, but I'm trying to tell you that I'm nothing like her. I might have gotten a little carried away with the charade, but it's over. Who you see now is the real me, Tiffany Warren, and this isn't who you want. You even told me—"

The words caught in her throat as he grasped her waist and lifted her, setting her down on the porch railing next to them, far enough from the post that she couldn't grab it to get her balance. She had to grab him instead. But he made that easy, lifting her gown enough to move in between her legs to trap her there.

She gasped. "Stop this."

"Hell no. We're going to find out who you're trying to convince of what, because I don't need convincing of anything, but you apparently do."

She didn't have a chance to reply. He held her face as his

mouth slanted across hers, so quickly reminding her of that night in the barn when she'd abandoned everything for what he made her feel. It was there again, that passion, blinding her to reason and logic, negating everything she'd just tried to tell him, and she didn't care! This was the one perfect thing they had between them, where their families didn't matter, where nothing mattered except each other. . . .

He leaned in closer. She held on tighter, deepening the kiss herself. It was ecstasy to hold him again like this, taste him again. How was it possible to want someone this much?

She was still thinking that when he pulled her away from the railing and she slid down his hard, strong body. She would have crumbled, her legs were so wobbly, if he hadn't been holding her tenderly now.

"I'll do anything for you—except make love to you on your father's back porch."

He sounded as shaky as she felt. Was she really going to walk away from *this*? From him? But she had to! God, what had she just done? She couldn't even upbraid him for it when she needed him on her side right now.

She latched onto what he'd just said, asking hesitantly, "Will you talk to your father and get him to agree to my suggestion?"

"No."

Her eyes flew up to his. "You just said—why not?"

"Who says I want it ended that way? Maybe I like the idea now, of marriage being the cornerstone of a new foundation." He let go of her and leapt over the railing.

She yelled after him, "You do not!"

He continued to head toward his horse out front, but she heard him laugh. "*Now* you sound like my Red."

Chapter Forty-Nine

TIFFANY WAS OUT OF breath, from laughing, from drowning. And her brothers, who surrounded her in the lake, wouldn't give up on trying to dunk her. Not that she had a chance of winning when they were so much stronger than she was. She finally crawled out of the water to catch her breath. The boys continued their antics, pulling each other under the water.

Sam had loaned her one of his shirts to swim in. Long-sleeved, buttoned up the front, it fell to her knees. She wore her longest bloomers with it. Not exactly proper swimming attire, but then no one was going to see her except her brothers.

She sat on the grass, leaning back against a tree trunk, as she watched them, though she wasn't actually seeing the boys now. Removed from the horseplay, she felt an onset of the sadness that had come over her last night. She was actually going to miss things about Montana when she left: the beauty, the openness, summer storms lulling her to sleep, even days like this, so crystal clear. And most of all Hunter. No one had ever treated her the way he did, no one ever would again. The teasing and the laughter that so easily broke down her defenses, the way he didn't hesitate to speak his mind with her. The man truly had an enjoyment of life to find humor in the smallest things, and it was infectious when she was around him. She'd never felt so close to anyone else, the way she did to him. But then he'd given her the most incredible experience of her life when he'd made love to her.

She wished she could package him up and take him home with her, but Hunter wouldn't be Hunter in the city. She couldn't ask him to make that sacrifice. They simply weren't meant to be. They'd known it all their lives. The attraction they shared wouldn't survive the differences in their ways of life and the hard feelings and animosity that had been bred into their families. Last night had proved that, when neither family could get through one simple dinner without arguing and the Callahans had left angry because of it.

The framing of the house that was supposed to be hers one day caught her eye across the lake and deepened her sadness. She could see the broken corner post and the pieces of framing hanging down. Hunter had said he'd tear it down.

It would have been so much easier if he'd stayed angry with her for deceiving him and his family. But after what had happened last night on the porch, and, worse, his mention of cornerstones and marriage, she knew he wasn't. She was going to have to be blunt and tell him that wasn't happening—and remind him why *he* should be relieved that it wasn't.

"Your logic confuses me, Red," Hunter said behind her. "I

got the distinct impression last night that you were trying to convince me you're nothing like my Jenny, yet here you are behaving like a hoyden with your brothers."

She leapt to her feet and came around the tree to find him leaning against it. "How long have you been here?"

"Long enough to see that you could have used some help against your brothers."

"Don't guns get too wet to shoot in the water?" she quipped.

He chuckled. "You know I didn't mean that kind of help."

She was embarrassed that he was seeing her like this, her hair dripping wet, clothes clinging to her. "Go away. This is a family outing."

"And we're going to be family."

Oh, God, that sounded nice, but *he* wasn't being logical. "You know you don't really want that. You've hated this betrothal as much as I have. Don't turn stubborn now just because you think I'm someone I'm not. I—I won't marry you. I'm going to go back where I belong. Be glad that I'm letting you off the hook."

Her own words started to cut deep. She hadn't thought it would hurt saying them! But his expression arrested her. He didn't believe her? He actually smiled.

"Your pa followed your ma back East," he said, coming away from the tree to maneuver her against it. "He did his courting there. You going to make me do that?"

"Courting at this point isn't appropriate."

"She didn't fight him every step of the way, Red. Why are you fighting me?"

She lifted her chin stubbornly. "She didn't know what the West was like yet."

"Do you really think she cared? She was in love. She just wanted to be with her man."

"Yet she left him," she stated, thinking she'd made her point.

He didn't think so. "Don't use that excuse when you admitted you don't know why she left. And you don't really want to leave, either."

"I—I do."

"Prove it," he whispered as he leaned in closer.

She could have turned away in time—no, she just didn't want to. She wrapped her arms around his neck, let him lure her into a few moments of bliss. It was. His kiss was pure magic. How could she give this up, what he could make her feel? Did she dare be selfish and marry him when she knew they'd both end up regretting it eventually?

"*This* is beautiful," he said against her lips. "This is two people meant to be." Then he stepped back, but he left his hand tenderly on her cheek. "Go tell your ma what you feel, what you really feel. She'll tell you this is where you belong."

"I can't, she's not—"

"She's in town. One of the hands just rode in and mentioned it. Half of Nashart remembers her, it's all they're talking about. I was riding over to warn you, in case you didn't know. The sound of laughter in the lake distracted me."

"But she said she'd never step foot in this territory again!"

He shrugged. "Maybe she felt she had to come to straighten you out."

Tiffany winced. "No, she's probably come to rescue me. If she's here now, then she left before she got my father's telegram. But she will be furious when she finds she came for nothing, that he and I are on the best of terms now."

"Need me to protect you? My pa might have been intimidated by her, but I've got more at stake. I'll fight the dragon for you."

Tiffany almost laughed. "She's not a dragon, she just doesn't mince words when she's angry."

Chapter Fifty

Rose stood at the window of her room in the Nashart hotel. She'd gotten a room in order to make herself presentable. She had to look her best today. She didn't see anyone outside waiting for her. They'd always been there, the watchers, and always in plain sight, no hiding. Parker had wanted her to know. The ones who had been watching her for years sometimes even nodded to her respectfully when she ventured out, they'd followed her for so long. Most didn't last a year before they were replaced or quit. It was a boring job, after all. It felt so odd, not having them following her anymore, so odd it would probably be a long time before she stopped glancing over her shoulder to look for them. But they were really gone. She had her life back. She might even get her husband back—if he could forgive her.

She couldn't believe how close she'd come to not finding out that this nightmare was over. She'd been in her hotel suite packing for her trip to Montana to find out what had made her daughter sound so panicked in her last letter and beg to be allowed to go home. There hadn't really been time for one more visit to Parker's house when her train was leaving in a few hours. She'd already been to that mansion five times since she'd arrived in Chicago, and each time she'd been turned away. There hadn't been any point in trying one more time. Yet she did. And she'd gotten in the door. And heard the last thing she expected to hear. Parker was dead.

He'd died two days ago when she'd felt so despondent she hadn't even left her hotel suite to take a walk or buy a newspaper. His household was in mourning, or at least giving that impression. The man had made her believe his death wouldn't make a difference, that his vendetta would continue from the grave. He hadn't counted on his wife, Ruth, not honoring his wishes.

"I can't give you back the years you lost, but I can assure you I won't throw good money after bad," Ruth had told her when she received Rose in her parlor that last day in Chicago. "My husband was wrong. He did many bad things that I was aware of, but I think this was the worst. He couldn't accept that our son was weak. He had to blame others for Mark's death when it was Parker's own fault for coddling the boy his whole life. To be honest, Rose, Parker's death isn't just your liberation, it's mine."

Ruth had said a lot more that day and offered what apologies she could, even mentioning a large sum of money. She called Parker brilliant when it came to business, but a fool when it came to family. She claimed she'd stopped loving him soon after they were married and admitted, "He never knew, that's how insensitive he was."

Rose had listened in a haze of shock.

That first day on the train was nothing but a blur. So many emotions made that grueling trip to Montana with her, hope, worry over Tiffany, even anger that Parker hadn't died sooner, but only one arrived with her in Nashart. Excitement.

Now, she was bubbling with it like a schoolgirl as she hurried down to the hotel lobby. A buckboard was waiting outside to take her to the Callahan ranch. She was going to collect Tiffany and take her straight to Frank. And then? She didn't know. She'd been given her life back. What happened today would determine if it could once again be a life worth living. . . .

"Well, well, you didn't waste any time, did you, Mrs. Warren?"

She knew that voice, that horrible voice. It wiped the color from her face as she slowly turned to face the man who'd threatened her all those years ago. The man who had shot Frank and promised to kill him if she didn't do exactly what he told her to do. She knew who he was, too. She'd spent a lot of money finding out. She'd wanted to put him so deep in prison that he'd never see the light of day again. But she'd been blocked at every turn. His boss was too powerful, had too many officials in his pocket. And William Harris had been Parker Harding's right arm.

She slipped her hand into her purse to grip the derringer she had in it before she said, "I spoke with Ruth Harding, Parker's wife. His vendetta is over."

"I know."

"She even had any mention of it stricken from his will. Their lawyer was a personal friend of hers, not his."

"I know."

Her eyes narrowed. "Then what are you doing here, Mr. Harris? And I'd be very careful with your answer. If you think to blackmail me into compliance again, for any reason, I'll kill you myself."

He had the gall to tsk at her. "Now is that really how you want to spend your homecoming? In jail for shooting an unarmed man? Perhaps you should know that I was never a gun for hire, Mrs. Warren. No set salary could compensate me adequately for what I do. Parker knew that. I earned a percentage of all the businesses I handled for him and will continue to handle for his estate. The more they earn, the more I earn. His wife knows my value. She's already assured me the deal I had with her husband will continue."

"But *not* the deal you had concerning me, so why are you telling me this? Parker's vendetta died when he did. Mrs. Harding has already dispatched notices of termination to the men following me and my husband. *This is over!*"

"I just find it ironic," he said in that same smug, unperturbed voice. "All these years watching Warrens, then we run into trouble with their enemies. Parker didn't know that yet. He was just told there was trouble with his new copper mine and gave me leave to fix it in my usual, efficient way. I'm here on business. Now that you're here, too, I'm seeing more options for how I might solve a few business problems."

He laughed as he walked away. Rose's hands were trembling. She should have shot him. He was just as guilty as Parker Harding was, for ruining her life fifteen years ago.

Sam grinned. "Yeah. He probably doesn't believe it's her. Probably thinks she'll disappear if he says anything."

Tiffany jabbed Sam with an elbow. "Why didn't *you* warn him she was in town?"

"I figured once we caught up with her, we should give you a little time with her first. Didn't expect her to just walk in the door."

No one did, least of all Franklin. He looked so incredibly surprised. And Rose—Tiffany had never seen her mother with such an expression. . . .

Tiffany suddenly burst out, "Oh, my God, you *both* still love each other!"

Their eyes immediately turned in her direction. Rose started toward the bottom of the stairs. "Tiffany, come down—"

Franklin cut her off, simply swinging Rose around and kissing her. There was no hesitation on Rose's part. She wrapped her arms around her husband—grabbed him hard was more like it.

"Well, who would've thought," Sam said with a chuckle, and elbowed Tiffany this time. "Want to go swimming again?"

"You mean leave them alone?"

"I don't think they're going to notice anyone else for a while."

They didn't go swimming again. Tiffany had been far too embarrassed when Hunter had found her doing that. They did vacate the stairs, though, to give their parents some privacy. But Tiffany was too curious to leave the house. She wanted to be available the moment her mother was ready to talk. She didn't expect to have to wait until dinner that night!

Rose and Franklin came into the dining room laughing, their arms around each other's waists. It was as if they hadn't

Chapter Fifty-One

TIFFANY CAME TO AN abrupt halt at the top of the stairs when she saw her parents in the hall below. She'd taken too long getting ready! But she'd been sure Rose would go to the Triple C looking for her first. Even if Hunter had steered her this way instead, she didn't think her mother would actually come *here*.

As she started to call out to Rose, her brother Sam whispered, "Shh."

She glanced to her left and saw Sam peeking from behind a wall at the drama unfolding in the entrance hall. He slipped around her and sat on the step directly below her. She joined him on the step and whispered, "No shouting?"

"Neither one has said a word yet."

"How long have they been staring at each other like that?" Tiffany whispered.

" 'Bout five minutes now, by my reckon."

Her eyes widened. "Without a word?"

lived the last fifteen years apart. Their children stared at them, speechless for a moment, then noisily fired off questions at the same time.

Rose held up her hands and in her usual indomitable way said, "Be quiet, children. Your questions will be answered if you still have any when I'm done explaining. I was under a threat of death, your father's death, to say nothing. But that threat is finally dead and buried. I've already told your father. So let me tell you now why I was forced to leave here all those years ago."

It was almost funny, how many times Tiffany's brothers opened their mouths to interrupt Rose as she told her tale, only to clamp them shut again. But Rose wasn't an adept storyteller. In trying not to leave anything out, she said things out of context. But she did finally piece it all together for them. It took most of the meal to do so.

Tiffany barely touched her food. She was shocked and horrified by the old man's cruelty and the violence he had resorted to, to get his revenge for something her parents hadn't been responsible for. His ruthlessness had touched them all, dividing their family, making sure they wouldn't even know why. That was the worst part of the whole tragedy—that Rose had had the burden of keeping this secret all these years, even from the people she loved.

"You should have told me, trusted me to deal with it," Frank finally grumbled.

Rose raised a brow at him. "How many times are you going to say that today? We both know exactly what you would have done. You would have hunted Parker down and killed him. But you can't kill a man that rich and powerful without paying the ultimate price for it. If you must know, I almost did myself. But he convinced me even his death wouldn't end it. He just didn't know his wife despised him and had no intention of carrying out his final wishes. My God, I wished I'd known that sooner."

"I thought those men watching your house were *your* guards," Frank said.

"No, they were Parker's men, and they had orders to kill you on sight. Why do you think I told you I'd shoot you if you ever showed up at my door again?"

"You were angry enough when you said it that I didn't doubt you meant it."

"Of *course* I was angry. I'd had to leave you to save your life, and part of his damn revenge was that I not tell you why. But you wouldn't let it go, and that was just making the pain so much worse."

"I'm sorry," Frank said, putting his hand over hers.

"Don't be. It's *not* your fault. I wish I could have found some way to tell you, but Parker was too thorough. He didn't just have men following me to make sure you and I never met up anywhere, he had you followed, too. You didn't know you were being watched?"

"How would I? I had no reason to suspect anything. If I did, I would have just figured it was the Callahans up to no good. I did see flashes in the hills every so often, like sun glinting off binoculars, but when I reached the spots to investigate, no one was around."

Sam interjected, "I guess it's a good thing you disguised yourself, Pa, when you came to New York with us."

"You didn't!" Rose gasped, and threw her napkin at Franklin.

He chuckled and handed the napkin back. "You think I could really go fifteen years without gazing on you?"

"*I* had to!" Rose exclaimed.

"But you knew why you had to, I didn't."

"But a disguise? So you did suspect something?"

"No, that was just so I could meet Tiffany. Well, it also made it easier for me to follow you around the city when you left your house. I did stay out of sight of your guards—thinking they worked for you."

"You're lucky whoever followed *you* never figured out what you were up to."

"It was a good disguise, Mama," Tiffany said. "He looked like an old man. I don't think even you would have recognized him."

"Why did you never tell me, baby?" Rose asked her.

Franklin answered. "She didn't know. You were pretty clear about my not coming to New York for any reason."

"I had to do it that way!" Rose cried. "You understand why, don't you?"

"Yes, now we do. But it didn't help Tiffany, thinking I didn't care enough about her to even visit over the years."

"I was afraid that if you showed up in the city even once, and Parker found out about it, that he'd change his mind about the revenge he'd settled on and simply have you killed instead. That was his first intention, you know. An eye for an eye. It was William Harris who talked him into this longer, never-ending revenge instead. Harris might even have thought it was a kinder version. At least you could have found someone else. It was only I who was never to have anyone ever again. But no one was to die as long as I remained alone."

Tiffany was nearly in tears. She'd listened to it all, but it was so unfair! Her parents had never stopped loving each other, and they would never have gotten back together if Rose didn't have that chance meeting with Ruth Harding. Rose could have gone on forever thinking she didn't dare be in the same room with Frank.

"No one has paid for causing our family this heartache," Tiffany said angrily.

"Harding is dead," Frank replied gently. "He'll never hurt us again."

"But he died naturally. He didn't get what he deserves. And Mr. Harris is still walking around, as if he had no part in it, still causing trouble for people. It's not fair they got away with this."

"Some things never are fair, baby," Rose said. "I have no proof Harris was involved. It's just my word against his."

"Which is all the proof I need," Frank said ominously, his anger apparent now. "That man nearly killed me and he ran you out of the territory. He robbed me of fifteen years with my wife and daughter!"

Rose glanced at Franklin sharply. "He's as ruthless as Harding, but he was still just a lackey following orders. Do you *really* want to stir up that pot now when this is over, when we can finally be together? Don't make me worry about you again."

"I won't go looking for him, but he better pray he never crosses my path."

Tiffany watched her parents. Rose put her hand over Frank's for that half concession. Tiffany had a feeling her mother wouldn't leave it at that, that she'd have more to say to him about it when they were alone. Tiffany could even understand why Rose wanted to leave it alone. She'd suffered enough. But it still wasn't fair!

Rose addressed her children again. "Ruth Harding did try to make amends. She offered me an incredible amount of money, which I turned down, of course. I have all I could ever want or need, my husband back. She's giving the money to you children instead, since you also suffered because of her husband's unconscionable actions. Small compensation for splitting a family apart, but I didn't turn down her offer."

"I don't want her guilt money," Tiffany replied bitterly.

"Then it can rot in a bank somewhere, so don't give it another thought." Rose stood up. "Now, come show me your room, Tiff. You and I haven't had a chance yet to discuss what you've been doing since you got here."

Tiffany groaned to herself, but led the way upstairs to her room. "Very nice," Rose remarked as she walked around it. "I knew Frank would make sure you felt comfortable here. Don't you feel silly now for trying to avoid him?"

"Mama, I had those feelings for the longest time. They weren't going to go away simply because you asked me to come here with an open mind."

Rose sighed and sat down on the bed, patting the spot next to her for Tiffany to join her. "All this suffering because I was too kindhearted to tell Mark Harding no when he asked me to marry him. It is my fault, you know. I tried to spare his feelings. I thought we'd do fine together just because we were friends. I did care for him. I just didn't love him, didn't even know what real love was, until I met your father. Now—cooking? Really?"

Tiffany laughed at her mother's exaggerated appalled look. "It was frustrating at first, but I was actually starting to have fun, figuring it out."

"I almost sent a cook to you instead of those books. But that would have been helping out the Callahans instead of pointing out to you that you weren't where you were supposed to be."

"But you wanted me to get to know Hunter, to give him a chance."

Rose winced. "Not really."

"What?!"

"If you wanted him, I wasn't going to dissuade you, but I was too selfish to *want* you to settle here when I didn't think I could ever come here again. I used the betrothal as an excuse to give you some time with your father. I had kept you from him all these years. It was time for me to share you. I know I should have just told you that. Instead I tried to manipulate a bad situation—which I hear you tried to fix. I commend you for your effort to put an end to the feud once and for all. I've actually had years to think about this. I even have a letter that I wrote to Zachary long ago that I would have sent to Zachary after you returned to New York, suggesting he continue the peace I arranged despite the marriage being called off. Now that I'm here, I can talk to him myself and add my sentiments to yours. But that's nothing you need to worry about now."

Tiffany frowned. "So you really don't care if I marry Hunter or not?"

Rose gave her a long look. "You know, regardless of Parker Harding's threat I was coming here to drag you home. I was going to sneak into town and sneak you out of it, without Frank knowing. I never dreamed you would run into the worst the West can show you."

"I know, a stream of bad luck," Tiffany said with a roll of her eyes before Rose did.

"Possibly. It won't be long before you don't even hear about train robberies like the one you witnessed, much less get caught in them. It was worse when I lived here. But you take the good with the bad, and the good far outweighed . . . I digress. The choice was, and still is, yours, Tiffany. Your father and I want you to be happy. If that isn't going to happen here, we'll take you back to New York and stay with you until you find your perfect man and get married there."

"Stay with me? It doesn't sound like you'll be staying in New York after I'm married."

"We won't. I fell in love with Montana as much as I did with your father. The happiest years of my life were spent here. Of course, I would have had that happiness anywhere, as long as I was with Frank. But there was something about this place that charmed me from the very beginning. I didn't have to stop myself from trying new things, fun things, just because someone would frown on it. People don't do that here. They aren't judgmental about superficial behavior."

"It's more relaxed here," Tiffany said, remembering Hunter's words.

"Exactly!"

"You can wear britches and wide-brimmed hats if you want to."

Rose chuckled. "They told you about that, did they?"

"And rope cows if you want to."

"Well—"

"And keep pet pigs."

"What? No!"

"Come here, Max," Tiffany called.

The piglet poked his head around the tub screen from where he'd been napping. He immediately trotted to the bed. Tiffany picked him up and rubbed noses with him.

Rose stared incredulously at them for a moment before she started laughing. "I guess you've already figured it out."

"I guess I have."

Chapter Fifty-Two

THE WARRENS RODE TO town that Saturday for the dance, either on horseback or in wagons, the family, the cowboys, even the servants, including the cook. No barn or building in town was big enough to hold everyone, not when people were coming in from all over the county for the event. There were no social barriers: cowboys, miners, lumberjacks, young and old, everyone was welcome.

Lights were strung in a field just outside town; a large square-dance floor had been built there for the occasion. Long before they arrived they could hear the musicians playing, not exactly music or instruments Tiffany was familiar with, but banjos, fiddles, and harmonicas. A few couples were already dancing, though the dance hadn't been scheduled to officially start until the sun went down and the heat of the day had passed. Dusk was just approaching. But dozens of tables were already laden with food and drink, with aromatic smoke from a half dozen roasting pits wafting over the area.

Tiffany thought the site looked and smelled wonderfully

festive! It seemed to her much more like a fair than merely a dance. Children were running about, mostly chasing each other. A horse race was taking place between three cowboys. Some lumberjacks were having a tree-climbing contest, which seemed rather silly with only four trees nearby and none of them tall. Even a drinking contest was taking place, which didn't bode well for those participants' doing any dancing later.

It definitely wasn't what Tiffany had been expecting, but it was no wonder Rose had been excited as soon as she'd heard about the social event. Tiffany wasn't sure if her mother just loved country gatherings or just loved being back in Montana with her family. Maybe it was a little of both. Tiffany was surprised to see her mother like this, so exuberant, so full of laughter and cheer—so unreserved. And not the least bit proper. Tiffany actually thought she wouldn't stand out like a sore thumb in her sophisticated clothing for once, not with her mother along. But Rose had surprised her in that regard, too, coming downstairs wearing a skirt and blouse with no bustle in sight.

"I left here fifteen years ago with just you and a valise, and it was half filled with your things," Rose said. "Your father stored everything I left behind in the attic, never giving up hope that I'd come back and wear those clothes again. I had my maid air some out, but I think it all needs a washing." Rose sniffed her own shoulder. "I smell a little musty."

"You have time to change," Tiffany suggested.

"Oh, no. I'll take comfort over fashion any day, even if it is a little musty."

While Rose was dressed in plain, everyday styles, her garments were elegantly tailored from expensive materials. Trust her mother to fit in here yet still retain her uniqueness. Tiffany, on the other hand, had donned her best day dress, replete with bustle, and she'd had Anna put her hair up. But she had nothing else in her limited wardrobe that would do, certainly not her kitchen outfit, which she wasn't going to be caught dead in again. Besides, she still had to make Hunter come to his senses and figure out on his own that silk and spurs just didn't go together.

Nashart's founders and people who had known Rose when she'd lived there converged on her as soon as they arrived. Tiffany had hoped to stay close to her mother, but the crowd of people welcoming Rose got too big.

Roy pulled her away and appointed himself her protector for the evening. He turned away the first three men who asked her to dance before she could say a word to them. He seemed to be disgruntled, but she realized it had nothing to do with her when she caught him staring at Pearl dancing with another man. Which reminded her . . .

"Do you want to talk about it?" she asked her brother hesitantly.

Roy glanced down at her. "Huh? Oh, her. No. She made it clear I was barking up the wrong tree."

"I'm sorry." Like hell she was.

"But maybe you can tell me what she meant when she said that I've got too many women in my house. There's always been women in our house. Most of the servants are women. Don't make a lick o' sense."

She put her arm through his, then she bumped her shoulder against his. "You weren't really looking to settle down yet, were you?"

He grinned. "Not really."

"Then don't give it another thought. More women come West every day . . . well, maybe not every day, but there should be more choices by the time you're ready."

"Or maybe I'll start a Warren tradition and just do what Pa did."

"It's nice to have choices."

"What's yours going to be? And answer quick, 'cause he's headed this way."

She spotted him at the same time Roy did. Hunter was weaving his way through the crowd in her direction. She tugged Roy toward the wooden platform. "Dance with me."

He laughed. "Hell no, I don't dance."

A cowboy nearby overheard Roy and said, "I do, and she owes me for making me scrub her floors."

Roy looked at her quizzically, and before he could object, one of the Callahan cowboys pulled her the rest of the way to the dance floor. He was all teeth, his grin was so wide. "First one to get you on the floor," he crowed. "I'm going to be bragging about this for a year or two—if the boss don't kill me for it."

She remembered him, just not his name. But he was definitely an exuberant dancer. She was actually almost out of breath before he relinquished her to another partner. She didn't actually get off the dance floor, just went from one partner to the next. She might even have danced with a miner, though it was hard to tell with the men all done up fancy in their Sunday best. With each boisterous twirl around the floor, she caught sight of Hunter, arms crossed, hat tipped low, patiently waiting. For what? For her to come to him?

She wasn't sure why she wanted to avoid him. Maybe because she was feeling a little vulnerable and too close to giving in to him. Despite everything that screamed they weren't right for each other, one thing whispered they were. She'd gone and fallen in love with Hunter Callahan.

Degan Grant was her next partner. She almost declined. Despite how many conversations they'd had, the man could still make her nervous. She would have guessed he wasn't familiar with any sort of dancing, and that this boisterous country dancing just didn't suit the gunman. Yet he did know how.

"I'll be moving on soon," he told her. "In case I don't see you again, I wanted to say it was a pleasure meeting you, Miss Warren."

"Moving on? Does that mean Zachary has agreed to a permanent truce?"

"That goes hand in hand with the wedding, doesn't it? But Zachary is here if you wanted to discuss it."

Maybe she ought to. He'd had enough time to think about her suggestion. It would probably be a good idea to hear his answer *before* her mother gave him her opinion about it. Rose might make the situation worse. Zachary might turn mulish instead of agreeable if Rose lit into him again.

"*You* should be sheriff here," she said to Degan.

"This town can't afford me. Besides, once the miners leave, Nashart will return to the peaceful town it used to be."

But they weren't leaving, and when had Nashart ever been peaceful with the Warrens and the Callahans living there? She decided to head off another disaster and seek out Zachary. But she was too late. When she finally spotted him, he was leading Hunter over to meet her mother.

Tiffany groaned to herself and turned about abruptly—and

smacked right into someone. She started to apologize, but her arm was grasped and he started leading her away.

"There's a man with a rifle aimed at your father," he said in a chilling voice. "If you don't come with me quietly, he's going to pull the trigger."

Chapter Fifty-Three

T HEY DIDN'T EVEN GIVE her a light, just shoved her in a storage room deep in the mine and left her there, taking the lantern with them. There was light beyond the heavy iron door, though. She could see it from the crack at the bottom of the door, and the shadow of someone's feet, whoever had been left to guard her.

Many people were at the dance, her entire family, but no one seemed to have noticed her being led off to the long string of horses, it had happened so quickly. Hunter, who had been watching her all evening, would have noticed if his father hadn't distracted him. He'd been waiting for her to leave the dance floor, and why the devil had he *just* been waiting? Why hadn't he claimed her for a dance himself? If he had, she knew this would never have happened. Or would they have taken him, too, if they couldn't get her alone?

She wasn't gagged, wasn't even tied, but she wasn't surprised that they hadn't taken that precaution. She'd seen all those buildings in the gulch—bunkhouses, offices, sheds. If anyone came looking for her here, they would search those buildings first. No one would think to look for her deep in the mine tunnel. No one would hear her either, if she got around to screaming. She hadn't yet. She'd been too afraid for her father as well as herself. That man who'd hied off with her had sounded so merciless. She'd actually been terrified of him, not knowing who he was or why he'd taken her—until they arrived at the mining camp. She prayed her father wasn't still in danger of being shot by one of Harding's miners because her mother had returned to him. Her family would be looking for her by now, and they'd have the law with them. Sheriff Ross had been at the dance tonight; she'd seen him swinging arm in arm with Mrs. Martin.

While she was still frightened, she was feeling angry now, too. That damn copper. What else could it be? She was beginning to wonder if these people were even real miners, or just criminals posing as such. More likely the latter, considering whose name was on the mine. Harding.

The door opened. She shielded her eyes from the sudden burst of light. "Just making sure they grabbed the right woman," she heard a masculine voice say. "I would have been annoyed if your mother was here instead of you, Miss Warren, especially since my note is being delivered to her."

He actually started to close the door again. "Wait! What has my mother to do with this?"

"She's going to assure me that the law stays out of it. In exchange, I'll give you back to her and abide by Mrs. Harding's wishes to let your father live. Your mother will once again be free to do as she pleases."

"She was already free to do that—"

"No, she only thought she was. All those years I worked for Harding, do you think I wasn't loyal to him? That I wouldn't honor his final wishes? He made me rich. A lot of money can buy a lot of loyalty."

"Honor? I don't think you care about honoring anyone's wishes or anything else, Mr. Harris. I think you just want this copper at any cost."

He smiled. "Very astute of you, but then copper isn't the poor substitute it used to be, and the vein here is worth millions."

"The Callahans have already refused to deal with you. The sheriff and the county judge both know that. You won't get away with this."

He tsked. "Of course I will. People change their minds all the time—with the right incentive. The Callahans are cattle-men. They don't give a damn about the copper."

"They care about the damage you've caused to the range."

"They'll get over it."

"That was you who tried to burn their house down, wasn't it?" she guessed.

He laughed. "No, that wasn't my idea. My foreman here was just trying to be helpful."

"You call that help?"

"Yes, actually. Too bad it didn't work."

"Did you have one of your men shoot Cole Callahan?"

"I think you ask too many questions."

"You did, didn't you?"

He shrugged. "That was an idea that just didn't pan out. Your family and the Callahans were supposed to be enemies; they just weren't acting like it enough to suit me. Figured to give your menfolk a little nudge to get the killing started so you Warrens could get rid of the Callahans for me. Problem solved. Still not sure why that didn't happen. But this is much more simple. You'll be released as soon as the mining rights are signed over, and Callahan should be here at any moment to do that. Your fiancé makes sure you come out of this unscathed, while your mother will have already convinced them not to retaliate. Everyone wins. I'll even still give them my original offer, just to keep it all nice and legal."

It was utterly galling, how pleased he sounded with himself. If he hadn't been blocking the doorway so she couldn't see beyond him, she might try pushing past him to get out of here before his plan succeeded. But she couldn't tell how many guards were out there.

"There's nothing legal about abduction and blackmail. For all your spit and polish, you're just a fancy-dressed outlaw."

He laughed. "I'm a businessman."

"You're no better than a common thug! Oh, and let's not forget kidnapper, arsonist, blackmailer, and murderer!"

"Oh, come now, I only shot your father once," he sneered. "The trick, Miss Warren, is not to get caught. I do pride myself—"

He stopped. Tiffany wasn't sure why, but Harris suddenly looked a little sick to his stomach. She didn't know he had a rifle barrel pressed to his back.

"I think I can dent that pride some, Mr. Harris," Sheriff Ross said in a lazy drawl, "for all the things the little gal just mentioned and then some. Funny thing about our judge. He gets mighty ticked off when his rulings are ignored. And for everything else I can now lay before him, they'll be tossing you in jail and throwing away the key."

"Tiffany?!"

Hunter shoved Harris aside to get to her, drawing her hard against him. "Tell me you're all right? That he didn't hurt you?"

"I'm fine—now," she assured him, though she was holding on to him just as tightly. Even with the sheriff's arrival, she hadn't felt relief until now. "How long were you listening?"

"The sheriff held me back. You were getting such a nice confession out of Harris, he wanted you to give him enough rope to hang himself."

"My parents must be frantic."

"They're outside tearing the place apart, along with our brothers, looking for you."

The sheriff's voice was fading as he prodded Harris and the guards out of there.

"Come on, I'll take you to them," Hunter added, but he didn't move, didn't unwrap his arms from her either.

"How did you know to find me back here?"

"Andrew's father led us to this back section. It would have taken us much longer to find you if he hadn't, they've got so many tunnels down here, including one around the cave-in that's on our land. Ross saw it on the way in. That's a direct defiance of the court order against them and is going to get them shut down for good."

"Completely? Well, it's nice that something good came out of this, aside from Harris going to jail. But Andrew's father? Don't tell me their last name really is Buffalo?"

"No, it was just obvious, they look so much alike. He was leaving, in fact, most of the miners were. Harris was overheard planning your abduction and the word spread through their camp tonight. They didn't sign on for things like this."

He *still* wouldn't let go of her. "Hunter?"

"I *know*." He started to release her, but suddenly squeezed her tighter, confessing, "I've never been so scared, Tiffany. I was the first one here. I didn't know where to look. Ross caught up to me just as Andrew's father did, to point us this way. I almost drew on the sheriff for trying to stop me from charging in here. I don't ever want to feel that kind of fear again. Marry me tomorrow—tonight. I don't think I'll ever sleep peacefully again if you aren't where I can protect you. Don't make me sleep on your porch tonight."

She almost smiled. He hadn't calmed down yet. It was making him unreasonable. "It's such a small world. That mine owner, Mr. Harding, ruined our lives long before he tried to ruin yours. I'm glad this happened, that Harris is going to be held accountable, after all. It really bothered me when I thought he wouldn't. But please, I *have* to let my parents know I'm safe. Get me out of here. We can discuss 'us' later."

"Porch it is, then."

She only half thought he was joking. He wasn't.

Chapter Fifty-Four

Rose had been furious that William Harris had threatened another member of her family and had tried to manipulate her once again. She simply thrust the ransom note at Zachary and told him, "Get my daughter back." But she'd calmed down after being assured that Harris was going to prison this time, along with a handful of his cohorts. Thanks to his arrogance in thinking he could get away with anything out West, they had so many charges to bring against him that he would be put away for good.

Zachary had been furious, too, but then he wasn't used to anyone's daring to manipulate him. He would have signed the papers, sent Tiffany on home, then shot Harris. But he felt better after Sheriff Ross assured him the mine would be shut down and gave him permission to close the mine entrance the easy way, with dynamite. Zachary lit the fuse himself.

The Callahans actually followed the Warrens home. Rose passed out the whiskey glasses, keeping one for herself. Tiffany didn't object that she wasn't included in that round of drinks.

She could have used one earlier, but with Hunter still in the room, she was enveloped in feeling safe. She'd always liked and appreciated his adamant desire to protect her no matter what, even before he knew who she was.

There was no mention of going back to the dance. Tiffany was the only one disappointed by that. Her brothers assured her there would be several more dances before the end of summer. They assumed she'd be there for them. They didn't yet know that Rose was willing to take her back to New York now. But then Rose didn't yet know that Tiffany no longer wanted to go back. However, her staying was dependent on Hunter. She still wasn't sure she'd be doing the right thing by either of them if she let just her own wishes decide their future—or lack of one.

Rose found a moment to tell her privately, "I like Hunter, in case you were wondering. If I had to pick a Callahan again, now that they're grown, I'd still pick him. He didn't blush, even a little, when he told me how he felt about you."

"Was that before you got that note?"

"Which he snatched out of his father's hands. I've never seen a man that big move so fast. His horse was long gone before we even got to ours. He's yours if you want him to be, you know."

Rose told Zachary the tale of the night she first met William Harris and how he'd blackmailed her into leaving her husband. They shared another round of drinks to celebrate his downfall. Nothing could ever bring back the lost years, but at least one of the villains in that old tragedy had gotten what he deserved.

"It felt good, us being on the same side tonight," Zachary admitted as the Warrens walked the Callahans to the door. "I'm willing to put the past to rest if you are, Frank."

Franklin offered his hand. It was a momentous occasion, the first time those two men ever shook hands. "I would have moved to New York to make my wife happy, but she *is* partial to this place, and I'll do anything to make her happy. Thank you."

Rose went one better and hugged the eldest Callahan, which actually made him blush. "Good, good," he mumbled. "Now maybe Mary will talk to me again."

Tiffany's brothers left with the Callahans to head back to town. It was still Saturday night, after all. Her parents hugged Tiffany for a long moment, now that they had her alone. They didn't say anything, just showed her how much they loved her.

Then Rose said with a yawn that Tiffany was sure was fake, "What a long day. I'm ready for some sleep."

"Sleep?" Frank chuckled as he followed his wife upstairs.

Tiffany watched them for a moment with a smile, then started up the stairs herself, but stopped when she remembered Hunter's silly remark about sleeping on the porch tonight. Just to be sure he'd been joking, she stepped outside.

And there he was. He'd already removed Patches' saddle so he would be comfortable for the night. It was on the floor next to the uncomfortable wooden chair Hunter was sitting in.

He smiled up at her. "What took you so long?"

She leaned back against the wall near him, even raised one knee the way he always did. "Because I didn't think you were really serious."

"Course you did, or you wouldn't be out here."

She didn't deny it. "Should I get you a blanket?"

He gave that a little thought before saying, "Today was one of the hottest days of the summer. Don't expect it to get too chilly tonight—or you could sleep here with me so we won't notice if it does."

"In the chair with you?"

"Why not? Well, you can sleep. I don't expect to get any."

"You really think there will be any more trouble? The worst offenders are in jail, and the sheriff said he'd arrange for the railroad to ship the rest out, east or west, in the next few days."

"I meant with you on my lap, I won't be getting any sleep."

"Oh."

The porch lamp wasn't lit, but ample light came from the parlor windows. However, for once, Tiffany didn't care that she was blushing a little.

She did look down, though, before she said, "Why didn't you ask me to dance tonight?"

"Because I was having too much fun watching you get the hang of it. Because I wanted you to have a good taste of one of our shindigs and see that we can have as much fun out here in the West as you do back East. Because I knew once I did have my arms around you, I wouldn't be letting go—and I can't wait any longer for that."

He leaned over to reach her and drew her onto his lap. With one arm about her waist to support her back, he tilted her chin so she'd look at him. She almost gasped, so much heated emotion was in the powder-blue eyes looking back at her.

"I want to marry you, Tiffany. I've never wanted anything in my life as much as I want you to be my wife."

"That's twice now you've called me Tiffany."

"Is it? Guess I'm getting used to it. But you know it doesn't matter what you want to call yourself, you're still the woman I fell in love with. I knew it the night I saw you with Caleb's new son, saw how sweet and tender you really are. There was nothing fake about that. It wasn't some role you were playing. That was you, plain and simple. Didn't take more'n a day for me to figure that out, that it was *all* you. Your daring to come to the enemy camp on your own, that took a great deal of courage. So did trying to put out a fire instead of running away from it. Wanting to rope a cow and laughing at yourself for how long it took. Befriending a pig of all things. Admit it. None of that was a lie. The only thing you lied about was your name."

"Maybe . . ."

"Maybe? That's all you have to say? You've been trying to convince me I don't really know you. I just proved I do. And I just asked you to be my wife! Not because we're already betrothed. And certainly not because your last name is Warren. I love you!"

"I love you, too, but—"

That's all he needed to hear to silence her with a kiss. Tiffany didn't want to wait any longer to taste him, either. To hell with her reservations. To hell with what he'd told her that day they went riding, told *Jennifer*, about why he didn't want to marry the Warrens' only daughter. And she'd thought too long that she couldn't have him. Now with that glimmer of hope that she could, it was like a dam opening, releasing all her emotions at once.

His kiss was exquisitely passionate. Her hand gripped his neck, but the position wasn't to her advantage, she couldn't feel enough of him. The one nice thing about that uncomfortable wooden chair was that it had no arms to keep her from straddling his lap. She moved rather quickly when she realized that. He was a bit surprised, but she was now facing him, her breasts pressed hard to his chest, her hands now holding his head, which was more even with hers. And she could feel him, between her legs, that hard bulge. She could even rub against him and she did. He was driving her crazy—no, she was driving herself crazy, because she could almost feel that dizzying excitement and overwhelming pleasure that she'd felt that night in the barn. It was there, wanting to spiral out of control, but just out of reach. So much passion, so much need, and she couldn't quite get to it.

She had no idea how he did it without actually moving her or breaking that kiss, pulling on a string, pushing down loosened drawers, but he was suddenly inside her, really inside her. His hands moved to her hips to guide her, but she didn't need help. She knew exactly what to do. It all converged at once, everything he evoked—passion, hope, love—bursting the spiral, wrapping her in bliss.

They sat there unmoving, breathing still heavy. Her hair had come loose, lay over his arms as he held her against him. She didn't want to stir yet, didn't want to give up a single inch of him. It was a remarkably comfortable position for such an uncomfortable chair.

Until she realized, "Oh, my God, on the porch?"

His laughter shook her body, still pressed to his. "Barns, porches, does it matter?"

She turned her head and lay it on his shoulder and kissed his neck tenderly. "No."

"I heard that *but* earlier," he said carefully. "That wasn't a 'yes, I'll marry you,' was it?"

She sighed. "I can't deny I have one last reservation, but it's a big one."

"Tell me."

"It was the day you told me why you didn't want to marry a Warren, that what you felt for them would always be there, deep down, under the surface. And it would get in the way, whether you liked her—me—or not."

He smiled wryly. "You would have to remember that. It's not that I didn't think it. I did, every time I was looking for excuses not to have to marry a woman I didn't love. Other times, I'd look at it from a more positive side, that, who knows, maybe I'd end up adoring her. So I actually did some shopping for her—well, ordering. Some odd catalogs come through here from time to time. I bought her some things I thought an Easterner might like. Don't laugh, but I've got crates of fine English china stacked in my room, vases, pretty little knickknacks, fancy painted porcelain teacups, when I had no idea if she even drank tea. I went overboard, on my optimistic days. Then I'd think of chucking it all in the fire, on my not-so-optimistic days. You drove me crazy before I even met you."

She grinned. "It's ironic that a few of those crates arrived here the same day I did."

He moved her back so he could hold her face in his hands. "Why don't you ask me why I shared those fears with you?"

"Why?"

"Because I was already thinking of *you* in a permanent way, and I didn't want you to think you were breaking up something that was fated to be. The real irony is that it *was* fated to be, we just didn't know it yet. Well, I didn't. You, on the other hand, cheated. You got to meet me long before I met you."

"Are you ever going to let me live that down?"

"I won't say another word—tonight." She laughed, but he added, "The suspense is killing me, Red. Are we getting hitched tomorrow or not?"

She kissed one cheek. "My mother did have a wedding dress made for me." She kissed his other cheek. "I just refused to pack it, since I had no intention of marrying you." She kissed his lips. "It will take at least a week to get it here."

He kissed her long and hard before he said, "Next Sunday then?"

"Next Sunday sounds wonderful."

"You'll have to move a bed to the porch for me." She rolled her eyes, but he added, "I'm not kidding. But next Sunday is a nice date. We might even get our house built by then."

"Now that's absurd. There's no way—"

"You'd be surprised, actually, I guess you will be. We've got carpenters, even masons, and one heck of a lot of people who will want to pitch in to see it happen. A barn can be built in a day. A fancy house will take a few days more. And you can design it however you want—if you want one here."

He was suddenly looking a little worried, for having jumped the gun. She assured him by saying, "I thought we might take a trip to New York after the house is finished. We can pick out furniture together. And I can show you where I grew up, introduce you to my friends—"

"And talk me into staying? I will, you know, if that's what you want. I don't care where we live, as long as we're together."

"You'd do that for me?"

"I'd do anything for you."

She wasn't really surprised that he'd say that. It was part of his charm, just one of the many reasons she'd fallen in love with him.

"Lucky for you, I'm partial to Montana sunsets," she teased. "Among other things. And I think we can find an empty bed for you in the house."

Drawn by his looks, roped in by his charm, her heart had been won by this man. It made her smile quite brilliantly to realize that her grandchildren were going to be cowboys after all.